NOWHERE BUT HOME

Also by Liza Palmer

More Like Her

Conversations with the Fat Girl

Seeing Me Naked

A Field Guide to Burying Your Parents

NOWHERE BUT HOME

Liza **Palmer**

WM

WILLIAM MORROW

An Imprint of HarperCollins*Publishers*

P.S.™ is a trademark of HarperCollins Publishers.

Excerpt from MORE LIKE HER copyright © 2012 by Liza Palmer.

HarperCollins books may be purchased for educational, business, or sales promotional use. For information please write: Special Markets Department, Harper-Collins Publishers, 10 East 53rd Street, New York, NY 10022.

FIRST EDITION

Library of Congress Cataloging-in-Publication Data has been applied for.

ISBN 978-0-06-200747-6

13 14 15 16 17   OV/RRD   10 9 8 7 6 5 4 3 2 1

FOR EVERYONE WHO THINKS THEY'RE TOO DAMAGED TO LOVE AND BE LOVED IN RETURN

Each time you happen to me all over again.

—Edith Wharton, *The Age of Innocence*

For Nada, who has lived through it all,
and usually patiently . . . you know who.

Bottle of water, Fig Newtons (snack size)

My mother was an unwed teenager from the Texas Hill Country. As it turned out, her parenting was questionable at best, criminal at worst. But as she stared into my squinty eyes on the day I was born, she vowed to do right by me. She'd name me something that would instantly give me social standing.

She blamed the fact that she was a pariah on her name: Brandi-Jaques Wake. It was just too easy to shorten her name to BJ. BJ Wake. She was a laughingstock, the town slut . . . and our mother. On that brightly lit morning, she did what she thought was right for her new baby girl. She gave me a name that would guarantee me entry into any castle.

"Queen Elizabeth," she whispered. "You're going to be famous."

"Name?" the girl at the concierge desk asks. I see her every day. I know her name is Keryn because she wears a name tag, just as I do. I have built entire narratives around the spelling of her name. It's her way of reinventing herself in the Big City, I muse. She's not just Karen from Small Town, USA! She's Keryn taking a bite out of the Big Apple one sassy mouthful at a time.

"Queenie Wake," I say, pointing at the name stitched on my dark blue chef's coat.

She doesn't look up.

"Have a seat and I'll let him know you're here," she says, typing busily.

I look around the hotel lobby for a place to sit and the tiny kiosk selling snacks catches my eye instead. It's past two PM and I have yet to eat besides nibbles and the occasional scrap from the kitchen. I buy a bottle of water and a pack of Fig Newtons. I sidle back into the lobby, hoping that Sassy Keryn will tell me it's time to see the boss. She doesn't, so I try once again to find a place to sit. I've walked through this lobby a thousand times, but never once sat down. I find a seat near the bar as the smooth jazz wafts through the 1980s once chic décor. I take a swig of my water and a big bite of my Fig Newton. I settle in, watching as the harried tourists push their way through the revolving door as if they've just run a marathon. As they make their way to the quiet of their hotel rooms, I can see them decide that New York is no place for "normal people" to live.

Which is exactly why I came here in the first place.

"Hey . . . yeah—he's actually at the main office over in the West Village. He wants you to meet him there." Sassy Keryn is standing directly over me as she hands me a business card. I look up at her and take the card that is just centimeters from my face.

"You're in the service industry, correct?" I say, standing. I glance down at the card. Keryn's swirly handwriting is sprawled all over the card, as if an eight-year-old girl with a can of pink spray paint and a bad attitude went rogue somewhere in an American Girl store.

"My job is to cater to the needs of the people who stay at the hotel, not the people who *work* at the hotel. The address is on the back. He wants you there in thirty," Keryn says, walking back to her station. I follow her, winding my way through a pack of German tourists weighed down with souvenirs.

"Did he happen to say what this meeting was about?" I ask, hoisting my backpack on both shoulders as I hunker down for a dash to the F train, just by Rockefeller Center.

"We had another complaint about the continental breakfast," Keryn says, smiling wide for another couple of tourists.

"About the food?" I say, stopped in my tracks.

"No. About you," Keryn says. A Japanese businessman steps forward as Keryn welcomes him to the hotel.

"About me?" I ask, nudging in front of the businessman. Keryn ignores me. I continue, "Am I about to be fired?"

"Probably," Keryn says with a smile. The smile is not for me, it's for the Japanese businessman. I wrench my fingers around my backpack straps as the Japanese businessman averts his eyes.

"That's just perfect," I say, flipping the business card back in Keryn's face.

"You'll need th—"

"I know where the head office is. He's my boss, too. I don't need the address," I say, turning away finally.

"You're welcome," Keryn says, her voice lilting.

I ignore Keryn and push through the heavy revolving door of the hotel. I put my head down and hurry to the subway. I'm on autopilot. Another job lost. Another kitchen I've been banished from. Another job where the food wasn't the issue, I was. At least I was at the McCormick Hotel the longest. Almost six months. That's progress, right? I trot past the Dunkin' Donuts in the Rockefeller Center subway station and take note. If all else fails, I can ask them for an application on my return trip.

"I'm not fired yet," I mutter, finally shoving myself through the subway turnstile.

I stand on the subway platform and allow myself a moment. I close my eyes and breathe in. I can win this job back. I can change. I'll plead my case. My food is good. It's better practice to keep an already existing employee than to train someone new. This guy's a businessman. He's got to know that. The rush of air signals the incoming subway cars, and I can feel the crowd shift forward on the platform. I open my eyes. Even after two years in New York, I've never grown tired of the subway. I think it's beautiful. I would never say that out loud, because it would surely brand me as a wide-eyed newbie just waiting to be taken down by this city. I can't help it. Despite mounting evidence that New York has apparently grown tired of me, I have yet to be anything but spellbound by it. As I board the subway, bound for the West Village, I can't blame New York for my inability to fit in. The city itself isn't cruel. It's just indifferent.

I tuck in next to the back of the car. I've never liked sitting on subways, always preferring to stand. I can't even settle into a simple mode of transportation without some quick exit strategy. My stomach roils as the subway jostles its way under the city. I practice my speech. I won't blow up. I'll listen. I'm thirty-one years old and I'm about to be unemployed. Again. I've got nowhere to go if this job doesn't work out. I negotiated a room in the hotel along with my salary. If I lose this job, I lose a place to stay. My hand grips the metal bar as I'm bumped and crowded. Even if Dunkin' Donuts is hiring, where will I live? Deep breaths. Deep breaths.

I exit the subway and run up the stairs. I rush the three or four blocks to the head office trying to steady my breathing. I find the intercom and push the corresponding button.

"Yes?"

"Queenie Wake to see Brad Carter," I say, trying to sound cool. The door buzzes open. I walk inside trying to smooth my hair, wiping the sweat off . . . everywhere. Get myself under control. More lobbies, more elevators, more long hallways until I find myself standing in front of a large desk. I've finally caught my breath.

"He's ready for you. Down the hallway. He's in the corner office," the woman says, her face kind.

"Thank you, ma'am," I say, her momentary kindness breaking through my guard, yielding an embarrassing slip back to my Texas roots. She nods and I know she's obsessing about me calling her ma'am. *"I'm too young for her to call me ma'am,"* she'll sob to her girlfriends over cocktails later than evening.

I walk down yet another hallway and see an open office door. I steel myself. I will win my job back. This is not my last day. I knock on the door, peeking in just a bit.

"Queenie. Come on in," Brad says, looking up from his desk.

"Thanks," I say, taking off my backpack and sitting.

Brad doesn't look up. He's typing something. I wait. My smile fades. I've met him only once before and maybe seen him a handful of times at the hotel. As he ignores me, I study him. You can tell, at one time, Brad was a good-looking guy. He's effortless and cool. Golden curls cut short, crinkled blue eyes from being out in the sun frolicking. Probably in the Hamptons.

I look around his office. I've never been in here before. The walls are laden with every pop-culture reference most people either don't "get" or wish they could forget. Hugh Grant's mug shot framed and signed by Divine Brown, her red-lipsticked lips kissing Hugh's cheek. A Shepard Fairey–style poster, but this time instead of President Obama and Hope being heralded, Brad's got Charlie Sheen and the word "WINNING." On the wall just to my left is a large painting that takes up the entire wall. Light brown strokes of paint cut a wide swath over the canvas. I can't make out what the painting is of. I blink and lean back just as Brad stops typing and checks his cell phone. I take in the entire painting. As he sets down his cell phone, sighs, and leans back in his chair, I realize what the painting is of. It's of Britney Spears and Paris Hilton in the front seat of a car. It's an artist's rendering of that infamous paparazzi gutter shot—quite literally—where we the public got to see every last inch of Britney . . . whether she liked it or not.

"I'm going to have to let you go," Brad says. I whip my head around from staring at the painting and meet Brad's disappointed, half-masted gaze.

"Why?" I ask, moving forward in my chair.

"Come on," Brad says, his voice offhand and cutting.

"It's not about the food," I say.

"Never is."

"So?"

"We're in the hotel business. The food's an afterthought."

"That's kind of bullshit."

"True."

"So?"

"You yelled at some poor schmuck from Iowa or whatever because he wanted to put ketchup on your eggs."

"Yeah, so?"

"That's what I'm talking about."

"Who puts ketchup on eggs?"

"Who the fuck cares?" Brad laughs.

"But don't you love that I do?"

"Not really, no." Brad has stopped laughing.

"What?"

"These tourists want some free food before they head out to buy mugs, T-shirts, and shit with I heart New York on them. They want to take pictures of the Statue of Liberty. And if they want to put ketchup on their eggs, we let them."

"But don't you want to own a hotel that's known for its cuisine?"

"I already do and it's definitely not the McCormick. I'm going to be renovating it later this year anyway."

"Well, then put me at another hotel?"

"You're kind of a bitch, Queenie. And . . . I get that—I mean, I've already got these other asshole chefs, don't get me wrong. But it's not as if you're known for any one kind of food, right? You cook what we tell you to cook. Adding your down-home whatever to our recipes every now and again isn't enough to have to deal with your attitude."

"Down-home whatever?"

"Yeah, you know, wherever you're from. The south?"

"Texas."

"Yeah. The south. I mean, if you came to me with some really cool southern recipes and tried to do something with the McCormick's menu, we'd be having a very different conversation."

"Why didn't you tell me that before?"

"I don't have to tell the other chefs."

It's as if the wind has been knocked out of me.

"And I don't have an attitude." My voice is a defiant growl in a feeble attempt to resurrect some shred of dignity from this meeting.

Brad just looks at me.

"Fine. Maybe I do, but it's because I'm passionate about food. That should be a good thing."

"Yeah, well . . . it's not. Plus? Your passion about food only goes so far, doesn't it? You're passionate when it comes to complaining about our menus, but not passionate enough to suggest any recipes of your own."

I'm speechless.

Brad continues, misidentifying my stunned silence as an invitation to enlighten me further. "People put up with a lot of shit when someone is talented. Believe me. But if you're just going to be another drone? You'd better be a quiet one if you want to continue to get work."

"I don't want to be just another drone," I say.

"Yeah, well . . ."

Brad's phone vibrates and he checks it. Tapping and scrolling through a few e-mails as I begin to have a nervous breakdown in a chair decorated with pillows that look like iPhone apps. I tug at the Twitter app pillow that's now folded itself into the small of my back. I bring it around and clutch it tightly. Brad smiles at something in the e-mail, absently flipping the phone back down on his desk. He looks up as if he's surprised I'm still there.

Brad continues, "I know you're living at the McCormick, so I'll be flexible with you moving out, but you *will* move out. We're done."

"Don't I get probation or something?"

"You were already on probation for telling that British dude that your bangers were probably bigger than his dick, so what would he know about it? Remember?" Brad's cell phone vibrates again.

"Oh yeah."

"Look, I've got to take this. I'll give you a good recommendation or whatever, so don't worry about that. You really are a good chef, I just . . . I can't have you in any of my kitchens." Brad picks up his phone and starts talking with whoever is on the other end. He extends his hand to me and I take it.

"Good luck," he whispers as we shake hands. He lets go of my hand, spins around in his chair, and continues talking on his cell.

"Thanks," I say, picking up my backpack. I stand and make eye contact with the painting. I just nod my head. Yep.

I was just fired in the shadow of Britney Spears's vulva.

2

Croque monsieur on country white bread, potato leek soup, a giant glass of cold water, and an old-fashioned doughnut

I've seen the movies: Small-town Girl with her "head in the clouds" moves to the Big City. There's a makeover montage. There's a tiny apartment with white twinkle lights; a lovably nosy landlord; and a brand-new group of quirky, irreverent friends. And the pièce de résistance: a scruffy-haired boy (usually named Logan) who adores Small-town Girl because she's different and not like those "Big City girls."

I counted on this mythology when I left North Star, Texas (population: 2,000), at eighteen years of age. I knew the lore. The movies. The books. I couldn't wait to leave everything behind so I, too, could gaze into a Tiffany's window in oversize sunglasses and opera gloves.

I was certain as I stumbled about New York that I'd soon

be welcomed into the ever quickening fold. I'd invite my impossibly beautiful and stylish friends over for dinner parties that would last late into the night. My tiny, twinkle-lighted apartment would be a gathering place with me at its center offering another plate of braised pork or "down-home whatever."

Still clad in my dark blue chef's coat from the kitchen where I'd just been fired, I stand outside of Brad's headquarters and grip my backpack straps. Tighter. Tighter. I know, without even having to look, that I am an unmitigated disaster to behold. I let the streams of people bob and weave past me on the sidewalk, choosing for once to just stop.

I can't be the only one faking it. I'm not the only lonely small-town girl drowning in this big city. I'm not the only refugee feeling invisible and alone. I'm not the only one who wants to scream, "NOTICE ME! I MATTER!" Maybe everyone is faking it. Maybe they're just better at it than I am. People walk around me on the street as if I'm not even there. It's quite something. I left North Star because I was tired of every move I made being tracked and judged by a cabal of gossiping ladies. I oftentimes wished I could go unnoticed as I moved through my life in that tiny town and now here I am. Utterly invisible.

Dreams do come true, kids.

I walk toward Twelfth Street and duck into DiFiore Marquet Cafe. Maybe I'll find momentary comfort in one of my favorite eateries. A place, by the way, I feel better about going to since I learned it's just called Marquet. Yes, I'd like a table for one by the window. I pass clutches of studying kids, hushed couples leaning toward each other across wooden tables, and late-lunching New Yorkers stealing away for a moment's solace. I order a croque monsieur, their potato leek soup, and the biggest glass of cold water they've got. I have one more paycheck coming and . . . I can't think about money right now. I just want to sit and gaze out this window. Of New York, but not *in* New York.

My sandwich and soup arrive quickly and I dive in. My mind goes blank as the tastes and flavors slide over my tongue, comforting me and bringing pleasure, however transitory.

What am I going to do after I finish this sandwich? I've got no job and no place to stay. I bring the spoon to my mouth and try to let the soup soothe me again. Did I really come all the way to New York to work at a Dunkin' Donuts in the Rockefeller Center subway station? Maybe this is an opportunity? I could take this as a call to adventure! A new city! A new life! A new shot at my elusive dream of belonging somewhere. A new chance at meeting that scruffy-haired boy named Logan. The sandwich begins to turn in my stomach. I take a long drink of my water.

I've worked in New York for two years. At four hotels, two restaurants, and one Starbucks. Before that I was in Los Angeles, San Francisco, San Diego, Las Vegas, Albuquerque, Taos, Branson, Aspen, Dallas, and Austin, where I was during and right out of college at the University of Texas. I don't have to stay in the U.S. What about Dublin? I could get a job at a hotel somewhere; they're nuts for comfort food, aren't they? "Down-home whatever" as Brad put it. Food that's good, but not great enough to tolerate someone being "kind of a bitch" is surely sweeping the Irish culinary world. I push away my plate and let my head fall into my hands. I rub my eyes and push my hair out of my face.

"Can I get you something else? Is the sandwich okay?" the waitress says, noticing my dramatic rejection of the food.

"The sandwich was great. Thank you."

"So just the check then?"

"Sure. Thank you," I say; the girl tears off my check from her pad of paper and begins to set it facedown on my table. I continue,

"Hey, are you guys hiring by any chance? I can do anything. I'm trained as a chef, but I can work behind the counter, wash dishes, whatever you . . . whatever you need," I say.

"Oh, uh . . . we're not hiring. For any positions." She slides the check across my table and can't look at me. She mutters a quick "Thank you," and leaves.

"I've been here before," I whisper to myself. I sneak a peek at the two girls next to me as they cautiously look away. To them, I'm now someone who mumbles to herself just after begging for a job. I feel wave after wave of nausea begin to roil. I quickly pay my check and hit the sidewalk at a pretty good clip. I need to be somewhere quiet and private. I'm on the verge of a meltdown of epic proportions and I can't let anyone here see me lose my cool. As I wind and dart through the streets of the West Village, I realize I've never said the word "home." Not even to myself. The place I'm looking for isn't here. I want to feel safe right now. I have no idea where to go to feel that.

My breathing quickens. The nausea continues to come in waves as my face flushes, alternating wildly between hot and cold. I'm on the verge of vomiting in public. I launch myself down the stairs into the subway, push myself through the turnstile, and try to regain control of myself as I wait for the train. The rush of air, the platform shifts forward, and we all board as a herd. I close my eyes, gripping the metal bar as we shift and jostle back toward Midtown. I probably wouldn't be the first person to vomit on this train. Hell, I wouldn't be the first person to vomit on this train in the last hour. No one here knows me.

No one here knows me.

I open my eyes. It's Friday night and everyone is getting off work. This train is alive with life and freedom. A man holding a bouquet of flowers sits next to a woman who carries a small present in a gold gift bag. An accordion player hops on at one stop, his wife holding out a hat for spare change. A young woman reads a book and tunes out the world.

It's not as if this city can't be home. It was just never *my* home. Actually, none of the cities I've passed through in the last decade has felt right. I can't remember the last time I felt at home.

I think of North Star. I've been back only once since I left at eighteen to go to college. The last time I saw Cal, my nephew, he was in diapers and now I hear he's going to be North Star's starting quarterback at just fifteen. My sister, Merry Carole, has made sure I've been kept up to date on the town gossip. She'll smile and be polite because she not only needs the business at her hair salon, but it's always been important for Merry Carole to fit in. Which is exactly why the people of North Star love keeping her out. I'm actually curious as to how they're dealing with Cal's prowess on the football field. However you praise the Lord, be it Baptist, Methodist, or Catholic, the true religion in Texas is football. So for a Wake to be the star quarterback? To be doing something good? Does not compute. Does not compute. Does not compute.

The train bumps and throws me off balance. I clutch at the back of one of the seats and am met with an annoyed gaze. Unrepentant, I lean once more against the back of the car.

I get off at my stop and ramble through Rockefeller Center's subway station, letting the sights and sounds wash over me. I stop at the Dunkin' Donuts, buy a bottle of water, ask if they're hiring, am rejected again, and then order an old-fashioned doughnut that I eat far too quickly. I climb the stairs as the old-fashioned doughnut only heightens my nausea and am thankful to finally be in the fresh air. I walk toward the hotel in a haze, trying to settle my stomach, the glaze from the doughnut still flaked to my cheek.

I stop in front of a department store display window. The scene is one of home and family. Faceless mannequins mix and mingle in an elegantly decorated room. Umbrella-festooned cocktails, tank tops, and summertime fun are on display for those willing to think they can buy it. Emblazoned in the window in big gold type it says, THIS IS YOU. THIS IS NOW. I read the words, my eyes losing focus. Then I see my own reflection in the window. My hollow blue-eyed stare is set off by my blotchy red-faced complexion. I look exhausted. My fine brown hair is matted to my neck and forehead. A lone bobby pin clings to eight hairs as the bangs I've been trying to grow out fly every which way. I clutch a bottle of water in one hand and a greasy doughnut wrapper in the other.

I am officially the Anti–*Breakfast at Tiffany's*.

I snap out of my haunted reverie and shuffle back to the hotel. I toss my now empty bottle of water and the doughnut wrapper into a trash can and begin the spiraling about money and jobs and shelter and and and. Lofty, philosophical reasons aside, the stark reality is that without this job and the hotel room that came with it, I simply can't afford to stay in New York. Sure, I can find another room for rent, with its communal, filthy bathroom at the end of a long, unlit hallway. I can put up another ad for roommates only to find myself spending less and less time at home and then watch as I devolve into only talking about "my annoying roommates" to anyone who will listen. I can crash in hotel lobbies for a while just like I did when I first got to New York. The bigger the hotel, the more nooks and crannies. And if someone found me, a simple lie about being locked out or getting in a fight with my boyfriend made everything better. But to what end? I've been on the run for going on ten years. I'm tired.

I push through the revolving door and into the hotel.

"Queenie?" A voice. I look up. It's Sassy Keryn. Great, *now* she knows my name.

"Yeah?" I ask, slowing my pace.

"Brad told me to give this to you?" She ends the sentence as if it were a question.

I walk over to the concierge desk and take the envelope in Keryn's hand.

"It's your last paycheck," Keryn says.

"Yep. Thanks," I say, turning my back on her.

"So . . . ," Keryn leads. I turn back around. She continues, "Brad also wanted me to let you know that your key card will be deactivated in three days."

Several thoughts crowd my brain as I stand in front of Sassy Keryn. First and foremost: I hate Keryn with a fiery passion. I have to focus the energy of the Big Bang not to haul off and punch her square in the face. I hate Keryn's faux-apologetic tone, letting the poor hick off easy after she got canned. She's a saint!

I can't believe Brad has given me only three days. Three days to find a new job and a new place to live in New York City in the middle of a recession. But most of all I hate that there was a tiny, fleeting moment where I let Keryn see those other emotions wash over me. I collect myself.

"Hey, thanks . . . I'm sorry, what was your name again?" I ask, folding my paycheck and putting it into the back pocket of my chef's pants.

"Keryn," she says, deflating.

"That's right. Hey, thanks, *Keryn,*" I say. She attempts a smile.

As I walk to the bank of elevators, I realize that New York has taught me one thing: hatred is not the opposite of love—indifference is. Being forgettable is way worse.

Trust me.

The elevator moans upward as I let the short-lived bliss of putting Sassy Keryn in her place linger for as long as possible.

I slide my key card in and out of the slot as the red light beeps green. Three days until that light no longer turns green. Does today count? Or is it two more days counting this one? I was too busy being a bitch to Keryn to ask. I slip the key card in my back pocket, as I've done for the last six months. I sit down on the bench at the end of my bed and watch as New York begins to twinkle just outside my window. It looks so beautiful from here—safe and sound inside. I pull my cell phone out of my pocket, heave a long weary sigh, and dial.

"Too Hot to Handle, this is Fawn." The breathy voice on the other end is my sister Merry Carole's longtime business partner and one of the only friends Mom ever had. Rumor has it that Fawn keeps the rhinestone industry in the black.

"Hey, Fawn, it's Queenie," I say, kicking off my shoes.

"Hey there, sweetheart. You okay?" Fawn asks, I hear the receiver being muffled and unmuffled as she tucks the phone into the crook of her shoulder, no doubt so she can continue to cut hair.

"Oh, you know. Is Merry Carole busy?"

"She's always busy, honey. I'll get her for you."

"Thank you, ma'am."

"Don't mention it, sweetie pie. Merry Carole! It's Queenie, for you. I don't know. She doesn't sound upset. I don't know! What does . . . I don't even know what that word means. Why don't you . . . come on over here and talk to her your own damn self then. I know. I told you I . . . I don't know. You can . . . sure, I'll take over, but I gotta finish with Mrs. Beauchamp's color. No, I . . . she's got twenty minutes on . . . see right there? Just put her under the dryer then—"

"You all right?" Merry Carole's voice bursts through the phone, but is muffled as she continues, "I don't want to hear it, Fawn. You can . . . there's a dictionary right there, why don't you look it up yourself? Well, it's not my fault you don't know how to spell it. Lord almighty. Queenie? Well, are you okay?"

"I got fired."

"Again? Heaven sakes, Queenie, you don't have the sense to come in out of the rain sometimes." Merry Carole muffles the phone again and continues, "She got fired! I know. She seems fine about it, I guess. What was this one? Six months, right? Some hotel. I don't even know—honey, how are you about it?"

"It's fine, you know. Same ol', same ol'."

Merry Carole is quiet.

I continue, "I know what you're thinking, but—"

"Don't you say this wasn't your fault, Queen Elizabeth. Don't you even think it."

"This jerk-off asked for ketchup and he was going to slather his eggs with it. What was I supposed to do?"

Merry Carole muffles the phone and continues to talk to Fawn. "Some poor man had the nerve to put ketchup on his eggs! Yes, ma'am! Right in front of her! It's like he didn't know who he was dealin' with! I know! Hahahahahahahahahaha!" Merry Carole says through the muffled receiver and the peals of laughter begin.

"It's not funny!" I say to no one.

"So what are you going to do now? Are you going to stay in New York or are you on to the next city?"

"I haven't figured that out yet."

"How long you got?"

"They've given me three days." I look around the room. Open suitcases with clothes strewn from them like blood spatter at a crime scene. I realize I haven't washed my hair with anything but a fun-size bottle of hotel shampoo in years.

"That's not a lot of time."

"I know." I think about maybe going to Philadelphia. Or Chicago? Maybe I could start fresh. Find something, shit . . . anything. Even in the abstract, I'm having a hard time giving up my dream of being in New York. I've wanted to be here my entire life. *"New York, New York! If I can make it there I'll make it anywhere."* Well, what if you can't make it here? What happens then?

"It's not the end of the world, but you can definitely see it from there. You've seen worse," Merry Carole says.

"I know." I tuck my legs underneath me as my mind darts around its darker recesses. As Merry Carole muffles the phone and directs Fawn through Mrs. Beauchamp's color, I hate that it's always about enduring and surviving. Crawling through and out of some muck to get to the other side.

Yes, I'll survive this. Merry Carole's right. I've seen worse. Much worse. But just once I'd like to simply . . . have something. Just . . . be. Get a job somewhere where someone isn't "taking a chance on me." I'm now officially pouting. My hangdog expression reflects back at me in the window. I look absolutely pathetic.

"I'm going to throw something out there and I need you to just think about it. Will you do that for me?" Merry Carole asks.

"Sure."

"As you know, the big Fourth of July festival is next weekend."

"Sure," I say. North Star's summer season is bookended by two big events: the Fourth of July festival starts it out with a literal bang and the North Star Stallions opening football game finishes it.

"Well, they're going to announce that Cal will be the quarterback for the North Star Stallions. We'll get our sign for the front yard and he's going to be presented with his varsity jersey in front of God and everybody. I know he'd love it if you could come back to see him."

"Next weekend?"

"That's right."

I look up and am met, once again, with my own reflection in the window. I stare back at myself.

THIS IS YOU. THIS IS NOW.

I don't know how else to cut it. I'm a shadow of who I once was. I hang my head. It's not as if anyone is going to mourn my departure. I never bonded with anyone in the kitchen—turns out people didn't really take to a bossy know-it-all who hammered them with cooking tips and tricks while they tried to dice that day's onion allotment. If I did hit it off with someone, it was still well within the boundaries of "work friend." Even walking out of the kitchen after work turned labored when there wasn't something cooking oriented we could talk about. It became clear that, unlike the other people in the kitchen, all I had was cooking. No family in the city. No history I cared to share. No hobbies. As long as I've been away from North Star I've been a cipher. And while I treasured the anonymity and the clean slate, it never dawned on me that I'd erased everything about me: good and bad.

I can't stomach quitting, never could. This will be temporary until I plan my next move. I'll recharge my batteries and really plan where to go—not just make another lateral move. I am also thirty-one years old and no longer believe the world begins and ends with North Star, Texas. I should be able to return without falling victim to the perception that I'm something to be hunted with torches and pitchforks. I will go back on my terms. It will not have the same power over me this time. I am older now. Smarter, I'd hope. Stronger.

"I think I can do that. It'd just be for a few weeks. Until I find a new job."

"Oh, he'll love it!"

"I can't wait to see him. I can't imagine how big he's gotten."

"He's not in diapers anymore, that's for sure."

"Okay, well, I'll settle things here and be there in a couple of days."

"Oh Queenie . . . this is just . . . I love that you're coming on home." Merry Carole muffles the phone and continues, "I KNOW! She's coming home! Can you believe it!? Well, where else has she got to go, though, bless her heart? Hahahahahahahaha . . . Who are you telling?! Yeah, she's coming back to see Cal get his jersey! I know! That's what I said, Fawn, aren't you hearing me over here! Queenie, honey?"

"Yes?"

"You be sure to call when you're on your way."

"I will."

"I just couldn't be happier. I'll see you soon then! Don't you just love saying that?"

"I'll see you soon. Bye," I say.

"Bye-bye now," Merry Carole signs off.

I beep my cell phone off and let it fall onto the bench. My haunted gaze stares back at me.

THIS IS YOU. THIS IS NOW.

I'm lost. I'm alone. I've got nowhere to go.

Nowhere but home.

3

Lipton tea and a 3 Musketeers

Several inconvenient truths have presented themselves in the last forty-eight postfiring hours. While I've bragged about living in the greatest cities in America, I have yet to actually become a part of any of them. I've worn the carpet threadbare on the tiniest piece of real estate these cities have to offer. I've created an agoraphobic triangle between the inside of a kitchen, the closest restaurant to catch my fancy, and whatever subway station is the nearest to the aforementioned. As I lay awake last night, I realized that it never mattered what city I was in, I never interacted with any of them. I vowed in the panicked haze of my last early morning in New York City that I would jump in with both feet to my next job in the next city. My future decisions can't be based on just not wanting to be in North Star, Texas. Deciding *not to be* somewhere is no choice at all.

As the sun comes up on my last day in New York, I put my

clothes in the same two suitcases I've been lugging around for ten years. As I fight with them while leaving my room, the door clicks shut behind me. No fanfare. Nothing. Instead, my last moments in that New York City hotel room were a frustrated symphony of various four-letter words aimed at inanimate objects. The elevator dings open and I step in with all the other exhausted tourists who are ready to go home.

I've already pulled around the 1998 Subaru Outback I bought in Brooklyn yesterday and parked it in front of the hotel. I bought the car for three reasons: 1. it was cheap; 2. it has a hatchback; and 3. it has New York plates. Apparently having a few epiphanies in the early morning haze doesn't trump sheer pettiness (thank God).

I walk through the lobby of the McCormick one last time. Sassy Keryn is not working today. Too bad. I go out the revolving door to where the car is parked with its hazards on.

"Checking out?" the doorman asks. I've worked with this man for six months.

"I used to work here," I say, opening the hatch and lifting in one of my bags.

"Oh, *oh*. You need help?" he asks, lifting the other bag in and closing the hatch.

"Oh, thanks," I say, now awkward. Do I tip him?

"Don't worry about it," he says, watching me fumble around in my jeans pockets for any loose change.

"Thanks again."

"No problem. Good luck then." I nod and smile.

I walk over to the driver's-side door and climb inside. The doorman walks around and shuts the door behind me. He scans the busy street and gives me a tap on the roof of my car when it's safe to go. I give him a wave and pull out from the curb.

The leaving is always so painless. One minute I'm in New York and the next I'm hurtling through Pennsylvania, Maryland, and then crossing into Virginia. I have officially left. But leaving one place means I'm going somewhere else, right? On to the next. I turn up the radio and sip the tea I bought just outside Roanoke.

After driving for sixteen hours the day before, I finally crashed at a motel just outside Birmingham, Alabama. The drive from New York to North Star is just over twenty-four hours and I completed a little more than half of it. Twelve hours to go. I called Merry Carole and let her know I'd be getting to North Star that night around dinnertime. She said she hadn't told Cal yet that I was coming. She did that not because she wanted to surprise him, but because she doesn't trust me. I've said I'm coming home a thousand times, then called with regrets from some new place.

In that scratchy bed, with the seemingly unending scan of headlights hitting my motel room window, I couldn't sleep. Guilt. Going home to Merry Carole and Cal made me feel apologetic and heavy. Did I abandon them? Or was it better for Merry Carole not having me in town? I wanted to believe my absence made it better. Merry Carole was always way more palatable without me around—well, me and my temper anyway. As I gathered my things early that morning, I knew the answer. I'd been selfish. I guess I just didn't know what else to do.

Despite promises several times to come home, I've only been back once. I put everything I had into getting into the University of Texas. When I did, I'd never been more proud of myself. No Wake had ever gone to college—Merry Carole chose cosmetology school and had worked up to owning her own hair salon by twenty-four. We are a family whose bad reputations are earned. Our ancestry is lousy with convicts, murderers, and drug addicts, and that's just the women. We come from a long line of beer-joint broads and low-life criminals. We have a pedigree of bastard children and their inconvenienced parents. This has always been our place in North Star, despite Merry Carole's tireless efforts to change the legend. Having a mother like Brandi-Jaques Wake only solidified our lineage. And there was never a father in sight. We were the babies trotted out to blackmail the men in neighboring towns. The men who'd had a good time with our mother and now regretted ever laying eyes on her. We had this man's nose, that man's eyes, and this other man's hair color . . . whenever it was time to pay the rent. Merry Carole counted up at least fifteen men who thought they were our father. This was not a happy revelation for them. We still don't know if we're true or half sisters. What we do know is we're the only family we've got.

· It seems apt that I would pull into North Star under the cover of darkness. I sit at the blinking red light on the edge of town, just off the highway. I remember sitting at this light when I decided to leave Texas for good. I'd gone to college, worked in restaurants in and around Austin, and had gone home to North Star for a couple of fateful weeks. I sat at this very light and knew I was destined for greatness . . . anywhere but in North Star. I was going to take on the world. I was going to show them.

The red light blinks. Welcoming me home. What's the exact opposite of a blaze of glory? I look around at my dusty Subaru, cut-off jeans, and think: me. This. This is what the exact opposite of a blaze of glory looks like.

I'm close to tears as I drive through the intersection and into the main square. The multicolored, exposed brick storefronts invite you to come on in! Air-conditioning! I pass the Homestead. The diner where you go to see and be seen. Old men talk about World War II and teenagers gather after football games. The Old West–style sign is still gnarled and just as tacky as I remember it. The church at the center of the town square is alive and welcoming. I roll down my window to hear the cicada song that so defined my childhood. Each storefront boasts its own rearing black stallion out front. North Star's Stallion Batallion: the booster club for the high school football team.

No denying it. I'm back.

I slow down in front of Merry Carole's salon, which is just on the outside of the town square, two large windows with "Too Hot to Handle" written in blue-and-red script as pretty and feminine as my sister. It's a beautiful aged brick building with red doors and trailing ivy. A rearing black stallion statue is proudly in front. This one, unlike the others, is emblazoned with a gold number 5—Cal's number. I pull down the long driveway to Merry Carole's house, just behind her salon, and turn off the car. I am hot immediately. I step out into the humid North Star air for the first time in years and it's as if I never left. It's been waiting.

"Aunt Queenie?" a man's deep and drawling voice asks.

"Cal, honey?!" I say, unable to control the emotion. He hurls a garbage bag into a bin just behind Merry Carole's salon and looks at me, his head tilted and curious. He still has the same blond hair he had as a toddler. But now it falls across his clear blue eyes with an ease I could never muster as a teenager. As he walks over to me, I notice he has that Wake swagger, which, now that I see it on him, is nothing to be ashamed of.

"What are you doing here?" Cal asks, lunging in for a hug. I am engulfed in pure power. If he squeezes me any harder, I'll break in two.

"You need to stop hugging me so I can see how truly giant you've gotten, sweetheart," I say, holding him away from me. He's wearing low-slung cargo shorts and a white tank top.

"What are you doing here?" Cal asks again. He continues,

"Does Momma know you're here?" Cal looks into the warmly lit house just behind us.

"She sure does. I think she wanted to surprise you. That and she didn't believe me when I said I was coming on home for real this time," I say, reaching up to swipe the bangs out of his eyes.

"I don't know why you'd want to," Cal says, with a sidelong glance and rolled eyes.

"Want to what?"

"Come back to North Star," Cal says.

"Well, despite the time apart, it appears we are definitely related," I say, laughing.

"Last I heard you were in New York."

"Yep."

"I can't believe you'd want to leave a place like that."

"It's just not what it's cracked up to be, sweetie. At least it wasn't for me," I say, lacing my arm through his and walking up the manicured pathway flanked by gold marigolds and white perennials (the North Star Stallion colors) to Merry Carole's crisp red front door.

"I'd like to put that statement into the column of things people say who haven't been cooped up in North Star their whole lives."

I can't help but smile.

Cal opens the front door and I am met with . . . *a home*. I haven't been inside a house, a real house, in years. I worked at this one restaurant in Las Vegas during the holidays and I got to attend the boss's Christmas party—meaning, I was on the catering team who worked the affair. Merry Carole decorates in that way I've always appreciated: not hip enough to be someone you're friends with but inviting enough to be like the friend's mom's house you coveted when you were a kid. There's abundant usage of the Lone Star flag, bits and bobs of Christmas whimsy (after her birthday and name), and the occasional black stallion; Merry Carole's house defies designer labels. I let it wash over me and breathe in the familiar smell of her cooking. I crane my neck past Cal and am now itching to see her. How have I been away for so long?

"Don't tell me! Now, don't you even tell me that that is my baby sister you brought in with you, Calvin Jaques Wake!" Merry Carole comes out of the kitchen, unlacing her Lone Star apron and poufing up her hair.

"He found me outside," I say, bringing Merry Carole in for a tight hug. The smell of her rose-water perfume mixed with Aqua Net tickles my nose just as it always has.

"I can't believe the surprise is ruined," she says, slapping Cal on the arm and then quickly smoothing it over to "make it better." He smiles, wrapping his arm around her.

"The surprise isn't ruined, Momma. It just happened outside," Cal says.

"Just . . . just look at you," Merry Carole says, her voice catching.

"You look just the same," I say, taking her in, my smile wide. Blond Texas hair as high as she can get it and the tightest wardrobe only she, and her Jayne Mansfield–like curves, could pull off.

The room falls silent as Merry Carole remains quiet, her face haunted and unable to hide that I, unlike her, do not look just the same. Cal, sensing her mood, rubs her back and tugs her closer. Great. It seems Merry Carole must be consoled by her only son to soldier on in the face of my gaunt appearance. My face flushes as my smile fades. The once welcoming living room now feels tight around me.

"You just look thin and tired, sweetheart. The drive must have really taken it out of you . . . I, uh . . . you need to eat and get out of those clothes. Then I'm gonna burn everything you brought with you. Oh, speaking of, Cal dear—can you go get Queenie's bags?"

"You don't have to . . . really," I say, trying to gather myself.

Merry Carole just looks at me. I dig my keys out of my pocket and flip them to Cal. He immediately heads outside.

Once Cal is outside, Merry Carole walks over to me, her eyes welling up, black mascara rimming them. Her hand is clutched at her breasts, a silver cross suffocating in their depths. I can't help but feel ashamed as she looks at me. What have I let happen to myself? Who have I become? Why didn't I notice how bad I'd gotten? How much of myself did I erase?

"It can't be all that bad?" I ask.

"You're home now," Merry Carole says.

"It's like you've seen a ghost," I say.

"No, no . . . time just goes by so fast is all," Merry Carole equivocates.

I see her studying me. This is not good. While I've always viewed Merry Carole as the only family I've got, Merry Carole has always treated me as her very own life-size doll. My entire childhood consisted of her dressing me up, doing my hair, and slathering me in makeup. She would hold entire beauty pageants in our backyard. I'd come out in different looks, her commentary peppering my walk down the plywood runway until she tearfully put a tinfoil tiara atop my perfect hair.

Merry Carole flips my lank brown hair over my shoulder, letting my split ends trail through her long fingers.

"Don't even think about it," I say.

"It's just . . . there's no body, no height at all. Are you using any products? Any products to speak of?"

"Yes, Merry Carole. I'm using a can of hair spray every day and this is the end result." I can feel my smile coming back. Having Merry Carole step back in as my constant caretaker makes me feel safer than I have in years. She and my split ends will be dueling in the town square at high noon.

"I don't even understand what you're talking about right now. And you're not wearing any makeup, not even lip gloss. I can't—" Merry Carole is beside herself. She wouldn't dream of going to the mailbox without her face on. I have visions of her house catching on fire and she takes a quick second to check her face in the mirror before fleeing.

"I showered this morning."

"A shower is just the . . . I can't deal with *this* right now," Merry Carole says, waving her hand over all of me to indicate that I am the offending *this*. The front door opens and slams shut.

"You've only got two bags?" Cal asks, carrying my two pieces of luggage.

"I travel light," I say. Merry Carole rolls her eyes at my clichéd answer.

"Where do you want 'em?" Cal asks.

"Oh, I, uh . . ."

"Not you, Queenie. Momma, where do you want 'em?" Cal says, laughing. As if I would know.

"Can you put them in the guest room, sweetheart?" Merry Carole says, turning for the kitchen.

Cal heads toward the back of the house with my two bags. Merry Carole motions for me to sit down at the dining table.

"Can I help with anything?" I ask.

"Not tonight. Tonight you are the guest of honor," Merry Carole says, bringing plate after plate of food from the kitchen. There are barbecued ribs, biscuits, corn on the cob, and on and on. My mouth is watering just looking at it. Cal emerges from the guest room, waits for Merry Carole to sit, and then seats himself. She slaps my hand as I reach out for the plate of ribs.

"We're saying grace, Queen Elizabeth," Merry Carole says, her eyes narrowed.

"All right then, Jesus," I say then quickly correct myself. "Sorry." Cal laughs.

Merry Carole takes my hand and Cal the other. We close our eyes.

"Thank you, Lord, for the feast you have provided us with and for your continued love and guidance. Thank you for blessing me with a strong, healthy boy who any mom would be proud of. But on this night I want to thank you for bringing my baby sister home safe and sound to us, oh Lord. In Jesus' name, amen." Merry Carole finishes, her eyes fluttering open as mascara streams down her face. She has yet to let go of my hand.

"Amen," I say, squeezing her hand and smiling as I try to swallow a wave of tears.

"Amen," Cal says, watching us like a tennis match.

"Now dig in so we can get to burning them clothes of yours," Merry Carole says with a wink.

4

Crow
(and two eggs over medium, wheat toast,
house potatoes, and a cup of coffee)

I sleep like the dead. I remember starting to think about New York and being back in North Star and where I was going to go next and then the sun cracks through the red, white, and blue window treatments, letting me know it's morning. I dreamed of nothing, and looking at the deep indentation I made in the little twin bed, I didn't move all night.

"Good morning." I yawn, walking into the kitchen.

"Good morning," Merry Carole says, turning around from the kitchen counter.

"Cal still asleep?" I say, pulling a stool up to the breakfast bar.

"Football practice starts at six AM. He should be home soon, actually."

"That sounds terrible."

"That's just the first practice. His second one is tonight when the sun goes down."

"So, where can I get a cup of coffee around here?" I ask.

"Right there in the coffeemaker," Merry Carole says, now leaning against the kitchen counter.

"No, I mean like buy a cup of coffee. Is there a Starbucks here yet?" I ask.

"You can go to the Homestead," Merry Carole says.

"I don't think I'm ready for that yet."

"Well, I heard there's a new coffee place called Around the Corner. It's fifteen miles outside of town," Merry Carole says, taking a seat at the table with her steaming mug of coffee.

"Maybe I'll try that," I say.

"Or you could just have a cup at home from that coffeemaker right there, you know—for free." She sips.

"I think I'm looking for stuff to do, you know? A plan," I say, hopping down off my stool and walking toward the coffeemaker. I pour myself a cup.

"The creamer is in the fridge." Merry Carole guides.

"Thanks." I pull open the refrigerator and am way too excited about the assortment of International Delight creamers that line the door. I choose the French Vanilla and pour it reverently into my mug. I breathe it in.

"You're welcome to help me out in the salon anytime you want. I know Fawn and Dee are dying to see you."

"I'd like that."

"Really?" Merry Carole is caught off guard.

"I mean, don't get me wrong, I'm not looking forward to telling and retelling the tale of the string of epic failures that have led to me returning to a town I basically gave the finger to lo those many years ago." I sit down at the dining room table and take a sip of coffee.

"Sure."

Merry Carole and I fall silent.

"Cal's a great kid," I finally say.

"Isn't he?"

"And he looooves you."

"He's all I've had through all—" Merry Carole stops herself. That guilt that settled on me in that motel room in Birmingham becomes heavier. Did Merry Carole want to go with me all those years ago? No. She loves North Star. Why don't I? With my single-minded kitchen life in all those cities, I didn't have time to ask these inconvenient questions. Finally. Something positive that came out of all those years. Merry Carole speaks quickly. "I don't mean to make you feel bad. I just . . ."

"No, you're right."

"I'm glad you're back."

"Me, too."

We are quiet.

"But you're thinking about the next city already, right?" Merry Carole asks, her voice clear, her eyes focused.

"Yes, ma'am."

"Is North Star that bad?"

"For me? Yes."

"That's just ridiculous."

"Are you trying to tell me they've gotten better?" I say, motioning to the world just outside Merry Carole's sanctuary of a home.

"Are you trying to tell me that whatever life you had in New York or Los Angeles or whatever that place was with all the turquoise—"

"Taos."

"Taos? Are you saying that Taos is worth what it took out of you?" Merry Carole motions at me and the shadow I've become.

"So you admit that they're still just as shitty."

"So you admit that all those cities were just shitty."

We are quiet.

"Cal's just like you. All he wants to do is leave," Merry Carole says, not looking at me.

"I know."

We fall silent again.

"If you're looking for something to do, you can go visit Mom," Merry Carole says.

"Please don't tell me you've been going there."

Merry Carole says nothing.

"I don't know what you think you're going to find. It's not like she can apologize or make amends," I say, sipping my coffee.

"It's called forgiveness, Queen Elizabeth. It's the Christian thing to do."

"Well, seeing as how she's dead and buried, I imagine it makes it a lot easier to forgive her." The last time I was in North Star I was feeling particularly dramatic and drove over to the cemetery that's just off the church in the center of town. I got out of my car and immediately crumpled into tears—the kind of tears that feel so vast it's alarming and mystifying at the same time. Then, just as quickly, I swept all those emotions aside and decided never to return. I do that a lot.

"Don't talk like that."

"You don't talk like that."

"Me? Me don't talk like that?"

"Don't you dare try and make a hero out of that woman. I swear to God," I say, leaning on the dining room table.

"I'm not making a hero out of her, for heaven's sake. I'm just saying that while you're back in town for the twenty minutes you plan on staying, you might want to drive by the cemetery and place a nice bouquet on her grave."

A moment passes.

"You ever think about her?" I ask.

The room goes cold. Merry Carole circles the rim of her coffee mug with her manicured fingers. Her face is twitching with all the energy it's taking to remain neutral.

"Sometimes," Merry Carole says, finally looking up to meet my gaze.

"I check on her, you know," I say.

"You what?"

"You can check on the prison Web site, you know . . . how she's doing, if she won all those appeals."

"She murdered two people in cold blood and got the death penalty—those appeals are offensive."

"She murdered her own husband and the woman he was cheating on her with in her very own bed. A woman who was her very best friend right up until she cocked that shotgun," I say, taking a sip of my coffee. My hands are shaking.

"Yvonne Chapman is a monster and that's all I'm going to say on the subject."

"Yvonne Chapman let us stay in her home for several weeks—right up until our mother got herself killed in it."

"How dare you take that woman's side."

"Honey, I'm not taking her side. I'm just saying that it's a bit more complicated than Yvonne Chapman being a monster."

"I know that. Of course I know that." Merry Carole's entire body is tight. Her mouth is pulled into a hard line. She just keeps shaking her head, like a child trying to get out of eating their vegetables. "Sometimes I wish it weren't . . . *complicated*, you know?"

"I know."

Merry Carole reaches her hand across the table and takes my hand in hers. I give her a comforting smile and she squeezes my hand tight.

It's easy to be detached about my mom's tragic end when I know it came as such a relief to Merry Carole and me. Whenever she was around, it was hell. So all we wished for growing up was for her to be gone and away. When the principal walked into my classroom on that ill-fated day with the news that she'd been killed, by Yvonne Chapman of all people, the first thing I felt was . . . free. Merry Carole was just eighteen, so she became my legal guardian and life got better for us, especially when Cal came along a few months later. I'm not delusional (well, not about this) to be afraid there aren't major repercussions because of her death.

It doesn't take a team of psychologists—or perhaps it would—to understand what I've been running from all these years. Why it's like a religion for me to travel light and keep moving should not be a mystery to anyone—least of all me. But knowing my mom was a bad person doesn't mean I understand why she didn't love us— didn't love me. Whatever that was at the cemetery was probably more about innocence lost or some other bullshit.

"Weren't you saying something about a cup of coffee?" Merry Carole stands.

"I don't want to fight. Please."

"I know that, I really do. It's just weird having you back."

"You're telling me," I say. The front door opens and shuts.

"Mom? Aunt Queenie?" Cal comes barreling into the kitchen, sweaty and red faced. He dumps his football pads by the door.

"Hey there," I say, smiling and happy for the distraction.

"You're still here," he says, his entire being exhaling.

"Of course," I say, my heart breaking.

"Your breakfast is ready, sweetie. It's warming in the oven. I've got to get to work." Merry Carole bends over Cal and gives him a kiss on the top of his head.

Merry Carole gives me a quick nod and hands me the directions for the coffee place that's "just around the corner" but apparently still fifteen miles outside town. I thank her hoping we're not mad at each other anymore. Back to normal? I don't know what our normal is, so maybe I'm just hoping that my New Car Smell hasn't worn off yet. Cal pulls his breakfast out of the oven and pours himself a cup of coffee.

"I'm heading over to that coffee place. The Around the Corner one?" I say to Cal. He looks pointedly at the full mug of coffee in his own hand as well as the mug in front of me.

"You know you have coffee in that mug right in front of you, right?"

"Yeah."

"Just checking."

"I just need something to do. I'm getting all contemplative, and that, I assure you, is not a good thing."

"I can definitely get behind that."

"You want to come?"

"I'll go with you to the Homestead."

"A negotiation, eh?"

"Maybe."

"I don't know if I'm ready for my coming-out party yet."

"Now's as good a time as any, right? I mean . . . realllly think about it."

Sighhhhhhhhh.

"You know I'm right," Cal says.

"You just want more food."

"How dare you."

"Fine."

I mope and pout down the hallway and take a shower with big shampoo bottles and everything. I put on what I think is my best outfit and then decide very quickly that everything I've brought is either checked pants for the kitchen, jeans, or black. Meaning, I have nothing to wear in the throes of this hot and humid Texas summer. I throw on a T-shirt and some jeans, which I immediately regret as the entire lower half of my body turns into a sweat-based soup just outside Merry Carole's front door. We walk the two blocks to the Homestead and by the time Cal opens up the door to the old diner my hair is smashed against my face and my entire body is shimmering with sweat. The sunglasses I put on to hide my horror at being back in North Star have fogged over due to the humidity.

The air-conditioning hits me in a welcoming burst. The Homestead is just as I remember it. A long counter stretches down one side, the grill and soda fountain just behind it. A large menu with the same twenty or so items on it is painted high up on the wall behind the counter so everyone can see—one whole side dedicated to just pie. Small wooden tables line the other wall leading to the back where the diner opens up to booths and waitress stations. The smell of grease and beef is kept to a minimum because of the owner Sheldon Brink's motto that his standards are as high as a good Texas woman's hair. Cal and I grab a booth near the back as I try not to notice the stares.

"Queenie Wake?! Rumor has it you were in town. It's not often we get a car with New York plates driving through town on a Sunday night. Most townsfolk are in church or home with their families."

"Hey . . . *hey,*" I say, quickly checking the girl's name tag—Peggy. Peggy? Oh shit—Piggy Peggy. She was a couple of years ahead of me in high school and hung out with the popular kids.

"I know! I'm not Piggy Peggy anymore!" Peggy gives me a quick twirl, letting me see her much thinner figure. If I remember correctly, and I know I do, it was her own bitchy friends who gave her that moniker.

"I didn't think you were ever Piggy Peggy," I say.

"Oh sure . . . sure. I know. I'm just . . . Wow. Look at you." Peggy folds her arms across her chest, tucking her pad of paper and the pencil under her arm as she gives me the once-over.

"Yep," I say, narrowing my eyes at Cal. Peggy shifts her gaze over to him.

"And look at this boy, huh? North Star's pride and joy! An incoming freshman and already he's going after varsity quarterback!" Peggy reaches out as if to pat Cal on the back, but then pulls back, deciding to just rest her hand on her hip. Going after? I thought he was already named varsity quarterback?

We all just stare and smile at one another—and by "we all" I mean everyone in the Homestead. While everyone has done their best to pretend they have continued eating and talking, I feel the gazes boring into me. I should never have come here. And by "here" I mean North Star. Coming to the Homestead was just the momentary craziness of not being able to say no to my nephew.

"Coffee?" Peggy asks, snapping out of her haze.

"That'd be great. Thank you," I say.

"Just water for me," Cal adds. Peggy clucks a quick you're welcome and is off.

"I shall set aside my momentary hatred of you for bringing me here for a second as I clarify—I thought you had that varsity quarterback position?" I ask, my voice just over a whisper.

"Oh, I do. Piggy Peggy's just pissed that her friend's little brother didn't get it."

"Is he older?"

"No, he's a freshman just like me. He doesn't even want it. He's a great wide receiver." Cal's confidence is unnerving, yet familiar. Sounds like me talking about cooking.

"Okay, here y'all go—one coffee and one water. What else can I get you this morning?" Peggy says, setting down our beverages, her pencil at the ready.

"I'll have the number two with my eggs over medium, wheat toast, and the house potatoes," I say, craning past Peggy to get a look at the menu on the wall.

"Cal, honey, what are you having?"

"I'll have the country breakfast with everything," he says, not having to look at the menu at all. I just shake my head and laugh.

"Gotta keep fueled up, I guess!" Peggy says, her laughter now more nervous. She smiles and retreats back behind the counter.

"She hasn't changed a bit. You know her own friends gave her that name—Piggy Peggy. I can't believe she's here and still just as obsequious as ever. Don't let her fool you, my boy—she'll no sooner give you an ingratiating smile than start a rumor that you started your period on the bus coming back from a field trip to the Texas Ranger museum in Waco," I say, pouring cream into my coffee.

"Hypothetically speaking?" Cal asks.

"I wish," I say, reliving every horrific moment.

"Cal Wake," a man strides over to our booth and extends his hand.

"Mr. Coburn." Cal scoots out of the booth and stands to shake the man's hand. My stomach drops as I look up at him. Everett Coburn. In North Star there are three families who are set apart from the rest, however unfairly. Well, four if you count the Wakes and you're talking about the low bar. But if you're talking about the gold standard of North Star, then it's the Ackermans, the McKays, and the Coburns. They're the closest things to royalty North Star's got. Just ask them . . . they'll be sure to tell you.

"You looked good out there this morning, son," Everett says, his hand firmly placed on Cal's throwing arm.

"Thank you, sir," Cal says. The man looks from Cal to me and I see the realization settle on his face. I set my jaw and stare right back at him.

"Everett," I say with a curt nod.

"You know my aunt—," Cal begins.

"Of course, son. Queenie, nice to see you again, " Everett says, his entire face lined with contained disbelief.

"I see you're just as quick with a lie as you always were," I say with a smile.

"A delight, as usual. Well, good luck out there, Cal. Queenie, welcome home," Everett says.

"Temporarily," I say.

"As always," Everett says, a polite nod to me while he disentangles himself from our booth as quickly as he appeared. Cal slides back in the booth.

"You know Mr. Coburn?" Cal asks as Peggy brings over our breakfasts.

"Yeah. I knew him," I say as he digs in.

Everett Coburn is the man I've been in love with my entire life.

5

Butterscotch hard candy

I need to cook something. I need to lose myself in something else besides the fractured light of my own memory. I'll cook a big supper as a thank-you for being so welcoming. I'll cook. And not think about crying at cemeteries, principals walking down hallways with squeaky shoes, and, most of all, about Everett Coburn—with his light brown hair that gets the tiniest flecks of blond just at his temples as the summer goes on. I'll cook and really not think about his powerful hand resting on Cal's throwing arm, the muscles threading up his arm like piano wire. I'll cook so I won't have to think about those green eyes pinwheeled in brown and yellow playing against his olive skin. The same green eyes that implored me to understand that he was marrying that girl anyway—even as we lay in my bed. No. I'll cook. It'll be fine. I've been not thinking about Everett Coburn for going on twenty years.

I walk into Merry Carole's salon with my plan. I open up the front door to the salon, and am met with country music, the hum of hair dryers, and gossip. As I'm pulling a butterscotch hard candy from the decorative bowl, it all screeches to a halt.

"QUEEN ELIZABETH!" Fawn yells, coming around the front desk and diving into me with a hug. She has always been a big woman; her ability to take up space astounded me. Fawn's ever changing hair color is now an orangey shade of red and cut in a diagonal razored style that should be reserved for teenagers. Her trendy clothes always one size too small and, as always, some version of a rhinestone cowboy boot on her feet. She hasn't changed a bit. She pulls away from me and settles her eyes on mine.

"Good to see you again," I say, smiling.

"Oh, she is thin, Merry Carole. Just a slip of herself. You said you been feeding her?" Fawn talks as if I'm not there.

"We had a proper Sunday supper," Merry Carole says, focusing on the hair she's cutting.

"You'd think after working in all those fancy kitchens you would have bothered to eat some of it," Fawn says, anxiously swiping my lifeless bangs out of my face.

"I was working in all those fancy kitchens making food for other people," I say.

"Look at you," Fawn says, her voice breathy.

Fawn is my mother's age and would like to think of herself as a maternal figure in our lives. But she's too much like our mother to be anything close to maternal. Merry Carole and I play our parts anyway. While Fawn and my mother trolled the bar scene back in the day, like two peas in a pod, Yvonne Chapman was the happily married friend who finished out their tight trio. Momma and Fawn would lament their love lives while Yvonne endlessly doled out relationship advice to the hapless duo, trotting out her happy marriage like a prize pig. When Mom stayed away for days at a time, Fawn and Yvonne would always come by with a couple of Happy Meals, an apology, and the assurance that Mom was doing the best that she could . . . she really was. We took the food, but could never quite swallow the excuses. I don't begrudge Fawn any of it. She wasn't our mother. She chose not to have kids and is now happily married to a roughneck named Pete who works the oil rigs on the Coburn back forty. And Yvonne? Well, she made her bed.

"I want to cook supper for you guys tonight if you can make it. All of you," I say, hoping that the customers don't think I mean them.

"We'd love that," Merry Carole says, brushing the freshly cut hair from her customer's shoulders.

"Pete and I are definitely in," Fawn says.

"Is Dee working today?" I ask, scanning the salon. Dee Finkel is my oldest friend in North Star. When I left I remember thinking how small her dreams were—she wanted to get married, have some kids, and work in a hair salon. *I* was going to set the world on fire. No, you go ahead and cut some old lady's hair in some back-water in Texas Hill Country. What an epic jerk I was.

"She's back in the shampoo room." Merry Carole nods toward the back of the salon.

"Six? Tonight?" Fawn says, trying to hammer out the details.

"Sounds perfect. Don't bring a thing," I say, walking toward the shampoo room.

"I can't wait!" Fawn says before launching into a diatribe about how worried she is about me.

I walk into the shampoo room and see Dee pouring big gallons of shampoo into smaller bottles of shampoo that are next to the washing stations. She looks exactly the same.

"Dee Finkel, is that you?!" I say, walking toward her.

"Dee Finkel?" Dee asks, still focused on the shampoo. I stumble a bit, thinking she would welcome me with open arms.

"It's Queenie. Queenie Wake?" I ask, my voice half of what it was.

"Oh my God, you're so funny! I haven't been Dee Finkel in years," she says, setting the gallon of shampoo down and wiping her hands on her apron. We hug for an awkward amount of time and I find myself patting her back to break free.

"It's so good to see you," I say, backing away from her. Of course she wouldn't be super glad to see me. I was a heinous bitch the last time we saw each other.

"How long are you back for?" Dee asks, her arms folded across her chest. She looks like an adult. A grown-up I'd see in public and think would certainly have nothing whatsoever in common with me. She looks healthy and vomit-inducingly happy. Her dark hair is more styled than it used to be. That's probably because she's the lowest stylist on the totem pole here and everyone's experimental head of hair. She's wearing flowery capri pants and a light pink sleeveless blouse to go with her usual (not today apparently) sunny outlook.

"Oh, I don't know," I say, my smile quickly fading.

"But not long though, right? You're already planning to go to some other big city, right?"

"I don't know."

"Okay, well . . ." Dee's face is tight. She starts to move for the shampoo again.

"If you're not Dee Finkel anymore, who are you then?" I ask, trying.

"I'm sorry?" Dee asks.

"If you're not Dee Finkel anymore, who are you?"

"I married Shawn Richter almost six years ago. You remember Shawn? He was a defensive lineman?"

"Sure . . . sure. I didn't even know you guys were dating?" I ask, glad that she's no longer trying to escape to the shampoo rather than talk to me.

"Yeah, we started dating a little after you left. His mom comes in here to get her hair done, so . . ."

"Sure . . . sure . . ."

"We have three little boys. I still want that little girl," Dee says, pointing to an array of framed photos at one of the stylist stations out in the salon.

"So you're trying to say that while I have come back to town low down and broken down, you—the former Ms. Dee Finkel—have gotten everything you ever dreamed of," I say, nodding and trying to smile.

"You could say that, yes," Dee says, her face flushing.

"I'm so happy for you," I say.

We are quiet. Terribly awkward and quiet.

"I'm so sorry for being rude before, but I just couldn't stand getting all friendly with you if you're just passing through. You and this town are like outta sight, outta mind. I guess I just miss you, is all," Dee says, speaking quickly, her face growing blotchier and blotchier as she speaks. Dee was always way too nice to be friends with me.

"You weren't rude, seriously. I don't know why I expect people to forget that I was terrible when I left here," I say, breathing a bit easier.

"You weren't terrible," Dee says.

"You're just too nice to say I was, but . . . I definitely was." We fall silent again. I hear cackling laughter from the front of the salon. Fawn. I'd know that laugh anywhere.

"I'm glad you're back however long you're staying," Dee says, her eyes darting around the room.

"You want to hug again, don't you?"

"You know me too well, Queenie Wake!" Dee pulls me in for a hug. A real one.

"I'm cooking tonight for everyone. I'd love it if you, Shawn, and the boys could come over," I say, knowing Merry Carole is always comfortable with a thousand people in her house. The realization that she gets to actually put the leaves in her dining room table will be like Christmas come early.

"Oh, you're sweet, but I don't think you really want our entire brood in your house. I barely want them in mine," Dee says.

"I certainly do. Six?"

"That sounds perfect. Means I don't have to figure out what to cook. That alone," Dee says, exhaling. I notice the salon has gotten quiet; so does Dee. We both look into the front of the salon.

Laurel Coburn. Or as I like to call her, that bitch Everett married. I hate that she's perfect. Her lemon yellow sundress, her leather sandals and pedicured toes. Her sunflower hair exists in its own bubble. Apparently it's not a slave to the humidity as everyone else's is. She is everything I'm not.

The door to the salon opens and Whitney McKay bursts through. Short black hair and elegant in that kind of way others, myself among them, might describe as "icy." Laurel Coburn and Whitney McKay, along with Piggy Peggy, are North Star's resident mean girls.

"So the rumors are true," Laurel says, taking off her sunglasses and staring right at me.

"Did y'all have an appointment today?" Fawn asks from behind the front desk.

"Oh, no thank you. We just had to see it for ourselves," Whitney says.

It.

Laurel and Whitney wait. I don't move. Merry Carole thanks her customer as she hurries out and then walks over to the women.

"I'm so glad you decided to pop in for a visit," Merry Carole says, her voice forced and high.

"How's Cal? I heard he has quite the appetite," Whitney asks.

"He's home napping, saving up his energy for the second practice," Merry Carole says, puffing up.

"Coach says he looked tired today," Whitney says, pulling her compact out of her purse.

"He certainly didn't say anything like that to me," Merry Carole says.

"Probably just the heat," Whitney says, touching up her face in the tiny mirror. I'm half surprised the mirror doesn't break from the pure evil staring into it.

Whitney used to be Whitney Ackerman before she married Wes McKay. Wes McKay is North Star's golden boy, former all-star quarterback and Cal's biological father. At seventeen, Merry Carole made the mistake of thinking Wes loved her. When she told him she was pregnant, he renounced her and the as yet unborn baby. Merry Carole was branded a gold-digging harlot, just like her mother, and Whitney took her rightful place as the long-suffering Lady of the McKay Manor. Merry Carole vowed never to make the mistake of trusting a man again.

"I hear West is doing well," Merry Carole offers, her voice painfully anxious. I settle into my stance, waiting to hear what Whitney will say of her "little brother," West Ackerman. West Ackerman was born just months after Cal. Coincidentally, West looks exactly like Whitney and Wes. Yet she's passed him off as her "little brother" for years. Whitney and her parents spent a year at her grandparents' house in Houston before West's birth. And oh, look at that, her postmenopausal mother brought back a little surprise!

Even West's name is a blend of the two actual parents' names! But this is a lie North Star allows. The Ackermans are a respected family who wouldn't dare be deceitful, whereas the Wakes are just a bunch of slobbering animals.

"West is the pride of North Star and of the Ackerman family name. He's got quite an arm, and he can catch," Whitney says, tucking her compact back into her purse. It dawns on me that West Ackerman is probably the kid Cal was talking about this morning. Of course he is. It makes sense that the powers that be in this town would want West to take over the quarterback position made famous by his father. Of course, Wes McKay is Cal's father, too. The citizens of North Star seem to keep conveniently forgetting that.

During Whitney and Merry Carole's little banter, everything comes rushing back. I can't believe I was so naive. There is no coming back to North Star on my own terms. I may be older and wiser, but we are still the villains. We are still the unwanted. We are still the ones parents point to and warn, "Don't brush your teeth and you'll end up like poor Merry Carole and Queenie Wake. Let a boy get to second base and you'll end up like poor Merry Carole and Queenie Wake. Cheat on that final and you'll end up like poor Merry Carole and Queenie Wake." Being Brandi-Jaques Wake's daughters means being branded a pariah.

We are North Star's very own bogeymen.

I hate that Cal has been dragged into all this history. He seems unaffected by it. Although I know from personal experience that outward appearances can be deceiving. Take right now, for instance. I look as though I haven't a care in the world. My face wears a breezy smile. My entire body is a testament to the yogic pose mountain—balanced and rooted to the earth. I sigh and breathe as if I'm not about to explode across this room and rip Laurel's hair out while screaming, "YOU STOLE MY MAN, YOU SOUL-

LESS BITCH!" at the top of my lungs. Nope. I am a practice in calm. I breathe in for the first time in minutes, hours maybe. I snap out of my trance. Laurel's eyes are still fixed on me. I love it. I love that I've always gotten under her perfectly moisturized alabaster skin. I steady my breathing—like a sniper focusing his target in the crosshairs.

"We'd better get going. I've got to get supper on the table for Wes and the kids," Whitney says with a particularly giddy under-tone.

"Great seeing you guys! See you at the Fourth of July festival!" Merry Carole calls out as they leave the salon.

The door closes. I begin to speak—

"Don't say a word, Queen Elizabeth. Not. One. Word," Merry Carole says, retreating to the bathroom.

The bathroom door slams behind her.

6

The Number One

Mom ran her restaurant out of an eight-by-eight-foot shack connected to the Drinkers Hall of Fame, the one bar in town. The restaurant was an old storage shed on a small corner plot of land and the only thing the Wake family ever owned. Almost as an afterthought, Mom nailed a board by the take-out window with the word WAKE branded into it. She kept the same hours as the bar and her entire staff consisted of Fawn, Merry Carole, and me. No matter what anyone in North Star thought of my mom, everyone agreed on one thing: she was the best cook in the Texas Hill Country. She was known for her barbecue and fried pies. But she was most famous for one particular dish. The dish people would drive hundreds of miles for was simply called the Number One. I imagine Momma was going to make a list of specials. The trouble was, she never got past the Number One. So there it sat at the top of the menu, alone, all by itself.

The Number One:
Chicken fried steak with cream gravy, mashed potatoes,
green beans cooked in bacon fat, one buttermilk biscuit,
and a slice of pecan pie

With Brad's words ringing in my head about my vague culinary vision, I decide to make the Number One for tonight's supper. After leaving the salon, I drive to various farm stands, grocery stores, and butchers. I handpick the top-round steak with care, choose fresh eggs one by one, and feel an immense sense of home as I pull Mom's cast-iron skillet from the depths of Merry Carole's cabinets. My happiest memories involve me walking into whatever house we were staying in at the time to the sounds and smells of chicken fried steak sizzling away in that skillet. This dish is at the very epicenter of who I am. If my culinary roots start anywhere, it's with the Number One.

As I tenderize the beef, my mind is clear and I'm happy. I haven't cooked like this—my recipes for me and the people I love—in far too long. If ever. Time flies as I roll out the crust for the pecan pie. I'm happy and contented as I cut out the biscuit rounds one by one. I haven't a care in the world. Being in Merry Carole's kitchen has washed away everything I left in New York, along with everything that's happened in the whirlwind of being back in North Star. Laurel's little tantrum at the salon is a distant memory. However dramatic and ridiculous she is, she also gets to go home to the man I've loved since I was in kindergarten. I focus back on the cooking. It's almost time for supper. The front door opens and closes.

Merry Carole walks into the kitchen with a bouquet of Texas yellow bells. I can see the emotion on her face as she approaches me. With everything warming in the oven, the last thing to do before the guests arrive is fry this steak.

"I know," I say, taking her hand.

"I can't believe you're cooking the Number One. I haven't . . . I haven't walked into a house with that smell in years. It smells exactly the same." Merry Carole dabs at her mascara.

"Let's face it, toward the end there I was in that kitchen more than she was," I say, lifting the steak out of the skillet.

"The kitchen is a lot cleaner than I thought it was going to be," Merry Carole says, scanning the already set dining room table and spotless kitchen.

"I guess that's the one positive by-product of working in all those fancy kitchens. If you don't have a clean workspace, there's hell to pay," I say, quickly swiping at the counter.

"It's like you were shipped off to the culinary army," Merry Carole says, setting the flowers on the counter and pulling a vase down from one of the upper cabinets. She arranges them quickly and sets them in the middle of the table.

"That's certainly what it felt like," I say, pulling my arm away from the splattering lard. The front door opens and slams.

"Whatever that is I smell, bless you," Cal yells as he walks through the front room.

"Chicken fried steak, my dear. Now go take a quick shower and put on something presentable. We're having company," Merry Carole says, reaching up to fuss with his bangs. She continues, "I wish you would let me cut these. Just a touch . . . You have such pretty eyes, sweetness and light." Merry Carole calling her varsity-football-playing son sweetness and light damn near melts my heart.

"Is that—" Cal stops. I'm sure he's heard the stories. Merry Carole sighs and drags her gaze away from Cal's overgrown bangs.

"It is, in fact, the Number One. You're in for a treat," I say, turning away from the stovetop briefly.

"I didn't think it really existed," Cal says, gazing into the kitchen.

"Oh, it exists, but if you don't shower up, it'll become a myth," Merry Carole says, pushing him toward the bathroom. He obliges, his gait quickening as he realizes what's in store.

"Tired, my ass. That boy is amazing," Merry Carole says, her voice breaking.

"She was deliberately messing with you," I say, taking the last chicken fried steak from the lard.

"West Ackerman is the pride of North Star," Merry Carole mimics.

"Does Cal know?"

"No!" Merry Carole shushes me, checking to see if he is out of earshot. The guests are due in minutes.

"He's in the shower," I say, washing the last of the dishes. I squeeze out the dishrag, take my apron off, and hang it back up. The kitchen looks just as I found it.

"He has no idea who West really is to him, so please, you can't breathe a word of it."

"Honey, I have no intention of telling him, but I do think you're kidding yourself if you think he hasn't heard the rumors. He'd heard about the Number One. Do you honestly think he hasn't heard about Wes McKay fathering not one, but two children illegitimately before his marriage to the Ice Queen lobotomized him?" I ask, giving the pitcher of homemade lemonade a quick stir.

"It was hard enough when Wes disowned us; I'm certainly not giving Whitney and her people the opportunity to do it again," Merry Carole says.

"You have a point," I say.

"I know I do. West is a good kid. Cal likes him. Maybe someday . . . ," Merry Carole says. She offers a small smile as the doorbell rings.

"Maybe," I say.

Fawn and Pete are loud and happy to be here. Fawn introduces me to Pete as Merry Carole waits by the open door greeting Dee and her brood as they mosey down the long driveway.

I offer Fawn and Pete some beer or lemonade. They mill around the kitchen as I pour them their glasses. Everyone is a bit taken aback. I don't know if it's because this is Momma's dish or that I'm making it. Fawn looks like she's seen a ghost as she breathes in the scents coming from the kitchen. Yes, it's the Number One, I say, trying to lighten the mood. Yes, Momma taught me how to make it. Yes, she finally admitted I made it better than she did toward the end there.

Then the entire house is alive and loud with bursting energy. I imagine it's Dee's brood. I excuse myself from Fawn and Pete and head to the front room. Shawn is a big man, barrel chested and powerful. I recognize him vaguely from high school. I doubt our paths would have crossed. Matter of fact, I don't think he and Dee really knew each other in high school, either. Football players tend to keep to themselves. Today, he wears a denim shirt tucked into khaki pants and a heavy gold chain with a cross. He's smiling and wrangling children as he steps inside Merry Carole's house.

"Queenie, this is Shawn," Dee says, keeping an eye on an errant child. We shake hands and my hand is lost in his.

"And who might you guys be?" I ask, looking at the little stair-step boys barely containing themselves.

"You asked for it," Shawn says, smiling.

"I certainly did," I say, laughing.

"Queenie, this is our oldest, Shawn Junior, and Chance is in the middle there, and the little one is Austin." The little boys are all under the age of six and wearing exactly the same outfit: khaki shorts and a short-sleeved denim shirt with sandals. Apparently, all of the Richter men dress exactly the same.

"Come on in, supper is ready," I say, just as Cal comes back from his shower. He joins us at the table.

"Sit, sit!" Merry Carole says as Fawn and Dee offer their help, clearly unaccustomed to being waited on.

Our guests sit and Merry Carole and I bring out the dishes one by one. The chicken fried steak, the cream gravy, the mashed potatoes, and the green beans cooked in bacon fat. I bring over a tea towel–lined basket filled with biscuits. Merry Carole asks if anyone needs a beer or some lemonade. Cal says he'll have a beer. Merry Carole brings him lemonade. Dee's boys think Cal is hysterical.

Merry Carole and I sit. I hold my hands out to Cal and Shawn for grace. Everyone looks to Merry Carole. We close our eyes and bow our heads.

"Thank you, Lord, for the feast you have provided us with and for your continued love and guidance. Thank you for blessing me with a strong, healthy boy who any mom would be proud of. Thank you for blessing us, oh Lord, with friends and loved ones who are with us at our table and with you in your blessed kingdom. In Jesus' name, amen."

"Amen," we all say in unison. Merry Carole and I are both fighting back a confused muddle of emotion as we pass plates, serve ourselves, and tell people we're fine. We laugh, recount stories (leaving out all of the messy details) of our childhood, and talk about football. It's a beautiful night.

"Dee says you're going to be in town for a while," Shawn says, as the meal winds down.

"Oh, does she?" I ask, giving Dee a wink.

"Oh, I uh . . . I was just thinking if you were planning on staying, I know of someplace that's hiring. If you're looking," Shawn says. The crowd erupts in laughter as Fawn tells a story about Mom's fryer catching fire one time and the drunken denizens of the Drinkers Hall of Fame offering their help by throwing their beer at the flames. I'm happy for the ringing laughter and Fawn's hysterical storytelling. I don't know how to answer Shawn's question. Shawn continues, "The job is temporary, if that helps."

"Any job can be temporary," I say, trying to lighten the mood and move Shawn along.

"But this job is temporary 'cause people can't seem to stand doing it longer than a few months," Shawn says, looking over at his boys to make sure they're not listening. They're not. My curiosity is piqued.

"What is it?" I ask.

"I work over at the prison, not the main one in Huntsville, mind you, but the one over in Shine—just a short piece down the road," Shawn says. I nod.

"He's the captain of the Death House team," Dee says, her voice a whisper.

"I'm not going to be there much longer, mind," Shawn says.

"It's just too hard on him . . . on all of us. We're going to get into local law enforcement. He's not far off from joining the county sheriff's," Dee says proudly, her arm laced around the back of Shawn's chair.

"So what would I be doing?" I ask.

"You know how they make last meals, right?"

"I thought Texas stopped doing that?" I ask. I remember reading the articles about Texas putting a stop to the long-standing tradition because of one particularly disgusting convict gluttonously ordering a decadent last meal and then not touching a bite of it.

"The new warden is ambitious," Dee says.

"He thinks he's going to be the next W," Shawn says with rolled eyes.

"He found some anonymous donor and has proclaimed he's still going to make the last meals for the condemned," Dee says.

"That's where you come in," Shawn says, motioning to the full-to-bursting plates on the table.

"You want me to make the last meals for the condemned? Are you serious?" I ask, my question breaking through the other conversations at the table.

"They'd be lucky to have you," Shawn says, his paw of a hand bringing up his beer bottle and taking a giant swig. Merry Carole is now listening to our conversation. Everyone else is riveted to Fawn's tall tales. Shawn continues, "Just think about it."

"I will. I appreciate you thinking of me. Thank you," I say.

"You don't have to decide now, either. You go in for the interview, see if it's even something you want to do, and then you decide," Dee says.

"It's creepy though, right?" I ask.

"It's definitely not for everyone. Shawn's only been the captain for a few months and he's just . . . well, we're ready for him to move on," Dee says.

"Last meals," I say, almost to myself.

"I've always looked at it like, if this is the law, then the least I can do is bring my integrity to the job," Shawn says.

"How many meals are we talking?" I ask.

"I've heard Huntsville can go up to two a week some months. But over at Shine we do more like three or four a month," Shawn says.

"And I never—"

"You never even know their names or what they've done, Queenie. I mean, you can ask, but it's not information you have to know. You get an order. That's it. They come over to the Death

House that morning and spend the day with the chaplain. I'll come get the meal from you and take it by four PM, and by six PM, well . . ." Shawn trails off.

"I always thought it was done at midnight," I say.

"No, ma'am," Shawn says, taking another pull from his beer. This is clearly not something he likes talking about.

"You know that the last-meal tradition started because people were superstitious about being haunted by the people they'd put to death?" Cal says, inserting himself into the conversation.

"Sweetie," I say, uncomfortable with him getting involved.

"Timothy McVeigh only wanted two pints of mint chocolate chip ice cream," Cal adds.

"You can tell a lot based on someone's last meal," Dee says.

"I have no idea what mine would be," I say.

"Really?" Dee asks.

"Oh absolutely . . . there's too much to choose from," I say.

"Strawberries. Just strawberries as far as the eye can see," Dee says.

"John Wayne Gacy wanted a pound of strawberries," Cal says. Dee looks mortified.

"How do you know so much about this?" I ask.

"We were just studying the death penalty in history. We got to talking about last meals," Cal says. Merry Carole stands and picks up the empty pitcher of lemonade. She motions for me to follow her. I excuse myself and follow Merry Carole into the kitchen.

"Are you talking about the death penalty during supper?" Merry Carole says in hushed tones and behind the open refrigerator door.

"Shawn asked if I wanted to make the last meals over at the prison," I say.

"He's not happy there, though, says it's no kind of place to work."

"I know."

"Are you thinking about doing it?"

"I mean, if I want to really get a good nest egg going for the next city, it would be nice to stop cutting into my savings," I say.

"You can work at the salon," Merry Carole says.

"I can do that, too. This would be only a few times a month. I wouldn't see anyone and all I would do is cook one meal."

"Yeah, one last meal for a murderer."

"What if . . . what if food can do for these people what it does for me, you know? Transport them to another time and place."

"These people are the worst of humanity. You can never forget that."

"I won't forget it. And look, I've worked in so many places I've probably already cooked for a murderer or two. Who knows?"

"You're not taking this seriously."

"I am."

"And now . . . now you come back into town and start working at the prison? What will everyone think?"

"Are you really asking that?"

"Well?"

"They'll think I'm a piece of white trash who should be mocked and ignored . . . oh wait, they already do."

Merry Carole is quiet. The pitcher is full of lemonade. We have to go back to the table.

"Just please don't talk about it anymore tonight," Merry Carole says, walking back toward the dining room.

"I won't."

"And, sweetie?"

"Yeah?"

"I think we're ready for your pecan pie."

"Yes, ma'am."

7

Leftovers

I didn't mention Shawn's offer to Merry Carole again. I couldn't stop thinking about it as I lay awake night after night in the tiny twin bed. It finally came to me that there was something drawing me to the job. Was it because I'd finally found a job where being intensely passionate about food was exactly what they were looking for? Or was it because "temporary" was right there in the job description? Was I identifying a bit too much with the people I'd be cooking for? Or was it simply because I'd sent out countless résumés and applied for several jobs from Dublin to Portland and heard either nothing or gotten polite rejections in response. Whatever it was, I couldn't shake it. I fell into a depressed stupor and started spending day after day on Merry Carole's couch, the words "come back on my own terms" pinballing around my dark and crowded head.

Worse yet, I began thinking about things: my life, my future, my past. These were not happy thoughts. Inertia had produced exactly what I'd always feared: contemplation.

I needed to act fast.

Once everyone was safely out of the house, I called the number Shawn had given me.

"Warden Dale Green's office, this is Juanita," the woman's voice was sugar and all business.

"Hello, ma'am, I was given the warden's number by Shawn Richter. About cooking last meals?" My voice is hesitant. Speaking about the job seems macabre.

"Oh, of course."

"I'd like to know if the job is still available?"

"It is."

Juanita is really making me work for this. Fine. Two can play this game.

"I'd like to apply for that job. What can I do to facilitate this?"

Juanita rattles through her spiel of fax numbers for résumés, background checks, fingerprinting, interviews, and what can only be described as "rigmarole."

"Thank you, ma'am. I appreciate that. Where would you suggest I start," I ask, scanning the scrawled notes I took of her directions.

"Fax me over your résumé, and I'll give it a look. I'll call you if I see something I like. If I don't, I won't."

"Yes, ma'am."

"Whereabouts you from, honey?"

"North Star, ma'am, born and bred."

"That'll help."

"Yes, ma'am."

"I'll be waiting for your résumé then," Juanita signs off. I skitter around the house, boot up Merry Carole's computer, and access my e-mail. I print out another résumé, type up another cover letter, put on something presentable, and walk into town.

The humidity soaks me through within ten steps. But the more horrifying realization is, I've just ambled out in public. Disheveled and with no time to put up walls, I am ripe for the picking. I keep my head down and make my way to the post office—where the one public fax machine in town resides.

As I walk through the town square, I notice the decorations for tomorrow's Fourth of July festivities going up. Red, white, and blue swaths of fabric hang from every balcony and windowsill. People have already lined up folding chairs along the parade route. If they couldn't find folding chairs, they've staked out their territory with masking tape, crime-scene tape, and lengths of rope. North Star's Fourth of July parade involves the entire town. If you're not in the parade, you're expected to be watching it from the sidelines. I hurry to the post office trying not to crumple my résumé and cover letter.

I arrive at the post office and wait in line. It's just ten AM, so the old men of North Star are gathered in the post office. They all have breakfast at the Homestead, travel over to the post office where they spend the afternoon talking to the workers about politics and the state of things. Later, they'll end the day at "the Mexican restaurant" and begin the entire tour again first thing tomorrow. I notice Felix Coburn, with his white shock of hair, in their ranks: he stands a head taller than the other men. His rangy frame is proof he's a man who works the land. His black cowboy hat rests in his mitt of a hand as his velvety voice intones through the historic building.

Felix is usually not one to while away the hours, choosing rather to run his family's 2,800-acre Paragon quarter horse farm. The Coburns have been breeding the finest Texas quarter horses since the early days, before there was even a registry. Augustus, their foundation sire, was a rodeo cutting champion; his line has produced winners in the rodeos ever since. In the 1950s, Paragon started a line of thoroughbreds with their foundation sire, Titus. Titus's line now boasts one Preakness winner, while other descendants have placed in all the Triple Crown events. A Paragon-bred horse is the stuff of Texas legend. And Felix is leaving it all—2,800 acres, two hundred horses, and the Paragon name—to his eldest son, Everett.

As I wait in line I try not to make eye contact with the man who made it quite clear to Everett that no son of his would take up with "one of those grubby Wakes." We were eleven years old and Everett had the wild idea that he could talk his father into changing his mind about my family. He wanted to be my boyfriend, he told me one day during recess as he presented me with a handmade card and a flower. I was beside myself. I'd loved Everett Coburn since the first day of kindergarten. I knew he felt the same, even then. We were just made for each other in that cheesy way people always claim to be in their marriage vows. He was my touchstone. Where I felt safe. I could survive every nightmarish night at home, just so I could return to school and see him and know that I wouldn't have to say a thing. He would just know how to comfort me. He shielded me from bullies, but knew enough to let me fight my own battles. We also knew, even then, that whatever we felt during those early years was something we had to keep secret. The Wakes and the Coburns were the alpha and omega of North Star. We knew this even before we could write our own names.

So when Everett announced to his father that he wanted to take Queenie Wake to the Saturday-night dance, all hell broke loose. He was never to see me again. The Wake women were evil, Felix warned. I would ruin him, Felix told his eleven-year-old son. Everett never let Felix see him cry, but when he got to me his green eyes were rimmed in red and his face was wet from tears.

He shook as he told me he couldn't see me anymore, and I remember looking at him and thinking, this is my love. This is my love and I'm going to fight for it—just as I fight for everything.

"They don't have to know," I said, taking his hands in mine.

"What?" Everett said, squeezing my hands tight.

"No one has to know, but us," I said, my mind clear.

"No one has to know, but us," Everett repeated.

"We'll know," I said, my breath catching as he stepped closer.

"We'll know," Everett repeated, just before he kissed me for the first time.

Everett and I were standing behind the band shell in the town square, hidden in the shadows. At eleven, we learned we could be who we really were only in the murky edges of North Star, but out in the light we had to be strangers.

"I'd heard you were back in town," Felix Coburn said.

"Yes, sir," I say, stepping forward in line.

"Not for long, I expect."

"No, sir."

I meet his gaze straight on. I'm not afraid of you, I repeat in my head over and over and over as those light blue eyes take my measure. My heart races. My breathing quickens. I'm not afraid of you, I will.

"Next?" the woman behind the window calls.

"Mr. Coburn," I say, signing off and walking forward toward the window.

"Ms. Wake," Felix says, putting his hat on. I don't watch as he walks out of the post office. I don't have to. I can feel when he's gone.

I hand my résumé and the cover letter to the woman behind the counter in a daze. My hands are trembling as she turns around and puts the sheets of paper into the fax and begins typing out the phone number. I hold my hands, trying to steady them. I close my eyes and try to calm my breathing. I can't do this again. I can't let this man—this town—have this effect on me every damn time. I'm thirty-one years old. I'm not eleven anymore. When do I stand up for myself or is that just not an option if I'm here in North Star? Do I have to leave North Star to feel as though I'm . . . human. Is that right? Do I belong anywhere? Is there anyplace I can go where I'm not just "a grubby Wake"?

As an eleven-year-old, I bought into the mythology. I looked at my mom and agreed with what people were saying about her. The piece I never understood was what her behavior had to do with Merry Carole and me. I never did any of the things she did. I was a good kid who loved the same boy my entire life. I worked at the family business until I got into the University of Texas.

Do the people of North Star honestly think Merry Carole and I are just like her? I'm sure Merry Carole getting pregnant at seventeen was an affront to one of the finest families of North Star. Of course, no one ever asked why Wes McKay, this bastion of North Star families, had a nasty habit of impregnating the young women of North Star. The sad thing is, from the looks of it, and in North Star that's not worth much, Whitney looks as though she really loves Wes. So Merry Carole and I are the women North Star thinks we are. The women you're with in the shadows, but not the women you take to the Saturday dance. We're the women you're infatuated with, but not the women you love. The women who raise your unwanted children alone. The women who ruin you. The more Merry Carole and I fight the chains of our mother's legacy, the more they bind us.

But North Star has always been about appearances. Without the Wakes, who knows who they'd feed on? They might have to take a look at their own pillars of society. I swallow hard as I wait.

It seems North Star and I are a lot alike after all. Contemplation is something we're both running from.

After years of being spit on, I thought I couldn't care less what anyone thinks. The thing I keep running from, the piece that makes me choke up even now—is that Everett cared. My Everett cared more about what the people of North Star thought, about what his parents thought, than he cared for me. He loved me . . . but not enough. We stole kisses under the bleachers during the big Friday football games. We lost our virginity to each other at a motel just outside of town when we were juniors in high school and swapped promise rings at the end of that school year. I began to call him Ever and thought it so romantic that our secret affair had borne its very own pet name. I never really get to have pet names, seeing as how my real name is just about as ridiculous as they come.

For years we relished every minute of our treacherous love. It made it dangerous. It made us feel like Romeo and Juliet fighting for our love in the most hopeless of worlds.

In our senior year Everett's parents set him up with Laurel. She was from a proper family. He couldn't find an excuse not to follow orders. Everett's parents had always suspected he'd never gotten over me, and this was their way of testing his allegiance to the Co-burn legacy. Laurel and Everett started very publicly dating and I became the mistress. And the sad part? The really sad part was that I felt lucky to have that.

I remember sitting in Fawn's double-wide during one of Mom's longer times away and thinking how much better than all these people I was. I was going to live on Paragon Ranch when Everett finally came for me. I was going to be welcomed into the family and trot through the town square on a Paragon quarter horse in the Fourth of July parade. I was going to be happy. But as our se-nior year wore on, it became harder and harder for me to watch as

Laurel swanned around town on Everett's arm. Despite his tortured whispers about really loving me, they were crowned prom king and queen as I sat at home with Merry Carole, no Mom, and a fussy newborn.

I grew uncomfortable with being Everett Coburn's dirty little secret.

We tried to keep away from each other when we were both at the University of Texas. As teenagers we had fantasies about stealing away to Austin and finally being together out in the open. But when Laurel also attended the university, it became clear that we were doomed sooner rather than later. We tried to stay away from each other, but we were each other's addiction. We always needed one more drink. Always hungry. Always craving more.

But the writing was on the wall. It was time for Everett to grow up, settle down, and become the heir to the Coburn mythology. As Everett and I went into our final year at the University of Texas, we were desperate and raw. We knew our time together was running out and that our life in the shadows was coming to an end. Whenever I left him, I felt half of a whole. He undid me. I knew my life was about to be slashed into eras: With Everett and Without. And a life without Everett was the one thing I felt I couldn't survive.

So I ran. I ran to Dallas so I didn't think about those brown-and-yellow-pinwheeled green eyes and the way our bodies melded into each other as if we were made for each other. And I ran to Aspen so I wouldn't remember the way he tugged his cowboy hat off whenever he walked into a room. And I ran to Branson to forget how his light brown hair curled and swirled around my fingers in the dark of the night. And I ran to Taos so I didn't think about how his face lit up when he saw me. And I ran to Albuquerque to forget how tightly he held me as I finally sobbed about my mom dying. And I ran to Las Vegas to erase how we lay in each other's arms that first time in that cheap motel just outside town, speechless and swept away. And I ran to San Diego so I didn't have to think about Everett and Laurel standing arm and arm, their parents beaming and proud. And I ran to San Francisco so I didn't have to make up another lie to Merry Carole and Dee for why I never dated anyone. And I ran to Los Angeles to forget how I didn't shed a single tear when he told me he was going to marry Laurel because their parents felt it was the right thing to do. And I ran to New York to try to understand why the man I loved didn't love me enough to be with me in the light of day.

"That'll be one dollar, Queenie," the woman says. I hand her a dollar bill and know now that I have to get out of North Star before I make any new memories to run from. One of those résumés has to work. One of those résumés will be my ticket out of North Star.

Before I think better of it, I burst through Merry Carole's front door and into the tiny guest room. My clothes are mostly in the dresser thanks to Merry Carole telling me that I wasn't "a hobo" and should put away my clothes like a normal person. I pull the smaller piece of luggage from the closet and pull open the zippered pocket on the inside. I pull out the mangled manila folder just inside. I dump the contents on the floor and sit down quickly next to the messy pile. I sift through my passport, my birth certificate, an old photo of Merry Carole and me, a baby picture of Cal, various slips of paper with old recipes and dish ideas I've had over the years. I pull my hand away from the pile as if the mere presence of it has set it aflame: the card Everett gave me when I was eleven and the dried and flattened flower that accompanied it. Pink construction paper with my name in blue crayon written across the top of the card. He's drawn a girl with a crown at the bottom; a crudely drawn horse grazes on lines of green grass that edge the bottom of the card. There is an arrow pointing to the girl with the crown and the word "YOU" next to it. I run my fingers over the rough construction paper.

"You," I say, a reverent whisper. At eleven, I was a queen to Everett.

I open the card and in no rhyme or reason are the words "your great!," "I love you!," "the lone star state," and "E + Q." He's drawn the same girl with the crown from the front of the card, but this time she stands hand and hand with a golden-haired boy holding a horse. Underneath the couple are the words "you and me forever." The little Crayola couple is smiling and happy. I sit back against the bed, carefully holding the pink construction paper card.

"You and me forever," I say, closing the card and letting my hand linger. I hold the card as a believer would cradle a Bible. Everett was what I believed in. And he made me believe in an us. He made me believe I would get out of the hellhole I was in and that I could be happy. He made me believe that I was lovable. I choke back the tears I've been running from for decades.

"It was cruel to show me that kind of love at all," I say, my eyes to the heavens as if saying my own kind of grace. I pull my knees in close and sob, my tears momentarily staining the pink card red. I can't catch my breath as that feeling of mystical vastness I felt at the cemetery overtakes me. I honestly don't know if I could stop crying at this point. I've been holding this in for years.

After an unknowable amount of time, my cell phone buzzes in my pocket. I'm shaken out of my nervous breakdown as I check the phone number—it's the area code for Shine. It's the prison. Jesus, Juanita is a study in efficiency. I sniffle and breathe; the phone buzzes again.

"Get it together," I bite out, wiping the tears away. One last breath and I answer the phone. "Hello?"

"Ms. Wake, this is Juanita from Shine Prison," she says.

"Sure, what can I do for you?" I say, my throat choking and burning less and less. My breathing is steadying, shaky exhalation by shaky exhalation.

"The warden would like you to come on in and interview for the position. Are you free this afternoon?"

"Oh wow," I say.

"Well?"

"Oh right. Sorry. Yes, I'm free," I say, standing. I'm still clutching the pink construction paper card.

"Great. How does two thirty sound?" Juanita says, going through directions and instructions on how to get to the prison. I walk into the kitchen, find an old receipt, and scrawl the information on the back.

"Two thirty is perfect. I'll be there," I say, finally.

"We'll see you then," Juanita says, signing off. I beep my cell phone off and look around the front room in a fog. I focus on the receipt with all the information in one hand and the pink construction paper card in the other.

"I guess only one of us knew what forever meant," I say, walking into my room and placing the card back into the recesses of my luggage.

8

Gentleman Jack Bourbon

As I drive over the river and through the woods to the Shine Prison just twenty minutes away, I call Dee and tell her what I'm doing. Her response is subdued. This particular job definitely has a ghoulish edge to it that might dampen the normal celebrations a new job would bring. This job might change me. I'd know the terrible things people are capable of. That isn't something I want to sign on for, but my life hasn't been free of that already. I've seen the dark side firsthand and I know the complicated relationship we humans have with right and wrong. I'm painfully aware of how human beings can turn other human beings into something that's below an animal.

I pull into the visitors' parking lot just outside the barbed-wire fences that surround the prison. Guard towers anchor each corner of the compound, and as I walk to the entrance I swear even the wind is hesitant to float over these parts. The air is still. The humidity follows me through the door like a monkey on my back.

"Queenie Wake to see Warden Dale Green?" I ask the woman behind the glass.

"I knew *the* Queen Elizabeth herself wasn't coming on down to Shine!" the receptionist says, laughing with the other woman in the front office.

"You probably get that all the time," the other woman says.

"Yes, ma'am," I say.

"Well, Queen Elizabeth, I'll be right with you. I've been dying to say that forever!" The women cackle together. They look like every other receptionist. Matching floral separates, sentimental doodads littering their desks, and yet they're here. The first faces visitors see when checking in at a prison. The receptionist looks up after talking a bit with another woman in the front office. She continues, "Juanita's going to come get you in a second. Go ahead and have a seat, Queen Elizabeth," the woman says with a wink, motioning to the bank of chairs just behind me. I thank her and take a seat.

Sterile. Beige. Nothing to observe or draw conclusions from. Every now and again a guard comes in and talks with the ladies in the front office. They are easygoing; it feels like any other office. Except. Except there are hundreds of men just beyond those walls who are behind bars. What am I doing here? I should just work part time at Merry Carole's salon. I don't need to be doing this. What do I think I'm going to find here? Is this—

"Queen Elizabeth Wake?" A round woman in a fuchsia blouse and flowery skirt comes through the front-office door. Her cocoa skin shimmers with sweat, as the heat of the day has sneaked into the waiting room with the opening and closing front door. Her sensible shoes squeak and settle as she walks over to me. I stand, wiping my palm on my pants as she approaches.

"Please. Queenie," I say, shaking her extended hand.

"We spoke on the phone. I'm Juanita," the woman says, motioning for me to follow her through the front office. I oblige. She continues, "Now, Warden Dale is right through here. He's ready for you to go on in, if that's okay by you." Juanita's shoes squeak down the long, sterile hallway.

"Yes, ma'am," I say, trying to take in everything. It's a wraith-like symphony of sounds. The echoes bouncing off the institutional walls are not unlike those of a schoolyard or a playground, but the speed has been slowed down so the voices are lower. My gut is telling me to run. The instinct of impending danger is on overdrive. The authoritative yells are vomit inducing and the voices they quiet are menacing and frenzied. I feel as though I've stumbled onto the front lines of a looming rebellion.

"Don't mind it. They keep to themselves and you get used to it," Juanita says, without so much as a look back my way. I nod and focus my eyes on Juanita's waddling floral skirt just in front of me. She continues, "Right through here." She opens a heavy metal door. The door shuts behind us and the rebellion is silenced. She walks through the anteroom, with its deep woods and rich fabrics. I follow close behind her. She knocks on the wooden door.

"Come on in," I hear from just beyond the wooden door. Juanita opens the door and motions for me to go through. She nods to the warden and closes the heavy wooden door behind me. I swallow. Hard. The warden continues, "Have a seat, Ms. Wake." The warden is a titan of a man. He stands way over six feet, but with the worn-in Stetson that he's hung on the antlers of the mounted stag behind him, I expect he's pushing NBA standards. The Stetson also probably hides a reddish-auburn hairline that's clearly receding. His skin is pale and his brown eyes are clear and bright. He extends his hand to me and he envelops mine.

"Thank you, sir," I say, not knowing whether to shake his hand, sit down, or do the hokey pokey.

"Please call me Warden Dale," he says, motioning for me to sit. He comes out from behind his desk and walks over to a drinks cart on the far wall of his office.

Warden Dale's office is decorated as if it were a hunting lodge. Along with the stag, he's got a stuffed wild boar, a six-point buck, and various and sundry varmints posed in threatening positions, which they most certainly were not in when shot by Warden Dale. Warden Dale's heavy wood walls anchor his dark leather furniture and expensive oriental rugs. He takes the stopper out of a crystal decanter and pours two glasses of bourbon. He walks over to me, hands me a glass, and clinks his glass to mine in a quick toast. He leans against his desk, just in front of me. He crosses his legs and I notice that his cowboy boots finish the ensemble perfectly.

"To the great state of Texas," he says, raising his glass.

"To the great state of Texas," I say, raising mine. We drink. Bourbon. I was right. My entire throat is warmed and I can feel the heat of the liquor trickle down into my empty stomach.

"Ms. Wake, I am a visionary," Warden Dale says, taking the glass from me and walking back over to the drinks cart. He pours two more glasses. I steady myself in the leather club chair.

"Yes, sir," I say, taking the second glass of bourbon. He leans against his desk once more, his cowboy boots crossed, self-assured in front of me.

"To the great state of Texas," he says, raising the glass.

"To the great state of Texas," I say, raising mine. We drink again. Warmth. Trickling. I focus my eyes.

"I believe in justice," Warden Dale says, taking my empty glass once again. He walks back over to the drinks cart and pours two more glasses.

"Yes, sir," I say, steadying myself once again. He walks back over to me and hands me a glass.

"To the great state of Texas," he says, raising his glass.

"To the great state of Texas," I say, raising mine. We drink. I set my empty glass down and continue, "Warden Dale, I'm going to stop you here. I was born in Texas and I'm probably going to die in Texas, so if you're trying to drink me under the table as some kind of rite of passage, it's never gonna happen. I worked next to a bar when I was in elementary school, and while your bourbon is better than anything they served there, I guarantee this will not end well for you. Shall we get down to business then?" I ask.

Warden Dale is quiet. I meet his gaze and wait. And wait.

I continue, "I've been bullied by worse than you, sir, and this little pissing contest is just a waste of my time." I stand and start for the door.

"Let's get down to business, then," Warden Dale says, a wide smile across his face. He motions for me to sit down. I oblige and he walks back around his desk and sets his half-full glass of bourbon on a Lone Star coaster next to his calendar. He continues, "I would like to offer you the position of cook here in the Death House."

"The Death House?"

"You'd be making last meals, but also cooking for the Death House crew," the warden says.

"How often would I be . . . uh . . . cooking?" I ask. One meal equals one life. What am I getting myself into?

"We've been running about three to five executions a month. We've been getting some down from Huntsville as well as some of our own convicts," Warden Dale says, his voice serious and heavy.

"Three to five," I say, deliberately not saying the other word.

"Executions, yes."

"Executions." I said it. The word gets caught in my throat. The warmth of the bourbon is all but gone and all that remains is the icy chill of who I'm cooking for.

"You would have a staff of two convicts—the Dent boys. I've handpicked them for you. They're a father and a son who went on one drug-filled crime spree, but have since found Jesus. They're harmless and perfect for your needs."

"Would I be cooking for the Death House crew every day or just when there was a . . . an—"

"Just when there was an execution," Warden Dale says, finishing my sentence.

I nod.

"You never have to know the name or what they've done. You just have to cook a meal and make enough of it for the four members of the Death House crew, and Captain Richter. Chaplain Boothe tends to keep to himself. And you can decide if the Dent boys get your meal, if you want."

"Yes, sir." Merry Carole was right. I wasn't taking this seriously. These are real people. Real people who are going to die. Real people who have done the worst things humans are capable of. I'm . . . I'm . . . "I'm going to need another drink, Warden Dale," I finally say.

Warden Dale stands and pours me another glass of bourbon. He does not pour himself one. I slam the bourbon down, letting the warmth move through my body. I breathe.

"Can I give you an answer at the end of the weekend? We've got Fourth of July festivities and I need time to think," I say, my mind a haze.

"Yes. Absolutely. I know it's a lot to take in. But you have to see this as an opportunity to be that last shred of humanity before these men and women meet their maker. You are offering them a bit of . . . *home*." We stand and he extends his hand to me.

"*Home*." I take his hand and we shake.

"Please think about it, Ms. Wake. I know you are the right person for the job."

"I will think about it, Warden Dale. You'll have your answer by Monday."

"Ms. Wake?" I turn around, my hand desperately clutching for the doorknob. I have to get out of here.

"Yes, sir?" I ask. Juanita is standing and waiting to walk me back through the Long Hallway of Echoes.

"I think you'll fit in here. Please think about it," Warden Dale says. I nod and walk with Juanita through the hallway and front office. I walk across the parking lot and sit in my car. I turn the key and blast the air-conditioning as my car idles. I turn off the radio and rest my hands on the hot steering wheel.

"I'll fit in here? At a prison. That's perfect. That's fucking perfect," I say, putting the car in reverse and hightailing it as far away from Shine Prison as possible.

Once I get back to North Star, I park my car and head toward Merry Carole's salon. I skirt the folded chairs and red, white, and blue streamers that Merry Carole has put out in front of her salon to mark off her territory for the parade. Country music, hair dryers, and gossip greet me again as I walk through the front door. Merry Carole is standing at the front counter talking to Fawn; she looks up as I approach.

"Laurel Coburn has an appointment in ten minutes, so talk fast and then get back to the house," Merry Carole says, flipping through her appointment book. Fawn scans the appointment book for further "issues."

"I'm not going to sneak out of here like a dirty little secret. I'm your sister," I say, hating that I'm begging not to be hidden from the light of day. Again.

"I just don't want a whole thing, you can understand that," Merry Carole says.

"I've done nothing. We've done nothing. *She* has a problem with us, remember?" I ask, my blood boiling.

Merry Carole just sighs.

"It's actually adorable that you think you can hide enough of yourself so these people will accept you, bless your heart."

"Well, they'll have to accept me after tomorrow."

"Why?"

"The parents of the starting team are automatically appointed to the board of the Stallion Battalion, so once Cal gets named QB1, they'll have to put up with me." Merry Carole flips a small mirror on the front desk around and checks her hair in it. A quick pouf, a lip-gloss touch-up, and she turns the mirror back around.

I don't say anything. My blood goes from boiling to running cold. I feel nothing but compassion for my beautiful sister. She must know those women will never accept her. She must know that they will find some loophole and not let her be part of the Stallion Battalion. How can she not know this by now? I guess for the same reasons I don't. We're constantly waiting for this town to be . . . fair. We're waiting for our home to accept us, as we accept it. I guess we're waiting for our "terms" to be considered.

But it's never going to happen.

"Five minutes," Fawn says, her eyes darting toward the door.

"I just want to talk to Dee and then I'll sneak out the back. I promise," I say.

"You guys can talk back in the kitchenette. And close the door," Merry Carole says, motioning to Dee to make it quick.

Dee and I walk to the kitchenette and I elaborately close the door behind us.

"Can you get away tonight? Maybe we can drink and talk?" I ask.

"Sure, sure . . . Shawn gets home around seven, I can meet you at the Hall of Fame at what . . . eightish?" Dee says.

"That's perfect. I'll meet you there," I say.

"Just real fast, how'd it go?" Dee asks, pulling a Coca-Cola from the minifridge and cracking it open.

"He offered me the job," I say.

"What . . . did you . . . are you taking it?" Dee plays with the top of her Coke can, dusting it and spinning the flip top around and around.

"I don't know. I honestly don't."

"Okay . . . we'll talk. Tonight. Now go on before we both get into trouble," Dee says, shooing me out the back.

That night, I walk down the same side streets Merry Carole and I played on endlessly as kids. The closer I get to the Drinkers Hall of Fame, the closer I get to the plot of land where Momma's restaurant once stood. It's dark enough that I won't have to really see it, but I know the terrain like the back of my hand.

I step up onto the curb and walk through the dirt and overgrown weeds that have overtaken where the shack once was. I just stand there looking at the emptiness. Haunted. The cicadas sing. The music wafts out from the bar. The leaves rustle at a rare summer breeze. And I just stare. Gone. It's gone. The eight-by-eight shack where I spent my childhood is gone and now just blackness remains. In a lot of ways. I let my head fall to my chest as I try to steady my breathing. I know Merry Carole hasn't sold this land out of some warped sense of loyalty to Mom. I wish she would. That way the failures of our family wouldn't live on as a black hole in the North Star landscape. A couple of people burst out of the bar just next door and it snaps me out of my unwelcome literal walk down memory lane. I turn and drag myself away from the gravitational pull of my disastrous family tree.

The Drinkers Hall of Fame. An induction ceremony no one

wants to be a part of. The Hall of Fame, as we call it, has stood on that dusty plot of land for as long as North Star has been a stop on the railway. It's been called the Hall of Fame since around the 1950s. Before that it was called every hackneyed Texan name in the book: the Two-bit Whore, the Hitching Post, Old West Tavern, Lone Star Saloon, the Cowboy, and the ever memorable Three Wise Men Bar and Grill (which never really caught on).

From the outside, the Hall of Fame looks like every other bar in a small town. Not really welcoming, but not scary either. But for us in North Star, it's our watering hole. The place where the lights are low enough and the music is loud enough so people think they'll have privacy—until the rumors about what they did are being whispered all over town the next day. I push open the creaky wooden door and try to prepare myself for what's just inside.

Steve Earle's "Feel Alright" hits me like a ton of bricks. The darkness blinds me momentarily as I blink to steady myself. A crack of the cue ball hitting a newly set up triangle of balls, a hoot and a cowboy boot shuffle, and the sound of beer bottles hitting the inside of a trash can wafts over me. I open my eyes and the room comes into focus.

The Drinkers Hall of Fame. Just like I remember it. The smoke-tinged dark wood floors set off the dark wood paneling nicely. The dark wood paneling goes well with the dark wood raftered ceiling. The beautiful dark wood raftered ceiling is complimented by the dark wood tables and chairs. And the dark wood bar brings the whole room together. The giant Lone Star flag on one wall is set off against several neon beer signs on the other. The pool table in the back of the room with the jukebox just behind it is where people go to loiter, lean, and observe. They've all "got next." Cowboy hats are pulled low and beer bottles are held close. Women drape themselves over their men, arms hung over broad shoulders clad in plaid shirts. The tiniest of dance floors invites you to sway close and don't you never let go.

"Queenie!" I can barely make out Dee in one of the dimly lit corners that's usually saved for lovers. Her pastel flowery separates are a beacon that leads me to the safety of her saved table.

"Hey there," I say, sitting down across from her and fighting the urge to hug her. We'll hug with our good-byes, I tell myself.

"I ordered you a Lone Star. I know how you like the puzzles," Dee says, twisting around to hook her purse on the back of her chair.

"What are you drinking?"

"Sea breeze," Dee says, taking a genteel sip from the tiny straw.

"I didn't know this place did sea breezes," I say, unable to keep from smiling.

"Yes, Queen Elizabeth—it's not just New York City that has all the fancy new cocktails," Dee says.

"I heard you were in town," Bec says, setting my beer on a coaster she flips deftly down first. Bec. Not Becky. Not Rebecca. And Bec? Bec is terrifying. Just the sort of waitress you'd expect in a bar like this. She's ageless and she's worked here forever. She used to let me sneak in to use the bathroom when I worked at Momma's shack. Merry Carole and I were positive she was a witch of the Hansel and Gretel variety.

"Hey, Bec," I say, taking a swig of my beer.

"That's all you got for me?" Bec says.

"No, ma'am," I say, standing and wiping my now clammy hands on my jeans. I extend my hand to her and she takes it, gripping tightly. We shake hands efficiently and I'm positive she's stealing my soul or channeling some long-lost relative who'll tell me in some spooky elsewhere voice that "Queeeen Elizzabetthhhhh, your grand-mamaaaaa looooves youuuu." I'm for sure going to have nightmares.

"I'm glad to see you safe and sound," Bec says as I take my seat.

"Yes, ma'am," I say. My posture is perfect.

"All right then." Bec pauses. The look. It's the same look we get from a lot of people. Not the ones who are actively wishing us ill, but the other minority. The other people this town looks down on. They're sorry about what happened to Momma. They're sorry we got a momma like that in the first place. And then they're just sorry. I nod and offer her a smile. A tight smile back and she's gone to the next customer.

"I swear to God, that woman . . ." Dee takes a long, dainty sip of her sea breeze.

"I know," I say. I look toward the bar. I'm hungry and those potato chips clipped to the Budweiser mirror are looking better and better.

"So, the job," Dee says, settling into her chair as Kenny Chesney wafts through the bar talking about me and tequila.

"I think I'm going to take it," I venture, saying it out loud for the first time.

"I've got to tell you, I just . . . Shawn hasn't been the same man since he's been working there, you know?"

"I can see how that would happen," I say, fidgeting with my beer bottle.

"He comes home after . . . well, after . . . and he's like a robot. He doesn't want to talk about it, he just wants to be around the boys. I think it has to do with just wanting to be around goodness, you know?"

"Yeah."

"I mean, from what he was telling me, it'll be very different for you. It's not like you even have to see who you're cooking for."

"I'm counting on that."

"I think that's what wakes him up at night, you know? The

faces." I nod. Dee continues, "So, you don't have to worry yourself with that. You just cook the meal and that'll be that."

"I know, that's kind of what I was thinking," I say.

"Is the money that good? I mean, it's not like you have any expenses here. Why . . . why take it if there's some question about it, you know?" Dee is being very careful with her words.

"As I was leaving, Warden Dale said that I was the right person for the job. That I'd fit in there. No one's ever said that to me before," I say.

"Really?"

"Yeah, I get these jobs and there's always all these explanations and addendums about 'taking a chance on me' and how hiring me is 'out-of-the-box thinking,' and on and on. This was the first time someone just flat out said they wanted me and only me."

"It sounds like you've made up your mind," Dee says.

"The last time I got fired, my boss talked about how I didn't have any passion for the food unless I was complaining about their recipes. Like I had none of my own, you know?"

"But you do."

"I know. So why didn't I make them?"

"Maybe because you've been making those same recipes since you were a kid? I can see how you would have gotten burnt out," Dee says.

"I guess."

"Maybe you thought you'd find another way to cook that you liked better."

"But I didn't. And then I just forgot everything. And started yelling at tourists for putting ketchup on their eggs."

"Chance puts ketchup on his eggs. It's disgusting."

"Different strokes, right?" I say, my stomach turning.

"I guess. Makes me think I've failed as a parent is what it does."

We are quiet.

"I don't know. Something about being able to cook food for real Texans, and that it has to be perfect? That's speaking to me something fierce," I say.

"I can see why you'd like that," Dee says, not making eye contact.

Dee continues in an awkward blurting out, "Laurel was in particularly fine form this afternoon. I think Merry Carole was right about not having you in the salon."

"I just think it's all so futile. Like there's anything we could do or have done already to make it so they don't hate us. It's their little pastime at this point. It'd be like taking away scrapbooking or making deals for people's souls. And Merry Carole playing into it isn't helping. They're going to smell it on her and . . . I just hate to think of what's going to happen," I say.

"Laurel's been different ever since the divorce," Dee says, taking another sip.

The bar sounds muffle around me. My breath is yanked from my body and I can only focus on that tiny straw in Dee's impossibly pink drink.

"The divorce?" My voice is raspy as I settle deeper into the tiny chair.

"Yeah, sure. She and Everett got divorced about a year after they got married. It barely lasted a minute," Dee says, her voice now a conspiratorial whisper.

Everett. I can't even form a thought. I just keep thinking his name inside my head. Everett. Everett.

"I didn't know that," I say, finally managing some kind of quasi-understandable succession of words.

"They said it was on account of her not being able to have babies, but . . ." Dee trails off.

"But?" I can't breathe.

Dee looks surreptitiously around the bar—she decides we're far enough away from the denizens of the Hall of Fame and curls her body over the wooden table. I can't breathe. I can't breathe.

"I know they're from good families and all that, but I just never thought there was anything between 'em, you know? She was okay in high school, but holy smokes, she just got meaner and meaner," Dee says, her voice a tiny whisper. I wonder if it's that Laurel has gotten meaner or is this what happens to the women who love Everett Coburn?

"Yeah," I say. I can't feel my body. I can't feel my face, but I start to feel the littlest of embers warming inside me. I haven't felt this heat in years, definitely not since I left North Star. We could pick up right where we left off. We'll take our place in the shadows and . . . and I can be whole again. Even if it's just for a little while. Or . . . or does he even love me anymore?

"You look like you're going to be sick," Dee says, putting her hand on my shoulder as if she were comforting one of her little boys. She continues, "Here. You want another beer?" I am definitely going to need something stronger if I'm going to process this new information.

"I think I'm going to need something a little stronger," I say, offering Dee a smile. "You want another?" I ask, pointing to her sea breeze.

"That'd be lovely, thank you," Dee says, leaning back in her chair in search of her purse.

I excuse myself and walk over to the bar in a daze.

I don't know what to do with this new information. Maybe the answer is right in front of me. I've been in town now for almost a week and I've heard nothing from Everett, notwithstanding his marital status. Maybe despite whatever I think happened in our past, he's moved on. I take in a deep breath. I can't . . . I won't believe that. I know I meant more to him than someone he could easily get over. Shit, I've seen every kitchen from here to New York and I can't rid myself of the memories of him. But maybe that's just me. I was always the . . . my breath catches . . . I was always the dirty little secret. I was the thing that contaminated the mighty Everett Coburn. I was the old paint workhorse that would sully the Paragon thoroughbreds. He was my one and only. But what was I to him?

"Hello, Mr. Mueller," I say, trying to steady myself. Mr. Mueller owns the Hall of Fame. He had a rocky relationship with my mother in the past. I don't blame him for it, she was not any kind of neighbor I'd like. But he liked her cooking, so he put up with her.

"Queen Elizabeth," he says, looking from under his low cowboy hat, the ever present toothpick switching from one side of his mouth to the other as he takes my measure.

"I'll have a bourbon and branch and a sea breeze for Dee, sir," I say, standing tall.

Mr. Mueller turns away without so much as a word. I continue to eye those potato chips.

"Why don't you just order them already."

Everett.

"I was going to offhandedly suggest that hey, Mr. Mueller, you know . . . screw it, why don't you throw in some of those potato chips while you're at it."

"Seems like a lot of work for a bag of chips," Everett says, leaning onto the bar and facing me.

God*damn*. He takes my breath away.

In the darkness of this bar, the hard edges of his face are shadowed and beautiful. The stubble that appears late at night outlines his jaw just as it always has. That crooked smile and those hooded, pinwheel-green eyes, the right one always a bit more squinted than the left. He makes me feel like I'm the only person in this room as he looks straight through me.

"These are on the house," Mr. Mueller says, sliding my two drinks across the knotty wooden bar.

"Sir?"

"Welcome home," he says in his gruff smoker's voice.

"Yes, sir. Thank you," I say.

"Now you really can't ask for those chips," Everett says, holding up three fingers. Mr. Mueller turns and goes to get what I know will be three bottles of Shiner Bock beer.

"Hoist with my own petard," I say, picking up my drinks. Everett smiles.

Mr. Mueller comes back over and cracks open three Shiner Bock beers. I can't help but smile.

"Thank you, sir. Hey, Mr. Mueller, you know . . . screw it, why don't you throw in some of those potato chips while you're at it," Everett says, nodding his head in the direction of my beloved chips. I sigh. I can't help myself. I sigh.

"All right then," Mr. Mueller says, turning to pluck a bag of chips from its hook. He sets the bag on the bar and nods to another customer as if to say, "May I help you?"

"Welcome home," Everett says, presenting me with the bag of potato chips. I take them, the plastic crumpling under my touch.

"Thanks," I say.

I can't help myself. I look straight into his eyes. Just as I've been doing my entire life. His eyes lock back on to mine and we just stand there. We're inches from each other for the first time in ten years and yet we're frozen. I can't breathe. Everett leans in mere centimeters, but it feels dangerous. A crooked smile and that right eye squints just a bit more than the left. I let out a laugh, trying to hide the nervous gasp that sneaked out as I feel the heat from his body nearing mine. I hear him take in a breath, his eyes still fast on mine. The sounds of the bar fall away and it's just us. Seconds. Minutes. Hours. Lifetimes.

The crack of the cue ball. The hoot and holler and the shuffle of a cowboy boot. The beer bottles hitting the inside of the trash can. Waylon Jennings singing about being a highwayman.

My hands are cold around the drinks. I scan the bar. I see a couple of cowboys from Paragon waiting for Everett and, more important, their beers. And Dee. All riveted. I clear my throat and look back at Everett. He's waiting. I smile and it takes everything I have to turn and walk back to my table.

"What was that about?" Dee asks, thanking me for her drink.

"Mr. Mueller gave me these free," I say, trying to get myself under control. I can see Everett walk back to the table where they all are. He sets the beers in front of the two cowboys and sits down.

"No, I mean with Everett," Dee says.

"Oh, nothing. It's nothing," I say, offering her my version of an offhanded smile.

"Sure looked like something," Dee says.

"So what's the plan for tomorrow?" I ask, trying to change the subject.

Dee starts talking about all the Fourth of July festivities tomorrow. Her oldest will be marching with his Cub Scout troop and the other two will be throwing tantrums about not marching with the Cub Scout troop.

My mind instantly wanders and settles on Everett. On the idea—the tiniest of ideas—that I could have him again. That we could be together—however temporarily. My throat begins to choke and burn. So many years of being trained to dream smaller and smaller, even my wildest dreams are mere bansai trees to the mighty oaks they could have been once upon a time.

Once upon a time before that bell tolled midnight and I had to go back to being a grubby Wake.

9

Buttermilk biscuits, honey butter, not enough coffee

After a fitful night's sleep, I inexplicably find myself sitting on the curb outside Merry Carole's hair salon. I'm holding a tiny American flag in one hand and a mug of coffee in the other. It's early in the morning and Merry Carole is urging me to wave my flag "like I mean it." She's dressed in an outfit I can only describe as Wonder Woman's lounge wear and keeps pointedly waving her flag at me.

"This is just the biggest day of the year, Queen Elizabeth, and you can't even muster up a little flag wave?" Merry Carole asks, poufing and poufing a head of hair that is already as high as it can get without someone thinking it's a cartoon thought bubble brought to life.

I wave my flag violently in her face.

"You're only hurting America, Queen Elizabeth," Merry

Carole says, checking herself in the reflection of her salon's front window.

"When does the football team come down the route?" I ask as she finally sits down.

"They're last, of course," Merry Carole says, producing the biscuits I baked last night when I couldn't sleep. I made honey butter for good measure. Merry Carole flips the red, white, and blue handkerchief back over the top of the basket filled with biscuits. Fawn and Pete lunge for the biscuits. She sets the basket down with the rest of the food and drinks we brought out here at the crack of dawn.

"Of course," I say, leaning back on my hands and stretching my legs in front of me, out in the street.

I've been coming to this parade my entire life. It's one of those things your hometown does that you think is ridiculous and yet you wouldn't miss it for the world. The entire town shuts down and everyone just has fun. Merry Carole and I would always stake out a place along the route. We'd gawk at the North Star queen and her court, the pack of zany rodeo clowns, the mighty North Star Stallions, and of course, the Coburns and their beautiful Paragon quarter horses. It was a day off for the bogeymen of North Star.

We hear the siren of the ancient fire truck and know that the parade is starting.

"Oh, here we go!" Merry Carole says, tousling my hair. I look over at her and we smile. I pull my legs in close and perch on the curb, awaiting the parade.

We watch as half the town walks by waving and we wave back. We wave our flags as antique cars pass by carrying members of the city council, small-business owners, and rodeo heroes. The rodeo clowns roll around the street in brightly colored barrels and tiny cars to the delight of the kids lining the parade route. We're laughing, patting backs, and passing food and drink to one another as the packs of North Star citizens pass by.

The float—and by float I mean a flatbed truck with silver tinsel along its bumpers—trundles by with the North Star queen and her court of three princesses. Merry Carole and I wave our flags and clap as the girls go by, but both of us are less than impressed. The North Star court is Laurel Coburn and Whitney McKay's domain. Merry Carole and I would have killed to be in that court—waving to everyone in those pretty dresses. It was all I thought about as a kid. I later denounced it as "lame," but I'm sure everyone knew sour grapes when they saw them. I certainly did. I could barely get the harsh words out before swooning into another fantasy about being crowned queen and Everett finally professing his love for me as he scooped me up onto one of those quarter horses and we rode off into the sunset. That was not quite how it played out. Laurel was queen to Everett's king and I was the lank-haired interloper who said the parade was for "losers" as I watched out of the corner of my eye. Everett came by later that night . . . when no one was around to see us together.

Take that, Queen Laurel.

The queen and her court pass by and Merry Carole and I clear our throats. "Their hair looks great," Fawn says to Merry Carole.

"Oh, thank you," Merry Carole says, looking at their high hair with pride. She poufs her own hair that much higher.

I can hear them before I see them. The clop, clop, clop of the Paragon quarter horses. Two by two. Riders in crisp white shirts, jeans, and white Stetsons ride majestic animals that defy the expectation of what a horse should be. The crowd hoots and hollers for the pride of North Star. A chill runs down my spine as they round the corner by Merry Carole's salon.

Felix and Arabella Coburn are right in front. Smiling and wav-

ing and looking down at all of us, as they always do. Right behind
Felix and Arabella is their only girl, Everett's sister, Florrie. Florrie
was actually kind of a badass—and not into being the queen of the
North Star court at all. She was one of the only female cutting
champions and is on her way to making the National Cutting
Horse Hall of Fame. She was a staple in rodeos in her time. Now
she's a sought-after rodeo judge and mother to her five little girls—
who trot just behind her in the parade. Florrie married well, had
beautiful babies, and is everything her parents could want. I always
thought Florrie and I could have been friends. She was never anything but cordial to me. I always thought she knew about Everett
and me, but never gave it away. She didn't say a word when Felix
laid down the law about never bringing a Wake into his home. But
I can't fault her for that.

Just behind Florrie's brood is the youngest Coburn—Gray.
Gray is catnip for the young women of North Star. He's the vet at
Paragon and perpetually single. I never saw any signs of him settling down, but I'm sure he'll bow to his family's pressure and find
a suitable wife. Until then, he's going to continue leaving a string of
broken hearts behind him. At Gray's age, Florrie already had two
babies and a successful rodeo career. Florrie didn't have the luxury
of freedom that Gray has. Neither did Everett, I suppose.

Ranch hands, rodeo riders, and the rest of the men and women
of the Paragon Ranch trot by two by two. I'm not breathing. I'm
waiting. He's always last.

Everett is riding by himself in the very back carrying the flag of
Paragon. He might as well be on a white charger instead of the
beautiful blue roan he's on. I can't help myself, and just like at the
Drinkers Hall of Fame last night, I let my eyes wash over every
inch of him. His crisp white shirt pulls tight across his broad shoulders. Stubble outlines his strong, yet always clenched, jaw. His full

lips are pressed in a hard line, nary a crooked smile for the waving citizens of North Star. His eyes are hooded as they search the crowd, intense and concentrated. His brownish hair is curling up from under the wide brim of his cowboy hat and I can see his neck starting to glisten from the heat. His bitten-down fingernails curl around the flagpole as the flag waves and flickers in the air just above him. His legs are powerful around the animal that he controls beneath him, but my eyes stop on the big silver belt buckle at his waist. I know it well and can't help but smile. I gave it to him as a joke when we were going through a rough time at UT. I told him that as long as he was going to act like the king of the assholes, there should be some sort of commemoration. Then I elaborately presented him with the belt buckle emblazoned with a crown on the front and an inscription on the back: EVER THE KING OF THE ASSHOLES. LOVE, QUEENIE.

I can't believe he still has it. I hate that I'm running through the same teenage list: this means that and that means this and Everett doing that clearly means this and because he did this one thing it means when that happens we'll do that, but we had that moment in the bar where our love for each other literarily froze us in time and on and on.

As Everett rides by he tips his hat, his eyes fast on mine. The crooked smile that's just for me. I hate that my face flushes and my body reacts to him as it always has.

Divorced.

The tiniest of voices inside my head offers up that maybe he never stopped loving me. His marriage to Laurel was doomed. And now? Now we can be together. We're adults, aren't we? I'll take this job and we'll start up again. I mean, what's worse? Running all over the world alone, becoming a shell of myself, or being back in North Star and being with Everett—in the shadows or not? Why are these my only options? Loving Everett means I'm either alone or his dirty little secret. I shake my head as he trots on down the parade route. He knows. I've never been able to hide what I'm feeling from him. What I could never understand was how, if he really did know what I was feeling, how he could treat me the way he did. He must think we're together in this treachery. We're both prisoners of the North Star law that says we can't be together. But that's not true. He chose not to be with me all those years ago. He could have taken a stand. He could have told his father exactly what he could do with his ideas about dating Laurel. He could have fought for us. He could have fought for me. He could have fought for true love. But he didn't. I didn't, either. I ran.

It's worse knowing he loves me. I keep waiting for him to do the right thing by it . . . by me. Now all we're bound by is pain and the knowledge that we can never be together, that we can never be truly happy. Knowing that the other is just as miserable—or at least hoping—is what connects us. What do we do? What do I do? I can't stop loving him and I'll never be able to hate him. Do I learn from New York? Do I try to muster up the ability to be indifferent to him? Is that the goal? There's no one else for me but him. He's the love of my life. So I hold out hope. I read into belt buckles and a tip of his cowboy hat just like I did when I was eleven. And I wait for his parents to suggest another worthy spouse who isn't me. Loving Everett has molded me, but it's also taught me that my love is something no one wants out in the open.

And then the crowd goes wild.

"Here he is! Here he is!" Merry Carole yells, jumping up behind me. I steady my legs after they turned to jelly seeing Everett and stand up next to Merry Carole.

The marching band launches into some unintelligible old standard as the cheerleaders jump and cheer down the parade route.

The drum major leads the band with an unparalleled enthusiasm. We're finishing cheers, spelling out our school name, telling the cheerleaders we will GO! FIGHT! WIN! And to every NORTH STAR we answer STALLIONS! NORTH STAR! STAL-LIONS!!! NORTH STAR! STALLIONS! Louder and louder. It's a thundering pack and the entire town is being swept away. The drums pound, the brass blares. It's all small-town glory with American flags waving as the marching band makes its way down the tiny parade route.

Then all we can see is a sea of black and gold. The football team looks more like a barreling horde of colts and puppies that have no idea how big they've gotten. And in the middle of it all is Cal. He's grinning from ear to ear and strutting down the center of town. My eyes well up; I can't believe what I'm seeing. He's being patted on the back and fallen over by his friends. The men and women of North Star are pulling him out of the ranks to shake his hand and give him a pat on the back. I can't believe it. I pull Merry Carole in close as she dabs to no avail at her trailing mascara. She's waving and calling his name. He's searching for her in the crowd and then all he can do is point, a huge smile breaking across his face. He is the happiest I've ever seen him.

"Wooohooooooooooo! That's my baby!!!!!! Woooohooooooo!" Merry Carole yells, leaping up and down. I smile and laugh as the football team passes.

"Which one is West?" I ask Merry Carole, my voice low.

Merry Carole points out another boy with blond hair.

"That's ridiculous. They look like brothers. It's crazy that people are walking around this town acting like they're not kin," I say to Merry Carole so only she can hear. She nods in agreement, but then goes back to hooting and hollering for Cal and the rest of the Stallions.

The thing is? This West kid looks . . . nice. He's walking with Cal and they seem to get along. Although it's not as if you can see my hatred for Laurel and Whitney emanating off my body or anything, so who am I to judge what's really happening?

"He looks like a good kid," I say, referring to a boy who could probably pulverize me with one swat.

"He really is. I don't know where he got it from," Merry Carole says with a wink, her voice low and cutting. The football team finally fades down the parade route as a line of policemen signal that the parade has come to an end.

"The dance will start at six PM this evening, and fireworks start at nine PM!" the policemen repeat as they walk down the parade route.

"Queenie, honey? We're heading over to the dance. You ready yet?" Merry Carole knocks and then opens the door. Her voice trails off when she sees me curled up in the fetal position in my tiny twin bed. Epiphanies about ballast and pacts of pain and misery cover me like a warm blanket. Merry Carole shuts the door behind her.

"I'm not going," I say, turning over on my back and facing her. She's in an entirely new outfit, new makeup, new hair. Merry Carole has more costume changes than Cher.

"What's wrong?" she asks, feeling my forehead with the back of her hand. Her hand is soft and it breaks through me. She sits down on the edge of my bed.

"I just can't face 'em," I say, letting my arm fall over my eyes. I can't bear to have her see me like this. Tears roll down my face.

"Okay," Merry Carole says, taking my hand away from my face ever so gently. She swipes my bangs off my forehead and scoots closer. Her rose-water perfume wafts over me. I am immediately comforted.

"I'm sorry," I say, truly meaning it.

"I know, sweetie," she says, smiling as my eyes flutter open.

"All the couples and . . . I mean, I could dance with you or Cal, but . . . ," I say, trying to make a joke.

"Cal won't want anything to do with us," Merry Carole says.

"Yeah, probably," I say.

"Can I give you a piece of advice?" Merry Carole says, still smoothing my hair.

"Sure."

"You can't let them get to you. They can't ever know that—" Merry Carole's voice cracks and she pulls a red, white, and blue handkerchief from the depths of her bra. She dabs her mascara and continues, "They can't ever know that you go home at night and cry yourself to sleep because they got to you." I sit up and pull her in for a tight hug. She breaks from our hug and continues, "I know what they think of me, but that doesn't mean that they get to think they broke me. Broke us. 'Cause they didn't. They can't. We won't let 'em. Now get dressed, and for God's sake, take a shower and be at that band shell by six so we can watch our boy get QB1," Merry Carole says, tucking the handkerchief back down into the recesses of her bra. She quickly wipes away my tears and stands.

"Okay," I say, swinging my legs off the bed.

"You could even wear one of my dresses," Merry Carole says, opening my door.

"Now you're pushing it," I say, standing.

"Six PM. I'll be right in front," Merry Carole says and closes the door behind her.

10

Strawberries and champagne

As I walk to the band shell that's in the center of town, I'm pulling and tugging at the top of Merry Carole's blue-and-white-striped dress that I'm nowhere near filling out. The red belt cinches at my waist. I hope wearing this very patriotic dress will convince Merry Carole that I'm 110 percent committed to these festivities. No more fetal positions and sobbing over spilt milk.

I make my way through the picnicking citizens of North Star, my bare feet just missing the laid-out gingham blankets, makeshift barbecues, and errant packs of kids lighting firecrackers to the dismay of their overheated parents. I'm headed for the area just below the band shell, by the dance floor with its red, white, and blue lanterns strung high just above it. The lanterns have yet to be illuminated, but I'm sure they'll add to the beautiful evening. I know I'll find Merry Carole there. I see the pink parasol first and my red-white-and-blue-bedecked sister second. She sits under the parasol like a 1940s pinup girl, all red lips and oversize sunglasses. So lovely. Cal is pouring some of Merry Carole's lemonade for himself and West.

"Queen Elizabeth, this is West Ackerman," Merry Carole says as West clambers to his feet, wiping his hands on his jeans.

"Ma'am," West says, extending his hand to me. I take his hand and his handshake is firm. He is a dead ringer, even more so up close, for Cal. The icy blue eyes and that strong blade of a nose— even the mannerisms. A shrugged shoulder here and a stifled laugh there. They are brothers in every sense of the word.

"Hey there, West, pleasure to finally meet you," I say, my face open and my smile easy.

"You, too. Cal was telling me that you're a chef and that you've been everywhere." We all settle on Merry Carole's blanket. Cal hands me a glass of lemonade. I thank him.

"I have," I say.

"And New York?" West asks.

"It's like nothing you've ever seen," I say, not wanting to burst the poor boy's bubble.

"I knew it," West says, looking from me to Cal and back to me.

"We'd better get on. Coach wants all of us backstage by six," Cal says. He and West pass their now empty lemonade glasses to Merry Carole with a polite thank you and stand.

"Pleasure meeting you, ma'am," West says.

"You, too," I say, looking up into the glare of the sun.

"Good luck," Merry Carole says, stemming the tide on a flood of emotion as the boys make their way to the stage.

"He's lovely," I say.

"I know. Like I said, I have no idea how he got that way," Merry Carole says, with a wry grin. She pours me some more lemonade and we fall into a comfortable, people-watching silence.

I scan the park and notice the clumps of families, laughing and celebrating. I can't find Everett or any of the Coburns. They're probably back at the Paragon stables seeing to the horses after their big parade outing. I can't find Laurel, either, but I don't look that hard. I'd probably be able to smell sulfur were she near. I see the McKays just off to the right. Whitney is attending to . . .

"Is that Wes McKay??" I ask, unable to believe my eyes.

"Oh, you didn't know? He got fat," Merry Carole says, her voice downright gleeful.

"Yes he did. Jesus," I say, taking in the man who used to be the model of athleticism. Now he looks like the model for the "Before" picture in a weight-loss ad.

"After his knee gave out, he stopped playing football, so . . ." Merry Carole trails off as if Wes's excessive mass is the logical result.

I take in the entire McKay clan. Whitney, Wes, a little boy and a little girl, Whitney's and Wes's parents, and various other grandchildren running around.

"Whitney and Wes's kids are cute," I say, unable to blame the adorable red-white-and-blue–bedecked children for their mother's meanness.

"Super cute," Merry Carole says, offering me some strawberries out of a red Tupperware bowl. I take one and immediately eat it.

"They look happy," I say.

"Do they? I never noticed."

"Your lies only hurt America," I sigh, with a mouth full of strawberry.

"Fine. I noticed." Merry Carole shifts in her lawn chair, recrossing her legs that go on for miles.

"He wasn't good enough for you. Even at seventeen," I say.

"Oh, I know." Merry Carole's answer comes out a bit too easily. She continues, "He just has to be good enough to be Cal's daddy. They've actually been getting on these past few years. Thank God for football," she says.

"And there's been no one since?" I ask, treading lightly.

Merry Carole lowers her sunglasses and gives me a ridiculous, cartoonish, dismissive look.

"Fine." I say.

Merry Carole is quiet. A vault. As she always has been. Of course, my decades-long affair with Everett is just as secret. For being each other's confidante, we sure don't know each other very well.

"Are you not even going to mention that I wore a dress?" I ask, smoothing out the blue-and-white-striped skirt.

"I know! Don't you look pretty."

"Thank you," I say, flushing.

"I mean, you could have finished it off just a bit. A lip gloss maybe. Some mascara. Maybe even done something with that hair, but . . . no, you look really pretty. I wish you'd dress up more," Merry Carole says, doing everything she can to not drag me back to the salon right that minute.

"Is that . . . am I thanking you again or . . ." I trail off.

"I'm sorry. You're right. You look beautiful," Merry Carole says, smoothing my bangs back off my forehead.

I smile and take another strawberry from the red bowl and bite into it. Merry Carole rushes a paper towel under my chin as the red juice drips and oozes out of my mouth. I thank her through a mouth filled with luscious strawberry.

The mayor of North Star climbs the stairs to the band shell, taps the microphone, and asks everyone to quiet down. Everyone obliges. Merry Carole sits up, getting her camera ready.

"Happy Fourth of July to the people of North Star!" the mayor says. He looks like every mayor of every small town anywhere in the country—gray haired, potbellied, and authoritative. One difference: in Texas, he's got on a cowboy hat.

The crowd claps, firecrackers go off in the distance, and we all quiet down as we await his next announcement.

"I'm not going to take much of your time because I know y'all see who's coming up right behind me," the mayor says, motioning to the growing mob of black and gold just off the stage.

The crowd hoots and hollers as the football team reciprocates with a big wave.

"After Coach Blanchard comes up here and announces your Stallion starters for this next season, we'll get this party started with a couple of great bands for your dancing pleasure and we'll end, o' course, with the fireworks spectacular," the mayor says. The crowd goes wild. The mayor continues, "So, without further ado, I give you your North Star Stallions!"

To a standing ovation, the marching band and the football team congregate just behind Coach Blanchard—who was just Reed Blanchard when Merry Carole and I went to school with him. He played football, but wasn't the star. He kept to himself, but wasn't a loner. He married his high school sweetheart, but then got divorced when they'd grown apart. His wife remarried and now lives a couple of towns over and they amicably share custody of their two little girls. He was always a good guy, fair minded and not easily swayed by public opinion. Most important, he was always nice to Merry Carole and me. But now he's the mythical Coach Blanchard—one state final under his belt and, with an even better team than that year, on the verge of winning the whole thing again.

"Reed looks good," I say, standing with everyone else and clapping for the team.

"I suppose," Merry Carole says, taking pictures of Cal.

"Now that he's divorced, would you ever consider—"

"How could I possibly settle down with one man when, according to the town gossips, I'm bedding every man from North Star to Austin?" Merry Carole's voice is tight, even though she's trying to make a joke.

"Reed's always been a good guy," I say.

"I thought Wes was a good guy, remember?"

"No one ever thought Wes was a good guy," I say.

"I know," Merry Carole says, laughing.

"I'm just putting it out there, is all," I say.

"Oh you are, are you?" Merry Carole asks, focusing back on the stage.

Reed's wearing a black baseball cap with a gold stallion on it, pulled low. His dark brown hair is cut in an almost militaristic style. His broad shoulders thrown back and his chest puffed out. Reed Blanchard's always ready to be the man people hold up as the shining example of decency.

"All right now. Quiet down. Let's get down to business," Reed says, his voice an annoyed sigh. Everyone obliges. The football team behind him settles down. Reed continues, "We've got some great boys coming out this season and I'm proud of all of them, but—" Reed motions for his assistants to bring out the lawn signs. The holy grail for proud Stallion parents across the town. These signs announce the player's last name, jersey number, and position he plays, along with the usual rearing black stallion. Every player gets a lawn sign, but—and *this* is crucial—the starting lineup's signs are black with gold writing as opposed to gold with black writing. Merry Carole hasn't breathed in minutes. Cal stands off to the side. His face is creased with worry. He's about to find out, along with the rest of us, if he's the starting quarterback. The suspense is killing all of us. Reed starts with the defense, wending his way through the offense. He announces each boy's name and presents him with his sign. A posed picture is taken with each boy, his sign, the now beaming parents, and an inconvenienced-looking Reed.

Reed announces that West will be starting as one of their wide receivers and the boy just looks relieved and happy. Whitney's parents (West's grandparents) make their way to the stage and are absolutely beaming as they pose for their picture. I look over at Whitney and Wes and they just look . . . broken. In all of this, I never thought about what it must be like for them not getting to be West's parents. And he's such a good kid. Wes takes Whitney's hand as she brushes away tears—that she'll pass off as tears of joy—and she collects herself long enough to take a few pictures of the big moment.

And then it's time for the starting quarterback—the coveted title of QB1. The fabled black sign is brought out, accompanied with much fanfare.

"This year we have an embarrassment of riches when it comes to quarterbacks. North Star is very lucky to have so much young talent, but I've decided that one player can lead the North Star Stallions to the state championships this year," Reed says. The crowd goes wild at the mention of North Star's team reaching the championships.

"I can't believe he's just a freshman—Cal Wake, come on up, son," Reed says, turning around and extending his hand to Cal. The rest of the football team proceeds to stomp on the stage as hard as they can. At first I'm thrown. Then they start chanting, "CWake!

CWake! CWake!" as the stage rumbles like an earthquake. Cal's face lights up and he takes a second to gather himself. I know he's holding back a torrent of emotion. Cal and Reed shake hands and I look over at Merry Carole to see how she's reacting to all of this. But she just shoves her camera at me and bolts to the band shell. The people of North Star go crazy as Cal raises his sign high above his head.

Wake.

The citizens of North Star are applauding for a sign that is emblazoned with the name "WAKE." I never thought I'd see the day. I snap pictures of Reed and Cal shaking hands, Cal celebrating with his team, and then Merry Carole taking her place by Cal's side. She's trying to keep herself together, dabbing at her mascara, poufing up her hair, collecting herself on her proudest day. Merry Carole, Reed, and Cal gather around the sign and the official photo is taken. She hugs Cal, shakes Reed's hand, and walks back and sits down with me.

As the rest of the football team is announced and presented with their signs, Merry Carole and I just sit in silence.

"I can't believe it," I finally say.

"I know," Merry Carole says, her eyes still covered by her oversize sunglasses.

We fall silent again.

"I thought . . . I thought for sure they were going to switch him out, you know? That, like everything else in this town—"

"It wouldn't be fair," I finish.

"Damn right," Merry Carole says, pulling out a bottle of champagne she's been hiding in her cooler up until now. I'm sure she thought she'd jinx Cal's chances if she brought it out early. She pops open the bottle with ease. She kneels on the blanket and pours the bubbling contents into our plastic cups.

"To Cal," I say, raising my glass.

"To Cal," Merry Carole repeats, clinking her glass with mine. We drink. In that moment I realize I didn't look to see what Whitney and Wes were doing as Cal was being named QB1. I didn't check and see what the enemy's faces looked like as we vanquished them. This is new. Every success was only half experienced while I searched the room for that one disapproving face. My glories were never mine, just a pie to throw in the face of my adversary. What would life be like if I was just happy? Not happy because it would drive someone crazy, but happy because I want to be happy? Celebrating Cal felt great. For once, I let happiness just live and didn't allow the stench of North Star's usual disapproval. As I sip my champagne, I realize I might like to try that a bit more in the future. Maybe those are my terms. And maybe that starts with taking the job at Shine Prison. It seems odd that such a grisly job could make me happy, but there's something pulling me to it. Something I want to figure out. So, instead of inviting everyone to look down on me, why don't I just decide what I want to do . . . and do it.

A band takes to the stage and the twang of country music floats through the town square. Couples take to the floor. Country western dancing's roots are firmly held in the waltz and polka genres, but there's an elegance and effortlessness to it that belies any modern take the dance could have. Couples move as one, and the older, more experienced couples barely touch the floor at all. Men in cowboy hats hold their women tightly as they guide them across the floor. Shuffling cowboy boots leave scuff marks on the wooden dance floor as the sun finally dips below the horizon and the day finally begins to cool down. The dance floor is awash in light from the red, white, and blue lanterns as the couples drift and sashay. Merry Carole and I sit, slightly buzzed off the champagne we drank too quickly because of the heat.

"I think I'm going to head home," I say, standing.

"Well, we sure appreciated you coming out today," Merry Carole says.

"I'm going to see what you've got around the house and throw together something for supper, if you're interested," I say, smoothing my skirt down in the back.

"Oh sure," Merry Carole says, taking out her cell phone.

"Are you checking in with Cal?" I ask, just about to head out.

"Oh . . . no, I'm sure he's off somewhere with the team," Merry Carole says, covering her cell phone.

"So you're not going to tell me who you're texting?"

"No."

"Fine."

"Fine."

"I'm going to assume it's a man and that you're passionately and quite secretly in love," I say, standing over her. Merry Carole just rolls her eyes and continues texting.

"Just go on now," Merry Carole says, shooing me away.

I walk across the park past the food booths that have been set out on the street at the edge of the town square. I think about the day, about Cal standing up there holding that sign over his head: WAKE. I trot across the main street in a happy haze, reliving it all. I turn the corner by the post office.

Everett.

"Oh hey," I say, caught completely off guard.

"Hey," Everett says, just as startled.

We stand there frozen once again. The live music floats throughout the town.

"Well, good seeing you. Hey, say hi to your folks for me," I say and continue walking down the street. I can't be alone with him. I won't set myself up for that. I have to get away from him or else—

"Queenie, it's just us here. Can we—," Everett says, turning around.

"Just how you like it, right?" I call, not looking back. My voice is breathy and desperate. The pain of being without him is fueling my anger.

"You should be real proud of Cal," Everett says, calling after me. I whip around.

"I am. He's an amazing kid," I say. Everett is slowly but surely, inch by inch, backing me up into an alley in between the post office and an antiques shop. The old brick walls of each building rise high above us as the dusky night becomes an inky black. I can hear the music in the distance, the occasional crack, crack, crack of a firecracker.

Everett is quiet. He leans forward mere centimeters, just as he did last night but without the safety of the bar, and the crowds of people in it. I feel outside of myself. My breathing quickens as he bends his head low and tilts it just enough for my entire body to react to him. His eyes are fast on mine and my heart races to catch up with the fantasies of what the next few moments might bring. I make my hands into tight fists, hoping this will keep them from reaching for him. His face is now inches from mine.

"An entire town is lit up just over there and we find the—," I say, my voice an intimate whisper.

"I've missed you," he says, taking his hands out of his pockets.

"Don't," I say, willing my voice not to break and catch.

"You look beautiful." Everett steps closer, his hand lacing around my waist and pulling me in.

"That's not helping," I say, my body restless and shaky.

"Be still." Everett just looks at me, his eyes washing over every part of my face. I slide my hand around him and hold on. He leans down and kisses my neck. I bring my other hand up and grasp

him. I'm losing my balance—always a problem around him. My
hand grips his shoulder, feeling his shirt shift and tighten over the
sinewy muscles just beneath. I slide my hand up and let my fingers
brush his glistening neck. Goose bumps dot his olive skin as I run
my hand farther up and explore the curls at the nape of his neck.

"You're finally back," Everett sighs, whispering in my ear.

Stillness. The air around us waits. Even the music in the distance takes a breath.

"Everett, I—" Everett covers my mouth with his and I can feel
his breath quickening. I feel alive for the first time in years as the
fireworks crack and pop high above North Star.

"Please . . . just—just give me a minute," I say, trying to catch
my breath. He tilts back, but only slightly. Something's different. I
can't breathe. He kisses me again and I feel claustrophobic. He's too
much. This is too much. I've been running from this feeling for
years and now with each kiss I can feel it bearing down on me. It:
the pain of knowing we can never be together. With each kiss he
peppers down my neck, I am forced to admit that the love of my
life will never really be mine. It's one thing to run from ghosts, it's
quite another to let them catch you. My eyes dart around the darkened alley and I catch the glint of his belt buckle.

"I can't believe you still have that," I say breathlessly, pointing at
the belt buckle. He looks down at his crotch and arches an eyebrow.
My face flushes red and I clarify, "The belt buckle, I mean the belt
buckle."

"Why wouldn't I still have it?" he asks. I study him. The man I
once knew so well that I could draw a map of his freckles from
memory. I gather myself. Everett tucks my long bangs behind my ear.
He covers my mouth once more with his. The cracking and popping
of the fireworks light our faces in the colors of the rainbow. Flecks of
red and blue color the side of Everett's face as he watches me.

"I thought when you married Laurel that—"

"That what? She had nothing to do with us."

His words hang there just as the smoke from the spent fireworks hangs over the town center. Something is different. I'm different. I *am* older. I *am* smarter. And most of all, I *am* stronger. The haze begins to lift. This isn't going to work. No matter how badly we want it to. In this age of princes marrying "commoners," it's easy to think that the days when one's social strata dictated who you married are behind us. As much as I hate that Everett is loyal to his family, it's why he's the man I've loved since I was five years old. Asking him to turn his back on them would mean eroding the very character that both mystifies me and makes me believe in better things. Maybe if I can believe I'm not my mother, Everett has to learn he's not his parents.

And maybe I need to let him.

I said I would come back to North Star on my terms. Maybe my terms start right here. With Everett.

"I can't do this again," I say.

"What?" Everett says. With the firework spectacular over, the live music has started back up. The citizens of North Star are beginning to wander out into the town square.

"I'm different now. Maybe I was always different, but just—"

"I don't understand," Everett says, reaching out to me. I step back. He immediately tenses.

"I didn't come back here to pick up where we left off."

"Why did you come back?"

"Because I had nowhere else to go."

"So you're off to the next city then," Everett says, folding his arms across his chest. His chin is high and defiant.

"No, I'd like to stick around and watch you marry another suitable woman who's not me," I say, stepping toward him.

"That was a mistake."

"A mistake I paid for."

"You're not seriously insinuating that I wanted that."

"You're a grown man, Ever." His brow furrows and I can tell my offhanded use of his pet name has shaken him.

"A grown man with responsibilities. It was the right thing to do at the time. My father was very clear about that."

"Always the good little soldier," I say, my eyes darting around the dark alley.

"It's probably hard for you to understand what it's like to have consequences for your behavior, or any responsibilities, for that matter."

"What?"

"Someone tries to be the boss of you and you what—quit? Get fired? Move on? That's how it works, right?"

I am quiet. Shaken. The thing about someone knowing you better than you know yourself is that you can't shut off their knowledge when it hits too close to home. He's right, of course.

"I never moved on from you," I say.

"No, you just left," he says.

"The night before you got married to Laurel. You couldn't have expected to . . . Could you have watched me walk down the aisle with another man?" I ask, stepping closer.

"No."

"You broke my heart, Ever," I say, laying my hand on his chest. He covers my hand with his and holds it tight. He dips his head and can't look at me.

"I did what was right by my family. You have no idea how . . . I tried to honor the family name. Shit, Queenie—my parents made it perfectly clear that the future of Paragon rested firmly on my shoulders. Dad would never let Florrie near the business, and

Gray's turned into some idiot playboy. And . . . I mean, this all would be a whole lot easier if I didn't love my parents and love Paragon, but I do." Everett's voice catches and he turns away from me. He continues, "But I fell in love with you and I didn't know how to handle that," Everett says, pacing around the alley.

"You didn't know how to handle that? What am I—a disease you caught?"

"What? No!"

"I knew your parents saw me as trash, but I never thought you did."

"I don't." Everett pulls me close and says, "I don't."

"Then why do you treat me like I am?" I ask, freeing myself from him.

Everett is quiet. He turns away from my gaze.

"Don't you think we get to be happy, Ever?"

"We're happy right now," he says, kissing me again.

"Are we?"

Our shared pain is palpable and yet I can't help but hold on to him. Even still.

I continue. "I'm taking a job over in Shine. I've decided to stay for a while," I say.

"Why are you telling me this?"

"I want you to stop me from walking away by yelling that you love me. I want you to sweep me up on one of your beautiful Paragon horses and let the entire town see how we feel about each other. I want what I've always wanted," I say, taking his face in my hands.

"Which is what?" Everett says.

"For you to be proud of me, proud of us. I want you to not be able to contain yourself and let everyone know that you're my man," I say, and it hurts. It hurts to say it out loud. It hurts to admit it.

"I am your man," he says, letting his forehead fall onto mine. His voice is low and frantic.

"Prove it," I say, pulling away from him and taking in the people streaming past us on their way home. Everett is quiet. Still. Tortured. I continue, "That's what I thought." I turn and finally walk away.

I don't look back.

I burst through Merry Carole's front door and straight into my little guest room. I strip off all of my clothes and wrap a towel around my body. I put Merry Carole's dress and all of my undergarments into the washing machine, measure the detergent, twist the knobs, and close the lid. I don't let myself think. I don't let myself stop. I press my lips together and try to erase the taste of Everett still on them. I walk out of the laundry room and into the guest bathroom, turning on the shower. I lock the door behind me and let the towel fall to the ground. My mind races with thoughts of Everett. I try to stay ahead of them as I step inside the shower, letting the water fall over me.

I feel light. The weight of loving Everett had held me so tightly for so long, it's all I knew. I feel a sense of panic move through my body. I steady myself on the tile wall.

"What am I going to do without him?" I whisper, the sobs finally coming. I let the water wash over me as I think of a life without Everett. No more fantasies. I need to see the reality of what we have become. We're not happy. Whatever momentary joy we have can never equal the love that's felt when you commit yourself to someone and decide to live out your days together. The peace of mind that comes from building a future with someone is not even in the same ballpark as the scraps we've been living on. Time. The promise of time is something we never got. What kind of future would we have based on a past and present filled with stolen moments?

The truth is, I came back to North Star because I left something here. And it wasn't Everett. Or Merry Carole. Or Cal. Or even my mother. I didn't leave it somewhere in high school or even as I sat at that blinking red light at the edge of town just before getting on that first highway that took me anywhere but here. No, I lost this when I was a little girl. And now I want to find it.

I want to be happy again. Be happy for the first time.

Maybe the first step is doing something just for me without judging it or fearing the consequences.

I shut off the water and step out of the shower. I wrap the towel around my body, grab another towel for my hair, and walk into my guest room. I find my cell phone and dial.

"Shine Prison, how can I help you?"

"Warden Dale Green, please?"

"Who may I say is calling?"

"Queen Elizabeth Wake." The woman puts me on hold and I settle on my perfectly made bed. The prison has music playing while you're on hold, which I find odd. As I try to towel-dry my hair, I find myself singing along with Johnny Cash's "A Boy Named Sue": *"Well, I grew up quick/And I grew up mean . . ."*

"Ms. Wake, happy Fourth!" Warden Dale says, cutting through the music.

"Happy Fourth to you, sir," I say.

"You got an answer for me, Ms. Wake?"

"Yes, sir. I would like the job, if it's still available," I say, my wet hair sticking to my damp shoulders.

"It sure is. I appreciate you calling me back. How about if you come on in tomorrow and have Juanita give you the walk through? I'd like you to cook the Death House crew supper that night and then we're going to need your last meal services this Friday. You can understand why I was pressing you for an answer," Warden Dale says.

"Yes, sir," I say. This Friday. My first last meal. I can do this.

"Now, Juanita's got today off, but I'll hand you back over to one of the other fine ladies at the front desk and she'll set you up with all the details. I'll see you at ten AM sharp tomorrow morning."

"Sir?"

"Yes?"

"Can I bring knives?"

"Pardon me?"

"Knives, sir? I have a set of knives I prefer to use."

"Oh, we'll have Juanita inventory them and you'll have to check them in and out when you come to work. That suit you?"

"Yes, sir," I say.

"Welcome to Shine Prison, Ms. Wake. And I'll see you tomorrow morning," Warden Dale signs off. Last meals and inventorying knives. This is going to be an interesting day. I beep my cell phone off and stand up. I get dressed, throw my wet hair up into a ponytail, and head to a hard-core German butcher I know is open in New Braunfels. Even on the Fourth of July that German flag flies high. I'll grab some chicken to fry up tonight, as well as a brisket for tomorrow's supper. I'll have to smoke it all night, and even with the time I've got, it can always go longer. This'll have to do. I swipe my keys off the table by the door and head out. I'm already listing appetizers and desserts in my head as I pull out of Merry Carole's driveway and past all the meandering citizens of North Star, the live music still floating through town.

11

Gentleman Jack Bourbon

"Why would you make a decision like that without even talking with me first?" Merry Carole asks as I appear in the kitchen fully clothed and exhausted after a night of checking on my twelve-pound brisket. After a whole night of smoking, I packaged it up and the brisket and I are finally ready to head over to Shine this morning.

"I did talk with you about it," I say, pouring coffee into a mug. I open up the refrigerator to get some creamer.

"You didn't say you were going to take it," Merry Carole says.

"I know, but I did," I say, pouring the creamer into the mug.

"I can see that."

"Don't you like that I'm staying?" I ask, checking the time: 9:00 AM. I have to get going.

"I do," Merry Carole says, cinching her robe tightly around her body.

"Then let's focus on that," I say, giving her a quick peck on the cheek before grabbing my canvas bag that's filled with the foil-wrapped brisket and my list of ingredients for the day's menu. I head for the front door.

"This isn't over," Merry Carole says, calling out to me.

"I know," I say, closing the door behind me.

I walk quickly to my car, before the early morning humidity wreaks havoc on my hair. I open the hatch, lovingly set the brisket inside, and close it up. The brisket smells delicious. I have a shopping list for today that I'll have to take care of once I check in. I hop into my car and drive through the town's center. I pass the alley where I was with Everett just yesterday. There's nothing I can do about that. I can't wait for him anymore. I've waited twenty years and nothing's changed. I did the right thing. I know I did. Now all I have to do is convince myself that this ache will go away in time. That I'll feel like myself again. That this newfound lightness won't begin to feel terrifying. I'm not alone—I have Merry Carole and Cal, just like always. The key is to take the little nugget I learned at the very end in New York. Just as finding adventure in a new city can't be about not being in North Star, finding love with a new man can't be about not being with Everett. Remember, I want to be happy. On my terms. I speed onto the highway and turn the radio up full blast.

I was told to park in Lot D. I scan the expanse around the prison and wonder how I thought I could just keep parking in the visitors' lot. I find Lot D, park, grab my knife case, my shopping list, and the brisket. I walk the interminable distance to the prison with a side of beef worthy of the opening credits of *The Flintstones*. The golden hills, silvery barbed wire, and the big sky are broken up only by the depressing puce color of the prison's outer walls.

I walk into the front office and find myself, once again, following Juanita and her sensible, squeaky shoes back down the Hall of Echoes. We settle into the anteroom where I sign contracts, waivers, and far too much paperwork. I'm sure I signed something where I wouldn't sue if I was injured in the line of duty. I don't think about any of it. I just read and sign. Juanita inventories my knives, I get my name badge and a key card. Then Juanita walks me through the various protocols and safety measures.

"Now, follow me," Juanita says, standing up and walking back into the Hall of Echoes. A guard stands just outside Juanita's door. "This is LaRue Banner. He's on the Death House crew." LaRue gives me a curt nod. He is a big man, like all the other guards I've seen. He's younger than I expected, his cocoa skin unwrinkled and perfect. He has dimples that—I'm sure he doesn't want me to mention—are adorable.

"This way, ma'am," LaRue says, leading Juanita and me out of the Hall of Echoes.

"LaRue is taking us out to the Death House. It's an annex right off the prison. You won't be cooking in the main prison kitchen where the convicts eat, you'll have your own private space," Juanita says. We're outside now. The heat is bursting through the early morning. It's already hotter than three kinds of hell out here. We're in this in-between space connecting the prison walls and the outside that is all fencing and razor wire. I look up to see the pacing guards in their uniforms, their shotguns held high. I imagine this corridor is used just by staff and convicts to get to and from the newly built Death House. LaRue doesn't look up at the guards, his pace is steady and measured. I find myself trying to stay as close to him as I can without causing an uncomfortable moment. We arrive at a small brick building just outside the prison walls. LaRue swipes his key card and the door clicks open.

"You won't be coming in this way, ma'am. There's a parking lot just behind, Lot B. That's for you. Your key card works in the door that leads right to the kitchen," LaRue says, motioning around the back of the Death House.

"I was told Lot D," I say, becoming breathless.

"*B* as in boy, not *D* as in . . . well," LaRue says, trailing off. "Right through here."

We all finish in our heads the sentence beginning with the *D*. D as in Death.

I walk into the sterile entry space and through one of two metal doors. I get the feeling that this is one of those terrible fairy-tale rooms, where you choose the wrong door, and . . . I take a deep breath. LaRue swipes his card and we walk through to a long, clearly bulletproof window with guards and desks just behind it. Four men in their brown uniforms are sitting on desks, talking on phones and speaking with each other. They come to a complete stop when we walk in. I see Shawn. He smiles, but then there's a change in his face. He walks over and buzzes us through.

"Gentlemen, this is your new Death House cook, Queenie Wake," Juanita says as the men stand. They all look basically the same. Sure, they're different races and ages, but the same thing emanates from them: do not mess with me.

"It's a pleasure," I say, my Texas drawl thick. All of the men look at me, then at the canvas bag. I continue, "And this is your supper," I say, lifting the bag a bit higher.

"Good to see you, Queenie," Shawn says, extending his hand. Juanita excuses herself and leaves me there in the Death House. Shawn turns around and addresses his men. "This is a good friend of my family, so I expect y'all will treat her right." This is not a question. The men nod and intone a "yessir." He introduces the men one by one. LaRue is the youngest, by far. Jace looks like he could be in prison himself. Shawn moves me past him quickly. Big

Jim and Little Jim look like guys you see at the end of a bar, a beer in hand, watching the Cowboys. They're all edgy and I can tell that they view the Death House as their territory. What I hope is that I'll win them over with this meal. With the success of the Number One the other night, I feel hopeful. Confident that Brad's harsh words about my passion are old news and behind me, I hope to be accepted into the fold of the Death House with one well-made supper comprised entirely of my own recipes.

As Shawn leads me back to the kitchen, I feel a sense of excitement. That can't be the right word, can it? I want to get cooking. I feel like this place is big enough to hold me. I know that sounds silly—it's what this place does: holds people. Why do I feel my most free in a place that cages people? Is it because the stakes are so high? That for once my intensity is right on target? That it's life or death and that one plate has to be perfect and I get to be as focused as I want and it's just another day at the office? Or is it because everyone here either has a gun or is a convict and my little sob story is just run of the mill? Maybe it's all of the above.

"The kitchen is down that hallway, we'll go there next. But I wanted to show you where the inmates go when it's their time," Shawn says, motioning to an unmarked metal door. He continues, "There is an outer room where the Death House crew congregates; there is a cell; there is a hallway with a clock, a phone, and a choice of religious reading material. There are five members of the Death House team because each one of us is in charge of a specific region of the inmate. As the captain, I handle the head and chest, should he try to rise off the gurney or resist. The Jims each handle a leg, and the younguns, Jace and LaRue, each handle an arm. Do you understand?" I nod. I get what Shawn is telling me. Each man handles a region. My mind spins and avoids trying to understand anything deeper than that. I try not to think about Yvonne Chapman and her clickable name on that prison's Web site that'll tell me one day that her appeals have been exhausted and she, too, will be sitting in some tiny cell somewhere with five men, each assigned to a region. My breathing quickens and I make a vow right there and then not to check that prison Web site again. Shawn continues, "And then there is the execution room. I need you to promise me something, Queenie," Shawn says, taking me aside. I am lost in thought. Yvonne Chapman. Complicated monsters. Lost. Spiraling around under the semantics of "each man handles a region of the inmate." Shawn repeats himself, "Queenie?"

"Yes," I say, my eyes darting back and forth from the unmarked metal door to Shawn.

"I need you to never come over here to this side. I made that promise to Dee when she found out you took the job. So, we clear?" Shawn asks, his eyes boring into mine.

"Yes, sir," I say, falling into line just like the rest of the crew. I refocus on Shawn and the task at hand and try to leave Yvonne Chapman in that far, faraway prison where she belongs.

"Good. Now come on," he says, walking toward the kitchen and away from that unmarked metal door. Shawn swipes his key card and we walk into a makeshift dining area and the kitchen just beyond. It looks like any other cafeteria and kitchen. The kitchen is immaculate, I can smell the cleaning products from where I'm standing. Crisp lines of cabinets over slick white floors. There are high, barred windows that light shines through, but are frosted to make anything blurry just beyond. I walk through the kitchen testing and inventorying what it has to offer. A workable cooktop, a nice-size walk-in, and plenty of preparation areas. I set the brisket, still in its foil, down on one of the counters. I'll reheat it (something I do, but other Texans swear against) and slice it about five minutes before everyone sits down. No passion, my ass.

"What's through here?" I ask, pointing to a door.

"Our parking lot." Shawn walks over, swipes his key card, and opens the door for me. Lot B. As in boy. Not D. Not D. Shawn closes the door and continues, "All right, then. I hear you're cooking supper for us today," Shawn says, leaning up against one of the metal counters.

"Yes, sir," I say, poking around in the kitchen some more. Tons of space in the pantry, work stations for the infamous Dent boys.

"Well, that just made my day," Shawn says, a smile breaking across his face.

"Mine, too," I say.

"Jace is going to bring in the Dent boys for you. One of the guards will always be in the kitchen with you. So you don't need to worry about that. They're harmless anyway. They're getting out in less than a year, so they've got no call to act out," Shawn says, scanning the kitchen.

"Good . . . good," I say, my mind mercifully busy. No time to think about yesterday. No time to mourn Everett. No time to fantasize about finding him and repeating yesterday over and over again. No. I have a meal to plan and the Dent boys to meet.

I hear the kitchen door click and Jace and LaRue walk through with two men just between them.

Guards. Guns. Convicts. Shackles.

Toto, we're not in Kansas anymore.

"These are them," Jace says, ambling over to Shawn and motioning to the two men. LaRue stands at attention behind the men. The older man is balding and slight. His rangy frame swimming in the all-white uniforms the convicts wear. The other man is basically a younger version of his father. He's taller and his head of hair is definitely on its way to going bald. They look like a couple of guys you'd see anywhere and not think twice about. If not for the shackles and chains, they'd look like a couple of hospital orderlies coming in to check on your bedpan. But I know better.

"All right, boys. This is your new work assignment. This here is Ms. Wake. She's from up in Hill Country—North Star. She's going to be cooking our last meals. Ms. Wake, this here is Harlan and Cody Dent," Shawn says, presenting me to the two men. The men don't make eye contact and nod their greetings. I nod back, not knowing exactly how to communicate with them. I don't want to get them in any kind of trouble or, for that matter, get me into any kind of trouble.

"Harlan here worked at diners all his life and works in the prison kitchen when he's not assigned here," Shawn says.

"Cody here bartended, so if you need some limes cut up, he's your guy," Jace adds. Shawn shoots him a look and Jace immediately recoils.

"May I?" I ask Shawn, motioning to see if I can approach the Dent boys. He nods. I walk up to the father, Harlan, "Would you mind answering some questions?" I ask, looking from Harlan to Cody.

They look to Shawn, he gives them the okay, and they nod.

"Mr. Dent—*Harlan*—what kind of diners did you work in?" I ask, not getting too close.

"I was a short-order cook mostly, ma'am," Harlan says, finally making eye contact. His eyes are a hollowed-out, dark blue. His skin is wan and he just looks tired.

"That's good. What's your specialty?" I ask.

"I can cook anything and cook it fast," he says, his chin rising just a bit.

"I bet you can," I say. Short-order cooks are masterful. To watch one of them in their element is to watch a genius at work.

"And you? Cody?" I ask, my voice strong and level.

"I didn't do much of nothing, but I did hold down a job at a couple of bars," Cody says.

"Before he robbed 'em," Jace says. Shawn shoots him another look. Jace recoils again. Cody tenses and deflates.

"Okay, we can work with that," I say.

"Yes, ma'am," Cody says, still averting his eyes.

"Now, boys, I'm going to need you to clean this kitchen while Ms. Wake meets with Warden Dale and goes out and gets what she needs for supper," Shawn says as LaRue and Jace bring out cleaning supplies and mop buckets. How much cleaner can this kitchen get?

"Yes, sir," the Dent boys say together.

"Come on with me now," Shawn says to me. I follow him back through the kitchen and out into the main room, past the un-marked door of horrors.

"They'll be perfect for you. A kitchen assignment, especially in the Death House, is a real plum. They won't want to mess it up," Shawn says as we walk outside in the purgatory between high prison walls and barbed-wire fencing. The heat beats down on us as we walk back into the prison.

"I'm feeling a bit overwhelmed," I admit as we walk down the Hall of Echoes.

"Yeah, that happens," Shawn says, his voice strong and sure.

"Are they going to be in shackles the entire time?" I ask, trying to get my bearings, to hold on to some normality about this new setup.

"No, they won't need to be, although that has been done in the past," Shawn says.

"How do they do anything?"

"Slowly and without killing anybody," Shawn says, leading me into Juanita's office. I just nod. Shawn continues, "But Jace'll be in there with you, so it don't matter."

"Warden Dale is ready for you," Juanita says, thanking Shawn. He says his quick good-byes and leaves us.

I walk through to Warden Dale's office still in a daze, exuding a false sense of first-day bravado. I notice we're not alone.

"Queen Elizabeth Wake, I'd like to introduce you to Professor Hudson Bishop." Warden Dale is practically bursting his buttons with pride at this professor person. I extend my hand to him. He takes it and smiles as we shake hands.

He's clearly not from here.

"Queenie, and it's nice to meet you," I say as Warden Dale motions for me to sit.

"And you," Hudson says. He's the sort of man whose appearance you don't have time to inventory because you're too busy trying to assess whether you should dive in or run for your life. Someone other than himself cuts his thick, black hair, and it's not the ancient barber in town who believes the only options are: (1) going into the military, or (2) just getting out of the military. Eyebrows that are naturally and quite dangerously shaped into a roguish arch set off his piercing blue eyes. His entire wolfish bearing was born to tempt. He exudes a confidence bordering on arrogance. I immediately feel out of my depth.

Once again, Professor Hudson Bishop is not from 'round here.

"Hudson here is a professor over at UT," Warden Dale says, walking over to the drinks cart. It's ten AM.

"I hear you're an alum," Hudson says, taking a glass of bourbon from Warden Dale. He continues, "Thank you, sir." Warden Dale nods and walks back over to the drinks cart.

"Hook 'em horns," I say, extending my pinky and index finger as if miming my very own shadow puppet. This man has turned me into an idiot.

"Hudson is writing a paper on death," Warden Dale says, handing me a glass of bourbon. He walks back over to the drinks cart.

"It's more about how knowing you're going to die—whether it's terminal patients or the men and women of death row—affects the human brain," Hudson says, lazily swirling his bourbon around in the glass.

"I imagine not well," I say. Warden Dale pours himself a glass and stands behind his desk.

"You'd be surprised," Hudson says, with a quick smile.

"To the great state of Texas," Warden Dale says, raising a glass.

"To the great state of Texas," Hudson and I repeat in unison. We drink.

"Where are you from originally?" I ask, holding my now empty glass.

"Is it that obvious?" Hudson laughs, holding his now empty glass. I'm impressed.

"I'm afraid so," I say.

"Santa Barbara, California," Hudson says.

"It's beautiful there," I say.

"Definitely," Hudson says.

"Well, we've got some business to attend to, Professor Bishop, so I will see you at the end of the day," Warden Dale says, standing and extending his hand to Hudson.

"Yes, sir," Hudson says, standing.

"Are you coming to supper?" I ask, looking at both Warden Dale and Hudson.

"Supper?" Hudson asks, clearly thinking the word "supper" is adorable. He and Warden Dale are both standing and I feel awkward that I'm the only one sitting. Should I stand? Do I stand? Wouldn't that be even weirder? And shall I stand, hand held aloft, while I proclaim that you will dine with me?

"Oh sure. That's a great idea. It'll be a good opportunity for

Hudson here to talk to the guards. We'll both join you," Warden Dale says.

"I'm thinking five thirty?" I ask. Warden Dale nods.

"I'll be there. Pleasure meeting you, Queenie," Hudson says, excusing himself from Warden Dale's office. Warden Dale takes my empty glass and walks over to the drinks cart with it. He does not refill it. He walks behind his desk and sits.

"Professor Bishop is one of my pet projects, Ms. Wake. It's just another example of how, as a leader, I am also a futurist," Warden Dale says.

"Yes, sir." I breathe deeply, trying to keep from laughing. I vow to use the word "futurist" at least ten times a day from now on.

"Here is your budget and a schedule of the upcoming executions," Warden Dale says, handing me two sheets of paper stapled to each other. I am jerked out of my concealed hysterics and reach for the pieces of paper. Please don't let it be a list of names. Please don't let it be a list of names. I scan the first sheet. The budget is not extravagant, but definitely something I can work with. Warden Dale has outlined how I will be paid. I will be paid hourly and will be expected to work the full day preparing the last meal. That sounds workable.

I gather myself and flip the sheet of paper over to look at the list. I exhale. It's not names, but dates. The first couple of entries at the beginning have an order, as well. Fried chicken, potato salad, tamales, tacos al pastor, fried pies, and homemade biscuits abound. As I scan what I'm being asked to prepare, I find myself getting excited. In just a few weeks, I've gone from being midguidedly passionate about some pasty tourist putting ketchup on tasteless eggs to trying to remember where Momma put all those old family recipes. After only wanting Texas in my rearview, I'm now chomping at the bit to dig into five generations of North Star dirt for inspiration. Whatever I think of North Star and the past I thought I left here, this food has always been what comforted me. It made me feel as if I belonged somewhere. It's where home was, especially when we had no home.

But then this darkness clouds over it all. Who I'm cooking for, when they're going to eat it. Where I am. I need to stay in the kitchen—mentally and physically. I will get my order and cook it to the best of my ability. I'll know that someone who really needs a little bit of comfort is receiving it. It's not for me to judge what they've done to land here. I can't get caught up in their crimes, the victims, and the victims' families—like Shawn said, this is the law, this is my job, so I will do it with integrity. I know this feels like a cop-out, like a child pressing her hands to her ears and screaming at the top of her lungs so she doesn't have to listen. And maybe there's some of that simply because I can't face the magnitude of what happens within these Death House walls.

It's not as if I haven't experienced violence in the past. I've been part of one of those victim's families that were visited by police reciting their robotic apologies at "my loss." It somehow seems fitting that I'm here. A part of this violent world again. As long as Mom was around, there were police in our lives: the sheriff driving her home when she'd had too much to drink, barroom brawls, jealous wives vandalizing our possessions (what little we had). The red and blue flashing lights outside our windows became less and less of an event and more and more of a common occurrence.

I was just sixteen when Momma was murdered. She was beautiful. Flaming red hair, big boobs, and porcelain skin like you couldn't believe. She had clear blue eyes that seemed mysterious and compelling. People couldn't help but stare at her as she swayed her curves to and fro down North Star's streets. Merry Carole's figure was clearly inherited. But Momma was someone I stopped trying to figure out long before she died. Those blue eyes that were so intoxicating to me as a child weren't mysterious at all. They were cruel and heartless. People were either stepping stones or obstacles, and that included her kids. Love wasn't something she was even capable of. It was an act she put on so a man would think she was the marrying kind, only to tell us to wait at the Dairy Queen while "she had company." Most times, the manager at the Dairy Queen would have to call Fawn or Yvonne Chapman when Momma didn't come for us. They'd come get us and we'd spend the night at their house, sharing a guest bed or curled up on the couch. Momma wouldn't come for us for days.

I'm sure there's scar tissue and buttons being pushed all through the rubble of what my life has become. But for me it was always clear: my family was Merry Carole and now Cal, too. And when I couldn't turn to Merry Carole, I had Everett. I also had Dee. Mom was someone we carried to bed, filled in for at the burger shack, and apologized for every day of our lives.

But that day.

The day the principal walked into my classroom, whispered in the teacher's ear, and motioned for me to follow him without so much as a smile is burned into my brain. I remember following him down the hallway and trying to inventory what I'd done wrong. I was sixteen. I thought, maybe they figured out I'd been forging Momma's signature on all my permission slips. Maybe Everett's parents had found out about us and we were going to be disciplined for that. But what would we be "charged with"? I had the tiniest of fears that something had happened to Merry Carole and the baby. She was pretty far along with Cal at that point and things had gotten almost unbearable for her at school. It was Laurel and Piggy Peggy's mission to make Merry Carole's life as excruciating as possible. Of course, Whitney was pregnant and shipped

off to her grandparents in Houston at that point anyway, so . . .
hindsight and all that. It never occurred to me that it was about
Mom. Her domain was in the outside world and she rarely infected
my school life. That was about to change.

I remember walking into the front office and seeing Merry
Carole there. She was sobbing and inconsolable. I ran to her,
crouching in front of her, pleading with her to tell me what was
wrong. Please. What's going on? I remember saying.

"Mom's dead," Merry Carole said, through sobs. It made total
sense and no sense at all. I remember taking a deep breath and
thinking, there it is. The news I've been waiting to hear for years.

"How?" I asked, not a tear falling from my eyes. I remember
being eerily calm.

"Yvonne fucking Chapman shot her!" Merry Carole screamed.
Merry Carole rarely swore, and I kind of loved that she screamed the
F word right in the front office. It was freeing and wonderful. And
no one could reprimand her for it. It was just going to be another
trashy thing we Wakes did instead of behaving like "proper folks."

"Yvonne Chapman? But where . . . where are we going to live
now?" I asked, unable to process Mom's death, so I reached for the
next big issue: shelter. Merry Carole was only becoming more hysterical. I pushed my fears aside and focused on calming her down.
She was too worked up. She was going to lose control, if she hadn't
already. Her crying had escalated into hysterics and she was struggling to breathe.

"Yeah! Her best friend whose husband Mom was fucking,"
Merry Carole said, her voice cracking and breaking as it shrieked
through the school.

"Okay, now . . . if we can just take this into a more private
place," the principal interrupted.

"Eat shit," I said, my head whipping around at the man who

seemed to be annoyed by how two girls were handling their only parent's death. I remember hating that I hadn't said something more cutting and brilliant in the heat of the moment. But I was sixteen, and despite wanting to be a grown-up, I wasn't. And I'd just learned that my mom had died.

"All right now," the principal said then, gripping me around the arm and pulling me away from Merry Carole. And that was when something just exploded inside me. Even all these years later I remember never feeling as terrified as I felt when that man pulled me away from my sister. I felt like a wild animal, clawing and wailing as he tugged us apart. So I punched him. I rounded on him with my only free hand and connected with the side of his bloated face. It was later documented that I "accidentally swatted him as he tried to calm me." But I was completely out of control. In those seconds I thought it was possible to simply combust. I remember being pulled off the principal by people, teachers probably. They held me back, picked me up, restrained me, and I remember thinking—all someone has to do is tell me it'll be okay. Comfort me and I'll stop, I screamed inside my head. I heard Merry Carole sobbing, and I fought back because they wouldn't let me be with her.

I howled, kicked, and finally freed myself only to lunge past the mob of teachers and administrators and wrap myself around Merry Carole, finally calming her and in so doing calming myself. Merry Carole and I held on to each other among the pacing, milling faculty as we let the reality sink in: we had no home, no possessions, no parents, and a baby on the way.

That was the worst day of my life.

So as I sit here today in the warden's office, I know a thing or two about identifying with the victim's family.

12

*Brisket, ranch beans, coleslaw, white bread, peach
cobbler, and sweet tea*

I have to pass under a guard tower, more razor-wire fences, and
another guard booth just to park in Lot B when I return from
shopping. I gather all the ingredients and transport them to the
back of the kitchen in one trip. My skill—some may say pig-
headedness—in trying to get everything in one trip being utilized to the hilt. I fumble with my key card, shifting and
sliding canvas bags filled with fixings on an elbow here, cutting
off circulation in a bended-back index finger there, and finally
the door unlocks. I push open the kitchen door. The silence
hits me immediately.

This is my first very own kitchen. I get to run it as I see fit.
I let that sink in as I arrange my ingredients in stations. I walk
freely around the space, breathing easy and getting more and

more excited. I have nine hungry men to cook for tonight and I've never been more ecstat`c. These are Texas men, all except Hudson, and this meal will . . . well, it'll be great. A smile cracks across my face and I feel light and happy. What does it say about me that I've never felt more at home than in this particular kitchen? I shake that off. I get to be happy. No more judgments. Whatever this kitchen is, it's mine and mine alone.

I walk out into the hallway, past the unmarked door of horrors, and find the guards at their desks. I see Shawn and walk toward him.

"You ready for the Dent boys?" Shawn asks, standing.

"Yes, that'd be great," I say.

"You going to tell us what you're cooking?" Big Jim asks, coming out from behind his desk.

"Where would the fun be in that?" I ask, with a smile. Big Jim laughs—it's a great big belly laugh that cuts the room open, easing tension and sweeping away the eggshells on the floor.

"I'll call for the Dents," Shawn says.

"I'll just wait in the kitchen?" I ask, motioning to the door.

"That'll be just fine," Shawn says, a tired smile curling across his face.

I walk back to the kitchen and set up where the Dents will be. I imagine Harlan will act as an assistant, while Cody will take on more of a sous-chef role, cutting and preparing. It won't be limes and maraschino cherries just yet, but maybe we'll get there. I search cabinets and pull out pots and pans, getting ready for a full day of cooking. And we're going to need every minute. I hear the kitchen door click and open.

"Here you go, ma'am," Jace says, presenting me with my kitchen staff, which consists of convicts.

"Thank you," I say with a tentative smile.

"I'm going to be with you in here today, if that's okay," Jace says, pulling up a chair by the door.

"Fine by me," I say, not liking the cut of his jib one bit.

"Mind yourselves, boys," Jace says as the Dents step forward.

"Okay, we have a lot to do," I say, pulling out the menu I scrawled late last night. The Dents pull in close, Cody leans across the counter and studies the menu. I continue, "I smoked a brisket last night, took all night, but it's worth it. We'll put it in the oven thirty minutes before to heat it up and then carve it just before we all sit down," I say.

"Yes, ma'am," Harlan says.

"And I think to get our bearings in here, I'd prefer it if you call me Chef. Clear?" I ask, my voice strong. The Dents nod. I continue, "I want to do ranch beans, a slaw, and we'll finish with a peach cobbler," I say. The Dents are quiet.

"My mouth is watering from over here, Chef," Jace says, leaning his chair back against the wall. He hits the word "chef" with just enough derision to let me know he thinks it's ridiculous. Those in male-stripper-name glass houses, *Jace,* should not throw stones.

"Wait till you taste it," I say, not looking up. Jace takes his *Statesman* newspaper and flips to the sports section.

"Cody, I want you to step in as what's called a sous-chef. It just means that you will cut and prepare all the food for Harlan and me to cook up. Does that make sense?" I ask.

"Yes, ma'am."

"Chef. Remember. And I'll walk you through how I like things done," I say.

"Yes, Chef."

"Harlan, I have a very particular way of doing things and I know you're actually a better cook than you let on," I say. Harlan's face flushes just a bit. I continue, "So I'm going to ask you to do the hardest thing a chef is ever asked to do. I want you to cook more like me and less like you," I say.

"Yes, Chef," Harlan says.

"Okay, so let's get started," I say, standing tall.

I set Harlan up first in charge of the ranch beans. Cody looks on, listening as I run through the ingredients. Jace makes a comment about why don't I just use the canned kind, craning his neck to find the immediately recognizable black can with the western-style writing, "Ranch-style Beans" that can be found in every kitchen in Texas. I hold my tongue only because it's my first day and I don't want Jace to take out my insolence on the Dents. I give him a charitable laugh and move on. He goes back to his newspaper. Harlan starts in on the ranch beans as Cody and I start on the slaw. He's cutting and preparing all the ingredients and we're officially off and running.

I settle in happily with my secret barbecue sauce where no one can see. I covertly add the ingredients and set it to the side. I check on Harlan and Cody periodically as the hours pass and they continue to cruise along. We're actually quite a good little trio. Cody is slow, and in the time it's taken him to prepare the ingredients for the slaw, Harlan is already through with the ranch beans and on to the cobbler. The day flies by. I am happier than I've been in . . . Jesus, maybe ever. I've never felt this at home in a kitchen this quickly. It throws me every time I look over at Jace and see his holstered gun or the clear outline of his bulletproof vest.

I'm in a prison, but it feels like home.

As the time for supper nears, I put the brisket into the oven for just a bit to heat it back up. Harlan finishes the last touches on the cobbler, while Cody stirs the ranch beans. I set the table with whatever institutional dishes and cutlery the small makeshift dining room has to offer. In the months to come, this is where everyone will congregate and share a meal the day of an execution. I want to make it as comfortable and homey as I can, hoping that this gathering place and this food can act as some kind of mental balm for what is in store. So we can eat and not be so alone in all this. I hope.

The table is set and I'm carving the brisket.

"That's a nice smoke ring, Chef," Harlan says.

"That's the nicest thing anyone has ever said to me," I say, with a smile. Harlan smiles and then we quickly hide our camaraderie from Jace and his holstered gun.

As the guards, Warden Dale, and Hudson gather around the table, I make up plates for the Dent boys.

"Eat," I say, setting a plate in front of each of them, knowing if I sound authoritative enough, they won't want to disobey my orders.

"Yes, Chef," they say, bending over the counters and settling into their meal. I'll make it a point to remember to ask Shawn if I can have a table and chairs for them in the future. I continue, "There's sweet tea in the fridge, help yourself," I say, walking out into the dining area with the brisket. All of the men are standing around the table. I set the brisket in the middle.

"Sit, please," I say, pulling my chair in and finally sitting down after a full day. The men sit once I'm settled. A full day has flown by. I've yet to notice how tired I am.

"This looks delicious, Ms. Wake!" Warden Dale says, sitting at the head of the table. Shawn is seated at the other end of the table, opposite the warden.

"Thank you, Warden Dale, and thank you for giving me this opportunity," I say.

"You keep cooking like this and you won't ever have to worry," Warden Dale says, taking the plate of brisket being passed to him from Little Jim. He takes it and serves himself. Everyone passes full plates and serves himself. I can see each one let the smells of the meal waft over them with closed eyes and memories of home.

"This brisket must have taken you hours," Hudson says, sitting next to me.

"A brisket like this takes all night, son," Shawn says, not even looking at Hudson. All of the guards laugh.

"Then you'd better walk me through how to serve this before I embarrass myself further," Hudson says.

"Definitely," I say, passing the brisket to Shawn, at the head of the table.

"You didn't have to agree so quickly," Hudson says.

"You can do it a couple of ways. The white bread and the barbecue sauce plus the brisket make a nice sandwich, like Jace is doing," I say, pointing to the now silenced doubting Thomas. I continue, "Or you can just have the brisket with or without barbecue sauce and with or without the ranch beans and slaw, kind of blending in, like turkey, cranberries, and mashed potatoes at Thanksgiving," I say.

"Isn't brisket supposed to be served with biscuits?" Hudson asks, serving himself some ranch beans.

The conversation at the table screeches to a halt. The guards and Warden Dale just shake their heads and continue talking and eating.

"I think from here on out, you just need to start actively censoring your thoughts and opinions. For your own safety," I say, laughing.

Hudson shoves a piece of brisket into his mouth while the entire table bursts into hysterics.

Whatever this place is, whatever happens within these walls, these people are human like everyone else. Even if we don't want to feel or understand what happens here, we still sit around a table and appreciate a nice piece of brisket and mocking an out-of-towner who doesn't understand that even when you've got three generations in the dirt here in Texas, you're still New People.

The Dent boys are returned to their cells after the kitchen is cleaned, and as I putter and fuss around the kitchen I think about the next time I'll be here. Friday. When I'm cooking my first last meal. I can't imagine how I'll feel, what that will be like, what that will look like. I'll make it—will it—to be about the food. I can't think about anything else. I say my good-byes to the guards, crane my neck to see if Hudson is still around (he's not), and slip out the back door of the kitchen.

The door to the kitchen clicks and Shawn strides through.

"Tonight was just wonderful. Thank you," he says.

"You're welcome. It was my pleasure," I say, packing up my knives.

"Warden Dale wanted me to give you this. It's for Friday," Shawn says, handing me a slip of paper. I know what's on this paper. I take it and steel myself.

"Thank you," I say. I open the piece of paper and read.

Inmate # CF785241:
Fried chicken, potato salad, biscuits, fried okra, buttermilk
pie (or chess pie), Blue Bell vanilla ice cream, and a Coke

I read and reread the last-meal request. It's been tweaked a bit since I saw it in Warden Dale's office. The inmate added Blue Bell ice cream. I read the meal again.

"You okay?" Shawn asks.

"Yes, sir," I say, folding the sheet of paper and firmly putting it deep into my pocket. I'm going to let the success of tonight remain a bit longer before I really digest what's on that paper.

I pull in Merry Carole's driveway to the larger-than-life lawn sign emblazoned with Cal's name and jersey number. Merry Carole has placed it in front of a pair of lawn lanterns that were already there before the sign arrived. How long has she been preparing for this? I shuffle down the manicured path and into the house. I'm exhausted. I've been up now for almost forty-eight straight hours. I haven't stayed up all night with a brisket in years. It's really the blessed combination of smoke inhalation, dried-out eyes, and utter exhaustion that I've missed the most.

"Hello!" I announce, coming through Merry Carole's front door. The last-meal request burning a hole in my pocket.

"In here," Merry Carole says from the kitchen.

The house is lit up and warm. As always. I happily sink into it every time. Merry Carole is sitting at the dining room table surrounded by books, opened binders, receipts, and a calculator.

"So how was your first day with the sign on your lawn?" I ask, pulling up a chair and taking in the scene.

"It was fine," she says, grabbing a store receipt from a shoe box and stapling it onto a sheet of paper. She slams the three-hole punch down and then threads the paper into the binder. She labels it, "Salon—Administrative."

"This is adorable," I say, leaning back and getting ready.

"What is? I am? I'm adorable?" Merry Carole says, sifting and slamming receipts down onto the table.

"Maybe it has to do with how you haven't had someone who's gonna call you on your shit for so long? But this? This is completely transparent," I say, motioning to her busywork.

"Which is it? Am I adorable or transparent?"

"Both."

Merry Carole stops. Deflates. The tiny papers shuffle and flutter across the table. She stands and marches into the kitchen. She pulls two beers out of the fridge, cracks them open easily, and comes back to the table. She hands me one, clinks bottles quickly, and sits back down, slumping in her chair. I have no idea what's going on and every minute she holds back, I get more and more worried. I cut in as she situates her legs under her in the dining room chair. "Where's Cal? Is everything . . . is he . . ."

"Cal's fine. He's out with West and some other boys from the team," Merry Carole says, offhandedly.

"You mean he's out with his brother," I say.

"Queenie, please."

"You mean, he's out with that unrelated boy who looks exactly like him and whose parents are ninety?"

"Now that's just mean," Merry Carole says, unable to stifle her laughter.

"Then what is it?"

"Apparently, I'm a whore again," Merry Carole says, taking a long pull from her beer.

"I'm sorry?"

"Oh yeah—haven't you heard? Cal only got QB1 because I'm screwing Coach Blanchard," Merry Carole says, threading her hands through her long blond hair that's damp from the shower. No pageant height and nary a product in use. She is (for once) au naturel. And she's as radiantly beautiful as ever.

"What are you talking about?" I ask.

"The orientation for new Stallion Batallion parents was today," Merry Carole says.

"Oh."

"Yeah." Merry Carole takes a long drag on her beer.

"And they were terrible." It's not a question.

"Of course."

"Which shouldn't be a surprise."

"But it always is."

"I know."

"I'm nice, Queenie."

"It doesn't matter."

"It should."

"It never does."

"The sad thing was, I walked in there thinking this time was going to be different. Why do I keep doing that?"

"I don't know," I say, knowing I did the same thing with Everett. Thinking this time was going to be different. Now that we're adults, he was going to sweep me up and finally admit to God and everybody that we're in love. But no. It was the same. It's always the same.

"I mean, let's not get crazy here. I got a whiff that it was happening within seconds and smacked that glazed smile on my face as quickly as I could, taking my place along the wall," Merry Carole says, her hand pointing to her plastered-on pageant smile as a game-show presenter would. She stands and reenacts the entire thing. Perfect. Breezy. Unaffected. We laugh. Her laugh crackles and breaks as it spirals down into the vast pain that is at the very foundation of us both. She sits back down and takes another swig of her beer.

"So what happened?"

"I'm in line at the stupid potluck just before we start planning the team barbecue, which you're coming to, by the way," Merry Carole says, her eyes laser focused.

"You're in a fragile state, so I'll agree to this. Now continue," I say, already trying to figure a way to get out of the team barbecue, a fund-raising event thrown by the Stallion Batallion. It's not *if* Merry Carole and I will be completely ostracized, it's whether or not we'll be able to have some barbecue before it happens.

"So I was ladling out some tacky punch and I hear these two women talking about Coach Blanchard. I give them the Smile. They, of course, don't smile back." I nod in agreement. Of course. Merry Carole continues, "And I hear one of them say, '*Her? He can do way better than that! Just like her momma, that one.*'" Merry Carole's smile fades quickly. The story has stopped being funny.

"What a bunch of bitches," I say.

"I'm . . . I wasn't even wearing something . . . I mean, this is my body. I'm not going to hide it because . . . I shouldn't have to apologize for looking the way I do." Merry Carole can't finish a thought or a sentence.

"Trying to understand rationally what those women were talking about is useless. They're catty bitches and the only way to put you back in your place is to make sure you feel as terrible about yourself as possible," I say.

"Mission accomplished," Merry Carole says, raising her bottle of beer.

"So it's the same old shit, then?" I ask, knowing this chatter well.

"Yeah, but I just hate to see Cal brought into it, you know?" Merry Carole's voice sputters and chokes.

"I know," I say, leaning across the table, through receipts and binders, to give her hand a squeeze.

"It's fine. Really. It just . . . it just caught me by surprise," Merry Carole says, taking her hand back. She begins to collect herself. Rebuild the walls. Armor back up with Aqua Net, push-up bras, and a well-placed "no, thank youuuuuu, ma'am."

"Well, it's not fine, actually."

"Yeah, but it's just the same old shit. Like you said."

"Don't you think it's a bit old, though?"

"I thought it was old back when I was walking around fourth

grade and these people were calling me the same exact names. So now it's just embarrassing that they haven't even tried to come up with something new."

"They're not known for their imaginations."

"Except when it comes to scenarios about me wanting to steal all their men. The ideas they get about my sex life." Merry Carole flushes. For looking and dressing much like a 1950s *Playboy* centerfold, Merry Carole has always been way too prudish for her own good.

"Do you have any idea what this round of rumors is about?"

"None." Merry Carole's answer is . . . suspicious.

"Uh-huh," I say, my eyes narrowing.

"I don't."

"Well, I don't believe you, but I guess you'll tell me in your own good time."

"What?" She is ridiculously putting on some faux-innocent bullshit routine. It's actually hilarious.

"The texting the other day and now this? There's someone in the picture that you're not telling me about. It's fine. It's your business, but if I'm going to defend you in the court of public opinion that is North Star's town square, I should have all the information."

Merry Carole remains silent. For a long time. And then . . .

"Reed and I—"

"I knew it," I say, my voice a bit too excited.

"We thought we were being discreet. I thought so, at least."

"They know everything that goes on in the entire great state of Texas, sweetheart."

"I know."

"Is it serious?"

"It was. It is. I don't know anymore. I tried to talk to Cal about it, how he would feel about me seeing someone, and it just . . . he got confused and I've just never seen him so upset." Merry Carole cinches her robe tight.

"What was he upset about?"

"I think he's afraid everything is going to change? I don't know—it's always been just us, you know? I think he also— I think the other boys on the football team might talk a bit about me. I think he feels like he has to defend my honor a lot and maybe he thought me seeing a man was like me being with some-one who talked about me like those boys on his football team did, you know?"

"I'm sure the boys on the football team talk about you. You're a beautiful woman," I say.

"I don't think they put it so lovingly, Queenie."

"I'm sure they didn't. Did you tell him it was Reed you were seeing?"

"No."

"But Reed's not that guy, so telling Cal that it's Coach Blanchard would have calmed him down about you being objectified, don't you think?"

"I don't know. It was the most uncomfortable conversation in the entire world. I thought talking to him about, well, *you know* . . ." Merry Carole shifts her eyes south. I get the point. She continues, "But this? This is a thousand times worse. Sometimes I think this is me paying for not being married to his daddy, you know? Then we wouldn't have this issue if he just expected me to be with—"

"Wes? Really?"

"I know. I just hate how the rumors are right, you know? They're right. I am seeing Reed. So what leg do I have to stand on to be righteous about it, you know? I just hope Cal doesn't get wind of it."

"You guys must think Cal doesn't get wind of a lot of things," I say.

"He thinks about football, girls, and rap music. I am relying on him being a selfish teenager—please don't burst my bubble."

"He's not a selfish teenager and you know it," I say.

"I knowwwww. Let's change the subject. How was the new job?"

We sit at that dining room table for another hour drinking beer and talking. It's glorious and just what I need. We talk about the orientation, Cal, the football team. We don't talk about the men we're not mentioning. We take apart the women of the town, again and again. Then we talk about the brisket and the new job. I don't tell her about yesterday (or the last twenty years) with Everett. I also don't tell her about Hudson. Not yet. It'd be like cutting out a picture of some movie star and announcing, "This is my new boyfriend!" It feels just as unlikely.

13

Country breakfast, coffee, Piggy Peggy's face

"Well, look at who stayed in town!" Piggy Peggy oozes as she almost leaps over to where Cal and I are sitting at the Homestead later that week.

"Oh hey," I say, narrowing my eyes once again at Cal. Everything related to the Homestead is, apparently, his fault. He smiles.

"*Oh hey!* Haven't had your coffee yet, I see?" Piggy Peggy says, making a face insinuating that I'm either in a foul mood, or based on her amateurish miming, drunk and/or having some kind of seizure.

"What's that you're doing there?" I ask, motioning to her solitary game of charades.

"Oh, you know," Piggy Peggy says, looking over at Cal.

"Nope, I don't," I say with nary a smile.

"You're just . . ." Piggy Peggy trails off as she launches into another bizarre bout of charades where she acts out what a bitch I'm being instead of just telling it to me straight to my face.

"I didn't know the Homestead had turned into dinner theater," I say, looking around the room.

"Oh," Piggy Peggy laughs, waving her hand at me to just stooopppppp. So crazy, she insinuates without a word. Again. God forbid she'd actually say something unkind to my face. I doubt Piggy Peggy is this tongue-tied about my less attractive character-istics when she's with her friends. I bet there's a lot to be said about me when I'm not around.

"I'd like two eggs over medium, some wheat toast, and your house potatoes," I say.

"And coffee?" Piggy Peggy asks, eyebrow arched.

"Sure," I say, not looking at her.

"Cal, honey?" Piggy Peggy's voice cuts across his name. The way she says it sends a chill down my spine. It's icy at best and downright disrespectful at worst.

"Country breakfast, please," Cal says.

"You sure do have quite an appetite, son," Piggy Peggy says, writing down Cal's order on her order pad.

"Yes, ma'am," Cal says, looking over at me.

"Just like your momma, I guess," Piggy Peggy's words are more mumbled than actually said.

"Ma'am?" Cal asks, looking confused.

"What did you just say?" I ask, standing and placing my entire buzzing-with-rage body centimeters from Piggy Peggy.

"Oh, you know . . . ," Piggy Peggy trails off, her eyes darting around at all the restaurant patrons who are now watching our every move.

"Nope," I say, stepping even closer.

"Aunt Queenie," Cal says, his eyes imploring me to sit down.

"I'm just asking Peggy to point out where the bathroom is," I say, loudly, so all can hear.

"Right back that way," Piggy Peggy says, her voice shaking.

"See? We're fine here," I say, for Cal.

"Fine. We're fine," Piggy Peggy says, clearing her throat.

"I would appreciate it if you would show me to the bathroom personally," I say to Piggy Peggy.

"Sure . . . sure," Piggy Peggy says, carefully turning toward the bathroom.

"Please don't kill Piggy Peggy, Aunt Queenie," Cal says, just as we step away from the booth.

"I wouldn't dream of it," I say with a quick wink.

Piggy Peggy walks toward the bathroom as a condemned man walks to the gallows. Maybe I should ask her what her last meal would be. In the tiny hallway that holds the bathrooms, I corner Piggy Peggy.

"I didn't mean nothing by it," Piggy Peggy says, bracing for the physical harm I mean to save her from. This time.

"Then why did you say it? To my fifteen-year-old nephew? What kind of person does that?" I ask, my voice a violent whisper.

"He should know what kind of woman his mother is," Piggy Peggy says, defiantly.

"What did you just say?"

"I just . . . he should know."

"Know about what?"

"That people are saying Cal only got the QB1 position because Merry Carole is . . . you know . . . with Coach Blanchard," Piggy Peggy says, still not making eye contact with me.

"Is that what you think?" I ask.

"What I think?"

"Yes. Is that what you think?"

"I don't know."

"You do know that you can think for yourself, right?"

"Of course I do."

"Then answer the question. Do you think Cal got the QB1 position because of a rumored relationship between Merry Carole and Coach Blanchard?"

"Well, Wake women . . ."

"Wake women, what?"

Piggy Peggy is silent.

"Wake. Women. What?" I repeat.

"People say Wake women are evil and will ruin you," Piggy Peggy recites. Felix Coburn's exact words.

"How can you even say that?" I ask, hating that I'm actually having this conversation with Piggy Peggy in the darkened hallway by the bathrooms in the Homestead of all places.

"Well . . ."

"Well, what? Jesus, Peggy. Just say it."

"Your mom? I mean, BJ didn't care whose man she was taking. Poor Yvonne Chapman put y'all up and look what happened to her. And then Merry Carole and Wes. I mean, that near broke Whitney's heart," Peggy says, in an almost mathematical tone. As if our rumored sexual conquests were just another string theory she's devised.

"We are not anything like our mother," I say, my voice strong and clear.

"Aren't you, though?"

"It's as if you want me to punch you in the face."

"I certainly do not."

"Then stop saying shit like that."

"My, my . . . your language, Queenie. My word."

"We're nothing like our mother," I say again, my voice dipping.

"Laurel's told us all about you and Everett, you know."

"What?" My words are a knee-jerk reaction. I don't even know I'm speaking. My mouth runs dry and I can feel the blood rush to my head.

"Everything," Peggy says, folding her arms across her chest.

"I don't know what that means. There's nothing between me and Everett," I say. Ouchhhhhh.

"Well, yeah . . . ," Peggy says as if it's the most obvious statement in the world. She continues, "But that doesn't mean you still didn't ruin him." Peggy's eyes are now fixed on mine.

"How did I ruin him?" My voice is tiny. Unguarded. Dangerously open.

"I don't know. I don't know how you people do anything." You people.

"Oh, is there a line?" a woman says, motioning to the women's bathroom.

"No, ma'am! It's all yours," Peggy says as we step back out into the restaurant. The cook dings the bell and Peggy perks up. She continues, "That's me. I'll bring you over your coffee." Peggy flips around and walks—nay, struts—back over to the kitchen. She can't wait to tell Laurel and Whitney about what happened here. She finally stood up to me! she'll say. She told me everything she's always wanted to say! And all I did was stand there and wonder how it all had come to this.

How did both Merry Carole and I turn out to be just like Mom?

"Everything okay?" Cal stands up as I slide back into the booth.

"Fine, darlin'," I say, my eyes hazy.

"It didn't look fine," Cal says, sitting.

"Maybe you're right," I say. Peggy walks over to our booth with our breakfasts. She sets down my mug of coffee.

"Anything else I can get for you?" Her voice is triumphant.

"Nope," I say, not willing to give her the satisfaction that her little outburst by the bathrooms has left me speechless.

"Just holler if you need something," Peggy says, her voice light and airy.

Cal and I finally leave the Homestead. I leave an enormous tip thinking that I can never let Peggy know she got to me, even though she absolutely did. In every way. Her words shook me to my core. I can be a lot of things in this world, but one of them cannot be "just like Mom." Because no matter how many cities I run to, how many kitchens I cook in—that truth will follow me everywhere. Am I my mother's daughter? How can that be?

Cal heads over to the high school weight room to work out and I make a beeline for the hair salon. I need to talk to Merry Carole. Now. I burst through the salon door and find the salon brimming with big hair, twangy music, and rip-roaring conversation.

"Hey there, Queenie," Fawn says, doing some busywork behind the front counter.

"Hey," I say, scanning the salon for Merry Carole.

"She's back in the kitchenette refilling her coffee," Fawn says without me saying a word.

"I appreciate it," I say, giving her a quick smile. I nod a quick hi to Dee as I walk by her. She's deep in conversation and blue rinse.

"So I had a nice little chat with Piggy Peggy at the Homestead," I say, walking into the kitchenette and closing the door behind me.

"Well, she works there, so . . . ," Merry Carole says, setting her Lone Star coffee mug on the small table and opening up the refrigerator in search of creamer.

"Sit down," I say, my arms folded across my chest.

"Don't be dramatic," Merry Carole says, pouring creamer into her coffee.

"Don't be flippant," I say, pulling out a chair and motioning for her to sit. She arches an eyebrow. Standing.

"I have clients, Queen Elizabeth." Merry Carole sighs, replacing the creamer in the refrigerator and closing the door. She stirs her coffee. The chair sits vacant as my folded arms slowly tire.

"She knows about Reed. How much longer are you going to keep this a secret? It only fans the fire," I say, letting my arms now fall to my hips. I stand there in that tiny kitchenette arms akimbo. Merry Carole blows on her coffee and couldn't look less impressed.

I continue, "You guys have known each other since elementary school and he's such a good guy. He's divorced, his wife has remarried. I'm sure his little girls will love you. You're single. What's the problem?" I ask, finally sitting. Merry Carole is quiet. Still. She finally speaks.

"The problem is he's Coach Blanchard and I'm the town whore," Merry Carole says, not making eye contact with me.

"You're not the town whore," I say.

"We both are, dear. Just like our momma," Merry Carole says, pulling out the other chair and finally settling in.

We are quiet.

Merry Carole continues, "So what exactly did she say?"

"Cal ordered the country breakfast and Piggy Peggy insinuated that he had quite an appetite," I pause and then put air quotes around "*just like his momma.*"

"That bitch," Merry Carole says, her face flushing red. She slams her coffee down on the tiny table.

"Yep."

"Why you gotta bring the boy into it? What did Cal do to any of these women?"

"He never bought into the party line, I guess. He never knew he was supposed to apologize for who he was, right?"

"Right. I tried . . . I hoped . . ."

"Honey, you get to be happy."

"Being Cal's mom makes me happy."

"I know it does."

"I don't think I know how to be in a normal relationship," Merry Carole says, her words chosen carefully, as if each is being excavated from deep, deep below the surface.

"Do you even . . . I mean, you've never actually been in a relationship. Any relationship, so . . . ," I say, smiling.

"What a mess," Merry Carole says, hunching down over the table, her head in her hands.

We are quiet for a good long time. I can hear the music and the gossip out in the salon. The refrigerator runs. The faucet drips. Our lives fall apart. My mind wanders over the information that Laurel knew about Everett and me. Laurel knew and confided in her friends about our affair. So they knew about it all then? How much did they know? Did they know I loved him? Do they know I still love him? Could they know if he loved me? Or if he still loves me?

"Reed and I have been seeing each other for over a year," Merry Carole finally confesses, her voice an exasperated sigh.

"And he asked you to keep it secret?" I say, my blood beginning to boil at the thought of another man asking another Wake woman to hide in the shadows.

"No. I asked him," Merry Carole says.

"What?"

"I just didn't want the scrutiny, you know?"

"Why would you want . . . what . . ." I can't make sense of this.

"He had just gotten divorced and everyone was coming out to see Cal play when he was over at the junior high. Cal was a star even then. So we just got to talking, I guess," Merry Carole says.

"You just 'got to talking'?" I repeat.

"It's more than Wes and I ever did, I assure you."

"What?"

"Months of flirting in the hallways, turned into a few awkward make-out sessions, and then that was capped off by one thankfully short . . . I don't even think you can call it sex; I mean, I was a virgin, but even I knew it was terrible," Merry Carole says, her face flushing.

"You were a virgin?" I ask, my eyes wide and my heart breaking.

"Of course," Merry Carole says.

"I didn't know that," I say.

"You don't know a lot of things."

"*That*, I know," I say, smiling. She laughs.

"I never went near another man. Why would I? Terrible sex after which he threw me over and called me 'a Jezebel,' which were his exact words, and then hey, looka that . . . I was pregnant. Not quite the fairy-tale romance I'd been dreaming of," Merry Carole says, her voice cutting and bitter.

I am quiet. This is the most my sister has spoken about her personal life . . . ever. EVER. The entire world feels as if it's fallen away and it's just the two of us here in this cramped kitchenette with just our secrets to nourish us. We shall never go hungry.

Merry Carole continues, "I didn't even like Wes, I just liked the idea of him. He was a McKay and I thought . . . this is my ticket out. People can't look down on me now if I am married to him. I wouldn't be a Wake anymore. I'm somebody, you know?" She takes a slow, measured sip of her coffee followed by a sour eye roll.

"I thought you—"

"Nope."

"But—"

"What does a seventeen-year-old know about anything?"

I fell in love with Everett when we were in kindergarten. Was I just in love with him because he was something I could point to and say, "See? I'm somebody. I'm a Coburn now." Am I any different from Merry Carole and Wes McKay?

"So Wes is the only man you've ever been with," I say. It's not a question.

"Until Reed," Merry Carole says, somewhat embarrassed.

"I can't believe you—"

"Can't you?" Merry Carole's face is hard and focused.

"What?"

"You were going to say that you can't believe I've only been with one man, right?"

"Maybe," I say, not wanting to give her the satisfaction of knowing that that was exactly what I was going to say, word for word. Merry Carole just looks at me. I continue, "Fine. Maybe I was going to point out the tragedy of One-minute Wes being your only sexual experience. I mean, what kind of whore are you?"

"You tell me," Merry Carole says, her laughter subsiding.

"Not a very good one," I say.

"But it's not like it's something you can't identify with, right?" Merry Carole's tone is strong. Her eyes are laser focused on mine. Her hands are tight around her steaming mug of coffee. She continues, "I mean, if we're going to do this . . ." I don't understand what . . . *Oh my God.* I can feel the blood leave my face. I can feel my mouth drop open. I am quiet, stunned. Speechless.

"How long have you known?" I ask, my words barely a whisper.

"Twenty years," Merry Carole says, her voice quiet.

"Of course you did," I say.

"Of course I did," she repeats.

"What . . ." I don't even know what to ask her first. I can't breathe. First Piggy Peggy and now Merry Carole. Who else knew? Everyone? My voice crackles as I speak, "Did everyone know?"

"Yes." One word. Simple.

"Oh."

We fall silent.

"How did my dramatic Spanish Inquisition of you turn into your Spanish Inquisition of me?" I ask. I walk over to the counter with the coffeemaker, open one of the cabinets, and try to find a mug.

"Because I'm your older sister and that's how this works. Take the yellow one with the flower on it. It's an extra," she says, guiding me through the mugs in the cabinet. I obey. I pour coffee into the little yellow mug.

"I'm so embarrassed," I say as I open the fridge to find the creamer. I can't look at Merry Carole. I can't face her. I've essentially been lying to her for twenty years. I've been lying to everyone.

"Well, that's just silly," Merry Carole says and yawns. She takes a sip of her coffee as I pour creamer into mine.

"Is it, though?" I stir my coffee.

"You were eleven. You thought no one would understand. It's actually quite . . . romantic," she says, her voice downright wistful.

"Romantic," I repeat. I think of our last time together. My face flushes as my body remembers Everett's touch. I sigh. The same yearning, ridiculous sigh I've been heaving for twenty years.

"It's not like he ever loved Laurel. Everyone could see that. Even Laurel, unfortunately," Merry Carole says, leaning forward into her gossiping position.

"How much do you know?" I ask, maybe not wanting to take in the horror or truly understand how transparent my entire covert life has been. I guess those shadows weren't as dark as I thought. As we thought.

"Everything," Merry Carole says, almost offended that I'd insinuate any less.

"Everything," I repeat. Jesus. Merry Carole's phone buzzes. She checks it and laughs. She turns the phone around so I can see it. It's from Fawn.

Dee says she won the bet. She texted first about y'all's little exchange at the Hall of Fame.

"For heaven's sake. There was a bet?" I ask, standing and opening the door to the kitchenette. Fawn and Dee are just outside the door. Fawn is still busily texting, unaware the jig is up.

"Oh, well . . . look at that, Fawn. There's no customers back here," Dee says, her entire face alight. Why didn't I ever feel as though I could share this with anyone, regardless of what they might think or feel? Why did I feel I had to be so alone with my secret?

"I can't believe you guys knew," I say as we finally walk out into the now empty salon.

"We didn't all figure it out at the same time," Merry Carole says, coming out from the kitchenette, her mug of coffee still in her hand.

"Merry Carole knew from the start," Fawn says, motioning to my sister.

"I found that adorable pink card he made you," Merry Carole says, her hand against her chest as if she's still emotional about it.

"I just thought you had a crush on him, you know, in junior high and all that," Dee says. This is like *This Is Your Life,* but the version where it's actually, "This is the life you thought you hid from everyone!" Dee continues, "But then I saw you guys one day as you were walking home from school, I guess it was freshman year? Y'all were holding hands and . . . well, it was sweet. He was leaning in and talking to you and you just threw your head back laughing at whatever he'd said. I'd never seen either of you like that, you know? Laughing like you'd heard the funniest thing in the world. I tried to ask you about it the next day at school, but you acted like I hadn't seen what I knew I had seen, so I just . . . I, well, I got my feelings hurt for a bit, but then just thought it was something you wanted to keep secret." Dee's face flushes.

"I'm so . . . I'm so sorry," I say, mortified. Every time I think I can't get more mortified the bar just keeps going higher and higher. Or lower and lower depending on how you look at it.

"I figured it out right after your momma died . . . was killed . . . whatever," Fawn starts. We all shift our focus to her. She continues, "I kept seeing him in that old truck of his, coming around, circling the house, and then he'd see me and speed on down the road like a bat out of hell. Until one night I was coming in from the market and I seen him crawling in your window when he thought I wasn't looking or what not. I didn't knock on your door all night, but . . . well, I heard you crying in there. And I remember thinking . . . thank Jesus, she's got someone in there with her. It was really the first time you'd . . . well, you'd let any of that out," Fawn says, growing more and more emotional as the story unfolds. I can't look at any of them. Reliving all of these moments from my past. Feeling the love I've cherished and treasured for Everett all these years grow too big for my chest again and again. Always fearing that one day it'll burst through and fly away.

We are all quiet. Swept away in the romance of it all.

"So did y'all also know about Ms. Merry Carole here?"

"No!" Merry Carole blurts out.

"Oh sure," Fawn and Dee say simultaneously.

"What?" Merry Carole says, her face flushing. A wide smile breaks across my face. Now this is the kind of scene I can certainly get behind. No more of that tragic slide show of my life, a life I know will no longer have Everett in it. I can't . . . I can't even bear thinking about it.

"You're talking about Coach Blanchard, right?" Fawn asks, just for clarification.

"Yep," I say, my eyes darting from Fawn and Dee to Merry Carole.

"Oh yeah, that's old news. They've been seeing each other for . . ." Fawn trails off and looks to Dee (not Merry Carole).

"About a year?" Dee works out, her face crinkled up and doing the math.

"About a year," Merry Carole clarifies.

"About a year," Dee repeats.

"I think they're actually quite well matched. What with Merry Carole and Cal and Coach Blanchard and those two little girls of his? It's just . . . well, I don't know why they're keeping it all secret," Fawn says, sitting down in one of the salon chairs.

We all look at Merry Carole.

"I want him to," Merry Carole says, striding over to the front counter and violently flipping open the appointment book.

"We don't have anyone for another thirty minutes," Dee says, her voice light.

"That's just fine," Merry Carole says, defeated.

"Why do you want him to?" Fawn asks.

"We were rejected once by someone I thought wanted to be Cal's daddy; I can't do that again. I can't risk that again," Merry Carole says.

"Reed Blanchard is not Wes McKay, and you are not that seventeen-year-old girl anymore," I say.

"But don't you see? All this? Makes me feel exactly that. Seventeen and helpless," Merry Carole says, searching for the word "helpless" deep in herself. Even the very word is hidden away.

"Oh honey," Fawn says.

"I spent my entire childhood being thrown over for a man. I know what that feels like and I am not going to subject my boy to that feeling. No, Reed and I—well, there's just no future there," Merry Carole says, the emotion bubbling up from so deep within her.

"But Coach Blanchard is—," Fawn says.

"Coach Blanchard is what?" Cal says, standing in the doorway to the salon.

The entire salon grinds to a halt. All of us. Horrified. We look from Cal to Merry Carole. She looks . . . pisssssssssed.

"What about Coach Blanchard?" Cal asks again.

"Oh hey, sweetie, we were just talking football," Merry Carole says, her cheeks flushed, her voice high and nervous.

"Oh okay. Can I borrow some money? A couple of the guys want to go catch a movie just to get in some air-conditioning," Cal asks, approaching a very relieved-looking Merry Carole. As Merry Carole and Cal wind through whose mother is driving the boys, when he'll text her to check in, and which movie they're seeing, I wonder where Everett fits in all of this. Merry Carole is so scared of being vulnerable that she's willing to forgo her own happiness to protect herself. Am I any different? What am I willing to do and put up with just so I can feel in control and protected?

"That was too close," Merry Carole says, watching Cal walk outside to meet his friends. She turns and speaks to the three of us as one. "I will figure out what I want to do about Reed in my own time. Until then, y'all need to stay quiet about it."

"That's all we ever are," I say.

"Queen Elizabeth," Merry Carole warns.

"Honey, I'm not going to say anything. Of course I wouldn't dream of it, but I do wonder what it is we're ashamed of, you know?"

"I'm not ashamed of my relationship with Reed," Merry Carole says.

"Oh, it's a relationship now?" I ask. Fawn and Dee move in closer.

"He's the best man I've ever known." Merry Carole is reverent. The entire room swoons. Merry Carole rolls her eyes and walks over to her station, readying for her next client. She continues, "I have to figure this out on my own. And if Cal has heard the rumors and asks me about it, then we'll cross that bridge when we get to it." We all nod in agreement.

"Now you and Everett, on the other hand," Merry Carole says, her voice cutting through Willie Nelson's twangs like a knife.

"There is no me and Everett," I say.

"What?" they ask in unison.

"Like you said, there's no future there. He loves his parents and Paragon," I say.

"And he loves you," Dee says.

"I know that. I do. And he knows I love him. But it's just not going to work out. We can't sneak around anymore . . . I don't think it makes us happy. We start getting sad about the situation pretty much right away. It wasn't always like that. Maybe when we were younger we thought it could be different? We had a chance. I think we both know we don't have a chance anymore."

Merry Carole, Dee, and Fawn are quiet. Sad.

"So that's it?" Dee asks.

"I don't want it to be, but I don't know what else to do," I say.

"Well, is there anyone else who could take your mind off Everett?" Fawn asks as delicately as she can.

"There is this guy at the prison. He's spectacular. Now *he* has the potential to be quite the distraction," I say, my voice almost as forced as the smile that cracks its way across my face.

"Queen Elizabeth, if you are about to tell me that you are dating a convict . . ." Merry Carole holds her broom in one hand and looks as though she's about to pounce.

"No, NO!" I say, not even realizing that's what it sounded like.

"Oh my God, I thought she was going to say that, too," Dee says, her hand clutching at her chest.

"No, NO? God, you guys. Right, I'm going to keep my decades-long love affair with Everett Coburn, pillar of society, a secret but announce that I've fallen for a convict and it's perfectly normal." No one thinks that's as hilarious as I do. I continue quickly, "Fine. His name is Professor Hudson Bishop and he's from California. He's smart and funny and holy shit, has black hair and these ridiculous blue eyes. And he's just . . . you just know he can DO things," I say, waggling my eyebrows.

"At the very least this Professor California can be useful," Merry Carole says, seeing her client come through the front door finally. Fawn walks over and checks her in.

"Useful how?" I ask, following Merry Carole. Dee listens intently.

"He'll make Everett jealous as hell," Merry Carole says just before greeting her next client.

14

Inmate # CF785241:
Fried chicken, potato salad, biscuits, fried okra, butter-
milk pie (or chess pie), Blue Bell vanilla ice cream, and
a Coke

It's Friday morning. Today's the day I make my very first last meal.

I went to the butcher and the farm stands yesterday. I brined my chicken for four hours, set the alarm, and then did a buttermilk soak for another four. The chicken will be spectacular. I drove out to this liquor store off I-35 that I know sells the real Cokes—in beautiful glass bottles from Mexico. Purists believe Mexican Coke is far better because they use refined cane sugar, not high-fructose corn syrup. I am one of these purists. I also purchase Coke in a can and the regular American Coke, which is in one of those beautiful light green glass bottles that's Americana personified. As I stood in that liquor store, I tried to think about what kind of guy this is—if it's a guy at all. It could be a woman, for all I know. Shine hasn't ever executed a woman, but Huntsville has. And I just stood there holding bottles of Coke I was about to buy for a person who was going to be put to death. In the liquor store where Everett and I used to buy condoms so no one would know.

"Today's the big day, then?" Merry Carole says, replacing the coffee decanter this morning.

"Yep," I say, pulling my buttermilk-soaked chicken out of the fridge. I place the Tupperware in grocery sacks and get them ready for transport. With the summer heat, I'm barely going to get the Blue Bell ice cream to the prison—even with all the ice and ice packs I've placed in the cooler.

I need everything to be perfect today. I lay in my bed last night and envisioned the day, the menu, everything. Where Harlan would be. Where Cody would be. The chicken crackling, the biscuits rising, the pie baking. All of it. I've envisioned everything but the person who will be eating the perfect meal I make. My heart sinks every time my thoughts bump into that reality.

"All right then," Merry Carole says, her face creased with worry.

"I know this is . . ." I trail off, pouring my coffee into my travel mug. I sit down at the dining room table.

"This is . . . what?" Merry Carole asks, clearly holding back a torrent of opinions.

"I don't know what this is yet, I guess," I say, my stomach in knots.

"And that's my worry," Merry Carole says.

"I know."

"You think this is just about cooking, but . . . ," Merry Carole says, letting just the tip of the iceberg break through.

"I know."

"You can't . . . it . . . this just pisses me off left-handed," Merry Carole finally growls.

"I know."

"Do you even know what this *person* did?" Merry Carole asks, her tone barely acknowledging that I'm cooking for a person.

"I don't want to know."

"That's fine."

"I know you're angry with me."

"I'm worried about you. There's a difference."

"You sound angry."

"Well, sometimes worry sounds like anger."

"I guess it does."

"I just . . . I just hate that you're going to have this in your head, you know?"

"We've had worse."

"Yeah, but that wasn't our choice. You're walking into this thing all on your own," Merry Carole says.

"I never thought about it like that."

"I know you didn't."

"Well, it's too late now," I say, standing up from the table. I walk over to the freezer and put the gold-rimmed pint of Blue Bell into the cooler.

"And why is that?"

"Because I said I would do it. And I'm not about to shirk that obligation. Apparently, I have a thing or two to learn about responsibility," I say, remembering Everett's words.

"Who said that?"

"Everett," I say, laying grocery sacks and coolers over elbows, shoulders, and fingers.

"Uh-huh," Merry Carole says.

"When you're ready to talk about Reed, I'll be ready to talk about Everett," I say, grabbing my car keys off the kitchen counter with the one finger that's not carrying food.

"Oh, ha-HA," Merry Carole says. I can't help but laugh.

"That's all you got?" I ask, walking past the dining room table toward the front door. The longer I'm in this house, the longer I don't have to be cooking for a murderer.

"It's early," Merry Carole says, standing. She walks over to the front door with me, opening it up wide. She continues, "Please be careful, baby sister."

"I will," I say, letting her kiss me on the top of my head like she did when we were little. As Merry Carole doesn't have her face on yet, this open door is as far as she ventures. She's concerned, but hasn't lost her mind. Merry Carole cinches her robe tight and watches me walk out to my car loaded down in groceries. As I slam the hatch closed, she gives me a tight wave. I wave back and shut the car door behind me quickly. I turn on the car, blast the air-conditioning, and focus. Focus on the food. Focus on the food. I reverse out of the driveway and head for the highway.

Focus on the food. Focus on the food.

I arrive in Lot B, passing through guard towers and razor wire. I unload all of my groceries, slide my key card into the door, and enter the dark kitchen. I make my way through the darkened space, find the light switch, and watch as the fluorescent lights flicker to life. The quiet of the room settles around me.

"Focus on the food," I say to myself. I shake my head, trying to turn loose the thoughts of complicated monsters, death, and lethal injections. I drop the groceries to the immaculate floor and try to get the feeling back in my overburdened fingers. I hear the click of the kitchen door. Jace saunters through.

"Hey, there," I say, pulling the Blue Bell ice cream from the cooler and getting it into the freezer first thing.

"I just wanted to make sure it was you. We have an alarm system. It beeps when anyone enters or exits the Death House," Jace says.

"Oh, all right," I say, unpacking the groceries. Jace hesitates by the door. I continue, "Is there something else?" I ask, realizing my laserlike focus could be taken as rudeness.

"First executions are hard and I . . . uh . . . I just wanted to make sure you were okay, is all," Jace says, clearing his throat. He doesn't know where to put his hands and finally rests them on his holster, his arms now akimbo. His concern catches me absolutely off guard. This is the same man I thought gave nerds wedgies in his spare time and now here he is . . .

"I don't know how I am, to be honest," I say, setting up Cody's station with all the potato salad fixings. Harlan has more talent, so he'll be better utilized with the chess pie and biscuits. I'll handle the chicken and the okra.

"That sounds about right," he says, with a curt nod. Jace is a big man, in his twenties—definitely younger than me. He's probably an ex-football player who didn't get that scholarship he was counting on. He's bullnecked, and up until now, I thought he was bullheaded as well.

"Yep," I say, still not sure how to communicate with him.

"Okay, then. I'll fetch the Dent boys for you," Jace says.

"Thank you," I say. He nods.

After he leaves, I pull Mom's skillet from one of the sacks and place it on the stovetop. I set up my fried chicken station: plates for dredging, paper bags for shaking, and lard for frying. I hook a dishrag to my belt loop, getting ready for the impending mess that happens when you dredge the chicken twice. In the quiet of the kitchen my mind wanders. Fried chicken and potato salad. What's this man trying to re-create? A picnic? An outing? A meal his grandma made? A chess pie is old school. It's basically a pecan pie without the pecans. Syrupy sweet. I think about the memories he must have about this meal. Innocent. Pure. Happy.

It's what we're all trying to do, right? Remember a time that was better. Re-create a moment of that memory as we let the crisp Coke bubble down our throats. Riding bikes on a summer day. Sitting on the curb and watching the streetlights come on. Playing in the sprinklers with a group of neighbor kids. We're all trying to salvage a time when we dreamed beyond our reality and thought monsters were under our beds instead of peppering our family trees. We're trying to harness those fleeting moments that turned our ordinary lives into something extraordinary. In the sepia haze of those memories, we are beautiful. I hear the key card click and try to gather myself. I've gotten downright sentimental in this hard-lined stainless-steel kitchen all by myself. I can't let it happen again.

"Chef Wake," Jace says, presenting the Dent boys.

"Thank you," I say, my voice softer than before. Jace nods, undoing their shackles one by one.

"Chef," Harlan and Cody say simultaneously.

"Harlan. Cody," I say, with a nod. Jace settles himself in a chair by the door. He flips open his newspaper and leaves us on our own.

"What have we got today, Chef?" Harlan asks, scanning the kitchen.

I go over the meal with the Dent boys, pointing out their stations, hoping they begin to think of these workspaces as their own territories.

"I'll be doing the fried chicken, but I've actually changed my mind about the okra. Harlan, I'm going to need you to do that, so I can get on that chess pie," I say, scribbling and scrawling all over my to-do list.

"Yes, Chef," Harlan says.

"We have until four PM and it's just past ten AM. We'll break for lunch and then get back to it," I say, scanning my list again.

"Do you know who we're cooking for?" Cody asks, looking to Harlan. Harlan nods yes.

"I don't want to know," I say, jumping in before Harlan has a chance to answer.

Jace flips his paper down and is now watching us.

"Yes, Chef," Harlan and Cody say in unison.

"I apologize for my rudeness. I decided early on that I didn't want to know anything about who we're cooking for. I need this to be about the food. If I know I'm cooking for some murdering sack of shit, I'm not going to be able to do it. Y'all get that?" I ask, my voice strong and clear.

"Yes, Chef," Harlan and Cody answer.

"Now let's get to work," I say, moving on.

"Yes, Chef," Harlan and Cody say. Jace brings his paper back up and flips the page.

The day is sublime in that way I'm just going to have to get used to if I continue working here. I fit. Whatever that means. I decide to walk Harlan through how I make biscuits, thinking we're probably going to be making them a lot. Cody looks on as he chops up the potatoes for the potato salad. I have to tell him twice not to peel the potatoes. I want them unpeeled. At least he has the good sense not to even ask where the mayonnaise is.

I start in on the crust for the chess pie. Cutting in the lard, carefully—knowing each one of those pieces will be a bite of heaven once the pie is baked. I chill the pie crust while we break for lunch. Harlan and Cody follow Jace back out into the prison, joining the other convicts for lunch. I eat the turkey sandwich I packed. When lunch is over we pick up the pace. The potato salad is perfect and in the refrigerator. Cody is cutting up okra and now Harlan is getting ready to fry it. The chess pie is done and the biscuits will go in the oven just before dinner. All I have to do is fry up a mess of chicken. I hear the key card click and see Shawn and Little Jim come into the kitchen.

"We can smell that all the way out in the hall," Little Jim says, his eyes closed as he inhales. Shawn says nothing as he walks over to me.

"You all right?" Shawn asks, his voice low.

"I'm focusing on the food," I say, trying ever harder to believe it.

"I'll be back in here in twenty minutes, you understand?" Shawn asks, his head dipped, his eyes fast on mine.

"I understand," I say.

"Good."

"When should I have supper ready for y'all?" I ask, scanning the room.

"Four fifteen should work fine. We eat when he eats," Shawn says.

It's a he. My mouth goes dry and I can't look at Shawn. I focus on my chicken. Focus on the food.

"Yes, sir," I say, my voice raspy and choked.

"All right then. I'll see you in twenty minutes," Shawn repeats.

"I'd better get to it," I say.

"Yes, Chef," Shawn says, with a quick wink. I force a smile. My stomach is in knots as the clock ticks down. Twenty minutes fast becomes ten. Then five. Harlan brings over a tray.

I stare at it.

I grab a stark, white plate from the shelf and place it in the center as if I were re-creating an inverted Japanese flag. Harlan and Cody just watch. We all stand there. I breathe deep and collect myself.

"Harlan, get me the potato salad. Cody, I'm going to need you to get that chess pie out of the fridge as well," I say, taking the most perfect pieces of fried chicken from under the paper towel that is now shiny with lard.

Four minutes.

I place three pieces of chicken on the plate. I put a serving of fried okra on a side plate and decide at the last minute to offer up a side of ranch dressing, just in case. You never know. Harlan hands me the bowl of potato salad and I scoop some out onto the plate. Cody places the chess pie on the counter, just next to me. "Harlan, why don't you pass me the biscuits?" I say, motioning to the oven where they're warming. He obliges, coming back over with the biscuits. I place three biscuits on the side of the plate. "Cody, why don't you grab me a bowl from up there?" I ask, pointing to a shelf I can't reach. He obeys quickly, setting the bowl next to the tray. Harlan hands me the Blue Bell ice cream without me even having to ask. I cut a piece of pie that's about as mouth-wateringly beautiful as you can imagine. I place it on a side plate as Cody scoops the ice cream out into the bowl.

Three minutes.

I walk over to the fridge and pull out the can of Coke, the two bottles—one Mexican Coke and the other American. I set them on the counter next to the tray.

Two minutes.

Harlan, Cody, and I stand there and gaze at it all. The glistening fried chicken, the potato salad, and fried okra. The biscuits still steaming from the oven. A ramekin of honey butter and another of ranch dressing set off the meal. The chess pie and the Blue Bell ice cream are just begging to be devoured.

"Well, goddamn," Jace says, now standing behind us. I don't look at him. I don't know what comes over me in that moment. I hold out my hands to Harlan and Cody, on either side of me. The men jostle a bit, making room for Jace, and we all join hands. We stand over the meal.

One minute.

"Bless this food, Lord. Let it transport and remind us all of better times. Let it cleanse and purify. Let it nourish and warm. In it, let us find peace. In Jesus' name, amen," I say, my eyes closed and beginning to well up.

"Amen," the men say, quickly dropping hands.

The key card clicks and Shawn walks into the kitchen.

"Queenie, it's time."

15

Garrison Brothers bourbon and branch

I slam the hatch of my car down and walk to the driver's-side door. I unlock the door and sit behind the wheel, clutching the piece of paper Shawn gave me as I left the kitchen. I start the car and blast the air-conditioning. I sit there letting the coldness hit my face. The car idles and strains through the blasting air-conditioning. My hands are clamped tight around the steering wheel. I watch the guards pace. Pace. I can't think. I can't form a thought. I feel as though I'm holding back a flood with the mantra "Don't let one drop spill or it'll all go." I'm taking shallower and shallower breaths, because even the idea of breathing threatens the dam. I am the gasp of air you take before you go underwater. The guard paces. The car yearns and sputters some more. My hands are still clamped down tight around the steering wheel.

The guards' supper was somber, but everyone needed it.

We passed food and were quiet. But we were quiet together. We said grace and even laughed once about Hudson wanting to put biscuits with his brisket. We didn't talk about why we were gathered. We just let the food warm us. Comfort us. Join us.

I cleaned the kitchen with the Dent boys after they'd eaten their supper. We were almost done cleaning when I heard the key card click and Shawn walked back through the kitchen. He was holding the tray with the convict's plate of food. He set the tray down.

"You did good, Queenie," Shawn said as he watched me eye the tray.

"He didn't like the dark meat," I said, pulling the tray over. Shawn didn't look at the tray.

"Why don't you go on home. The Dent boys'll do this last bit," Shawn said as he motioned for the Dent boys to clear this tray stat. I grabbed the tray and placed each one of my arms around it, protecting it.

"No," I said, quiet but dangerous.

"All right now," Shawn said, used to dealing with crazy.

I remember breathing. And refocusing on the tray. On what was left. I remember not wanting to touch anything. I restrained my own hands in an attempt to control myself. In an attempt to control anything. Shawn just looked drained.

"I don't mean to be troublesome. I just want to see. Just give me a minute," I said, trying to ease up after a hard day. I didn't need Shawn feeling responsible for me after all he'd been through. But I did need him to let me see what was left. I needed to study the ruins.

"All right," Shawn said, backing away.

"I'm fine. Thank you, Shawn," I said.

Shawn nodded and looked over at Jace, who was at his post by the door, then he left the kitchen.

"He sure liked that ranch dressing you put on there," Cody said, motioning to the empty ramekin. Cody didn't touch the tray either.

"I know," I said. I still wonder if I put enough. Did he want more? Should I just put ranch on every tray from now on? Jesus. From now on.

"He ate everything," I said, finally touching the plate.

"The guilty ones do," Harlan said under his breath.

"The guilty ones do," I repeat now as I am in my car just thirty minutes later. Who had I just fed? It'd be easy to find out. All I would have to do is ask or turn on the news. I don't want to know. I can't know. I can't set this precedent. It'll infect the cooking. I know it. I let my head fall, my forehead touching down on the steering wheel. I breathe. "The guilty ones do," I repeat again, my voice a rasp.

I open the piece of paper.

Next Tuesday
Inmate #HB823356:
Tamales, ensalada de noche buena, cabrito served with
rice and beans, orange soda, churros, and a pack of Star-
burst

I read and reread Shawn's scrawled writing. Whether I like it or not, I begin to think about the person (man? woman? murderer? innocent?) behind this order. I know that this is a traditional Mexican Christmas dinner. The tamales and the ensalada de noche buena give that away. I've never cooked goat (cabrito) before: I'll have to tinker with that this week. But what dawns on me as I stare at that crumpled piece of paper is that I have to ask Shawn a question about this person. One question and I'll be off and running. I pull my phone out of my pocket and dial the direct line to the guards' station just inside.

"Death House." It's LaRue.

"Hey there, LaRue, this is Queenie Wake."

"Oh, hiya, what can I do for you, Queenie?"

"Is Shawn still around?" My hands smooth and crumple the tiny sheet of paper.

"Yes, ma'am, he's right here." LaRue puts me on hold. The air-conditioning blares as I wait. The dusky evening begins to darken further.

"Queenie? Everything okay?" Shawn asks.

"Oh absolutely. I just . . . I had a question about next Tuesday's order?" I smooth the paper out once more.

"Sure, go ahead," Shawn says.

"I need you to ask this . . ." I trail off.

Shawn jumps in, "Gentleman."

"I need you to ask this gentleman where his grandmother is from."

"You want me to ask him where his grandmother is from?"

"Yes, sir."

"Do I get to know why?"

"He ordered tamales. They're one of the most regionally specific foods out there. The thickness of the masa, the filling, roja, verde . . . I just hope it's not Oaxaca, I have no idea where I'll get a banana leaf th—"

"All right. All right. I get it," Shawn says.

"I don't want to make the wrong kind," I say.

"I'll let you know," Shawn says. We say our good-byes and I beep my cell phone off and just sit there. The darkness has officially fallen as I watch the guards pace back and forth on the prison's walls. The blinding floodlights focus and search, focus and search.

I'm jolted out of my purgatory of reverie by someone knocking on my window. I whip my head up, numb and confused. I gather myself just enough and roll down the window; the humidity streams in.

"Hudson, right?" I ask, my mind everywhere and nowhere. I tuck the piece of paper in my pocket, realizing too late that to do so makes me squirm and wriggle in my seat. I shove it down deep and focus.

"You need a drink," Hudson says, his hand now resting on my car door.

"I need to—"

"Follow me," he says, tapping my car twice and walking to his car a few parking spaces down.

"I appreciate th—," I start, but he's already getting into his car, the engine revving to life. "I *could* use a drink," I say to myself, watching as he pulls out of his parking space. I quickly pull out my cell phone and text Merry Carole so she won't worry.

"*Today went fine. Need a drink. Stopping for one with Professor California.*" I send the text and back out of my parking space. My phone buzzes as I'm just about to put the car in drive.

"*You okay?*"

I text back, "*I'm good. We'll talk in the morning. Night-night.*"

Hudson drives past guard towers and razor wire and out of Lot B. Just as I'm about to follow my phone buzzes again.

"*What will North Star do with two town whores? It'll be an embarrassment of riches. Be careful. Call if you need a ride.*"

I text back, "*Will do. Xoxo.*"

I follow Hudson down the street that takes us away from the prison. Takes us away from today. I stare at his red taillights as my mind continues its vigilance with the dams, walls, and panic rooms it's built in the last few hours. Growing uncomfortable with the silence, I turn on the radio and follow Hudson as we wind through the hills just outside Shine to somewhere only he knows. With so much thought about futures and pasts lately, it's nice to be with someone who is firmly in the here and now.

After twenty or so minutes, we arrive in a town just east of North Star called Evans. Evans is where Hollywood goes to film a "quaint Texas town," with its main street done up just so and its inhabitants fully aware of how appealing the town is. I only know Evans because North Star beats their football team handily every year. Hell, everyone beats the Evans football team each year quite handily.

Hudson pulls up in front of a picturesque bed and breakfast that's off the main street. We get out of our cars and walk toward each other in the empty street.

Of course, this is where Hudson is staying for the summer.

"The bar's just over here," Hudson says, motioning toward the next block over.

"Oh good," I say as we begin walking.

"You seem relieved."

"I thought this might quickly be turning into a whole 'come on in for a nightcap' thing." He smiles back in a way that makes my face flush. We pass warmly lit homes with families sitting on porches sipping lemonade. Doing everything people not from here think small-town life is about. Evans's townspeople wave and call out to Hudson by name. Everyone knows everyone here—especially the out-of-towners. A lot of the talk is about how hot it is and how Hudson probably wishes he was back in California. He laughs and says the food is better here. Before I know it, we're in front of the local watering hole. It's called the the Meat Market. Get it? Even Evans's bars are endearing.

The bar is better than I would have thought given its name and location. It's dimly lit—albeit self-conscious. The wood paneling isn't smoke stained and as old as the railroad, it's actually tasteful and adds warmth to the room. Hudson and I walk past a pool table and weave through the bar crowd. The crowd is dense and loud. Young. These are college kids home for the summer. A lot of girls in short skirts and cowboy boots sing along to Carrie Underwood as they hang on each other and warn their suitors they're not above taking a Louisville slugger to both headlights.

I need bourbon.

The crowd moves and sways as Hudson and I inch our way through. It's a Friday night and this is the only good bar for miles. As the crowd jostles, Hudson takes my hand and leads me on toward the bar. So easy. Just like that and no one is looking, no one is gossiping, and no one is wondering why a man like that would hold the hand of a woman like me. I squeeze his hand tight as we approach the bar.

"What are you having?" Hudson yells over the din.

"Bourbon and branch," I yell back.

"What?" he asks, leaning in close.

"Bourbon and branch. Garrison Brothers, if they have it," I say, my breath fluttering his black flips of hair.

"I don't know what that is, but I'm getting two," he says, leaning forward on the bar. The chiseled-jaw, cowboy-hatted bartender (who looks like he does some stripping on the side) leans forward and offers Hudson a kind—if not somewhat stereotypical— "Howdy."

"I'll see if I can find a table," I yell, scanning the crowded bar.

"The quieter the better," Hudson yells over the noise. I nod and edge my way out toward the patio. The outside area is much quieter and a lot more authentic than I expected. A welcome discovery. The patio furniture is easy and relaxed. Swamp coolers and fans make the temperature only a bit wet and muggy. Even with all these amenities, there are very few people out here. It's perfect. I find a wooden bench in a distant corner, situate the canvas striped pillows, and settle in. The wooden table is scarred by numerous drink rings, knotty flaws, and even a few carved-in initials. Some older women cradle their Lone Stars a few tables over. They crouch over their table in a drunken sway, their hair matted, their spirits dashed. They are the "last call" women. They remind me of Mom. I realize I'm staring. Maybe I'm just brain dead after today. I didn't sleep at all last night and I can't imagine tonight will be any better.

Next Tuesday. Oddly, it's not the traditional Mexican Christmas that gets to me, although this inmate trying to re-create a happier time is tragic. It's the Starburst. It seems so childlike to want candy. The two older women hoot and holler as a drunken frat boy stumbles by them. I'm actually thankful for the jolt. It's too early to be depressed about the next meal. I've got work to do. I have to experiment with the cabrito, and once I know where his grandmother is from, I can start doing my research on what kind of tamale we're talking about. Once again, Queenie . . . focus on the food. Focus on the food.

"Here you are," Hudson says, walking over to the table two drinks in each hand, four total.

"You're a genius," I say, reaching for two glasses.

"Cheers," Hudson says, clinking glasses with me as he settles himself across from me, his wooden chair skittering under his weight.

"What are we toasting?" I ask, downing my drink in one gulp.

"Life," Hudson says, downing his.

"Ironic," I say, reaching for my other bourbon.

"Is it?" Hudson says, pulling his other bourbon close.

"I can't figure out if you're being purposefully obtuse or just being a dick," I say, downing my second bourbon.

"Probably a combination," Hudson says, downing his second.

"Hmm," I say, eyeing him closely. I scan the patio for a cocktail waitress. I need a beer. We need beer.

"So branch is just water. A bourbon and branch is just bourbon and water," Hudson says, looking over his shoulder for the cocktail waitress as well.

"It's water that comes right from the land where the distillery is. It's not just any water," I say, finally getting the cocktail waitress's attention.

"But it *is* water, just the same," Hudson says, just as the cocktail waitress approaches.

"What are y'all drinking?" the cocktail waitress says, dropping a couple of Lone Star beer coasters onto our table.

"Apparently, we're drinking bourbon and fancy water," Hudson says.

"Bourbon and branch, hon," the cocktail waitress says, looking to me. We share a "yes, he's not from here" moment.

"Two Shiner Bocks, please. And water when you get the chance. Just *regular* water," I say, my accent thick enough to make up for Hudson's languid California drawl. The cocktail waitress gives me a quick nod and is off into the bar.

"So," Hudson says, leaning over the table. The two bourbons are beginning to warm me, making my brain happily hazy.

"So," I say, guarded. It wouldn't matter if I saw Hudson coming out of a burning building saving a puppy and a baby, something about him makes me think he's up to no good. Let's face it, if I saw him coming out of a burning building with a puppy and a baby, I'd probably think he started the fire.

"We can not talk about it, we can talk about it until the bar closes, or we can get drunk. Your call," Hudson says, bringing his face ever closer to mine.

"I don't know what I want, to be honest," I say. My mind is a minefield. Desperately searching its darkened depths, but terrified of what it might find, it then retreats into the light once more. I think about Merry Carole and Cal and that makes me happy. I think about my day in the kitchen and that makes me happy. I think about Everett and become mournful. I look at Hudson sitting across from me and I feel . . . curious.

"I'm actually an expert on these things, if that matters," Hudson says.

"An expert on what it feels like to cook for a murderer?" I ask. The cocktail waitress approaches our table, her body visibly reacting as she hears the tail end of my sentence. I smile. She puts our beers and a couple of glasses of water down. I thank her and she leaves. Great.

"You cooked for a triple murderer today, if that counts," Hudson says, taking a long pull off his beer.

"What?" I can feel the blood drain from my face and I feel like I'm going to be sick.

"You didn't know?" Hudson asks.

"No," I say, my voice quiet. Asking Shawn about the next guy's grandmother and now this? I can feel the light cracking under the closed doors in my mind. I can't do this. I can't live like this. If I'm going to do this job, then I need to talk about it. This isn't working. This can't be about me shutting myself off even more. I've been doing that for too long and this is getting even worse than before.

I continue, "I told myself I didn't want to know. That if I focused on the food, then whatever they did wouldn't infect me, if that makes any sense," I say, my eyes on his. Piercing blue, even in this light.

"It makes total sense, but it's just not possible," Hudson says.

"I'm realizing that now," I say, taking a pull on my beer.

"It takes the term 'elephant in the room' to a whole new level," Hudson says. I can see him thinking and processing. It fascinates me to be around someone when I have no idea what he's going to say or do next. How his mind works is an absolute mystery to me. He seems different from anyone else I've ever known.

"I know it was naive," I say, starting to peel the label off my beer.

Hudson sits back in his chair, cradling his beer. He is thinking. He looks up at the tin roof of the patio as Patsy Cline wafts through the bar's speakers. I watch him, searching his face as he starts and stops a thousand sentences.

"It's interesting though, isn't it? Before I decided to come to Shine this summer, I did a ton of research on the death penalty and all that. And aside from the Texas Department of Criminal Justice having a fantastic Web site, they also cater to the somewhat morbid," Hudson says.

"How so?" I ask, leaning forward.

"They have a place where you can see who's next in line, you know? And they also have this list of who has already been executed and what their last words were. And inevitably the last words are gorgeous . . . downright poetic. I mean, if you told me some great thinker or writer said them, I'd believe you. But then you click over and see what this guy did to get there? Fuuuuck," Hudson says, trailing off and taking a swig of his beer. I am quiet. I know exactly what he's talking about, because I've been checking a very similar Web site to follow Yvonne Chapman.

Hudson continues, "And for a while I thought, just don't click over, you know? Just read these beautiful words and think of it like some great injustice was done and this is some misunderstood hero, but it's not. It's some dipshit who held up a gas station and killed the poor schlub who had the misfortune of being behind the counter."

"That's exactly it," I say.

"I know," Hudson says, still contemplating.

"I read about—shit, even Ann Boleyn, right? What she was thinking and what must she have felt in those last few feet? I just . . . to know you're walking to your death. And yes, I'm infusing my own humanity where there might be none, but even at our basest we are all still animals who don't want to die. I don't care how right with God you are or how long that chaplain talks to you," I say, speaking of things I didn't even know I'd thought about.

"The myth that people can possibly be ready to die is one of the cruelest," Hudson says, taking another long swig of his beer.

We are quiet.

"I haven't talked about life and death in a long time," I say, curling my foot up beneath me on the bench. I'm closing in on myself. I'm thinking about that day. The principal and his squeaky shoes, being wrenched away from Merry Carole, complicated monsters, and a mother with the cruelest blue eyes I've ever seen.

"I think about it all the time," Hudson says.

"I hear you're an expert," I say with a beleaguered smile.

"Yeah, well."

"What does that mean?" I'm happy we're moving on to another subject. I'm also happy we talked about it. I feel . . . better. Lightened ever so slightly.

"It means I'm trying to be heard in a room of screaming people, I guess. My opinions and thoughts are . . . completely new and revolutionary. This whole summer is about trying to put some power behind my words," Hudson says, gesticulating wildly.

"You're here to keep it real then. Get a little street cred," I say.

"Academics are hard core, yo," Hudson says.

"That was painful," I say.

"I know—I was midway through it and I could have totally stopped before the 'yo,' but I didn't. I just went for it," Hudson says, laughing.

"Yeah. *Totally,*" I say, poking fun at his Californianisms.

"Don't even get me started on the way you people talk, or should I say the way y'all talk," Hudson says. I drain the last of my beer. Hudson continues, "You want another round?" He scans the room for the cocktail waitress.

"No, I've got to get home. My sister will be waiting up for me," I say, wanting to just crawl into my bed and dream of anything but Shine Prison.

"I'll settle up the tab and meet you out front?" Hudson says, draining his beer.

"Sounds good," I say, standing. Hudson stands. I keep forgetting how tall he is. How did I get here? Sitting at some snobby bar in Evans, of all places. And with him. I don't know if I could have had that conversation with anyone else. Whatever happens with Hudson, I am grateful he was here tonight.

"What are you thinking?" Hudson asks.

"What?" I ask, caught off guard.

"What were you thinking just then?" he asks, standing in front of me now. My face colors as though I've been caught red-handed. Can this motherfucker mind-read? Hudson continues, "Oh, you're totally telling me now. It's good, huh?" He folds his arms across his chest.

"I was just thinking that even though I have no idea how I landed at this bar of all places, I'm happy I did," I say, deciding to tell the truth (some of it anyhow).

"Is that all?" Hudson asks, stepping closer. I look up at him.

"And that you're taller than I thought," I say, finally making eye contact with him.

"Am I?" he says.

"I don't know if you're being purposely obtuse or just being a dick," I say, his body so close now.

"Probably a combination," Hudson says. He slides his hand behind my waist and pulls me into him. I'm caught off guard and hear myself (horrifyingly) gasp. "Oh well, that's kind of adorable, isn't it?" he asks, just before quieting me with a kiss. His mouth is warm and I can feel him smirking even now. I hear the older women at the other table making comments. There might be hooting and hollering. As the humidity settles in around us, I can hear Miranda Lambert singing about the house that built her. I can't help but smile. In front of God and everybody, Professor Hudson Bishop kissed me.

And you better believe I kissed him back.

"You sure you still have to get home?" Hudson asks, as we finally break from each other.

"I'm sure," I say, not moving one inch.

"Then you'd better get going," he says, pulling me in again. My heart swells as Shine Prison falls away. Hudson is fast turning into the antidote for the horror of what goes on in the Death House. I break from him again.

"Time to go," I say, with a smile.

"Fine. Meet you out front?" he asks, swiping my bangs to the side.

I nod and walk into the bar before I get lost in him again. The music is pounding and loud, couples move and sway across the tiny dance floor. I shift and jostle through the crowd and find myself unable to think straight. What happened out there?

As I stand outside the bar among the ostracized smokers, it hits me. I've been as much a party to the Wake mythology as everyone else. They thought I was a whore; I became someone's mistress. They thought I was a deadbeat; I showed up at Merry Carole's door with nothing.

I've lived my life based on what "they" think. Who are they? They don't love me. They don't know me. And they sure as shit don't care about what happens to me. Yet every decision involves thinking about what the judgmental and anonymous "they" would think.

What would *they* do if I stopped caring what they think?

"You ready?" Hudson asks, greeting me with another kiss. I can't help but let him, finally soaking up the freedom of it all.

"Yeah," I say, as we finally break apart. He takes my hand and we start walking back to his bed and breakfast.

"The thing about this B and B is, they have—," Hudson says, as we approach my car.

"It's not going to happen," I say. It's time to stop allowing others to cast me as the whore and/or the deadbeat. And it has to start right now. Despite wanting to go up into that bed and breakfast and do profoundly unadorable things with Hudson, I can't. I need to start believing I'm worthy of being courted.

"Ever?" *Ever.* My brain sputters over Everett's pet name. I quickly collect myself.

"We'll just have to wait and see."

"I don't know if you're being purposely obtuse or just being a dick," Hudson says, kissing me again.

"Probably a combination," I say, unlocking my car door and climbing inside. He slams my door shut. I reach over my shoulder for my seat belt as I start the car.

"New York plates, huh?" he says as I roll down my window.

"Yep," I say.

"Oh, this is going to be fun," he says, with a raised eyebrow. Hudson stands back from the car and steps out on the empty street. I give him a wave and pull out into the night.

I drive the few minutes home and find myself at that red blinking light at the edge of North Star without really knowing how I got there. The last meal. Hudson. Epiphanies about playing my part and being faithful to a man who was never faithful to me. I'm officially a zombie at this point. I pull down Merry Carole's driveway, pull my now empty canvas bags out of the hatch, lock my car, and make my way down the manicured pathway, past Cal's glorious sign and into the darkened house.

I walk through the dark and empty house to my bedroom. I push open my bedroom door and flick on the light. I put the piece of paper with my next last meal written on it on top of my dresser and decide to keep it folded. Closed. I pull my pajamas out of the dresser and begin to undress. The air-conditioning clicks on and the clunk of the fan startles me. I take a deep breath and continue undressing. Focus on the food. Think about the next meal and envision the day, cooking perfection. Tamales. Cabrito. Churros. I walk over to my dresser, unfold the little piece of paper, and start scrawling ideas I have about the meal. I'll serve the churro with a Mexican hot chocolate. I can do the Mexican rice that I learned while I was in San Diego. I didn't learn the recipe from one of the other chefs, mind you, but from this amazing man they only let wash the dishes. I traded him my ranch beans recipe for it. It was absolutely worth it. This is the good. Herein lies the balance.

I enjoyed my day more than I should have. What kind of person enjoys making last meals for triple murderers? That's just it, though, isn't it? Me. I don't know why or how, but I did. I didn't even know I still knew those recipes. It's not as if they're written down anywhere. Mom learned them from her mother and on up the Wake family tree. No one wrote anything down. It just wasn't done. I pull on my tank top and scrounge through my luggage, pulling a little notebook from its depths. I grab the pen from my dresser and flip the notebook open. And I write. From beginning to end, I walk through my first last meal—what I cooked, the recipes, the processes, what worked and what didn't. My hand is hurting as I finish, the house still so quiet. As I flip the pages, rereading my work, I feel a surge of emotion. I'm proud of myself. My attention to detail and the respect I have for the food of Texas catches me off guard. I didn't even consider changing these recipes or evolving them. It never occurred to me to reimagine the fried chicken or think of a new way to prepare chess pie. No. Those recipes are bigger than me. As I relive my last meeting with Brad in New York, I'm proud that I've at least learned one lesson since I've been back in North Star: it's one thing to have an ego about one's cooking, but it's a whole other to have an ego about oneself as a chef. Reclaiming those magnificent black-and-white moments of our past can only work if I am true to the recipes. True to their history by making them just as Texans have been doing for hundreds of years. Just as my family has been making them for hundreds of years.

I think about opening up my own little place. Cooking this kind of food. I never wanted my own place before. My dream was to be the executive chef in someone else's kitchen. What does that say about me? But now? With these recipes, my family recipes, pinballing around in my head, I can't shut off the idea of my own place. My own kitchen. Maybe even ask the Dent boys to work there (when they get out prison, that is). I could find a place in Austin, maybe do one of those food trucks, maybe look a bit into something in California. I close the notebook and tuck it back into my luggage. The quiet of Merry Carole's house settles around me. I smile. There must be a part of me that takes pride in being a Texan after all. The part that loves a good brisket.

I think about the black hole that our plot of land has become. Could I open up my own place there? Could I exorcise the demons and start fresh?

I crawl into bed, finally realizing how exhausted I am.

And I lay there.

I close my eyes. They open. Wide open. My eyes adjust and I can begin to make out the shadows of the dark room. I toss and turn but can't get comfortable. I lick my lips and taste bourbon and Hudson. How different he was from Everett. Playful. Fun. Light. I turn onto my side, punching at my pillow. I close my eyes again. Triple murderer. Fried chicken. What about that ranch dressing? Should I always include it? Could I have done better? I flip onto my back and stare at the ceiling. A plot of land and a notebook filled with recipes. My own kitchen. It's no use. I flip off my bedding and walk out into the hall. I look down toward Merry Carole's room. Her door is cracked just a bit. I take this as a sign that she wants me to come in. I creak down the hallway, past Cal's room, and push Merry Carole's bedroom door open.

"You awake?" I ask, my voice just above a whisper. I hear Merry Carole shift in her bed.

"I am now," Merry Carole says.

"I can't sleep."

"Come on then," Merry Carole says, flipping the blankets back and making a space for me. I walk over and crawl into Merry Carole's bed. Just like when we were kids. I fidget and situate. She continues with a sigh, "Working at that prison has made you jumpy."

"Probably," I say, now on my side facing her in the dim light of her bedroom.

"So?" Merry Carole asks.

"It was phenomenally weird," I say, still unable to put today's experience into words.

"Phenomenally weird," Merry Carole repeats.

"I love working in that kitchen. It's all kinds of wrong, but I love it. I get to make this perfect meal, and I've just never felt so at home," I say.

"I can understand that."

"But . . ."

"But . . . ," Merry Carole repeats.

"And that's the part I'm having trouble digesting. The 'but.'"

"Yeah," Merry Carole says, her sentence trailing off.

"I tried not knowing, but that just made it worse."

"That feels like a whole new level of denial to me."

"It absolutely was."

"So how do you continue to do this then?" Merry Carole sits up and rests her head on her hand.

"I guess I know what I have to know," I say, my words as confused as my thoughts.

"And what does that mean?"

"I have no idea," I say. I flip onto my back, trying to get my breath. I wish I could say that my change in position has warranted some clarity. It hasn't.

"Maybe it's just a case-by-case deal then? You take on one meal at a time and see how you feel after each one. When the bad outweighs the good, you stop," Merry Carole says, pulling the blankets up and smoothing them over me.

"That's brilliant," I say.

"You don't have to know everything now," she says.

We are quiet. I'm not sure whether she's dozed off or is just thinking. I finally am able to take a deep breath and close my eyes.

"I told Reed we needed a break," Merry Carole says, breaking the silence.

"Oh Merry Carole."

"I know. I just can't. The town is too small, and if it ever got back to Cal—"

"Cal would be lucky to have Reed in his life," I interrupt.

"It's been just us, you know? I can't risk it. I would never want him to feel like we did—always second to whoever Momma was seeing at the time."

"Honey, it's just not the same thing. It really isn't."

"I know that almost ninety-eight percent of the time, but it's that two percent that keeps getting me." Merry Carole's voice hitches.

"Yeah, but you're never going to be one hundred percent on anything."

"But you see, you're wrong. I can be one hundred percent about Cal not being upset if I just shut things down with Reed. See? Problem solved. One hundred percent."

"So you don't get to be happy, then. You don't get someone in your life?"

"I wouldn't say that."

"Do you think there will ever be a time when you think, without asking his opinion of course, that Cal would accept the man you finally deemed worthy of being part of your family?"

"That feels like a leading question."

"Well. Do you think Cal wouldn't consider the fact that you've never brought any man around, ever. Until now? And it's basically his father figure? The man he respects more than his actual father?"

"I know this seems silly to you."

"It does not seem silly at all. I'm walking around with the same shit you are, trust me."

"I know you are."

"Cal's not holding out any hope that you and Wes are going to get back together, is he?"

"No. No way."

"Okay, good."

"I'm just happy they have some kind of relationship now. He goes over there for dinner once a week. And I have to give it to Whitney—she's been nothing but nice to Cal. And their two kids—"

"Their three kids."

"Well, yeah, that . . . but the two official kids love Cal."

"And you're positive he doesn't already know about Reed?"

"I'm not positive of anything."

We settle into Merry Carole's bed, pulling on the covers like we always did. I knead and push the pillow into the proper position as Merry Carole tugs on the sheet that I've pulled too far to my side.

"So, Professor California. Tell me his real name again?" Merry Carole asks.

"Hudson," I say.

"When am I going to meet him?"

"I don't know," I say.

"He can come with you to the team barbecue," Merry Carole says, flipping onto her side and finally settling in for the night.

"I don't even know if I'm coming to the team barbecue," I say.

"Don't be ridiculous." Merry Carole pulls the blankets up over her shoulders.

"Right," I say, trying not to smile.

"You're also coming to church with me on Sunday," Merry Carole says.

"What? What are you talking about?" I ask.

"And I get to pick out what you wear," Merry Carole says, kissing me on the top of my head and settling back onto her pillow. She continues, "It's late. Get some sleep."

"I missed you," I say, my voice tiny in the darkened room.

"I missed you, too," Merry Carole says. I sigh. She continues, "But you're still coming with me to church."

"Fiiiine," I say, unable to hide my smile.

As I tuck myself in tight, I think about the idea of happiness. Lying here with Merry Carole is as close as I've gotten in recent years. It's utterly blissful. I haven't felt this safe in a long time. What if I stayed in North Star? I could have this all I want. Merry Carole and Cal. Dee and her brood. I think about Hudson and am grateful for tonight. There's something to be said for not knowing anything about a person. It's a refreshing change from everyone knowing everybody's business. I pull the blanket up and begin to drift off to sleep. A single thought dances around the edges of my brain, threatening my dreamy imaginings of staying in North Star.

Everett.

I close my eyes ever tighter and push those brown-and-yellow-pinwheel green eyes as far from my brain as I can. I sigh and finally drift off to sleep.

16

Cabrito stew, cabrito kebabs, grilled cabrito, cabrito chops, and pork tamales

I spent all Saturday starting to experiment with the next last meal's recipes while Cal watched TV. Shawn called last night and said that the inmate's grandmother was from the mountain area just outside the city of San Cristóbal de las Casas. As Cal watched the game, I finally finished my research. I nearly lost it when I realized that the tamales from this region use a banana leaf, but I managed to find a small Mexican market just a few towns over that actually sells them. All I have to do is heat them up the day of and everything will be fine. It's a more difficult version of the tamale, using a light, sweet mole in the pork filling, but it should be delicious.

It's now early Sunday and I hear Cal moving around the house in the haze of early morning. I check the clock, it's just after six. I slept okay, but still had nightmares. The kinds of nightmares in which you're running through Escheresque mazes and never quite find a way out. It's been only two days since I made my first last meal. I have a little over a week until my second one and I'm already obsessing, as evidenced by my pork tamale and cabrito cook-a-thon yesterday. I need to busy myself. I flip off my sheet and walk out into the house. Cal's in the kitchen trying to stem the tide as an avalanche of plastic bags filled with my tamale experiments tumbles out of the freezer.

"I just wanted some ice," he says, picking up a couple of bags and stuffing them back inside the already full freezer.

"I know, I'm sorry," I say, picking up the remainder of the bags and finessing them back into the freezer.

"First you make me an omelet and don't tell me until after I've finished that I just ate goat," Cal says.

"But when you fell for the goat soft tacos later that day . . . ," I trail off. Cal shudders.

"Where do you even get goat?"

"I found this great butcher who had all this different stuff," I say.

"Different stuff? Wait, I don't even want to know. I'm sure I'll be tricked into some more experiments soon enough," Cal says, finally getting that glass of water.

"You're up early." I say, smiling. Cal rinses his water glass and places it on the dish strainer.

"So are you."

"I'm going on a run; you're welcome to join me," Cal says, walking out into the dining room. He sits down and starts lacing up his gym shoes.

"I think I will, actually," I say, surprising even myself. This is exactly what I was looking for.

"Really?" Cal says as I walk down to my bedroom. Merry

Carole walks out of her bedroom, cinching her robe tightly around her.

"What's going on around here?" Her voice is a yawn.

"Aunt Queenie is going with me on my run," Cal says.

"Really?" Merry Carole says, stopping in my doorway as I pull out an old pair of sweats from a dresser drawer.

"Really," I say, sliding the sweats on. I rummage around in my closet and pull out my gym shoes and walk back out into the front of the house with Merry Carole.

"Church is at nine fifteen, so I'll have breakfast ready for y'all when you get back," Merry Carole says, walking into the kitchen and flipping on the coffeemaker. It burbles and shudders to life.

"Oh yeah," I say, lacing up my shoes.

"Yeah," Merry Carole says, folding her arms across her chest.

"I forgot about that," I say, standing.

"I didn't. I'll have your outfit picked out by the time you get back as well. Now run along," Merry Carole says, shooing us out the door.

"Don't open the freezer, Momma," Cal warns.

"What? Why?" Merry Carole says, eyeing the appliance.

"Just don't. And don't ask what was in those soft tacos, either," Cal says. I can only smile as I see Merry Carole's face turn pale.

The early morning mist settles around Cal and me as we walk down the driveway and out into the town square. Cal begins to stretch. I mimic him as much as I can.

"So how's practice?" I ask, stretching my leg back in a way no one is really comfortable with.

"Good," Cal says, now on to another stretch. I try to catch up.

"Good," I repeat.

"Momma says you're coming to the team barbecue," Cal says,

folding over, his fingertips brushing the pavement. I bend over, almost vomit, and stand back up.

"Yeah, I can't wait," I lie. I decide then that pinwheeling my arms is probably just as good as what Cal is doing. Cal straightens back up. And stares.

"What are you doing?" he asks, placing his heel on the curb and bending back over.

"Stretching," I say, placing my heel on the curb next to him.

"Uh-huh," Cal says.

We are quiet.

"So do you have any friends on the team? A girlfriend maybe?" I ask as all the blood rushes back to my head. Cal switches feet and I follow. I can hear him chuckling as he bends over.

"You mean are people as mean to me as they are to you and Momma," Cal says.

"Yeah, I guess," I say, caught off guard.

Cal stands and I follow. He meets my gaze.

"As long as I keep playing football the way I do, people will be nice to me, but it's not like I think it's real or nothin'. I just want to get to UT," Cal says. He looks down at his watch and messes with the buttons. Setting the stopwatch, probably. A stopwatch that will most certainly end in me having a coronary on some back road of North Star.

"Oh," I say, hating that he knows this at his age, but happy that he's able to tell the difference.

"You ready?" he asks, motioning to the open road.

"As I'll ever be," I say. Cal and I start to jog down the street, past the Homestead.

"Some people are nice . . . *for real,*" Cal says, his breath completely regulated. I, on the other hand, am going to die.

"That's good," I cough out. We head out of the town square and into the maze of streets that leads out of town and into the rolling hills and plots of land as far as the eye can see.

"You all right?" Cal asks, trotting along like a colt.

"Sure . . . sure," I say, keeping stride while trying not to notice that he's probably going at half his normal pace. We run past a more upscale neighborhood just on the outskirts of the town square. We pass several houses that have their own signs boasting a North Star Stallion in their midst. My breathing steadies and I begin to enjoy the syncopation of our steps. Within ten minutes there are no houses. I'm reminded of how isolated all of these little Texas towns are. They were built around the corresponding railroad stations of old.

"How was your first last meal?" Cal asks, looking straight ahead.

"It was weird," I say, looking at the low white fences, the high grass, and the grazing cattle just beyond.

"What did he order?" Cal asks. Is his pace getting a bit faster?

"Fried chicken, okra, potato salad, a chess pie, and some Blue Bell ice cream," I say, my mouth watering even now.

"Chess pie?"

"It's old fashioned. Basically a pecan pie without the pecans."

"That seems kinda pointless. This way now," Cal says, merging left onto another road.

"It's good. Real sweet, though," I say, noticing that this new road is turning into a hill. I'm going to kill this kid.

"He was a bad guy, you know. Real bad," Cal says, looking around to check my reaction.

"Yeah, I heard," I say, not wanting to remember it.

"I'd think cooking for someone who deserved to die would be better than cooking for someone who didn't, though, you know? Like someone who was innocent?"

"Yeah, I guess," I say. I think of those damn Starburst. I push the nightmarish thought out of my mind as quickly as I can.

"Not that you like cooking for either."

"I do, actually," I say. I can feel a line of sweat run down my neck and along my spine. My legs are starting to burn. The hill is getting steeper. Cal's pace is unchanged.

"You enjoy it?"

"I mean, I don't like the whole death row aspect, but I don't know. Cooking in that kitchen feels like home to me," I say, too tired to lie.

"That's weird, Aunt Queenie," Cal says, laughing.

"I know. Trust me, I know," I say, leaning forward just a bit as the hill gets steeper still.

We climb the hill. Although we don't speak, my labored breathing is loud enough to be a tad distracting. Cal keeps checking on me. Past plots of land each surrounded by low, vertical, white fences with barns in the distance. Cattle meander along, not bothering to look up at us. As we make another left, I begin to orient myself. I know this land. I know where we are. I turn my head and see Paragon Ranch just up over the rise. Nothing but land behind the metal gate that arches over the one road in.

When I was in school we all got to take a field trip to the Paragon Ranch. As we walked through the well-tended landscape, the stables, and into the main ring where they train the horses, I remember thinking how beautiful it all was. Felix Coburn sitting tall on the most gorgeous horse I'd ever seen, his Stetson bigger than all outdoors. Arabella Coburn, small, but fierce, controlling those horses (and the cowboys) as she leaned against the bars of the ring. I looked up to her. She was everything my mother wasn't. Strong. Loyal. Proud. People respected her. Feared her.

When I saw her again, I remember the look on her face after

Everett asked if he could take me to the Saturday dance. She was at the school and I remember thinking that if I could just talk to her she'd like me. I walked up to her, and the teacher she was speaking to called me by name. As Everett came up behind me, she snatched him close, as if to protect him from infection. They left quickly. The hallway emptied out. I was eleven. I was understandably crushed.

I know what she did was wrong. I was an eleven-year-old kid and she was an adult. She was obviously misguided. But knowing it and acting on it are two very different things. Leaving North Star allowed me to live in a vacuum. I could create endless monologues about Arabella Coburn and tell an imaginary Laurel exactly what I thought of her as I showered and got ready for a day in some faceless kitchen in some new city. I could yell into the night sky that Felix didn't know me and how dare he tell Everett I'd ruin him. It was my own private bubble where I could kick and scream and these ghosts couldn't hurt me. They existed in an abstract snow globe that would collect dust on the sill until I was ready to shake 'em up again.

But now that I'm back, I realize how vulnerable I feel. How that eleven-year-old kid is never far away. From me or Merry Carole.

And on we run.

This entire plateau belongs to Paragon. I look from the metal gate to over the rolling hills. The view is spectacular. The wheat-colored landscape stretches on forever. As I stare down the main road, I see Everett ever so slowly ambling along as the mist crawls and hovers over the very hills his family owns. I'd recognize him anywhere. His cowboy hat sits low as he walks along with—I crane my neck. It's Arrow, Everett's dog.

When Everett was eighteen his family's chocolate Labrador had a litter of puppies. Arrow was the runt. Everett took to him immediately. He always did have a habit of choosing the underdog. They became inseparable. When Everett drove through town in that old truck of his, Arrow was always right up in the front seat, sitting tall with his face out the window trying to catch the wind. When we shipped off to college, Arrow had to stay with the Coburns . . . and he was a nightmare. All heart and no brains. He spent his days attacking drapes and getting himself locked in closets, eating kitty litter, and making himself sick when he lapped up a bottle of the best bourbon Felix had mistakenly left on the counter. Everett always defended that dog. When he finally came home after college, he and Arrow took up right where they'd left off.

"Hold up a sec?" I wheeze to Cal. I stop and clutch my side.

"You all right?" Cal asks, beeping off his stopwatch.

"Yeah, just a stitch," I say. Cal nods and runs over to the long, white, vertical fence. He begins doing push-ups.

I stare at the slowly ambling pair. Arrow must be thirteen or fourteen by now. He looks frail. I watch as Everett slows his pace, waiting for the now barrel-bodied dog to catch up. I can hear Everett talking to the dog; I can't make out any words from as far away as I am, but the tone is easy and loving. This is how he spends his mornings? Everett stops altogether as Arrow, in his ornery way to the last, has decided to lie down right where he is. Everett just shakes his head, laughing, and bends down to him, caressing his muzzle and petting him. In time, he helps Arrow back up by lifting the dog's haunches, steadying him as he struggles to get his footing. The unlikely pair walk on, out of sight.

"You ready?" I ask, wiping away tears that I'll blame on the glaring sun.

"Yeah. You okay?" Cal says, fiddling with his stopwatch again.

"Sure . . . sure," I say, tearing myself away from the point on the horizon where Everett and Arrow are.

I gather myself, take a deep breath, and run and run and run. I need to flush the grief I feel for what Everett and I had. That sweetness I just saw with Arrow was what I always loved about him. It's not as if I understood in the beginning what it meant to fall in love with someone. I knew love didn't mean that things were going to work out or that it made people nice. Love, to me, even at a young age, was complicated. I knew it didn't stop people from leaving or from hurting you. Love seemed to give people a free pass to treat you poorly. How many times had I heard the words "I love you" right before someone did something terrible?

When that feeling bubbled up inside me about Everett, I didn't automatically default to love. It was different, purer. In the beginning, we didn't put any barriers or rules on it, we just knew that there was something there. An understanding that we were the same in ways we couldn't comprehend. There was a safety in knowing that.

It wasn't until I grew up a bit that I realized real love is more about the beauty of the everyday. It's not an accident that every love story seems to end with the couple walking off into the sunset together. I think about Everett and Arrow walking the Paragon land every morning and how I had no idea he did that. I know things about Everett only the most intimate connections yield and yet I have no idea how he spends his mornings.

I catch up to Cal as we finally begin to go down the hill. Our footfalls are syncopated as we begin our descent.

"So you're going to stay then? In North Star?" Cal asks, not looking at me. I stumble a bit, my feet tangling as I absorb what he's asked and what it took to ask it. I right myself quickly.

"I've definitely thought about it, but I don't know, sweetheart. I don't know," I say, seeing Everett still heavy on my mind. Cal picks up the pace down the hill.

"I want you to," Cal says, looking back at me now with those ice blue eyes. He gives a curt nod and looks away quickly.

Emotion chokes my throat. My breathing grows more and more shallow as he turns to see my reaction once more. I offer an ineffective smile and a nod, knowing if I stay it means that snow globe might as well be shattered. We run on in silence.

Cal and I get to the bottom of the hill and begin running through town. He smiles back at me, but then looks away. I smile, trying to breathe deep, deep, deeper.

We arrive home and the heat seems to have followed us down that hill. We eat and shower. There may have been a quick tantrum in there (by me) about having to go to church. When I get out of the shower, I find a bright orange short-sleeved sundress and some wedge-heeled sandals waiting for me on my bed.

"I assume you have undergarments," Merry Carole says, leaning in my doorway.

"It'd suit you for me to go commando under this thing, right?" I say, toweling off my hair.

"Please don't embarrass me, Queen Elizabeth," Merry Carole says. She's dressed in a demure outfit. Somber colors, high neckline, and hem past the knee. Her hair is high, yet reverent. Her makeup is respectful, with its more natural shades and pinkish-hued lip gloss.

"I'll try."

Merry Carole closes the door after herself and I put on the orange sundress as if it's a costume laid out for me by the wardrobe department. Today, Queen Elizabeth Wake, you'll be playing the part of a respectable townsperson who is not an utter failure.

Merry Carole, Cal, and I walk into the town square in our Sunday best.

The town church sits in the exact center of North Star. The

Texas Hill Country is known for its beautiful painted churches, which were built by the early Czech and German settlers. Our church is not one of the famed painted churches, but it is beautiful. Its white steeple rises high into the big sky, and the church looks just like you'd want a small-town church to look. The reverent North Star citizens stream in through the large wooden doors. I see all the familiar faces. Fawn and Pete. Dee and her brood. Shawn looks happy as he carries his youngest into the church. Whitney and Wes, their two kids, follow behind. As we near the church, I smooth my dress down, clearing my throat. It's gone dry all of a sudden. My legs are tired and sore from this morning's insanity, but I'm happy I went. Maybe just nuts enough to go again, if Cal will have me.

We walk through the big wooden doors, past the ushers, and down the main aisle of the church. Huge beams stretch and web their way across the barnlike ceiling. The simple design of the church and the pews is a nod to German engineering. Clean lines and function over form. Merry Carole stops and motions for Cal and me to go into the pew first. We oblige. I smooth my skirt again and sit on the hard wooden pew next to an older couple who smile at me as I settle in. I smile back and begin to scan the church, telling myself the entire time that I'm not looking for Everett.

Merry Carole's body is controlled and tight next to me. She's making eye contact with everyone and no one at the same time. Her posture is perfect and she keeps pressing her lips tightly together, smoothing her lip gloss from one to the other. When she's not doing this, her eyes are scanning the church as she anxiously bites the inside of her cheek. As I watch the circus that is Merry Carole's feelings, I see Everett, Arabella, and Felix Coburn settle into the pew just beyond Merry Carole's. They greet Florrie, her husband, and their brood as Gray smiles and charms his way through the bevy of adoring single ladies who've gathered around him. I lean forward in the pew just enough so that Everett can get a perfect bead on me. He does. He's caught completely off guard once again. I can see him see me, not really believe it's me, process that it is, and then look instantaneously drained. I remember this morning and seeing him unguarded as he walked along with Arrow. How beautiful it was to see him unencumbered with the weight of our relationship. I lean back in my chair, completely comfortable with using my fifteen-year-old nephew as a buffer.

The music, the pomp and circumstance, the ladies' fans, and the spoken and repeated words echo through the church as I stand, sit, and kneel in front of God and everybody. I catch glimpses of Everett during the service, but still force myself to seem unaffected. In the quiet of the church, I let myself relax and get swept away in it all.

As we file out of the church, Merry Carole guides us over to the edge of the front lawn. Cal and I oblige, but I wonder why we don't just go straight home. As I'm just about to ask, I see Reed Blanchard walk by with his two little girls dressed in their Sunday best. Reed and Merry Carole share what can only be described as a longing gaze.

"You could go over there," I say, after Cal has excused himself to catch up with some of his friends.

"I just can't, but I will go see if I can find Fawn and Dee. I'll be right back," Merry Carole says, and walks over to where Fawn and Pete are speaking with some other people Merry Carole knows I'd have no interest in spending time with. She falls quickly into conversation. I can see her exchange looks with Reed. It's heartbreaking. Their entire body language is a sigh.

"I didn't expect to see you here."

Everett.

"You keep forgetting who my sister is," I say. He laughs and it actually pains me. He's in his Sunday best, hair combed, clean shaven. A far cry from what he wore this morning.

"How are you?"

"I'm good," I say, meaning it.

"Good. I saw you up at Paragon this morning," Everett says.

"I went running with Cal."

"I was wondering why he was a little late today. Now I know."

"I wasn't that slow."

A moment passes.

"Did you know everyone knew about us? Like everyone?" I blurt out, the sun hitting my eyes as I look up at him. The question comes from everywhere and nowhere at the same time. I'm just as shocked as Everett.

"What?"

"Yeah. Piggy Peggy enlightened me in the Homestead the other day. Told me they all knew, Laurel . . . everyone," I say, my voice robotic and calm.

"She did what?" Everett's eyes flare and his entire body stiffens.

"Yeah, she laid it all out for me. It was actually a pretty stirring tale of how I ruined the great Everett Coburn. Or at least that's what people say," I say, placing my hand over my eyes to shield them from the sun.

"Right. Peggy can never just say something on her own. God forbid she has an original thought."

"That's what I told her."

Everett is quiet.

"Queenie, I'm sorry," Everett finally says.

"I know. Me, too," I say. The truth. I stare over to where

Merry Carole and Cal are standing with Fawn and Dee. Everett stops me.

"Do you want to talk about it? We could meet up later."

"We've been talking about this for going on twenty years, I just—"

"I waited for years for you to come back. I can't believe we're already over," he says. It's not a mournful statement, Everett's pissed.

"We never started," I say.

"Queenie—"

I interrupt him. "No. Enough. *Enough.* I saw you walking with Arrow this morning and never knew you did that. I pride myself on thinking I know everything about you, but the fact of the matter is, I don't. I know what a mistress knows. I've never even been inside your house."

"You can come over tonight."

"I just—after Cal and I ran this morning, I was brushing my teeth and there was this moth just circling, circling, circling the light. She just kept pounding herself against it over and over. Senseless. No thought for her own safety or mortality. She was dying— she was killing herself. So I turned around and shut off the light. And just like that, she flew away."

"And in your mind you're the moth in this scenario," Everett says.

"Of course," I say.

"Of course," Everett repeats, with a bitter laugh. He continues, "Let me tell you what happens when you turn off that light. The moth waits. In darkness. With nothing to live for. And when the light returns, he can't wait to hurl himself at it once more regardless of imminent death. It's worth it."

"How dare you," I say, tears welling in my eyes.

"How dare I what?" Everett's brow is furrowed and confused as he leans in closer.

"How dare you act like I had any choice in us being apart," I say, wiping away a rogue tear. I continue, "Look around. These are your people, Everett. Not mine. No one stopped you in the Homestead, warning you about ruining poor Queenie Wake. No one ever casts you as the bad guy."

"You remember when I grew my hair out? In . . . what was it?"

"Eleventh grade," I say. We both smile.

"I got such a talking-to about that hair that I finally had to cut it. 'No son of mine is going to be walking around this town looking like a roughneck.'"

"You never told me that."

"Sometimes it's just as hard always being cast as the good guy."

"I've never thought about it like that."

"You think it's hard being a Wake, try being a Coburn."

"I would love nothing more than to pick right back up where we left off, but we can't. Piggy Peggy was right."

"Piggy Peggy is an idiot," Everett says, his eyes flaring.

"Which makes it all the more annoying that she was right. You love your parents. I had a complicated relationship with mine—"

"To say the least."

"Right," I say, laughing. I continue, "But we're not them. We have to take what we want from our family and leave the rest behind. I'm not my mom—"

"No, you're not. I've always told you that."

"I know. I know you have," I say, tears now streaming down my face. Everett hands me his handkerchief and I take it. His face is flushed and those green-pinwheel eyes are now rimmed in red.

I continue, "But you don't see people as cut and dried, as your parents do. You saw me. You loved me despite my last name. Even

Arrow, for crissakes. You saw the good in that dog when no one else did."

"Not all the time. Trust me," Everett says with a laugh that lets more emotion loose than he was ready for.

"I think you have to figure out how to be yourself and also be the man your parents want you to be. I won't be responsible for you turning your back on your parents. You'd be miserable, and I love you too much to ask you to do that."

I can see him winding through every scenario until he arrives at the same one I did. He finally nods, his lips tightly pursed, his brow furrowed.

"We get to be happy, Ever," I say. I dab at my eyes once more with his handkerchief, finally handing it back.

"Keep it," he says.

"I don't need any more souvenirs from you that aren't actually you. It hurts too much," I say, placing the handkerchief in his hand.

"Please," he says, his hand pressing the handkerchief into mine. His hand lingers. He looks back at me. I give him a smile, a genuine smile for once, unguarded and vulnerable.

"Thank you," I say, closing my hand around the handkerchief. I look up into his eyes and in the quiet of this hidden corner in the churchyard, the sun streaming down, I say, "I love you."

"I love you, too." He just looks lost. So sad it breaks my heart. I nod once more and try to keep myself together long enough to turn away from him. As I walk away, my legs almost giving beneath me, I dig through my purse and mercifully pull my sunglasses from its depths. I shove them on my red, blotchy face as the tears begin to stream down my face. I leave him standing there and join Merry Carole again. She wraps her arm tightly around my waist and pulls me close. Fawn and Dee are watching me like hawks.

"Queenie, you remember West," Merry Carole says. I gather

myself quickly, thankful that my sunglasses will mask my red-rimmed eyes.

"Good to see you again, ma'am. Cal says y'all went on a run this morning. I may just join you one of these days," West says, offering his extended hand.

"I'd like that. I mean, I'd like it only if you're slower than Cal," I say, embarrassed that my voice is a little shaky.

"He's faster," Cal says.

"Then it'll be a shame you can't join us," I say, calming down.

Cal and West both laugh. Shawn and Pete ask them how practice was this past week as I watch Felix and Arabella introduce Everett to a nice-looking woman dressed in her Sunday best. It's clearly a setup. Merry Carole looks from me to the little vignette and I can feel her whole body tense.

"I'm okay . . . in that kind of dead inside way," I say in a hushed tone to Merry Carole, a beleaguered smile breaking across my face.

"Oh yes, I'm well acquainted with that feeling," Merry Carole laughs. I can't help but join her.

"West, there you are!" Whitney says, inserting herself into our little circle.

"Hey, sis," West says. Whitney's entire body deflates. Her smile falters and I can see her flinch at the word "sis." Once again, despite all of her terribleness, not being able to claim this delightful boy as her son must kill her. I wouldn't wish that on anyone. Even Whitney McKay. Merry Carole may have been blackballed, but at least her boy knows who his momma is.

"We'd better get on, you know how your mom needs all day for Sunday dinner," Whitney says.

"Yes, ma'am," West says, politely saying his good-byes.

"Come on then," Whitney says, urgently pulling him away.

"We'd better get on, too," Merry Carole says.

"Queenie, we'll see you in the salon tomorrow?" Fawn asks. This is not a question.

"Yes, ma'am." I say my good-byes to Dee and her brood. Shawn and I don't speak about Friday. I imagine he doesn't talk at all about what goes on at Shine Prison.

"All right then. You girls be good. Bye now," Merry Carole says.

We start walking home, past the loitering and laughing groups of churchgoers. Cal walks along on the curb, in front of us, his arms outstretched to help him balance.

"He used to do that when he was little," Merry Carole says as we watch him.

"He's such a great kid," I say.

"So, you and Everett—"

"Done. For real this time. He has to figure some stuff out. So do I, for that matter," I say.

"Dee texted that she was concerned. Said you looked real upset," Merry Carole says. I can't help but laugh.

17

Assorted types of churros offered with Mexican hot chocolate, café con leche, and/or a ramekin of cajeta

I made churros all day yesterday and I've set them on different plates in front of Fawn, Dee, and Merry Carole the next morning at the salon. I've used different types of sugar and fried them at different temperatures and for different amounts of time. For dipping, I've made a batch of café con leche and Mexican hot chocolate made with cinnamon (*canela*) and just a pinch of cayenne pepper. I also offer a small ramekin of cajeta, which is a caramelly concoction made from goat's milk that I may have become obsessed with lately. I know which combination is my favorite, but I want to see what someone else thinks.

"I need some real coffee to balance out all this sweetness; I'm going to brew another pot. Everyone wants another cup, right?" Fawn asks. We all can't say yes fast enough. She laughs and walks back to the kitchenette.

"If you keep feeding us like this, I'm going to have to join you and Cal on your morning runs," Merry Carole says, dipping a churro into her Mexican hot chocolate. Dee dips her churro into the cajeta again.

My cell phone begins ringing in my pocket. I immediately think of Warden Dale. Has someone . . . is it . . . ugh, I can't think about it. I check the caller ID. An 805 area code. I don't recognize it right off. It could it be one of the restaurants finally calling me back about those résumés I sent out in what seems like eons ago. As the phone rings again, I get this bolt from out of the blue—do I want a job somewhere else? I look at the plates of churros and Fawn, Dee, and Merry Carole sitting around enjoying them. That little black hole of a plot of land. My eyes dart from them to the ringing phone.

"Who is it?" Dee asks.

"I don't know, but . . ." The phone continues to ring.

"Well, why don't you answer it, for God's sake?" Merry Carole says.

"Hello?" I ask, walking out of the salon to the disappointed moans of Fawn, Dee, and Merry Carole.

"Hey, Queenie, it's Hudson," he says. I'm relieved and then immediately flushed with delight.

"Hey there," I say.

"I hope you don't mind that I asked Warden Dale for your number. I told him it was urgent business," he says. I begin pacing in front of Merry Carole's salon. The three women watch me pacing, like a tennis match.

"That's only slightly creepy, I suppose," I say, unable to quit smiling.

"I thought you'd be swept away by my ardent need to find you," Hudson says, in a faux (and quite terrible) British accent.

"Aaaand now we've hit full-blown creepy," I say, laughing.

"Wait until I start wearing your skin as a shirt. Don't you want to know what the urgent business is?" Hudson asks.

"Always," I say, laughing.

"So these people were talking around the breakfast table this morning—you know B and Bs, they want everyone to eat together. It's fine, but slightly annoying, you know what I mean? Anyway— these people were talking about how there was this super-secret restaurant in North Star that only the locals knew about. Apparently, this woman used to serve—"

"She used to serve meals out of her back door. Yeah," I say, knowing exactly what Hudson's talking about.

"You know it!" Hudson says.

"Maybe I do, maybe I don't," I say.

"Okay, you can blindfold me or do whatever you want, but I want to eat there tonight," he says. The invitation to blindfold him and do "whatever I want" sets off a mental chain reaction that ends with me flushing in embarrassment.

"At least the meal will be worth it," I say.

"Worth what?"

"When I have to kill you after," I say.

"Oh sure . . . sure. So do you want to come get me or can I meet you somewhere?" Hudson asks. I look into the salon at Merry Carole, Dee, and Fawn. They are staring at me as if I'm an animal in a zoo enclosure.

"You can pick me up at my sister's hair salon at five thirty," I say. I give Hudson the address to Merry Carole's salon and we say our farewells. I beep my phone off and can't wipe the smile from my face. I look up into the salon and see my reflection in the window. Smiling. Happy. Coming back to North Star was the right thing to do. Whatever happens next, I'm happy I came back. Even if it ends up being just for a little while. This is me. This is now. As I pull the door open to the salon, a thought crosses my mind—what happens when that phone rings the next time and it's a job offer? What then? I walk back inside the salon.

"That was Hudson, wasn't it?" Dee asks, her face expectant.

"Yes, it was," I say.

"And?" Fawn asks.

"He heard about Delfina's place; I guess they were talking about it at the B and B where he's staying—"

"He's staying at a B and B?" Dee asks.

"Yeah, over in Evans," I say.

"That boy's from money, peanut," Fawn says.

"What? No, he's a professor over at UT," I say.

"Who stays at a B and B in Evans for the summer?" Fawn presses.

"It doesn't matter. Look, you guys will be able to check him out tonight. He's picking me up here," I say. Fawn squeals with delight as Dee cautiously smiles. Merry Carole just looks worried.

"What time?" Merry Carole asks.

"Five thirty," I say.

"Piggy Peggy will be here at five thirty," Merry Carole says.

"Will she?" I ask, my voice unable to hide the fact that I know damn well exactly where Piggy Peggy will be at five thirty.

"Queen Elizabeth, this is my place of business—," Merry Carole starts in.

I interrupt, "Come on. She has it coming!" Dee and Fawn watch Merry Carole.

"She kind of does," Dee says, her voice quiet.

"Look, he'll walk in, we'll act like it's not even any of Piggy Peggy's business, and it'll all be fine," I say, my voice giddy with excitement.

Merry Carole just sighs. Then nods in agreement.

"Thank you!" I say, walking back to the kitchenette. I continue, "Does anyone else want some coffee?"

"I do," Dee says, following me back. She continues, "Shawn said you did real good the other day," she says, pouring herself some coffee. She opens up the fridge in search of creamer as my entire body deflates.

"Yeah?" I ask, now pouring myself a cup.

"Said the meal was downright beautiful," she says, not looking at me.

"Well . . . I appreciate him thinking so," I say, genuinely touched.

"He's worried about you," Dee says, putting the creamer back in the fridge and shutting the door.

"I'm worried about me," I say, bringing my steaming mug up to my nose. I inhale.

Dee is quiet.

I continue. "What is it?" My entire body is in a holding pattern. Do I want to hear what she's about to say? It's clearly a big deal.

"Shawn's leaving Shine. He starts up with the sheriff's at the end of summer," Dee says, speaking quickly.

"That's amazing," I say, relieved.

"You're not mad?"

"Why would I be mad?"

"He thought . . . well, we thought you'd feel left behind, you know?"

"I couldn't be happier for you guys. Honest to God. I'm so glad he's getting out of there. It was just . . ." I trail off.

"He was turning into someone else, Queenie," Dee says, her voice barely a whisper.

"Oh sweetie," I say, stepping closer. She gives me a smile, trying to be strong.

"I'm so happy he's getting out," Dee says, tears now streaming down her rosy cheeks. I set my coffee down and pull her in for a hug. I can feel her trying to steady her coffee as she hugs me back.

"I'm going to spill my coffee!" Her giggling is contagious and I love that she's laughing. We break from our hug and check for spillage. There is none. "You going to be okay out there by yourself?" Dee asks.

"I honestly don't know how long I'm going to be there. I talked to Merry Carole about it and I'm going to play it meal by meal. When the bad outweighs the good, I'll leave," I say, robotically repeating what we decided. I'm still unable to absorb what really happens in the Death House down down down to where it settles in my psyche. It's somewhere. It's feeding my subconscious. I've been dreaming of deathly metal doors and empty trays coming back with just bones on them. I shake my head. Enough of that.

"Leave and go where?" Dee asks.

"I don't know. I thought that phone call was a job offer. I applied all over, but . . . " I trail off.

"But what?"

"I just don't know anymore," I say, overwhelmed. I'm surprised by the feelings that bubble up in that moment. The idea of my own kitchen. My notebook of recipes. This is what passion feels like. This is what it feels like to let the genie out of the bottle and actually admit I want something more. Something of my own. And as much as I hate to admit it, Brad was right about me. My attitude about cooking was the same as my attitude about everything else: I defined myself by what I wasn't, not what I was. I don't know where I'll go, just not North Star. I don't know who I am, I'm just not my mom. I don't know what food to cook, but your food sucks.

"Know about what?" Dee asks.

"I was thinking about opening my own place. Maybe in Austin or one of those food trucks," I say.

"Or you could open up your own place where your momma's shack was. Sure, it needs some work, but it's still y'all's property," Dee says. It sounds as though she's been practicing this pitch for quite some time.

"I can't say I haven't not thought about it," I say.

"You can't say you haven't not thought about it? I don't even know what that means," Dee says.

"I have thought about that option as well," I say.

"Okay then. We'll just leave it at that," Dee says.

We are quiet. Just something to think about as we make our way back to the front of the salon.

Dee continues, "I personally love that Piggy Peggy is going to be here when Professor California gets here." Dee laughs and walks back over to her station.

I spend the rest of the day sweeping up hair, filling shampoo bottles, and making appointments in the salon. When my unscientific tasting was over, the women chose my favorite version of my churro and we voted for the Mexican hot chocolate as well as that cajeta concoction that we all secretly want to bathe in later. We laugh and talk about the day's events, all the while checking the clock, awaiting five thirty. I catch Merry Carole texting someone a few times, but decide not to bust her on it. I figure it's Reed and am glad that she hasn't cut off communication with him. I'm happy she's at least conflicted.

I head back to the house at around four thirty to get ready, take a shower, and put on one of Merry Carole's sundresses. I had to battle the three of them all day not to "fix my hair." I don't need to have Hudson walk in and be able to see my hair from the street.

As I blow-dry my hair, I can't help but stare at my own reflection in the mirror. The freckles that dot their way across my nose, the pale skin that burns at the hint of sunshine, the pale blue eyes that always seem to be prying even when I look at myself. I borrow some of Merry Carole's hair products to make my brown bangs stay put as I sweep them off to the side. I put on some mascara and lip gloss as the clock ticks down.

And I stare at my reflection.

I feel silly then stupid then terrified. What if I trot Hudson out in front of Piggy Peggy only to have him . . . no. Stop. I close my eyes and steady my breathing. I wonder if this is what getting your hopes up feels like. To me, it feels childlike. Silly. Like I should know better or something.

As I collect my purse from the dining room, I make a vow to myself. Tonight I will use words like "excited" and "invigorating" instead of "terrified" and "nervous." I'll think of it as if I'm on a roller coaster, jolting into that electrifying click, click, click of the climb before that first heart-racing drop. This is a good thing no matter how it turns out. Being with Hudson means I don't have to think about the past or the future. I just get to be blissfully entrenched in the present. He doesn't know who my momma was and he doesn't care. When he walks into that salon tonight, he's not trying to give the finger to Piggy Peggy and the North Star establishment (like I am), he just wants some good barbecue.

I walk back into the salon and see Piggy Peggy at Merry Carole's station. Her hair's separated with bits of tinfoil and she's wearing a black-and-hot-pink smock that makes her torso formless and mountainlike. She's absently flipping through a tabloid and looks up as the front door of the salon dings. The cartoonish terror that overtakes her as she compares how she looks with the state I'm in fills me with glee.

"Hey, Peggy," I say, my voice calm and sweet.

"Oh, hey," she says, sitting up straight in her chair, trying to minimize some of the damage.

"You look amazing!" Fawn says to me, coming out from behind the front desk. She twirls me around as Dee gives an excited little clap. Merry Carole finishes with the last of Peggy's tinfoils and walks her over to the hair dryers. She asks if she can get her anything, Peggy snorts a quick no and Merry Carole lowers the dryer. Merry Carole sets the timer for twenty minutes and pats Peggy on the leg with a smile. Peggy smiles. Merry Carole is walking over to the front of the salon, so she doesn't see it, but I watch Peggy wipe off the spot on her pants, as if to disinfect it, that Merry Carole patted. My blood boils as I try to contain myself.

"Don't even. I know exactly what she did. She thinks in a salon filled with mirrors she can get away with doing crazy things like that. Now, let's talk about how pretty you look," Merry Carole says, her face lighting up at the sight of me. She smoothes my hair down a bit, curling a tress under with her fingers. She slicks my bangs down as I inhale the rose water and Aqua Net that wafts around her.

"Why does she come in here then?" I ask, as she pulls the shoulder of the sundress straight across my shoulders.

"Because I'm the best," Merry Carole says.

"They're all nothing if not vain," Fawn adds under her breath.

"I love that they have to come here," I say.

"Oh absolutely. You can talk smack all you want, but if you want your hair to look its best, you've got to do some groveling," Merry Carole whispers, through her giggles.

"Funny how there's always a bit of a wait whenever they're trying to make those appointments," Fawn says.

Merry Carole's eyes widen, and I know without having to look that Hudson has pulled up in front of the salon. My stomach drops.

I feel nauseated. No. Remember. I feel invigorated . . . and nauseated.

"I am excited," I say, my voice robotic.

"You need to get it together, is what you need to do," Merry Carole says, her hand on my shoulder grounding me.

"Holy shit, Queen Elizabeth," Fawn says. I turn to see Hudson walking toward the salon.

He's parked his dark gray Audi and is beeping it locked as he hops up on the curb, his pace quickening. He's wearing a dark blue polo tucked absently into the front of a pair of khakis, his leather belt visible. His black hair is still wet from the shower and it looks like he hasn't shaved in a few days, the black stubble outlining his ridiculous jawline all the more.

"Everett *who,*" Dee whispers, her mouth hanging open.

"Okay, let's all get it together," Merry Carole says, walking over to the front desk as if on urgent business. She just stands there, not knowing what to do with herself. She flips the appointment book open with a flourish. Fawn and Dee look around the salon, not unlike a couple of kids looking for a hiding place. I don't take my eyes off Hudson, but I can feel Piggy Peggy watching this entire scene from under her hair dryer. Hudson opens the door and bursts into the salon.

We are all staring right at him when he enters.

"I know my hair needs a trim, but . . ." Hudson runs his hand through his damp hair. I can smell the shampoo from here.

"No, no . . . ," I say, laughing. I walk up to him and usher him into the salon. Piggy Peggy's dryer whirs on in the background. I continue, "Hudson Bishop, this is my sister, Merry Carole Wake. This is Fawn Briggs. And this is Dee Richter," I say, introducing each of the women. They shake hands and I can see them all blush a bit as he greets them.

"So you guys all know about Delfina's then?" Hudson asks, stuffing his hands in his pockets. I can't stop smiling.

"That sounds an awful lot like you're looking for confirmation that such a place even exists," Fawn says, her husky voice adding to the allure.

Hudson laughs, nodding in agreement. We say our good-byes and just as we're leaving I turn to see Piggy Peggy, staring. Her entire face filled with amazement and disbelief. I turn and walk out the door that Hudson is holding open for me and feel somehow cleansed. They may rule this town and control the gossip, but to-night?

Tonight I won.

18

Barbecued pork ribs, coleslaw, white bread, and a slice of peach pie

"Queen Elizabeth Wake, get your bottom in this house," Delfina says, tugging me inside by the arm.

"Yes, Mrs. Delfina," I say, while being squeezed and crunched to death by a tiny woman pushing seventy. She pulls me close, wrapping her arms around me and reaching up to kiss me on the top of my head. She's always been a tiny woman, not an ounce of fat on her. And the way she cooks, she should be as big as . . . well, as the people who eat her food.

"And who's this fine-looking man you've brought with you?" Delfina shunts me aside and takes Hudson's hand, acting like a schoolgirl.

"Mrs. Delfina, this is Hudson Bishop. He's not from here," I say.

"You're telling *me* he's not," Delfina says.

"Ma'am," Hudson says, his face coloring.

"Get on out back now. Pansy will bring y'all a plate," Delfina says, shooing us out into her backyard. I nod and oblige her. We walk out the back door and onto the patio.

"We don't order?" Hudson whispers.

"Delfina brings you what she's cooking and you say thank you," I say, whispering.

"This night just keeps getting better and better," Hudson says, taking my hand and squeezing it tight.

Delfina's Place is known only to locals and apparently patrons of a particular B and B in Evans. Delfina Mack is part of the DNA of North Star. She started cooking at her momma's side as soon as she could walk. I used to hang around here a lot as a kid, picking up whatever I could. Delfina knew I didn't have much in the way of a home life, so she obliged me. Although, sometimes she would try to wheedle Mom's recipes out of me and vice versa. It's hardly an understatement to say that the two women were competitive.

We walk out into the backyard; swamp coolers clunk and boom on the edges of the potholed lawn. The huge smoker sits over on the side of the backyard, Delfina's only son at the helm. The smell of oak and barbecue permeate the air around the small house. Delfina was always on one side of town and Mom was on the other. Delfina uses oak for her barbecue and Mom (and me) always used hickory. People said that you could tell where North Star was solely based on the competing smells that met in the air just above the town. That little weevil of an idea pops back up. Our plot of land. It's still there.

"There's a table in the back," Hudson says, gesturing toward the table. I nod and smile, finding myself a bit distracted by the possibilities. About a lot of things. I hold Hudson's hand a bit tighter.

Plastic chairs sit around small tables, and benches line a big wooden community table that runs down the center of the lawn. White Christmas lights are thrown absently over wash lines, but it's perfect. Delfina's Place is heaven on earth. Everyone talks and laughs over the swamp coolers, eating the best food this region has to offer. I wonder where I would fit in. Would I carve out my own place just like Momma did? Would I do better? The same? Different? Where would my cooking fit into North Star's tradition?

Hudson and I settle into the table in the back of the yard.

"Queenie Wake, well, look at what the cat dragged in," Pansy Mack squeals, setting down two sets of cutlery wrapped in paper napkins. Pansy is one of Delfina's nine daughters. All nine girls are named after some kind of flower. Her oldest and only son, however, is simply named Steve.

"Hey there, Pansy," I say, smiling.

"And who do we have here?"

"Pansy Mack, this is Hudson Bishop. He teaches over at UT," I say, looking from Pansy to Hudson.

"Nice to meet you," Hudson says, offering his hand. She takes it and shakes it ever so slowly. Pansy is all big tits, blue eye shadow, and cackling laughter. She's been married more times than I can remember, but she's also the first person to buy you a beer or bring you a plate if you're going through something. She's also the same person who makes a point of reminding the Wakes that they're a bit lower than the Macks in the town bogeymen pecking order.

"Y'all want some sweet tea, lemonade, Coke, or a Dr. Pepper?" Pansy asks, scanning the full to bursting backyard. With the community table stretching down the middle, combined with the smattering of tables on the fringes of the lawn, there are about thirty people here tonight. Pansy and Daisy, the youngest Mack, are the only waitresses Delfina needs. They are a well-oiled machine.

"Two sweet teas, please," I say.

"You guys don't have something a little stronger, do you?" Hudson asks.

"Aren't you just the cutest?" Pansy says, walking away from us with a flourish.

"If they don't offer it, you don't ask. They also really don't have any hours. They're open as long as they have food and close when they run out," I say, settling into the rickety plastic chair.

"Thank you so much for bringing me here," Hudson says, leaning over and giving me a kiss. It catches me so off guard that he pulls back. "Is that okay? That I do that?" I smile and think of Merry Carole, nonetheless an odd thing to think of as a beautiful man is kissing me without any thought of who sees.

"Delfina has rules," I say, my face coloring.

"Does she now?" Hudson says, looking around at the clientele.

"We want her food, we abide by her rules," I say. I quickly look around to make sure no one was watching. We are kind of tucked into the back, so maybe . . . I scan the crowd. It's a hot summer night at the most popular restaurant in North Star. Maybe no one saw. Then my eyes fall on a particularly crowded table set up close to the house. We must have walked right past it.

Laurel. Whitney. And an entire cabal of mean girls staring right at us.

I take a deep breath and continue scanning the crowd as if my heart didn't just stop at seeing them. Laurel takes her napkin out of her lap and excuses herself.

"Excuse me," I say, getting up to follow Laurel into Delfina's, where the bathrooms are. I wind my way through the crowd in a fugue state. I don't know what I'm going to say when I get there, but apparently having shoot-outs by restaurant bathrooms is going to become a thing. So . . . two for two.

I walk through Delfina's, making sure to keep to the plastic pathways. I walk down the long hallway, past all the family pictures, pictures of Jesus, a picture of Ladybird Johnson, and a poster of the Dallas Cowboys cheerleaders. I come to a skittering halt as I see Laurel at the end of the hallway, waiting outside the one bathroom.

"Who is he?" Laurel asks, without any greeting.

"A friend," I say, slowing my pace as I near her.

"He's not from here, right?"

"Of course not."

We are quiet as whoever is in the bathroom takes their time.

"Where's Peggy?" I ask, smoothing my skirt, fussing with my skirt, unable to keep still.

"I don't know. Home, I guess," Laurel says absently. I knew it. Laurel watches as I come to this smug realization. It might have ended with a sniff. Laurel continues, "What was that?"

"What?"

"That. That little hmmpf," Laurel says.

"I was just realizing that when it comes to town gossip, Peggy is your friend, but when it comes to hanging out as friends, well . . ."

"This is my going-away dinner," Laurel says, with a sigh.

"What?"

"It's pretty self-explanatory," Laurel says.

"Going away to where?" I ask. The person inside the bathroom flushes the toilet. We both see this as some kind of ticking clock. We have only so much time.

"I got engaged. I'm moving to Dallas to be with him," Laurel says, her chin raised.

"Congratulations," I say, genuinely shocked. The water turns on inside the bathroom.

"You're surprised?"

"Yeah."

"What's here for me?"

"Your family, your friends . . ." I trail off. *Everett*.

"My family and friends are happy for me. I'm finally moving on." The person inside the bathroom pulls paper towels from the bin and we can hear them wiping their hands dry. I am quiet.

"Why are you telling me this?" I ask.

"Because we're stuck in a hallway waiting for the bathroom. And . . . because it's about time we—" Laurel stops. Thinks. She heaves a big sigh.

"No, I get it." I do. The person comes out of the bathroom, excusing herself as she winds through us and down the long hallway. Laurel steps inside the bathroom and closes the door behind her. I wait. The hallway begins to close in around me. Laurel is leaving North Star. She's moving on and finally ready to take a chance on being happy. And I'm back. Here. I hear the toilet flush and the water go on. Paper towels. There's a moment of quiet as she probably checks her makeup. She opens up the door.

"And Everett?" I ask, finally daring to say his name. Laurel lets out a bitter laugh. She just shakes her head. She folds her arms and I can see her running through a thousand different thoughts (none of them kind, from the looks of it).

"Your friend looks nice. Maybe it's time for you to move on, too," Laurel says, her eyes fast on mine. I never noticed how delicate she was, maybe because whenever she looked at me, she was tense and pissed. Or maybe . . . was she just in anguish? This entire time?

"Good luck in Dallas," I say. I offer her a smile. It's tentative, but genuine. She gives me a cold, but polite nod and slides past me out into the hall. I step inside the bathroom and close the door behind me.

I put my hands on either side of the sink to steady myself. I always thought Laurel was the winner in all this. She got to swan around town with Everett and plan a wedding and walk down the aisle and see him standing at the end. She got to share his family name and think about building a family. Why didn't it ever occur to me that she was just as unhappy as I was? Of course she was. She got to swan around town with a man who was in love with someone else. She got to plan a wedding and walk down an aisle to a man who was forced into marrying her. She changed her name, her entire identity, hoping it would make a difference. It didn't. Her last-ditch effort to build a family and present Everett with something that would interest him, commit him, and make him happy. And not even that worked.

Laurel Coburn and I are more alike than I ever knew. Such a stupidly simple realization. I feel like I just walked outside and "discovered" water was wet. Either that or I'm trapped in some terrible romantic comedy where the music swells as the two enemies realize howwww verrrry aliiiiiiike they reeeeeealllly are. I'm a fool. So is she. All these years.

I pat my face with a wet paper towel, trying to compose myself. What a mess. I throw the paper towel into the trash can, take a deep breath, and open the bathroom door.

Now let's see about this moving-on business.

I walk out through the backyard and see that Laurel's group is getting ready to head out. They are standing, hugging, and overloading Laurel with gift bags, cards, and bouquets of flowers. There is crying and pronouncements about being invited to the big Dallas-size wedding. Laurel shoots me a quick look and a smile. And then she's gone. Just like that.

I walk past the wooden community table and find Hudson in the very back of the backyard. I lean down and kiss him. He puts his hand on the back of my head and pulls me in close. He's immediately passionate. Without a second thought.

"What was that for?" Hudson says as I settle in across from him.

"It's all the barbecue. It just gets to me," I say, flipping my napkin onto my lap.

"Then we should come here more often." Hudson laughs. Pansy Mack comes over and sets two plates in front of us. She sets another plate down with raw white onion and dill pickle slices. She sets down a bottle of Tabasco in the center of the table.

"Cut that out before Momma sees y'all," Pansy says, patting Hudson's shoulder and lingering just a bit too long.

"Yes, ma'am," I say as Pansy sets the two cups of sweet tea down.

"Now, *you* should know better, Queen Elizabeth," Pansy says, her eyes narrowed. There it is. Like a slap in the face. The past infecting my beautiful present. Don't be like your slutty momma, Queen Elizabeth.

I smile a tight-lipped assent as she walks away from me, tut-tutting me in the process.

"What was that about?" Hudson says, hunkering down and into the food now wafting up between us. It smells delicious.

"My mother had a bit of a reputation," I say as easily as I can. The last thing I want is for this to become a topic of discussion. I take a sip of the sweet tea and calm myself down.

"Had?" Hudson says, taking a big bite out of his ribs. His face is now covered in barbecue sauce.

"She died a while back," I say, scooping up some of Delfina's coleslaw. I luxuriate in it and let it erase, if only momentarily, the sludge left over from Pansy's condescending warning.

"Oh, I'm sorry. Do you mind me asking how she died?" Hudson asks, wiping his face and searching the table for more napkins. He pulls a handful from the basket that sits in the middle of the table.

Sigh.

"She was killed when I was sixteen," I say, woodenly. Eating. The ribs are perfect. Pay attention to this and not Hudson's questions. I close my eyes to really taste the sauce and the perfectly smoked meat. I open them and find Hudson just staring at me. He has a slight tinge of barbecue sauce around his mouth.

"Queenie . . . are you serious?" Hudson asks.

"Why would I joke about something like that?"

"Why would you mention your mother was killed and then casually take a bite of your ribs?" I set down the ribs and wipe my face clean. I take a long drink of sweet tea. Hudson waits.

"I don't mean to be casual about it, I really don't," I say. I stop. Think. I continue, "I haven't talked about it for so long, mainly because everyone knew. There was nothing left to say. And we don't really talk about things here, if you know what I mean. Plus, I liked that you didn't know; does that makes sense?"

"It does."

"It's one of those things in your past that you do a countdown on until someone knows it about you. And then it's three, two, one . . . and they're looking at you different," I say.

"And your dad?" Hudson asks, his voice quiet.

"Never knew him. Like I said, my mom had a reputation that was well earned, if you get my meaning," I say, not having the heart to spell it out for him.

"Jesus," Hudson says.

"Come on, let's eat. I don't want to ruin th—"

"So when you're cooking these last meals—wait, is the person who killed your mom in the system?" Hudson asks.

"Are you interviewing me for your paper now?"

"I've always been a curious person and never really had any boundaries, so . . ."

"Clearly."

"You don't have to answer, but I'm going to stare at you searchingly until you do."

"Yes. She's in the system."

"A woman, interesting. Did you know her?"

I just take a deep breath and arch an eyebrow.

Hudson continues, "Too far? Okay, but just that last one. Then I'll stop. For now."

"We knew her."

"So no other family? Mom dead, no father?"

"I have Merry Carole and Cal," I say, not liking how this dinner is going.

"Yeah, but . . ."

"No 'yeah but' . . . we're fine."

"Either you're ridiculously well adjusted about this or you, my dear, are in for quite the breakdown when the time comes," Hudson says.

"Fingers crossed for the breakdown!" I joke. I want to get away from this conversation. I'm sorry I brought it up at all. Oh wait. I didn't. I was scolded by Pansy Mack and now I'm being grilled by Hudson.

"If it helps, I've been studying criminals and death and the psychology of mortality and loss for years," Hudson says.

"You must be a big hit with the ladies back home. Your first-date small talk is delightful."

"A, I *am* a big hit with the ladies back home. B, my small talk is out of the ordinary and layered, and C, so this is a date then?"

I take a bite of my ribs and ignore Hudson's little list. He takes this as his cue to continue.

"What I've found as a by-product of my research is the fallout this type of death has on the families. It's always shocking how ill prepared they are for the loss, despite how they felt about the person. I mean, these are criminals here, their relationships with their families are always complicated. But still. I mean, even if it was bad, and it usually was—right? Even if it was bad, these families still defined themselves by their dearly departed. They were the good ones and the dearly departed made life interesting. Without them they have a hard time trying to find their own identity. I mean, right?" Hudson stops and waits for my opinion on the subject of whether or not my identity is wrapped up in my mother. If he weren't so right on with his assessments, I would have thrown my entire sweet tea at him a long time ago.

"You tell me," I say, ripping open the wet nap Delfina always puts in the basket along with her ribs. I begin wiping my hands, the sterile smell invading my nose.

"I mean I only know what my research tells me. But judging from the cartoonish steam coming from your ears right now, I'm either right on the money or need to shut up. Probably a combination."

"Or you're just being a dick," I say.

"Well, that's a given. I mean, if I may be so bold, what I found was even in those cases where the relationship was strained, it's the day-to-day stuff. That startling moment when your guard is down, which usually happens in a grocery store or sitting on the toilet, when you realize, tragically, that someone is gone. Like, off the face of the earth gone. Never gonna come back—"

"All right. Enough," I say, my breath quickening.

"Queenie, you've been through some real shit here."

"You think I don't know that?"

"Oh, I know you know it. That sounds ridiculous . . . *I know you know it,* but it sounds like, and this could be total bullshit Psychology 101 and the fact that everyone in California—including me—has been in therapy forever, so you can take what I have to say or leave it—" Hudson collects himself. He continues, "You're strong, Queenie. That's clear. I just hope you will also allow yourself to be—" Hudson stops. Thinks. He sits back in his chair. I'm not breathing. I haven't taken a breath in minutes. His eyes search the heavens and he runs his hand through his hair, the shampoo wafting over the smell of barbecue, fresh and clean. "I just hope you allow yourself to be affected. Got to, if that makes any sense . . . what's the word I'm looking for?"

"Vulnerable," I whisper.

"Vulnerable," Hudson repeats, nodding.

"If I may be so bold," I say.

"Please."

"These 'subjects' you speak of so cavalierly, they're people. Not data. You might want to curb your utter joy at their falling apart because it backs up your theory," I say, balling up my wet nap and throwing it on the table.

"I'm sorry. I went too far."

"I'm sure you do that a lot."

"I've been known to in the past, yes."

"I love that you're passionate about what you do, but you don't get to automatically know that shit about me just because you studied it at some fancy school."

"You're right. Shit, I'm sorry." Hudson settles himself in his chair, and even through my spiraling rage at his lack of boundaries, I can see him struggling to make this right.

"Okay, here's the deal. You need to tell me one thing about yourself that you have never told anyone. Then we're square," I say, my voice softening. Hudson looks away and just lights up. Relieved. He nods and sits back in his chair. Thinking. A smile every now and again, some more devious than others. He leans forward.

"So . . . this is . . . okay, no. I deserve this. Okay . . . so when I was younger . . . see my eyebrows—" Hudson leans over the table and stares directly into my eyes. Those piercing blue eyes that set off the black hair and eyebrows were one of the first things I noticed about him. It's hilarious—and probably a ruse—to think he doesn't know that.

"Yes, I see your eyebrows and this better get a lot juicier than just something about your eyebrows," I say, having to look away. Damn.

"When I was younger—they're thick, right? And like super black and I'm pale and the brow just went all the way across. Total unibrow. It was terrible. And at the time, I thought there was nothing I could do. I knew it looked bad, the other kids made fun of me relentlessly. It was a testament to the academic excellence of the boarding schools I went to that the insults were so unendingly imaginative. A lot of Neanderthal jokes, which would inevitably lead to the whole Homo erectus pantheon of options, whole dialogues about evolution and how I'd clearly been skipped, I mean . . . it was—" Hudson stops and just shakes his head. He continues, "I finally met this girl, and after a few months of what I thought was flirting, she leans over one night—and you know, I think I'm going to kiss her, and she says, 'You know, I have a great waxer.' And she's just looking at my eyebrows."

"Eye*brow*," I say, correcting him.

"You're so mean. That's so fucked up," Hudson says, howling with laughter. I can't catch my breath I'm laughing so hard.

"So yeah. I wax. I'm a waxer. I get waxed," Hudson says, taking a bite of his coleslaw.

"That's fantastic," I say.

Hudson picks up his ribs and digs in. I let Delfina's cooking comfort me as it always has. The sweet tang of that barbecue sauce was always a tonic for what ailed me. Seems it still is.

As the hours pass, we eat and laugh and in no time Hudson is walking me back to Merry Carole's salon. The tension of earlier this evening is not forgotten, but the sting of it has lessened. As Hudson slows in front of his car, my stomach is in knots. I'm excited, but wary of him. I went from being his dinner guest to his test subject in three seconds flat and that makes me nervous. I also hate that he's right. About it all. Of course I'll never tell him that. The salon is dark and I know Merry Carole is waiting for me back at the house.

"Hey, Aunt Queenie," Cal says, trotting back from his second football practice. I am so thankful we weren't doing anything embarrassing.

"Oh hey, sweetie. Hudson, this is Cal, my nephew. Cal, this is Hudson Bishop," I say, introducing the two.

"Nice to meet you, sir," Cal says, easy and open.

"Nice to meet you," Hudson says.

"I'd better be getting on," Cal says. He makes his farewells and runs the rest of the way until he's inside, looking back suspiciously only once.

"You've got a real football player in your midst," Hudson says.

"We do. He's such a good kid," I say, unable to help myself.

"Yeah, definitely," Hudson says. He's not listening to me, I realize. He's focusing on my face. My mouth. I watch those intense blue eyes fix on my lips.

"You make me nervous," I say, my voice quavering. Damn.

"Do I?" Hudson says, stepping closer. He tilts his head just so, his eyes still fixated on my mouth.

"I don't know if you're being purposely obtuse or just—"

Hudson cuts me off. "Being a dick. Oh *absolutely*," he says before leaning in for a kiss. He wraps his arm around my waist and pulls me closer. I can't help but smile. I feel him smiling. I let out a laugh as we break apart. The world comes speeding back into my consciousness as I hear a dog barking in the distance. I wrench my gaze away from Hudson for the smallest of seconds and see Everett idling at the stop sign in the center of town. Arrow's barking out the window at some passersby, but my focus falls on the man driving. How long has he been sitting there? He is unreadable, and the moment that passes between us couldn't have been more than a couple of seconds. Hudson is saying something. Saying something.

"What?" I ask, focusing back on him just as Everett drives off down the street and back to the Paragon Ranch.

"When can I see you again?" Hudson asks.

"Cal has a team barbecue on Saturday. It starts at three PM. You can come to that," I say.

"Sure," Hudson says, with a shrug. No big deal.

"I'll see you on Saturday," I say. One more kiss and he hops into his car and pulls away. Out of North Star.

I smooth my skirt again. I have to stop doing that. If ever there were a nervous tic, this skirt-smoothing thing would be it. I head back toward Merry Carole's house, anxious to tell her about my night—Laurel, Hudson . . . all of it. I let the thought of me moving on bounce and ping around in my head like a pinball.

19

Coach Blanchard's brisket, coleslaw, and not enough Shiner Bock

As the weekdays zoom past, and Tuesday looms, I find myself in a kind of limbo between understanding the new way of things and beginning to understand what this means for me going forward. I now have information I didn't have before. Laurel was just as miserable as I was. Everyone knew about Everett and me. I played as much a part in my being cast as an ostracized, worthless loser as the town of North Star did. These are facts. The hard part is switching these facts for the myths and rumors that I've based my entire life upon. I was lied to by people I thought knew better. But I gathered my own information and sifted it through a filter of self-hatred and doubt. What happens if I switch my old filter for a new one? A new one, where anything is possible, even for Brandi-Jaques Wake's daughters.

* * *

Merry Carole, Cal, Hudson, and I walk into the team barbecue that Saturday carrying a six-pack of Shiner Bock and some coleslaw I made the night before. Are they peace offerings, maybe? Are we hiding behind them, as if the beer and coleslaw will shield us from the first line of fire as we enter the barbecue? Most definitely.

"CWake!" another football player says, charging at Cal. He gives the boy a hearty handshake. They are swept away into the fold of the already raging barbecue.

Reed's house is on the outskirts of town, a simple one-story home with French doors that open out onto the backyard. Close to a hundred people mill around from the inside to the outside of the house. Ladies with fans and men with a cold beer in one hand and an opinion about the upcoming football season in the other. Reed has taken up his place at the barbecue and holds court as a group of men gather around. Merry Carole glances his way. She sighs. Reed's two little girls are with his mother for the weekend. Their presence is missed, but noted. My plan to have Merry Carole stay after at the party and patch things up with Reed can be put into action now.

"So football is kind of a big deal in Texas, huh?" Hudson asks. Merry Carole and I open our mouths to speak, but Hudson continues, "I'm kidding. I've seen *Friday Night Lights.*" He smiles.

"You look beautiful today," I say to Merry Carole as she keeps fussing with her dress.

"Thank you," she says, breathlessly. She decided to go with a bright yellow shirtdress, a black belt cinched at her impossibly tiny waist. She's been waiting to wear this outfit for weeks. Black and gold—the team's colors. She continues, "I'm sure someone will tell me I look like a floozy."

"If they're using the word 'floozy,' how big a threat can they be?" I say. Hudson laughs. Merry Carole loosens up a bit. She's not alone.

"Thank God you brought that one. It's all anyone will be talking about," Merry Carole says, motioning to Hudson. He's already cracked open a Shiner Bock and is taking a long drink. He's wearing a loose plaid shirt that he's once again only half tucked into his relaxed-fit Levi's. His worn-in leather belt just underneath is visible and becoming more and more inviting every day.

"That one, huh?" Hudson says, offering us a beer. Merry Carole and I decline Hudson's offer. We need to be stone-cold sober for these festivities. Whether we like it or not.

"Merry Carole and Queenie Wake." Whitney McKay and Piggy Peggy float over to us followed by a phalanx of no less than four indistinguishable women. Now that Laurel's off to Dallas, it looks like Whitney has taken her place on the throne. I probably know Whitney's Gang of Idiots from school, but their high hair and Easter egg–colored wardrobes all blend together into what is fast becoming this barbecue's terrifying first line of offense.

"Nice to see you, Whitney. You look lovely," Merry Carole says with a polite nod.

"Team colors. Bless your heart," Whitney says, giving Merry Carole the once-over. Merry Carole wants this too much. Women like Whitney get a whiff of that longing and it's hunting season.

"Queenie," Whitney says, with a curt nod.

"Whitney," I say, with a sniff. I can't even look at Hudson. I can feel his grin from here. He can barely contain himself. He folds his arms across his chest, tucking his open beer bottle under his arm.

The women stand in front of us, unmoving. Staring at Hudson.

"Ladies, this is Hudson Bishop. He teaches over at UT," I say, presenting him for inquiry.

They titter and nod their greetings.

"And how did y'all meet?" Whitney asks. She damn well knows the answer, but wants to hear me say it.

"Queenie and I met over at Shine Prison," Hudson says.

"Did you now? Isn't that sweet," Whitney says.

"I don't think anyone would call it sweet. What was your name again?" Hudson asks.

"Whitney," Whitney says, her facade cracking for just the slightest of moments. It's the most beautiful thing I've ever seen.

"It's Whitley, right?" Hudson asks.

"*Whitney,*" she corrects.

Hudson lets the moment hang just long enough as he takes a lengthy pull on his beer. He continues, "Anyway, I'm going to go take a look at that barbecue. Excuse me, ladies." He gives me a quick wink and ambles over to the barbecue, falling quickly into conversation with the already gathered men.

Then it's just us. Merry Carole and I facing off against a group of women who look as though they're about to feast on human flesh.

"How long is this little standoff going to take, Whitney? This coleslaw needs to be refrigerated sometime today," I say, annoyed. Merry Carole tenses next to me. I will myself to take it easy. Well, easier. The party crowd mixes and mingles around us.

"Oh, is that left over from Shine? I do hope we won't have to eat the food you served to a convicted murderer," Whitney says, clutching her pearls.

"He was a triple murderer and he ordered fried chicken," I say. Whitney and her Gang of Idiots are actually taken aback.

"Even for you, Queenie Wake, that's low," Piggy Peggy says, looking from Whitney to me. Yes, Peggy, you delivered your line perfectly.

"You'd know," I say, stepping forward. She flinches.

"All right now. Come on," Merry Carole says, her voice measured, but strong.

"Control your dog, Merry Carole," one of the other women says. They all think it's hilarious.

"That's quite enough. That's quite enough," Merry Carole says, her face coloring.

"Why don't you call in Coach Blanchard to help you?" Piggy Peggy asks, her voice raspy with excitement.

"No, ma'am. We can handle our own business," Merry Carole says, her voice becoming more and more eerily calm. The women don't know what to do with Merry Carole. Me, easy. I'm the uncontrollable dog. But Merry Carole is a pillar of calm. She continues, "Now if there's nothing else, I'd like to see if my son needs anything. Queenie, the refrigerator is through the French doors and to the right." Merry Carole's face colors as she realizes she's said too much. Her knowledge of the ins and outs of Reed Blanchard's house is obvious. Whitney doesn't even attempt to suppress her joy. Merry Carole gives Whitney and her Gang of Idiots a polite nod and goes off to find Cal in the crowd.

"If you'll excuse me," I say. The women ooze off into the crowd like a big blob of hate, looking for their next victim. No wonder Laurel had to get out of this town. I walk into the kitchen and come face-to-face with Everett.

"Jesus Christ," I say, unable to help it. This barbecue is like a haunted house.

"Hey, I didn't quite recognize you without some male model hanging all over you," Everett says, taking a long pull on his beer. I open the refrigerator door and finagle my coleslaw onto an already stuffed shelf.

"Oh, does that bother you? Is that hurtful to you? Seeing me with someone else? I mean, if I could only understand how that could possibly feel . . . ugh, it's soooo hard to imagine such a thing!" I say, my hands in fists and dramatically thrust to the heavens.

"Queenie, come on. He's ridiculous," Everett says, motioning out to where Hudson is standing with the other men.

"I like him. He's nice," I say.

"You like him and he's nice," Everett repeats, slamming his beer down a bit too hard on Reed's tiled counter.

"Yeah. I like him and he's nice. Is that so revolutionary?" I ask.

"Is his shirt tucked in or isn't it? Did he go to the bathroom and not quite tidy himself up after? I mean, I don't get what that look is about," Everett says, gesticulating wildly at Hudson and the of-fending plaid shirt.

"What's happening over there?" I ask.

"Nothing," Everett says. His voice subdued. Caught.

"How was that nice lady your parents were setting you up with on Sunday? Talk about ridiculous," I say, walking past him and out toward the backyard. Everett reaches out and stops me. He leans down and speaks softly, intimately, into my ear.

"Go ahead and have your fun with Mr. I Like Him and He's Nice. I know how this ends and so does he." Everett's eyes are locked on mine. Green, brown, and yellow pinwheels intense and focused.

"So does he what?" Hudson asks, standing in the open French doors, partygoers hustling past him. Everett straightens and ap-proaches Hudson. In that moment, I honestly don't know what Ev-erett is going to do. With everyone outside, the three of us are alone.

"Everett Coburn," Everett says, extending his hand to Hudson.

"Hudson Bishop," Hudson says, shaking his hand. Everett looms over Hudson, I'm sure reveling in the few inches of height he's got on him.

Oh. My. God.

"I was just saying that I knew how this thing between you two ends," Everett says, his voice low and threatening. He folds his arms and juts his chin high. I'm speechless.

"It seems the only thing between us two is you," Hudson says, walking over to where I am. He slides his arm around my waist and tilts his head just so.

"Damn right," Everett says.

Everett flicks his gaze from Hudson to me and turns and walks outside.

"He seems cool," Hudson says, walking into the kitchen and pulling a couple of beers from the cooler.

"Yeah, he's super sweet." He cracks them both open and hands me one. I take a long drink. Once again, I'm in that limbo. These are facts. What I'm supposed to do with all this new information, how I'm supposed to live, is the part I keep getting hung up on. Shit, if I had known Everett would react like this, I'd have trotted out a boyfriend way before now.

"So, are these your friends? Here? This is what your friends are like?" Hudson asks, taking another drink of his beer.

"He's an ex. It didn't work out. This is a very small town and I come from a long line of screwups," I say.

"Who doesn't?"

"Apparently, everyone but us."

"I think you're looking at this all wrong."

"That wouldn't be a first," I say. Hudson laughs. I watch Everett fall into conversation with Reed and some of the assistant coaches just outside.

"It's a simple equation really: the amount of money you have corresponds directly to the recognition of your family's . . . shall we say, *eccentricities*. Now, let's take my family, for instance. My father thinks we don't know he sexually harasses every single secretary he goes through and I, unfortunately, mean that literally. My mother who, I'm pretty sure, merely sidelined her true sexuality and a lovely woman named Jackie to marry my father in her early twenties for the trust fund that accompanied him on his wedding day. Aunt Jackie, as she's now known, is actually the best role model I've got, which is just perfect. Which brings us back to the original equation. My father comes from money, has even more power than that, and therefore his degree of eccentricity is swept under the rug, tolerated by the Santa Barbara elite and never questioned. I imagine that same equation is in play here in North Star. You scratch the surface of any family and you're going to find dirt. Unfortunately, my darling Queenie, you were dealt a disreputable mother with no money or power to balance it out," Hudson says, taking a long, long swig of his beer. He continues, "Am I close?"

"And I thought my family was crazy," I say.

"Ha!" Hudson says.

"Hey, y'all—can I have your attention?" Reed is standing next to the smoker, his coach voice in full force. Hudson and I exit the house and crowd into the backyard. I wedge in between a couple wearing matching T-shirts with their son's number on it and Merry Carole.

"Everything okay?" I ask.

"It's fine. You?" Merry Carole answers, her jaw still clenched.

"Yep. Fine," I say.

"I'm sure we can talk about it later," Merry Carole says, focusing back in on Reed. I take Hudson's hand and pull him close. He gives me a smile and I squeeze his hand. I don't know what to say or how to react to what he's told me.

"I want to thank y'all for coming out to the barbecue. The team sure appreciates everything y'all do for us. Thank you to the Stallion Batallion for being the best booster club a team could ever want. I would like to particularly thank the Paragon Ranch for donating all of the food and drink you see here today. Everett Coburn, come on down, sir," Reed says, scanning the crowd. Everett makes his way to Reed through the congratulatory, back-patting crowd.

"Ah. Now everything makes sense," Hudson says.

"Yep," I say, not able to look at him.

"A whole opposite-sides-of-the-track thing. How adorable," Hudson says. I don't answer him. Once again, that switch in him. It's as if he sees people as these little plastic army guys he can bat around on his bedroom floor.

"Everett, every year we choose someone from the community to do the coin toss at our opening game; we'd love it if you would do us the honor this year," Reed announces, presenting a large golden coin and hoisting it in the air. The crowd goes wild. I keep my eyes on Everett. He hates shit like this.

"Thank you so much, Coach. On behalf of the Paragon Ranch, I would consider it my privilege," Everett says, taking the coin and shaking Reed's hand. People are hooting and hollering as pictures are taken of the two men.

Merry Carole and I are as quiet as the grave.

I don't see Everett again. As the barbecue winds down, Hudson and I settle into a couple of plastic chairs and laugh and talk the entire time. Merry Carole joined us after about an hour and we even got her laughing, despite herself. We ate brisket, drank beer, and decided that my coleslaw was definitely better than Delfina's. Cal came over and introduced his friends, West among them. This led to Merry Carole and me whispering the torrid tale of West

Ackerman's lineage. Hudson could only gloat, insisting that his theory about wealth trumping eccentricity was proving itself to be true sooner rather than later.

As the sun finally set, Merry Carole fussed around the house, cleaning up, and made sure Reed was looked after in every way, except to join him in publicly declaring their love for each other. I catch them a few times in nooks and corners, whispering and pleading with each other.

"Do y'all want to come home with us or . . ." I trail off, plopping down next to Cal and Merry Carole.

"Cal, honey?" Merry Carole asks.

"I can walk home from the McKays, Momma. They're doing that big after-party thing at their house," Cal says.

"Is that your version of asking for permission to attend this 'big after-party thing'?" Merry Carole snaps.

"Yes, ma'am," Cal says.

"All right then. But I don't want you staying out too late, and drinking is just out of the question," Merry Carole says, her brow furrowed. It's as if it's just dawned on her that her little boy is becoming a man.

"Yes, ma'am," Cal says.

"I don't need to tell you that you're already working with a stacked deck, my love," Merry Carole says, her voice lowering.

"Yes, ma'am."

"People are just waiting for you to fail," Merry Carole says.

"Honey, he's going to a party at the McKays, not leaving for a weekend in Bangkok," I say. Cal can't help but laugh. Merry Carole softens just a bit.

"I know. I know," Merry Carole says, fussing with Cal's hair. He is ever so patient with her.

"So Hudson and I are going to take off. You'll be okay?" I ask, my eyebrows raised.

"Sure. Sure," Merry Carole says; unbelievably, she picks up what I'm putting down.

"Merry Carole, I'm sure I'll see you again," Hudson says, extending his hand to her. She takes it.

"Pleasure seeing you again, Hudson," Merry Carole says.

"Take your time now," I say over my shoulder as Hudson and I make our way to the front door. Merry Carole shoos me away as her face colors.

As we drive through the empty streets of North Star, I'm happy. I had a good time today, against all odds. It started out a bit rough, took an unexpected turn, but leveled out rather nicely. They can't get to me if I don't let them. If I'm sitting there laughing and having fun, claiming my space; they can't huff and puff and blow my house down.

Go ahead and have your fun with Mr. I Like Him and He's Nice. I know how this ends and so does he.

Where do I put this "fact" in the library like purgatory that is my brain these days? I can testify and monologue all I want about being over Everett, but when he leaned over and I felt his breath on the side of my face, I knew it was all bullshit. I craned my neck to look into those eyes of his because I couldn't help myself. It took all I had to not dive into him and kiss him right there. Please don't let me be the only one who thought that.

"You all right?" Hudson asks as he parks in front of Merry Carole's salon.

"It was just a long day," I say, unclicking my seat belt and turning to face him. Hudson leans across and kisses me. I break from him. Feeling tired. Maybe I'm conflicted about Hudson. Or Everett. Who knows? "I'd better head in," I say. I get out of the car, slamming the door behind me. I walk around to his side and lean down.

"Your friends are super nice. I had fun today," Hudson says.

"You're a really good liar," I say, kissing him again.

"I know," Hudson says. He puts his car in gear and pulls away. I watch his red taillights dim in the humid haze of the evening. The center of town is quiet except for the cicadas singing their song.

Go ahead and have your fun with Mr. I Like Him and He's Nice. I know how this ends and so does he.

As I walk down the manicured path, past Cal's football sign and into the darkened house, I can't get the words to stop repeating in my head.

Everett knows how this ends? What does he know that I don't?

20

Inmate #HB823356:
Tamales, ensalada de noche buena, cabrito served
with Mexican rice and beans, churros with Mexican hot
chocolate and cajeta, Fanta orange soda, and a pack of
Starburst

While I was shopping for Tuesday's meal, I found myself in the candy section staring at all the different kinds of Starburst. When did there get to be ten thousand different flavors of Starburst? Back in my day there was just the one kind and everyone ate all the red and pink ones before passing off the yellows to friends as a "kind gesture." But now? Summer Fun Fruit? FaveREDs? Tropical? Sweet Fiesta? What's a Flavor Morph? I grabbed one of each, just in case.

Then it was Tuesday morning. Today I'll make my second last meal for a man who's trying to re-create Christmas. Could I get some dramatic, last-minute phone call telling me the inmate has been pardoned? I've loaded all the groceries into the car after not sleeping very well and am pouring coffee into my travel mug.

"You're leaving early," Merry Carole says, cinching her robe closed.

"This one's going to be tough," I say, tightening the lid on my travel mug.

"Remember—"

"I know," I say, cutting her off.

"When it's too much, we'll have another conversation," Merry Carole says, coming into the kitchen and pouring herself some coffee.

"I think we're probably going to be having that conversation sooner rather than later," I say, feeling utterly exhausted after this week's ramp-up.

"Well, you let me know," Merry Carole says.

"Cal's on his run. He just left," I say.

"Good."

We are quiet.

"Meaning, if you want to talk about things . . ."

"Oh. Oh, no thank you," Merry Carole says, politely.

I wait. Merry Carole stares out the sliding glass doors and into her backyard. The sun is coming through and her blue eyes twinkle in the morning light. I begin to walk toward the front door, but turn around.

"When I first got here you were . . . bigger," I say.

"You mean fatter?" Merry Carole smooths her robe over her curves.

"Of course not. I mean *bigger*." My arms shoot in the air like an explosion.

"Honey, using the same word but only adding your own personal game of charades to the mix doesn't make it any clearer."

"It feels like you're disappearing. A little," I say, hating how harsh the words sound.

"Does it?"

"Yeah."

"Maybe a little."

"Anything you want to talk about?"

"Not yet, no. No, thank you."

"Okay." I nod.

Merry Carole gives me an obliging smile.

I continue, "Should I be worried? Because now I'm worried."

"No, it's good. I honestly don't think I'm ready to even say it out loud. Funny, isn't it? I need it to just be mine a bit longer," Merry Carole says.

"That makes a lot of sense," I say.

"I know it does."

"So we'll talk later?"

"I'm sure you'll be crawling in bed with me later tonight," Merry Carole says, walking with me as I head toward the front door. She opens it for me and I step outside.

"Yeah, probably," I say, unashamed.

"Go on now. Good luck," she says, with a wave. I unlock my car and climb inside. The quiet of the car surrounds me. Focus on the food. I buckle my seat belt, back out of the driveway, drive through the town square and past that flashing red light and onto the highway. Radio turned high. Mind busy. Running through the day. Envisioning the perfectly made plate. And nothing else.

I pull into Lot B, gather my canvas bags filled with supplies and groceries, and trudge to the back door. I manage to swipe my key card without having to drop all my groceries and step inside the darkened kitchen. I turn on the lights, and as they flicker on I await Jace. The kitchen door clicks open and he walks in.

"You're here early," Jace says, his hand resting on his gun.

"I didn't get any sleep last night," I say, setting my knives down.

"Nobody does," Jace says.

I look up from the counter and really make eye contact with him for the first time since I've worked here. His clear brown eyes are heavy and bloodshot. He has eyelashes any woman would kill for and I can't believe I haven't noticed them before today. What I notice most of all, however, is how worn out Jace looks.

He continues with an obliging nod. "I'll grab the Dent boys for you," Jace says. He excuses himself and is about to leave me in the kitchen by myself.

"Does it ever get any easier?" I ask.

"No." No hesitation. He turns around.

"Why do you do it?" I ask, almost unable to hold his gaze.

"I don't think I've ever thought about it. Maybe that was on purpose. It's a good-paying job and I've got a wife and kids," Jace says, looking uncomfortable.

"I'm sorry if I've—"

"It's no problem," Jace says.

"Thank you for being in here, Mr.— I don't think I even know your last name," I say.

"Murdoch. Jace Murdoch. And yours?"

"Wake," I say. His face changes. Just a bit. Enough.

"You related to BJ Wake?"

"Yes, sir."

Jace just nods. I brace myself.

"She used to own that shack over in North Star. She made this chicken fried steak, what was it called . . . the Number One. That's right. My mouth's watering just thinking about it. Well, no wonder you cook the way you do, girl. Damn. Your momma was the best there was. Ain't that something. Always wondered what happened to her. Now I know! She had you and you're doing the cooking for that family. Ain't that something." Jace smiles wide and is as animated as I've ever seen him. I just keep smiling and nodding. It's brightened his mood thinking about my mom's cooking. His heaviness is momentarily gone. He sighs and walks out of the kitchen in search of the Dent boys.

Ain't that something, indeed.

I put the groceries into their proper places and set up the Dent boys' stations once more. I pull pots and pans from the cabinets while I refer to my notes about the day's schedule. The door clicks and Jace and the Dent boys walk in.

"I'll be right here," Jace says, settling into his chair by the door. He flips open his paper and begins to read.

"Chef," they say in unison.

"Harlan. Cody. This is going to be a tough one today," I say, setting my notes on the counter in front of us.

"Yes, Chef," they say.

"Harlan, we're going to do the tamales. We're going to have our own little tamalada," I say.

"Tamalada, ma'am?" Harlan asks.

"Oh right. Sorry. It's a tamale-making party. Women gather, gossip, and make tamales," I say. Harlan and Cody just look at me. I continue, "I realize we're doing our own very special version today." The men can't help but crack a smile.

"I doubt you'd want to hear the gossip we have to tell," Jace says from behind his paper.

"I expect not," I say, my voice playful. I continue, "We have to mix the masa, spread it on the banana leaves, and fill and roll them. Cody, I'm going to have you put together the ensalada de noche buena, but that won't happen until much later. Until then, you're going to be in charge of the cabrito dish," I say, scanning the list.

"Cabrito?" Cody asks.

"Goat," I say.

"Goat?" Cody asks.

"It's actually quite good. But it can be a little tough. They don't have much fat on them," I say.

The Dent boys are speechless.

I continue, "My point being, it takes a bit to cook. So you'll be doing the Mexican rice while the pinto beans simmer." I walk Cody through the Mexican rice dish as Harlan checks on the pinto beans.

"Chef, I don't see anything about salsa here," Harlan says, scanning the list.

"Oh shit," I say.

"No problem. I can do a red and a green with the stuff you bought. We'll be fine," Harlan says, picking through the vegetables that I have.

"You're a lifesaver," I say. Harlan allows himself a small smile.

And we're off.

When Jace says it's time to break for lunch, I can't believe hours have gone by so quickly. The Dent boys file out and I sit on one of the stools and eat my turkey sandwich. I pace around the pots and pans, stirring, tasting, and checking the time. When the Dent boys arrive back an hour later, we hit the ground running.

I pull out the big pot with a steaming rack in it and put it on the stove. I set up the rest of the tamale assembly line on down the counter.

I stack the banana leaves next to the stove. I put the bowl of masa in front of Harlan and set down a piece of plastic wrap and a spoon. He eyes them suspiciously. Cody is next to the pork-and-sweet-mole filling.

"Now, watch me," I say.

"Yes, Chef," the Dent boys say in unison.

I pull a banana leaf from the stack and hold it next to an open flame. It immediately softens and becomes pliable. I walk over to the bowl of masa, take a heaping spoonful, and put it in the center of the banana leaf. I grab the plastic wrap and set it over the masa. I smooth the masa out using the plastic wrap to make it as smooth as possible. "Leave enough on the edges so we can fold these leaves over, remember," I say. Harlan and Cody nod. Jace wanders over, enthralled with the process. I pull the plastic wrap off and show them the smooth layer of masa just beneath. I take some of the pork from the skillet on the stovetop and then some of the sweet mole and put it on top of the pork. "Always remember to not over-fill. Less is more in this situation." They all nod. Including Jace. I settle the now filled banana leaf on the counter. "Now. The folding. Y'all ready?" They nod. "Fold it toward you, just to halfway, see? The other half away from you. Now the bottom, now the top," I say, lifting up the little green bundle of goodness for viewing.

"Toward you is first," Cody says.

"Exactly," I say.

"Like an envelope," Jace says.

"Right, exactly. Then you put them in this big pot here where we're going to steam them," I say, placing my finished bundle in the pot.

"You don't tie 'em up with something?" Cody asks.

"These banana leaves are big enough so that we don't have to, but if you find it getting away from you just use strips of another leaf as twine, you know? On both ends," I say, using my little bundle as an example.

"But that's only if we mess it up," Cody says.

"Right," I say, with a smile.

"So we don't want to be doing that," he says.

"Right," I say.

"Let's do this," Harlan says, walking to the front of the assembly line. Harlan takes a banana leaf and holds it next to the open flame and the leaf softens. He moves to the masa, puts a heaping spoonful on the leaf, and grabs a piece of plastic wrap.

"The only thing this stuff ever sticks to is itself," Harlan says, fighting with the plastic wrap.

"You made it look so easy," Cody says. I can't help but smile.

"It's like getting a linoleum bubble out, you know? Smooth it out," Jace says, doing the motions with his hands as well. Harlan watches him and turns around and tries again.

"There it is," Cody says, as Harlan lifts away the plastic wrap victoriously. Harlan gives him a wide smile.

"Now the filling," I say, pointing to the two skillets. Harlan spoons in the right amount and pauses before he has to fold.

"Toward you is first," Cody says, his hands doing the motion as well. Harlan nods.

"Toward you, away from you, bottom, then the top," Harlan narrates his folding. He flips the little green bundle over and there it is.

"You did it!" I say, patting him on the back.

"Well, all right there. Look at that!" Cody says, beaming at the finished tamale.

"Well, looka there," Jace says.

"Ha, well look at that," Harlan says, flipping the little bundle over again and again.

"Now, put it in the pot for steaming. Cody? You ready?" I ask.

"As I'll ever be," Cody says, grabbing a banana leaf. Jace meanders back over to his chair and newspaper.

Cody stumbles through his first tamale, but gets it sooner than he thought he would. We move and work, keeping pace like an old waltz. Weaving in and out we soon find that it works better to stay at one station and just pass the tamale down the line. I, of course, end up at the masa-smoothing station. In no time we've got our pot ready to start steaming.

"How's the cabrito coming?" I ask Cody as we put the lid on the tamale pot.

"Good . . . I think. I mean, I don't know, Chef," Cody says, walking over to his cabrito.

"Have you tasted it?" I ask.

"No, Chef," Cody says.

Everyone's quiet.

"You know she's going to make you taste it," Jace says, from behind his paper. We all break out laughing. Cody takes a fork and spears a tiny piece of cabrito. He puts it in his mouth, wincing dramatically with his eyes closed, and chews.

"It's good! It just—," Cody starts.

"Tastes like chicken?" Harlan finishes.

We all can't help but laugh. I hear the kitchen door click open as our laughter subsides. Shawn walks into the kitchen.

"Smells good in here," he says, scanning the room.

"Thank you," I say, happy he's here. Can I be here without him?

"Y'all have a little over an hour, so I just wanted to see how you were doing," Shawn says.

"Good . . . good," I say, my eyes flicking over to the clock on the wall. I can't believe we have only an hour. I watch Harlan and Cody come to the same realization.

"Okay, I'll be back then," Shawn says.

"And I'll have your supper ready by four fifteen," I say.

"I'm looking forward to it," he says. Shawn walks out of the kitchen and when the door closes we scatter immediately.

"Cody, start on that ensalada. Harlan, how's that salsa coming?" Cody goes over to his station and starts peeling the citrus and chopping the apples and the beets. I stir the Mexican rice and the pinto beans de olla that we made earlier today. The cabrito is ready to go and the handmade corn tortillas I found at a local market taste perfect. Harlan watches the tamales as he makes his salsa.

I start in on the churro dish.

"Chef, we've got ten minutes," Cody says, walking over as he finishes his salad. My churros are bubbling in the deep fryer, the Mexican hot chocolate sits steaming in a mug next to the ramekin of cajeta that Cody is eyeing. Harlan grabs the tray and a couple of plates. He sets them on the counter and walks over to us. There is a reverence to his actions. I feel the emotion begin to bubble up as the clock ticks down. I pull the churros from the deep fryer and place them in the awaiting sugar mixture. Cody rolls the churros through the sugar as I drop one after the other in. He sets the finished products on a towel-lined plate, covering up the growing pile. The churros are done. I walk over to the tray with the Mexican hot chocolate and the ramekin of cajeta. Cody follows me with the plate of steaming churros.

The tray. Once again, we just stand around it. Harlan places a plate in the middle of it. I find myself slowing down or maybe it just feels that way. Cody brings over the skillet with the cabrito, placing a serving on the side of the plate. He dishes out some Mexican rice and the pinto beans. Harlan heats up some corn tortillas and places them on a separate plate, covered with a paper towel. He sets his salsa down next to the tray.

"Chef?" Harlan offers his salsa up for my tasting. I take a fork and take a small bite of the salsa.

"Oh, that's damn good, Harlan. Damn good," I say. Harlan gives me a quick nod, but he can't help but let a smile sneak to Cody. Jace wanders over and I give him a quick taste. He nods his approval. Harlan puts a small bowl of the salsa next to the tortillas on the tray.

"Cody, can you grab the orange soda in the fridge?" I ask. He obliges quickly.

I wrap the churros in parchment paper and place them next to the Mexican hot chocolate and cajeta on the side of the tray. They're still steaming and glistening with a dusting of sugar. I walk over to the last canvas bag and find the Starburst. All six kinds. My hand curls around them. Candy. Re-creating Christmas.

"He's young, isn't he?" I ask, without looking at anyone.

"Yes, Chef," Harlan says.

"I knew it," I say, nodding. Nodding, I put the Starburst on the tray and stand back.

"The tamales!" Cody says, running over to the stove.

Two minutes.

Cody pulls four steaming green bundles from the big pot and hot-potatoes them over to the plate. He has to place them on top of the cabrito and Mexican rice, as there's no more room anywhere on the tray.

One minute.

I look from Harlan to Cody then to Jace. We all join hands once more.

"Bless this food, Lord. Let it transport and remind us all of better times. Let it cleanse and purify. Let it nourish and warm. In it, let us find peace. In Jesus' name, amen," I say.

"Amen," the men say.

The key card clicks and Shawn walks into the kitchen.

"Queenie, it's time."

21

Merry Carole's mac 'n' cheese

He didn't eat the Starburst.

As I sit in my car after the guards' supper and after we cleaned up the kitchen, I can't stop staring at the colorful assortment of candy now littering my passenger seat. Shawn thought I'd want them. I didn't have the heart to tell him that they were, quite frankly, the last thing in the world I'd ever want.

He ate the tamales, the cabrito was gone, the rice and beans peppered the tray as he made soft tacos from the handmade corn tortillas. He dipped the churros in the cajeta and, based on the stain left on the mug, it looks like he actually just drank the Mexican hot chocolate. He picked the pomegranate seeds out of the ensalada and really ate only the citrus. The orange soda cans were crushed and bent. He was angry. Scared. Who knows?

But he didn't eat the fucking Starburst.

I watch the guards pace as dusk turns to darkness. This meal was harder in every way possible. I'm already over an hour late to meet Hudson and yet I don't move. I just need to sit here in the quiet of this car and run through tonight's events. The guards didn't really eat as much as the last time. That could have been about the goat more than anything else, come to think of it, but I don't think so. The Dent boys ate their supper at the table and chairs Shawn brought in for them sometime last week. Shawn stopped Jace before he took the Dent boys back inside the prison and before I escaped out the back door to the safety of Lot B.

"We just got word that your next meal is this Friday," Shawn said. Harlan, Cody, and I just looked at each other. We had ten days between the last two meals.

"That's quick," I said.

"The next two meals you're going to be cooking are for convicts brought in from Huntsville," Shawn said. Harlan and Cody were deathly quiet.

"Is that a thing? Is that bad?" I asked.

"They're usually higher profile," Shawn said, choosing his words carefully.

"Oh," I said.

"Here's your next order," Shawn said, handing me a slip of paper. I took it, but couldn't unfold the paper.

"Do you have the next one? The meal after this?" I asked.

"Why don't we take one meal at a time, Queenie," Shawn said.

"Oh, all right," I said, feeling embarrassed.

"I'm just . . . I know how focused you can be," Shawn said.

"Sure . . . *sure,* and I appreciate that," I said, unfolding the slip of paper. Harlan and Cody crowded around.

Inmate #8JM-31245:
Barbecue, vegetable plate, baked beans, sweet tea, fried
cherry pie, and an apple

I'm almost catatonic as I hold the little slip of paper in my hand now. Harlan, Cody, and I didn't need Shawn to go into what "barbecue" meant. Classic Texas barbecue is a beef brisket, sausage, and ribs. A "vegetable plate" is traditionally a potato salad, raw white onions, and pickles. Not quite what most people would call a healthy vegetable plate, but this is how we do it in Texas.

As I roll down my window, hoping a rare summer breeze will find its way to me, I think about that damn apple. It's the unique, individualized requests that affect me. First it was the Starburst, and now this apple. I'm already winding myself up about being the one who has to choose the last apple this person ever eats. And I can't even bite into it. What if it's mealy? Bruised? Why didn't he just ask for a fried apple pie? I won't have long to obsess about it and I certainly don't need the time to practice or research. I could make barbecue in my sleep. And because this meal is going to take me two days to prepare, I really only have tomorrow off. This is a good thing.

I run Shawn's words through my head over and over again. My next two meals are for high-profile inmates transferred from Huntsville. What does that even mean? Why would they do that? Enough. Just . . . drive, Queenie. Get to the bar and have a well-earned drink. Get to the bar and see Hudson. Everything will be better.

As I drive to Evans, I think about the night ahead. I just want to lose myself and not think about any of this. The Death House. High-profile inmates being shipped in from Huntsville. A lot of things.

I finally pull up to the bar with my mind set. I'll knock back a couple of bourbons and let Hudson take me away fr—

"Hudson?" I ask, realizing I know one of the drunken twosome stumbling from the bar.

"I didn't think you were coming," Hudson says, straightening up. The woman he's draped around catches the hint and gathers herself.

"Clearly," I say, looking from him to the woman. She is *that* woman. The woman you pick up in a bar one night who you couldn't pick out of a lineup the next day. Thin, blond hair, questionable makeup, and a giant neon sign over her head that says you can take her home and never have to call her again.

"Can you excuse us?" Hudson says to the woman, motioning for her to go back in the bar. She stumbles inside.

"You don't know her name, do you?" I ask.

"I think I knew it at one time," Hudson says. That sinking feeling about Hudson rises to the surface. We're all little plastic army men he's moving around some battlefield on his bedroom floor. Objects. Not people. Hudson continues, "You really should have called."

"No, I'm actually glad I didn't," I say, turning back around and heading to my car. I don't need this bullshit.

"So that's it?"

"Yep."

"Is this about the other night? At Delfina's?"

"You mean you don't think stumbling out of a bar with another woman on the same night you're supposed to meet me is enough of a reason for me to take off?" I ask, approaching him.

"Well, a departure yes, but this feels a bit final."

"Does it?"

"Well, yeah."

"Good. Because it is," I say, continuing to my car. Hudson follows.

"I'm only here for the summer, what did you think was going to happen?"

"Shipping off to war, are we?"

"What?"

"You're heading back to Austin, Hudson. To teach. You're acting like this is your last night ashore."

"You being hilarious about this is really inconvenient."

"Then I'll just be on my way."

"I think it's about that guy—that coin-toss guy. I'm a professional, remember?"

"How about you save your condescending, dimestore psychoanalytic bullshit for a time when you don't have Barbie Fucksalot waiting for you." Hudson looks over his shoulder and back at the girl by the bar.

"It doesn't take a fancy degree to know what's going on with people, Queenie," Hudson says, pulling out a cigarette and lighting it. Of course I didn't know he smoked.

"Oh, I get it now."

"Get what?"

"You like to play with your food, don't you?"

"What?"

"When you came at me at Delfina's the other night, I knew something was off about you."

"There's nothing off about me." He takes a drag off his cigarette.

"Sure there is. People are interchangeable to you. I mean, look at this. I wasn't here, you got another one. No harm, no foul." I motion to the other woman, still by the bar.

"That's not—"

"You've got nothing, so you find people to feed off of. To empty.

So you can feel something. And then you go home to your absent, lecherous father and your martyred, shallow mother and tell them tales about what a bad boy you were, hoping they'll finally pay attention to you. See? No fancy degree needed, just like you said," I say, my voice getting calmer and calmer.

"That theory only works if I can add a bit of an addendum."

"What?"

"The trashier the girls the better."

I slap Hudson's face without thinking. He actually looks shocked. He claps his hand on his cheek and his eyes flare momentarily. And then he smiles.

"Watch your fucking mouth," I say, pointing at him. My finger is one inch from his face.

"Oh, did that hit a bit too close to home?"

"You know it did," I say.

"Hey, you guys okay?" The woman stumbles over to us from her perch by the bar. Hudson wraps his arm around her as she tumbles into him.

"You're not as unique as you like to think," I say to Hudson.

"Neither are you," Hudson says, tugging the girl closer. She flicks her cigarette into the gutter.

"He waxes his eyebrows," I say to the woman, pointing at Hudson.

"What?" She tilts her body back and takes a better look at Hudson. He turns away from her and they stumble back into the bar. Hudson doesn't look back.

I climb inside my car and watch as they walk down the pristine Evans street, and past the adorable B and B I will never see the inside of. The Starburst shift and slide on my front seat as I get on the highway and drive toward North Star.

I made a meal for a young man today who was too young to

know any better. At least that's what everyone kept saying during supper. *"Too young to know any better." "He didn't have a chance,"* they repeated. They felt worse about this kid than they did about the first man I cooked for, because they felt he wasn't responsible for his actions. I imagine the family of the store clerk he shot would think differently.

Hudson. I should be angrier. Instead, I can't stop thinking about Everett. I get off the highway and find myself driving through the town square, past Merry Carole's house and on into the hills where Cal and I run every morning. It's black as pitch up here at night. I drive past the Paragon gate and think. I know he inherited some land from his grandparents. I remember us going and taking a look at it. I slow my car to a snail's pace as I try to remember. I turn off the radio and roll down the window. I make a few turns. Wrong ones. Flip a U-turn. Another couple of turns and a few dead ends later and I'm pulling down a long dirt road that I recognize. There it is. At the end of the dirt road. Everett's home.

I shut the lights off like they do in the movies, but it's too late. The porch light comes on and the front door opens. Everett. Arrow is just behind him, barking and wobbling in the doorway. He's calming the old dog and telling him to cool it.

I roll to a stop, finally turning off the car. I don't know why I'm here. My stomach is somewhere in my throat. I collect the Starburst on my passenger seat and crawl out of my car, slamming the door behind me. I can see it in Everett's entire body when he realizes who it is. He walks forward and out onto his porch. He's wearing a white T-shirt and some plaid pajama bottoms and is barefoot. His hair is uncombed and he's wearing glasses. Everything about how unguarded he is right now breaks my heart. Maybe that's why I'm not mad at Hudson. Because the first thing I thought about after driving away from Evans wasn't what I'd lost with Hudson, it was what I'd lost with Everett. Hudson never had a chance. Of course, he knew that.

"I didn't know you wore glasses," I say, walking the apparent nine miles to his house from where I parked.

"Ah, yes. I'm going blind in my old age. I didn't know you knew where I lived," Everett says.

"You showed this land to me once. When you first got it," I say, stepping up onto the porch. Arrow waddles over to me, tail wagging, still half-barking. "Hey, boy . . . look at you. All grown up. That's a good boy." I hold my hand out to let him smell it and he finagles an entire pet out of the opportunity.

"That's right, but you haven't seen the house yet. You brought candy?" Everett asks, stepping aside and gesturing for me to come inside. Arrow launches himself into the house first.

"No, I haven't seen the house. And this is the last-meal candy that I don't know what to do with. He didn't eat it," I say, walking inside Everett's house, holding the handful of Starburst aloft. Everett shuts the door behind me.

Everett's house is not as grand as I would have thought based on the amount of land around it. Arrow waddles over to his dog bed, his feet skidding a bit on the dark hardwood floor. He plops down and sighs, letting his head fall on the cushion, still watching our every move.

"I know. He's getting old," Everett says, walking over to the large gray sectional and shutting off the sports recap playing on the flatscreen TV. The flat screen's positioned over the large fireplace that anchors the far wall. The great room is just that. Great. High ceilings with exposed rafters soaring to and fro. French doors and wood paneling. Warmth and light combined in a way that makes you want to sink into Everett's house with a cup of tea, a good book, and watch the seasons change. This isn't helping the situation.

"He's such a great dog," I say, not knowing where to stand or why I'm here.

"No, he's not," Everett says, looking just as awkward.

"I'm sorry I barged in on you," I say.

"I'm glad you did. Can I get you anything or did you just want to eat last-meal Starburst?" Everett walks through the great room and gestures for me to follow him. I oblige, still clutching the Starburst.

"I don't know why I brought them," I say, walking into his kitchen. Open shelving and a well-used wooden country table invite, but don't overwhelm you. He opens up the refrigerator and pulls two beers out. He cracks them both open and hands one to me. I take a long drink.

"Do you want to talk about it?" he asks, pulling out a chair and sitting down at the table.

"He was a kid. I knew it, too. His last meal was clearly trying to re-create Christmas. And he asked for Starburst, but then he didn't eat them. I'm finding it's those little personal things that are getting to me. The other guy ate the ranch dressing that I just happened to add at the last minute. I mean, what if I hadn't added it?" Everett sets his beer down on the table and reaches over and pries loose the Starburst from my hand.

"I'd heard you were making last meals," Everett says, setting the stack of Starburst down on the table.

"Yeah."

"How's that working out for you?"

"Not good, but good. It's weird, I know, but the part where I'm in that kitchen and we're making this luxurious, once in a lifetime meal and everything has to be perfect—that fits. I don't think I've ever been happier. But it's this. This," I say, motioning to the Starburst.

"Yeah, I can see that being tough."

"Your house is beautiful," I say, looking around.

"Thank you."

"Okay. I'd better head home. Thanks for the beer and for listening," I say, walking over to the trash can to throw my beer bottle away.

"You don't have to go," Everett says, standing.

"Yes, I do." I can't look at him. With his glasses and his messed-up hair. In this house that I can't sink in and stay forever. I shouldn't have come. I shouldn't have seen what it is I can't have. It's better than I could ever have imagined. I grab the handful of Starburst and Everett steps forward.

"Queenie." Everett puts his hand on my arm and it immediately soothes me. I lean into him and close my eyes. I can't look at him or else I'll stay. I breathe. Think clearly. I open my eyes.

"I have to go," I say, forcing out the words. I bend around his body and walk toward the front door. Everett follows.

"What did you mean the other day about knowing how this ends?" I ask, turning away from the door and facing Everett.

"You and me. That's how this ends," Everett says, stepping closer.

"How do you know that?"

"Because it's the only thing that keeps me going."

"But—"

"Did you ever stop to think that I wanted to go with you? That night you left?"

"What?"

"Did you ever consider the possibility that I wanted to leave North Star as much as you did, but couldn't?"

"No."

My simple answer catches Everett off guard.

I continue, "You seem to think I possess some superhero level of confidence or ability to read your mind. I felt rejected and lost right up until I hit that blinking red light at the outskirts of town. I mean, I'd seen the movies. I thought you were going to come running down the street—preferably in the rain—and stop me from leaving," I say, my voice hollow and far away.

"But I didn't."

"No."

"I was waiting for you to burst into that chapel—you know, when they say let him speak now or forever hold his peace. I imagined you saying something like, 'I object!' and then coming down the aisle, taking my hand, and leading both of us out of there."

"But I didn't."

"No."

We're quiet for a long time. Standing in that great room with the weight of our past hanging between us. Arrow snores loudly in the corner.

"I'd really better be getting home. Merry Carole is probably waiting up."

I step forward, hesitating just a bit, and pull him in for a hug. I feel him sigh and then wrap his arms all the way around me, pulling me in even closer. I nestle into his chest as he folds over me. I sigh, the softness of his T-shirt against my cheek.

"It was good seeing you," he says, right into my ear. Low. A whisper.

"You, too." We break apart and I shift the Starburst from one hand to the other.

"And now that you know where I live . . ." Everett trails off. I smile and nod as he opens the door for me and we walk out onto the porch. I walk down the steps and climb back into my car, scattering the handful of Starburst onto the passenger seat once again.

I start up the car and turn on my headlights. They light up Everett standing on that porch. I take a deep breath and turn my car around and make my way back down that long dirt road.

I drive back through North Star in a daze. He wanted me to stop the wedding? So both of us kept waiting for the other one to step in and save us from ourselves. I pull down Merry Carole's driveway, shut my car off, and just sit there for a second. The silence of the car soothes me as the heat builds from the closed windows and my buzzing energy. I grab my knives, leave the Starburst, and walk inside the warmly lit house.

"You're home early," Merry Carole says, sitting on the couch with Cal.

"Yeah," I say, walking toward the kitchen in a daze.

"Have you eaten dinner?" Merry Carole calls from the living room.

"I had lunch," I say from the kitchen.

"There's leftovers in the fridge. I made my macaroni and cheese," Merry Carole says.

"Oh nice," I say, pulling the casserole dish from the refrigerator. I serve myself up some mac 'n' cheese and wait in the kitchen as the microwave spins. Merry Carole walks into the kitchen.

"You okay?" she asks, craning her neck to make sure Cal is still in the living room.

"I may have just slapped Hudson in the face," I say.

"What happened?" Merry Carole asks.

"I was late to the bar and he was already leaving with another woman," I say.

"Oh," Merry Carole says, taken aback.

"But it's fine. He's not—"

"He's not Ev—"

"Well, there's that. But there was something off about him," I say.

"You're not just saying that?"

"No, he had this switch. It's like people became objects really quick. It was weird."

"Is he a sociopath?"

"I don't think so. I don't know—wow, maybe. He started talking to me about victims' families and how they feel this and that happens and what did I think and had I experienced that when my mom was murdered—at Delfina's he was talking like this."

"What? Why would he do that? That's none of his business."

"I know. I think because it's what he's studying he forgot that he just doesn't get to demand that information. He treated me like one of his test subjects."

"That's crazy."

"I'm glad I didn't get any further with him," I say.

"No, it's good that you're completely in love with someone else and therefore incapable of starting up anything new with anyone else. How is . . . everything else?" Merry Carole gives me a quick wink and smiles. I choose not to share with her my little detour to Everett's house right at this particular moment.

"It was a tough one. He was young. And . . . I knew it, you know? I just knew it. He wanted candy, but then he didn't eat it? It was Starburst. Did you know there's like ten thousand flavors of Starburst now? But why wouldn't you eat it? Shawn gave it back to me and . . . what am I supposed to do with it? I don't want to throw it away because . . . I just don't want to throw it away. I don't want to eat it, either, because that just seems particularly gruesome. And if I give them away it's like . . . hey, little girl, here's a dead murderer's candy. Ugh, I don't know. So the candy's in my car and I wish it would just disappear. Then Shawn came in and said my next meal is this Friday and it's barbecue, which means—"

"An all-nighter," Merry Carole finishes.

"Exactly," I say.

"Well, maybe we can make it fun. Invite Fawn and Dee over," Merry Carole says.

"Oh my God, that'd be great," I say.

"Then we'll do that," Merry Carole says. The microwave dings and I pull the dish out and find a fork.

"You were going to tell me something?" I ask.

"I'll tell you later," Merry Carole says, checking the living room once again.

"You're kind of freaking me out," I say, burning my mouth as I try to eat Merry Carole's mac 'n' cheese too soon.

"Don't be. It's good. Trust me," Merry Carole says.

"If the situation were reversed, you'd have me tied up in some torture chamber right now making me talk," I say, eating another bite too soon. My taste buds are now officially burned beyond recognition.

"True," Merry Carole says. Cal walks into the kitchen.

"What are you guys whispering about?" Cal asks, leaning on the breakfast bar.

I look from Merry Carole to Cal and back to Merry Carole.

"Your momma and I were just tal—," I start in.

Merry Carole interrupts me. "Baby boy, I have some big news." I almost choke on my mac 'n' cheese.

"What . . . what is it?" Cal asks, looking from Merry Carole to me.

"Don't look at me, I have no idea," I say. Merry Carole puts her hands on her hips and looks down. She takes a deep breath and steadies herself. Cal and I just wait.

"Momma, what's going on?" Cal asks again. I look at Merry Carole.

"Honey, Reed and I, you know, Coach Blanchard?" Cal and I nod. Merry Carole continues, "Coach Blanchard and I are . . . well, he proposed. He wants to marry me."

Cal just stands there. Time stops. Merry Carole looks petrified.

"I knew y'all were dating, but I didn't know it had gotten so serious," Cal says.

"You knew we were dating?" Merry Carole sputters. I look like the cat that swallowed the canary.

"Sure. For about a year now, right?" Cal asks. Merry Carole just nods. She's starting to lose it. I take her hand, squeezing it tightly.

"I'm sorry I didn't tell you, sweetie. I didn't know how I felt about him and I didn't—"

"How *do* you feel about him?" Cal asks.

"I love him," Merry Carole manages.

"Then you should marry him," Cal says.

Merry Carole begins to cry, which quickly turns into happy hysterics. As do my tears. Cal comes around the breakfast bar and sweeps her up into a hug.

"Why are you crying? Momma? Why are you crying?" Cal asks, squeezing her tighter and tighter. The tears run down my cheeks as I watch my sister completely break down. Cal's lip quivers, he's trying hard to be the last one to break. His eyes well up and the tears begin to fall.

"I was so scared to tell you," Merry Carole says.

"Why?" Cal leans down close, wiping her tears.

"Because it's always been just us. You're the best thing that ever happened to me and I never wanted to risk it." Merry Carole takes a hankie out of her robe pocket and blows her nose. She takes a deep breath, but the tears still stream down her face. I am quiet, hysterical, but quiet. Merry Carole squeezes my hand tightly. I sniffle and grab a paper towel, blowing my nose.

"You and Coach Blanchard. Getting married," Cal repeats, almost to himself.

"Yes," Merry Carole says. She looks terrified again as Cal searches her face.

"Aren't you supposed to have a ring?" Cal asks.

"I have it, but told Reed I wouldn't wear it quite yet. He wanted to propose with all you kids around. I want it to be a surprise when you see it," Merry Carole says.

"I like Coach Blanchard," Cal says, trying to figure this all out.

"You do?" Merry Carole asks, her voice cracking.

"Yeah," Cal says, nodding.

"What do you think about us becoming a family?" Merry Carole asks.

"I think I'd like that," Cal says. His voice is a hopeful whisper.

"You would?" Merry Carole squeaks out, the tears starting again.

"Yeah," Cal says.

"I would, too," Merry Carole says, pulling him in for a hug.

I just stand there and watch, clapping my hand over my mouth and trying not to cry too much. Merry Carole holds Cal tightly in her arms. She smooths his hair and assures him it's going to be okay as he just nods and lets her comfort him.

"I'm so happy for you," I say as they finally break apart.

"I'm so happy for me!" Merry Carole says, tears still streaming down her face.

"So, maybe invite Reed and his girls to our little barbecue," I say, taking another bite of the mac 'n' cheese. Cal leans back on the breakfast bar.

"What little barbecue?" Cal asks.

"We are not inviting those little girls over here so you can serve them murderer meat," Merry Carole says, pulling a glass from the cupboard.

"Murderer meat?" Cal and I break into hysterics.

"You know what I mean," Merry Carole says, pouring herself some water.

"Honey, they don't have to know who some of the meat is being cooked for. We'll grill hamburgers and hot dogs while the murderer meat smokes away," I say. Merry Carole is thinking. Cal and I wait.

"Fine. This might be a good thing. Have everyone together," Merry Carole says, looking at Cal. He smiles, but he's still mulling this over.

"I'm off to bed. Early day tomorrow . . . oh wait. Do I . . . do I tell Coach Blanchard I know? Do I still call him Coach Blanchard? Or . . . Reed? Or Mr. Blanchard? . . . Or . . . " Cal trails off, not daring to suggest he call Reed Dad.

"I'll let him know you know, sweetie. You can ask him about it if you want. We'll do it together," Merry Carole says.

"I think I can talk to him about it," Cal says.

"We can talk to him together, if you want," Merry Carole says.

"No, ma'am. I think I want to do it on my own," Cal says.

"Okay," Merry Carole says, walking over to him and putting her arm around his shoulder.

"Night night. Aunt Queenie, see you tomorrow morning for our run? West is meeting us at the bottom of the hill. So be ready," Cal says.

"Yes, sir," I say, already tired. Cal gives Merry Carole one last hug and walks into his bedroom, closing the door behind him. Merry Carole walks back into the kitchen. I just stare at her.

"What?" Merry Carole says, opening up another cupboard. This time she pulls out something a bit harder than water. Bourbon.

"I will refrain from saying I told you so about Cal knowing far more than you give him credit for because I have to ask— how long have you been holding on to that?" I ask, gladly getting out two glasses for us.

"Days. It's been terrible."

"Terrible?" I ask. Merry Carole pours us each a glass and we clink glasses before drinking. I lean back against the counter.

"I just saw this—" Merry Carole starts crying again. She pulls her hankie out of her robe pocket and wipes her nose. She continues, "I just didn't think I got to be happy." Her body shakes as she cries, tears streaming down her face.

"Oh sweetie," I say, pulling her in for a hug.

We hold each other in that kitchen for minutes, hours . . . who knows? We hold each other because maybe we finally believe that even we get to be happy.

And it feels terrifying.

22

One Dairy Queen double-dip swirl

Cal is quiet the next morning as we get ready to go on our run. I start a thousand conversations with him to which I get only one-word answers. Even though he'll quicken the pace, I'm thankful West will be joining us. Maybe he'll get Cal to talk. I slept like shit last night, tossing and turning. The meal. Those damn Starburst still sitting in my car. Hudson. Everett. And then I thought about Merry Carole and Reed and felt cautiously happy again.

Cal's quietly stretching and I'm loudly pinwheeling just outside Merry Carole's salon.

"You're going to have to talk to me, you know. I'll wear you down. See, people around here never talk about anything and that's kind of one of the reasons I left because I looooove to ta—"

"Aunt Queenie, what are you doing?"

"I don't know," I say, pulling my leg up behind me. We are quiet again. I can't stand it. I launch in again, "Are you scared? Do you think it's going to change stuff? I mean, what are you thinking?" I stand over him arms akimbo, brow impossibly furrowed, demanding that this poor fifteen-year-old boy talk about his feelings before it's even dawn. What kind of monster am I?

"It's just weird is all," Cal says, fiddling with his watch.

"Weird how?"

"It's like when you see one of your teachers in the grocery store, you know? You don't recognize them when they're not in their place. And it's not good or bad or scary or any of that, it's just . . . " Cal trails off. He shrugs.

"Different," I finish.

"Yeah. I mean, are we gonna live with them? Are they gonna live with us? Are those two little girls my sisters now? Are they going to mess with my stuff? And—" Cal stops. Abruptly. He puts his hands on his hips and looks off into the early morning quiet.

"What?"

"I just never had a dad before," Cal says, looking back at me. He continues, "But what if I don't . . . what if I don't do it right, you know?" Cal asks.

"Do what right, baby?" I ask, not moving too quickly to comfort him. I don't want to spook him.

"You know, be a son or whatever," Cal says.

"Honey, anyone would be proud to call you his son," I say, trying to keep it together.

"My real dad wasn't even proud to call me his son until I could throw a football. I mean, Wes is all right now—he's cool enough. But what if Coach Blanchard is the same? I mean, what if I get injured? What if I don't get into UT on a football scholarship? Will they . . . will they still care?"

"Honey, grown-ups can be just as screwed up as kids," I say.

"Oh, I know," Cal says, laughing.

"And your daddy loves you, it was just complicated in the beginning," I say.

"Complicated," Cal repeats.

"I know that sounds like a cop-out and I'm certainly not going to make excuses for Wes McKay, but—"

"But what?"

"This is going to work out, Cal. Things work out sometimes. And you're one of the good guys," I say.

"You know how you just—I don't know." Cal fidgets with his watch again.

"What?"

"I don't want to get my hopes up is all." Cal looks right at me. As pointedly as a fifteen-year-old boy can. Those clear blue eyes could cut through bone. I take a deep breath as I hear my exact words propelled back at me.

"It's okay to hope," I say. Cal's face softens. He looks down at the ground. Blond bangs falling into his eyes, chin resting on his chest, Cal allows himself the smallest, most private smile. From ear to ear. He looks up at me, his eyes damp and his jaw tensing and nods. I watch him as he lets the idea of hope wash over him. He sniffles, swipes at his eyes. He takes a deep breath, seeming to shake off the previous conversation.

"You ready?" Cal asks, beeping his watch. He sniffles again.

"Yeah," I say, smiling.

Right on the outskirts of town, West is waiting for us. He's pulling one of his legs back in a stretch and when he sees us he begins hopping in place, wriggling his arms around. As if he's going to launch himself into outer space. I'm screwwwwwwed.

"You're going to need to lower your expectations of today's run, sweetheart," I say as we approach this jumping bean of a boy. West just laughs and the two boys grunt an early morning hello to each other. West falls in with us as we leave the residential area and head into the hills just beyond North Star.

The early morning haze covers the ground as we climb the hill leading up to Paragon. My stomach is tied in knots at the thought of seeing Everett and Arrow meandering along on their morning walk. As our syncopated footfalls carry us up up up, I think about the numbness I felt when I was gone. Shutting down is easier than this. Long looks and proclamations of love only to say, "Okay, catch you later . . ." Who does that? Now it seems so endlessly masochistic with a nice twist of stupidity.

We break the rise of the hill and Paragon Ranch comes into sight. I can see Everett and Arrow walking toward the road. I actually do need a bit of time to rest. West's pace is almost double what Cal and I usually do. Yeah. That's why I'm stopping.

"Can we take a second?" I ask, lurching over to put my hands on my knees and catch my breath. West and Cal slow to a stop. Cal is used to it and walks over to the low fence and he and West start doing push-ups. Everett and Arrow amble over to the fence. Everett's cowboy hat is shielding his eyes from the morning sun, but even with that his right eye is crinkling up with that crooked smile.

"I'm dying," I wheeze.

"The key is to walk with an aging dog and not try to run with two of North Star's top athletes," Everett says, hitching his leg up onto the lower plank of the fence.

"I'm seriously going to have a heart attack," I say. Arrow flops onto the ground. Bored with standing, clearly.

"Is that the Ackerman boy?"

"You mean the 'Ackerman' boy," I say, putting giant air quotes around Ackerman.

"Wow, they just look embarrassingly alike, don't they," Everett says, shaking his head.

"He's a sweet kid, though, astonishingly," I say.

"Yeah, how'd that happen?" Everett says.

"That's what I said," I say, finally starting to catch my breath.

Cal and West walk over to where Everett and I are.

"Mr. Coburn," Cal says, extending his hand.

"How're you doing, son?" Everett says, taking his hand and shaking it.

"We're just waiting around for Aunt Queenie here," Cal says.

"I'm dying," I say.

"Everett Coburn," Everett says, extending his hand to West.

"West Ackerman," West says, shaking Everett's hand.

"You guys are going to have quite the season," Everett says.

"Didn't you play football?" Cal asks.

"I did, but I wasn't as good as you guys. I always had to work harder. You know how there's always one kid on the team who's not quiiiite as good as everyone else, but the coach keeps him around because he's 'got heart'?" Everett puts air quotes around the words "got heart."

"Oh definitely," the boys say in unison.

"That was me," Everett says.

"We have one of those this year, too," West says, without irony.

"You ready, Aunt Queenie?" Cal asks.

"Yeah, I guess," I say, trying to stand up straight.

"It's all downhill anyway," West says.

"See you at the opener," Everett says.

"Yes, sir," the boys say in unison.

We say our good-byes and begin running down the hill and away from Everett and Arrow, who has yet to get up. I can hear

Everett trying to convince him to get a move on. The old dog isn't buying it.

After I shower I head up to the salon clutching my cup of coffee. I open the front doors to find Merry Carole standing nose to nose with Whitney McKay. It's odd seeing Whitney so soon after leaving West. Once again, we're all shocked that he's such a good kid given his . . . origins. Dee and Fawn are begging the pair to back off and take it easy. I set my coffee cup down quickly and jump into the center of the two women and push them apart.

"That's enough," I say. Whitney jerks forward like she's going to make some last-minute jab at Merry Carole. "I won't hesitate to punch you in the face, Whitney. You know I'll do it, so govern yourself accordingly." I wave her off as she backs away immediately. "Now what's going on in here?"

"This bitch told me that my ring was a cubic zirconia piece of trash that Reed bought just so he could . . . I can't even say it!" Merry Carole is fuming. "I wasn't even supposed to be wearing it . . . I was just showing it to Dee and Fawn," Merry Carole says.

"Why didn't you just throw her ass out?" I ask, as if Whitney isn't in the room.

"It just kind of got away from them," Dee says, stepping into the fray.

"I was just repeating what I heard, Merry Carole," Whitney says.

"It's a lie and you know it. Right? You know it's not true. Whitney?" I ask, stepping forward. This has gone on long enough.

"I don't—"

"You didn't hear anything of the kind. So what's this all about then? And trust me, your minions aren't here and you're outnumbered. We are not above locking you in this salon until you talk," I say, motioning for Fawn to lock the salon door.

"You can't lock me in," Whitney says.

"You're the one who started this fight, it's not our fault if we have to finish it," I say. Merry Carole pulls her hankie from her apron pocket. She dabs at her mascara as she waits for Whitney to speak. I sigh. I shift my weight as Whitney's eyes dart around the room. "The truth shall set you free, Whitney." My twang is deep and thick. The clichéd words have the desired effect. Whitney rolls her eyes and lets loose with the smallest scoffing laugh. I step forward. She flinches.

"Fine. Fine," Whitney says, poufing out her hair just so. I turn around and realize that she's looking at herself in the mirror like a three-year-old.

"Um . . . Whitney? Yeah, we all know why you pick on Merry Carole, so . . . this will be one of those teaching moments where this is more about you learning how to talk about your feelings than actually enlightening any of us," I say.

"Oh, y'all know why I pick on Merry Carole?"

"Yes," we all say in unison.

"Well, then, why do I have to say it? I mean, can I at least have some coffee or something?" Whitney says, looking around the salon desperately, as if she's crawled through the desert for a week without a drink. Dee just sighs and walks back to the kitchenette.

"But don't say nothing till I get back," Dee says, calling out from the kitchenette. We all stand in silence. Whitney studies her fingernails and I settle into one of the salon chairs. I catch Merry Carole looking at her engagement ring.

"Hurry up, Dee," Fawn yells back to the kitchenette.

"All right, all right. I'm coming," Dee says, presenting Whitney with a mug of steaming coffee.

"Bless your heart, thank you so much," Whitney says, settling onto the bench by the hair dryers in the middle of the salon.

"Our first client is in thirty minutes, Whitney. So . . . ," Merry Carole says.

"Fine. Merry Carole was always so pretty. And then when she and Wes had their whole thing, well, it just did me in," Whitney says, not looking at anyone.

"And?" I urge.

"And nothing," Whitney says.

We wait.

"Honey, we all know," I say.

"You all know about what?" Whitney asks, her face draining of all color.

"West is an amazing kid, you know," I say.

"I know," Whitney says, her voice cracking. Whitney's entire demeanor changes and she just melts at the mention of West.

"Does he know?" Merry Carole asks, stepping forward.

"My parents won't let me tell him," Whitney says.

"Do you have to do everything your parents tell you to do?" Fawn asks.

"Well, yes," Whitney says, pulling a hankie from her purse and dabbing at her mascara with it.

"You're a grown woman, Whitney," Dee says.

"I know that. I just don't want to scare him or freak him out after these years of him thinking I'm his older sister."

"Are you sure he doesn't suspect anything?" I ask.

"I've come to find out that people know a lot more than you think they do," Merry Carole adds, Cal's nonchalant admission to knowing of her and Reed's relationship still thick in the air.

"But that's not really true, is it? I mean, look at poor Laurel," Whitney says, accompanied by a cartoonish reaction that wishes she could scoop all of those words back up and shove them right down her throat.

"What about poor Laurel?" I ask, stepping closer.

"Oh, you know," Whitney says, blowing on her coffee. "This has three sugars in it, right, Dee?" Dee rolls her eyes and nods that it does. "Bless your heart."

"Don't try to change the subject. What about poor Laurel?" I ask.

"You mean about her marriage to Everett?" Merry Carole prompts.

"Why they never had kids?" Fawn fishes.

"Well, yeah . . . I mean, Arabella did a real number on Everett after Felix had that little scare," Whitney says.

"What little scare?" I ask, trying not to sound too anxious.

"He had a stent or a shunt or something . . . something with an *a*?"

"An angioplasty?" Dee asks.

"Yeah, that's it."

"What does that have to do with them getting married?" Merry Carole asks.

"Arabella all but blamed Everett. Said Felix was worried that if something happened to him, there'd be nobody to take his place."

"Why did Everett need to be married to take over Paragon?" Dee asks.

"They're horse breeders. All they do is think about pedigree and bloodlines. And Arabella was worried about Everett not marrying the right kind of woman. No offense," Whitney says.

"None taken," I say.

"I remember Momma telling me that Arabella went the whole nine. Made a big show of it. She took Everett down to the hospital, and with Felix lying in the bed, all the tubes and cables or whatever hanging all over him, she begged Everett to do the right thing so Felix could . . . well, she basically said so Felix could get better . . . so that he wouldn't die. What would you have done?"

"I would have married Laurel," I say. We all stand there staring at Whitney. Maybe this town can keep a secret after all. Well, until Whitney gets hold of it anyway.

"See? You guys don't know everything," Whitney says.

"Obviously," I say, barely able to speak.

"Whitney, don't you think West deserves to hear it from you?" Merry Carole asks.

"Hear what?" Whitney asks. We all just stand there. "Oh. *That,*" she says, deflating.

"On the off chance that he's heard even one bit of the rumor?" I ask. Whitney crumples in her chair. It's dramatic and kind of ridiculous. I swear I catch her looking at her reflection, although this is probably the first time she's talked about this in years.

"You can handle your business any way you want, but taking it out on Merry Carole has to stop," I say.

"I'm not the only one, you know," Whitney says, sniffling.

"Oh, I know," I say.

"So—"

"You stop. They stop," I say.

"You know Cal really likes West. It's a shame they don't know they're kin," Merry Carole says.

I can see the idea of Cal and West, and moreover the Ackermans and the Wakes, being family ruffle Whitney. But then something kicks in. Her face calms and she resolves herself to the task at hand. That's the piece my mom never had. Whitney is going to do this because it's the right thing to do for West.

23

Hamburgers, hot dogs, potato salad, homemade potato chips, lemonade, and a Texas sheet cake

I do my rounds. The butcher. The farm stand. The farm where I buy fresh eggs. I found a local apple farm just over the hill and if the perfect apple isn't in this bag, I don't know where it is. I am running myself ragged so I don't have to think about Everett being trotted down to that hospital where Felix lay dying while Everett's own mother tells him that he's basically the cause of it. I slam my hand on the kitchen counter.

After my morning run with Cal and West, I prep the wood and get the brisket in the smoker early Thursday morning. I stack and settle the wood, pondering the idea that Arabella Coburn and BJ Wake are a lot more alike than I had previously thought. I haven't been able to even look at Everett since I found out. Why didn't he tell me? Of course he wouldn't tell me. That's so him. Shit, that's so us. Going through this stuff and thinking we needed to shoulder it all ourselves.

I set up my station: My barbecue sauce, my sopping brush, meat thermometers, the works. It's supposed to be close to 104 degrees out here today, so I also bought a pretty good–size kiddie pool. I catch a glimpse of myself: drinking my morning coffee in a pair of cut-off jeans and a tank top, filling up a plastic kiddie pool with the garden hose. I am the picture of class and good breeding. Momma would be so proud.

"So I'm telling Reed and the girls to be here by . . ." Merry Carole trails off.

"We want it to cool down some, so I'm thinking seven to seven thirty?"

"That sounds fine; the girls usually get to bed around eight, so we can always set them up in my bed right inside," Merry Carole says, closing the door behind her and walking out into the backyard.

Merry Carole's backyard is a testament to what one woman can coax her fifteen-year-old son into doing. The lawn is mowed within an inch of its life and the flora and fauna around the surrounding fence consist of overgrown shrubs and bushes. I've set the smoker up in the back of the yard where there's a concrete slab; no need to set this place on fire. The kiddie pool sits in the middle of the lawn, much to Merry Carole's displeasure. The patio is furnished with a lovely table and chairs that'll do nicely for tonight's festivities, although if the heat doesn't break we might have to eat inside.

"Honey, I don't think I even know these girls' names. You just always call them 'the girls,'" I say, turning the hose off and curling it back up.

"Oh right. Amelia is six and Rose is four. I bought them these little dresses for the opening game? Black and yellow, of course. The girls really liked them. Even Reed's ex-wife said she was happy I was . . . you know, when she came to pick them up for the weekend. She congratulated us, said the dresses were cute. I just . . . Queenie, I have always wanted little girls," Merry Carole says, her face a mixture of terror and excitement. I've been seeing that a lot lately.

"Are you okay?" I ask.

"Sure."

"Honey." Merry Carole looks inside the house.

"He's at practice," I say, now seemingly knowing Cal's schedule better than Merry Carole.

"We had dinner over there last night, you remember?"

"Sure. Did everything go okay?" I ask.

"It went fine. Better than fine. It was . . . perfect. Too perfect. Everyone was on their best behavior and I just felt . . . Cal was sitting there like he'd never even met Reed, when I know for a fact that Reed had been yelling at him not two hours before about letting go of the ball earlier. Cal hangs on to that ball way too long. Thinks because he's quick he can just hang out in the pocket for hours. I just want to, you know, get past all the niceties, I guess," Merry Carole says, sitting down on one of her patio chairs.

"Yeah, well, wouldn't we all." I walk over and sit down next to her.

"I hope today they can loosen up, you know? Remember that we actually know each other."

"Tell them to bring their swimming suits. They can play in the little pool," I say.

"They are not going to play in that dopey little pool."

"If you bring those children over here to this house and they see this dopey little pool and don't have their swimming suits, you're going to have some naked children on your hands," I say.

"Fine, but it may just be too hot," Merry Carole says.

"We'll cross that bridge when we come to it," I say as the temperature rises. I continue, "Have y'all set a date?"

"What?"

"You and Reed? Have you set a date?" I ask.

"Oh . . . I don't know."

"You don't know?"

"I know we don't want anything big." Merry Carole is acting downright shifty.

"So something small. Like how small?"

"Queenie, it's not going to be in the next few weeks, so I don't even know if you're going to be here." She fixes her gaze on me and doesn't let go. A raised eyebrow only accentuates her doubt at my staying.

"Honey, I would stay for your wedding," I say, standing. I walk over to the smoker and fidget with my station. Shifting the bowl one inch to the right, waving away a few flies.

"Dee says she talked to you about Momma's shack."

"She did."

"And?"

"I can't say I haven't thought about it," I say.

"You can't say you haven't thought about it? What does that even mean?"

"I've never really thought about having my own restaurant until lately. Making these recipes, having a kitchen of my own—it's definitely making me think."

"It's our land, Queen Elizabeth. This house and that land are the only things we own and that land is yours if you want it."

"Mine?"

"Well, it's ours, but if you stay you can live on it, work on it. Have it."

"Why . . . why would you just—"

Merry Carole stands and walks over to me. As she gets closer, I can see her close her eyes and just inhale. The hickory smoke is signaling that the Wakes are back in business.

"You seem happy," Merry Carole says, her voice easy and calm.

"If I stayed, I would have to deal with Everett," I say. Out loud.

For the first time. I hate that he's my reason—always is my reason—for running away from North Star.

"Yes, you would."

"I didn't know any of that stuff that Whitney was talking about," I say.

"Neither did I."

"I just don't know what else I can do. I don't know how to make this work. I don't know if I can be here and not turn into this crazy person who just gazes at him longingly and sighs," I say.

"You do do a lot of sighing."

"I nearly hyperventilated the other day, for crissakes," I say.

"Cal loves having you. I love having you. You can't tell me that you're not having fun catching up with Fawn and Dee?"

"No, they're great."

"And isn't it time we concentrated on that rather than what Piggy Peggy thinks?"

I look at her. Purposefully.

Merry Carole continues, "Fine, *fine*. I'm totally full of shit." She laughs. And laughs.

"Yes, you are," I say.

"But me not telling people about Reed is not the point of this conversation, Queen Elizabeth."

"And are you going to wear the engagement ring outside this house?"

"I am certainly thinking about it," Merry Carole says. I can't help but laugh. Merry Carole continues, "I want you to think about staying and doing something with our land. You can't work at that prison forever, so if you want to stay, that could be a great option."

"Honey, I think about that plot of land and I just get—"

"Emotional?"

"Overwhelmed. I feel claustrophobic just thinking about walking back in there. When I met Dee at the bar, I stood there staring at that black space where the shack used to be and I just froze," I say, trying to steady my breathing. I continue, "I was stuck in that shack almost every day after school. I never thought a person could be ignored in such a tiny space. No matter how long I spent in that shack with Momma, it was always the same. I was a means to an end just like everyone else."

"She's gone now. She can't ignore us anymore. She can't use us anymore. There are no ghosts on that land, trust me. All I'm saying is that you love to cook. You apparently love to cook Texas food and I can attest to the fact that you're damn good at it. Why let Mom win again? Why not open up your own place? You said yourself that you love having your own kitchen."

"I do. I love it."

"Honey, you belong here. This is your home, Queen Elizabeth."

"I just don't know."

"Do you remember that first morning after you got here? You kept asking where you could get a cup of coffee even though you had a cup right in front of you?" Merry Carole asks.

"Yeah," I say.

"Drink the coffee that's right in front of you, Queen Elizabeth."

"It just all seems too close, you know?" I say, still feeling trapped.

"It's good to be close. Maybe take a walk over there after church on Sunday and look at it with fresh eyes. Can you promise me that?"

"Yes, ma'am," I say.

"I'm going to ask if you did, and I always know when you're lying, Queen Elizabeth," Merry Carole says.

"I know," I say.

"Okay then," Merry Carole says, kissing me on the cheek. She continues, "I've got Grandma Ackerman's color in ten minutes, I'd better head over. But I'll check in every now and again, and you can count on us around seven." Merry Carole blows me a kiss and goes back into the house, closing the sliding door behind her.

I walk over and stand in the kiddie pool, wiggling my toes in the cold water. The temperature is already climbing and it's not even eight AM. I sip my coffee and think about being close to someone. I spent my life thinking about love and closeness in the context of Mom. Loving Mom felt like running after a train that never stopped. Then I started defining love by what it felt like with Everett. Loving Everett felt like dunking my head in a bucket of ice and then setting myself on fire. Over and over again. Over and over.

But loving Merry Carole? Tears spring immediately to my eyes as I think of the life I've shared with her. Loving Merry Carole is the best of everything. I'll walk over after church. But she's deluding herself if she thinks there are no ghosts on that land.

I spend the day basting and trying to stay out of the heat. I watch terrible daytime television and run up to the salon when I can. I find Cal's cowboy hat on the bookshelf and decide to wear it. I need the shade it offers. If nothing else, it's designed exceptionally well. This is what I tell myself as I get another glimpse of myself in the sliding glass doors. Smoking brisket, standing in a kiddie pool in cut-off jeans, a tank top, and a broke-down cowboy hat.

This is you. This is now.

"At least I don't have a piece of straw hanging out of my mouth," I mutter, tearing my gaze away from my reflection. I've got the hot dogs and hamburgers in the kitchen, ready to go. I figure Reed can handle those on the little grill I'll get ready for him so we can eat sooner rather than later. I'll focus on the meat (or murderer meat as Merry Carole likes to call it) in the smoker. I also did a potato salad, some homemade potato chips, and I'll make a Texas sheet cake later on. I hope the kids will get a kick out of that.

As seven PM nears I hop in the shower and try to wash the smoke and heat off of me to no avail. My eyes are bloodshot and I can't stop coughing. I put my cut-off jeans back on and find another tank top that's not stained with barbecue sauce (yet). Once the salon closes, Merry Carole fusses around the house, cleaning and dusting. Cal takes a shower and is still . . . off. Not himself. And I get it. He just needs some time, but we all can't help but worry.

At seven, the guests arrive.

"So let me get this straight. You're smoking a brisket and we're having hot dogs?" Pete asks. Fawn shushes him and tells him the brisket is for "my job." She actually does giant air quotes around "my job."

"I'm doing sausage and ribs, too," I say, with a wink.

"Now you're just being cruel," Pete says, bending over to pull a beer from the cooler. Fawn and Pete settle in around the table. Merry Carole has the fans going and a big swamp cooler set up so the temperature is somewhat comfortable. Of course, all bets are off by the smoker. Which is where I am.

Shawn and Dee arrive with their brood. The boys are wearing eight coats of sunscreen and swimming trunks. Dee is overloaded with canvas bags filled with dry clothes, toys, hats, and plastic bags filled with goldfish crackers. The boys clutch their special swimming towels to their chests as they file out onto the patio like ducklings. Merry Carole has suggested that if the pool looks scary to the boys, we can also just turn on the sprinklers. The boys eye them both. Shawn makes his way back to me as the boys walk over to the kiddie pool. They circle it suspiciously.

"This is for tomorrow then?" Shawn asks.

"Yes, sir," I say.

"Smells great," he says.

"Thank you," I say.

"So you all set?"

"Yeah, of course."

"There might be a bit more of a crowd tomorrow, but you won't see much of it," he says.

"Why would there be a crowd?"

"Like I said, the next two meals you're making are for higher-profile inmates, so with that comes the media and the people with the signs and the candles," Shawn says.

"Oh right," I say. "Of course."

"Don't you worry about that, though," Shawn says, his eyes going from me to the boys. Merry Carole has turned on the sprinklers and the boys are running through the cold spray and into the kiddie pool as their grand finish. Shawn smiles as he watches them.

"So when's your last day?"

"Oh . . . right. Dee said she was going to tell you."

"I hope you don't mind—"

"No, no . . . I'm just so used to keeping it a secret."

"Do the other guards know?"

"Yes."

"Who's going to be captain?"

"Big Jim. He's been there the longest. They'll bring in a new guard to take his place on the leg. They'll do fine," Shawn says, his eyes floating back to his boys. The smile returns.

"So when's your last day?"

"Third week in August," Shawn says.

"That soon?"

"Not soon enough, if you ask me."

"I'm happy for you," I say.

"Hopefully, you'll be right behind me."

"I'm thinking you're probably right," I say.

The sliding glass door opens and Reed and his two girls walk through. They meander out onto the patio while Reed closes the door behind him. The little girls stop and wait for him. They stick close.

"There you are!" Merry Carole says, walking over to Reed and the girls. They brighten up at the sight of her. Thank God. She crouches down in front of them and they lunge into her with hugs and stories of their day. Everyone else at the party may as well not be here.

Merry Carole continues, "Hey, y'all, I don't know if you know Reed's little girls? This is Amelia and this is Rose." The two girls stand there in their pink bathing suits, all little bellies and chubby legs. Their silken blond hair is done up in two little ponytails, and I find myself impressed with Coach Blanchard's ponytail prowess.

"Hey, y'all," Reed says, waving to everyone.

"Excuse me, Queenie," Shawn says, walking toward the patio. There's football to talk about. The sliding glass door opens again and Cal comes out fresh from the shower. He looks awkward and moves around the patio politely. I can see that he's making a beeline for me. Reed stops him. I can see Cal watching Reed as he speaks, at first apprehensively, but soon enough he relaxes. Reed is talking to him normally. Cal's shoulders sink down and I can see his hands come out of his pockets as he begins using them to gesture. Cal throws his head back and laughs. Reed leans forward and continues talking through Cal's laughter. I immediately look to Merry Carole. She is riveted. She looks over at me and just . . . smiles. I can see her breathe for the first time in days. Reed gets Cal to help him on the grill and they spend the next hour or so talking and serving up hot dogs and hamburgers. Amelia and Rose have taken quite a fancy to Dee's boys and now all five of them are running through the sprinklers and leaping into the kiddie pool for their big finish.

I bring out the potato salad, the homemade potato chips as Reed and Cal bring over the hot dogs and hamburgers. We shift and squeeze, but we're all finally seated around the table. I look at Merry Carole.

"Y'all, I'd like to say grace, if that's okay?" Everyone nods and agrees. The children eye the food hungrily. I hold my hands out; on one side it's taken by Cal and on the other by Rose. As my hand curls around the tiny four-year-old's hand, I can't help but let it affect me. She looks up at me with these giant blue eyes, still in her swimsuit, her hair slicked back from the water. And she smiles. Beautiful. Open. She pulls her hand (and mine with it) up to her nose and scratches it. Another smile.

Come on.

Merry Carole speaks, "Thank you, Lord, for the feast you have provided us with and for your continued love and guidance. Thank you for blessing me with a strong and healthy boy any mom would be proud of. Thank you, Lord, for the friends and family who have gathered here today. Thank you for sprinklers and hot dogs on a summer day. In Jesus' name, amen," Merry Carole finishes, her eyes fluttering open as the tears start to come.

"Amen," we all say together. Everyone begins to pass around food. Rose has yet to let go of my hand. I curl my fingers tighter and resolve to dine one-handed this evening.

It is a loud, raucous dinner. Hooting and hollering and arguing about football. Rose finally decided she needed the use of her other hand somewhere around her second hot dog. I excuse myself and walk inside in search of the Texas sheet cake. Merry Carole and Reed follow me.

"We thought we could make the announcement with the cake," Merry Carole says as Reed takes a bottle of champagne and a bottle of sparkling cider out of a grocery sack.

"Oh, that's perfect. Do y'all want to carry the cake out?" I ask.

"No, you go on ahead, Queenie. It looks really good," Reed says, twisting the metal cage off the top of the champagne.

"Oh, don't pop it in here. I'm sure the girls will love to see it,"

Merry Carole says, her hand resting on his arm. He melts at her touch. He looks from her hand to her face and lights up as she smiles at him. He's such a stoic man usually that seeing him so affected by her childlike excitement renders me speechless. Love. The promise of time together.

Reed opens the sliding glass door for Merry Carole and me. I can see Cal take in what's happening. And he smiles. From ear to ear. He looks from his mom and Reed to Amelia and they share this little moment. It's just a small smile and then a recognition that they can't ruin the surprise. I see Amelia straighten up and try to hide her smile in the least covert way possible. Apparently not giving away the big announcement involves telling Rose she needs to clean her face of some of the ketchup. Rose obliges.

I set the cake in the middle of the table and all five children immediately get onto their knees and inch closer to the cake. I sit back down between Rose and Cal.

"We wanted to thank y'all for coming out here tonight. I know it's a weeknight and we've all got an early day tomorrow. It means a lot to us," Merry Carole says, lacing her arm around Reed's waist. Dee takes the napkin from her lap and dabs at her already teary eyes. Fawn just squeezes Pete's hand, looking at Merry Carole and Reed. They can barely contain themselves.

"I'm here to tell you that Merry Carole has made me the happiest man alive by saying she'd finally marry me," Reed says, pulling the engagement ring from his pocket. He clumsily opens the box and with trembling hands kneels down on one knee and reaches up to place the ring on Merry Carole's finger. The crowd goes wild—we're clapping and oohing and awwwwing. Reed stands and kisses a weepy Merry Carole. But before anyone can speak, Reed continues, "And she's given me something—" Reed's voice catches. It's just as much a shock to him as it is to all of us.

"Daddy? What's wrong?" Amelia asks, her little brow furrowed. Dee leans over and comforts Amelia as Rose absently reaches for my hand. I am there and take it once again. I smooth my hand over Cal's back as we all hold back a wave of emotion.

"Nothing, baby girl. I just . . . I thought I knew how much pride a man could feel by being your daddy." Reed can't help but smile as Amelia and Rose sit tall. He continues, "But to think that I now have a family . . ." Reed gets choked up again. There's not a dry eye in the house. He manages one last sentence. "And a son any man would be proud to call his own." The tears stream down our faces as Reed walks over to Cal. Cal stands and is immediately enveloped by Reed. I look up and see Cal close his eyes and then, embarrassed, hide his face in the crook of Reed's neck. Reed puts his hand on the back of Cal's head and smooths his hair, comforting him. I hear Dee sniffle and ask Shawn to pass her her purse. She needs her tissues, she says when the boys ask her why. Fawn just leans on Pete, watching as Cal and Reed hug. I look from Cal and Reed to Merry Carole. She's officially crying, dabbing at her mascara to no avail.

I look over at Rose and she just smiles.

"Cake," she says, lifting up her hand (and mine) to point at the decadence she feels is being ignored in the center of the table.

"Who wants cake?" I ask, to Rose's delight. Reed takes his place next to Merry Carole and they share a kiss only when they think they're not the center of attention. I see Merry Carole whisper "I love you," as they stand together. He wipes her tears and says he loves her, too.

"We'd love some," Dee finally squeaks out, as her boys begin to revolt against all the gushy stuff that's clearly taking time away from the important things in life.

Like cake.

24

Inmate #8JM-31245:
Barbecue, vegetable plate, baked beans, sweet tea,
fried cherry pie, and an apple

I load my canvas bags filled with groceries, other supplies, and the barbecue into my car the next morning after my run with Cal and West. Cal is getting back to his old self, although he's still a bit fragile. From the normalcy of West's conversation, I'm guessing that Whitney hasn't talked to him yet. I hope she does. I trust she will. I saw Everett and Arrow this morning. We made small talk as I wheezed and tried to catch my breath, all the while screaming in my head, "Why didn't you tell me what your mother did?" Instead I just begged for water and told him I'd see him tomorrow.

"You heading out?" Merry Carole says, coming out of her bedroom cinching her robe. Last night's party went on until a little after eight thirty, but with the kids there were baths and bedtimes for all. I, on the other hand, set timers and checked on my brisket all night. I am worn out as I pour coffee into my travel mug and look forward to coming home right after this meal. Pure exhaustion is the only thing that's keeping me from getting melancholy about not driving over to Everett's beautiful home for a drink after.

"Yeah, I just want to get this day over with," I say, twisting the lid tight on my travel mug.

"I'll wait up for you," Merry Carole says. She reaches up to the cabinet for a coffee mug and I catch a glimpse of a sparkle.

"Well, look at that. Are you wearing your engagement ring?" I ask, walking over to her and grabbing her hand.

"Yes," she says, downright defiant. She holds out her hand, finally flashing the diamond proudly. It's a beautiful ring, and more beautiful that she's finally letting herself wear it—even after Whitney's little cubic zirconia dustup the other day.

"And are you going to keep it on outside this house?"

"Yes. And I'm going to meet Cal over at the Homestead for breakfast. Then I might just pop on over to the post office for absolutely nothing at all," Merry Carole says, giddy.

"Damn right you will," I say, the emotion of yesterday still near at hand.

"Okay, you'd better get going. I'll tell you how far Piggy Peggy's mouth dropped open, don't worry. I'll also make sure she knows how you had to dump Hudson for being too clingy, not to worry," she says.

"You're a genius," I say, grabbing my keys off the counter. Merry Carole walks over to the door and opens it for me. She stands aside as I walk out into the morning air.

"I'll be here when you get back," she says, shielding her eyes from the already glaring sun. I nod and she gives me a quick wave before closing the door behind me. I climb into my car, put my key in the ignition, and . . . the Starburst. Gone. I turn the key and remember that my keys were next to the door when I left this morning on my run. They were on the counter when I returned. As I back out of Merry Carole's driveway I imagine my sister sneaking out in her pajamas without her face on, grabbing those Starbursts, and throwing them into the abyss.

I wanted them to just disappear and she made it so. Love. I drive through the town square, past that red blinking light and out onto the highway with a smile on my face from ear to ear.

Things sometimes work out.

I park in Lot B, gather up all my canvas bags, and trudge the few feet to the back door of the Death House. I didn't see any media or anyone with signs or candles, but then again I'm early. Maybe they get here later? Maybe I'll see them on my way out? I slide my key card and the door clicks over. I turn on the lights and as they flicker on I await Jace. I set my canvas bags on the ground and start unpacking. The kitchen door clicks and I stand up.

"Hey there," Jace says, standing at the door.

"Hey, yourself," I say, going back to what I was doing.

"You ready for today?" Jace asks.

"Yep," I say, setting the brisket on the counter in its tinfoil wrapping. I unpack the ribs and the sausage and set them out, as well.

"Everyone's all amped up about today," Jace says, stepping forward.

"Oh yeah?" I ask, setting up Harlan and Cody's station.

"You don't know, do you?" he says, his hand resting on his gun.

"No, sir. I prefer not t—"

"We're puttin' down the Teacher's Pet," Jace says. I look up at him.

"That serial killer?" I ask.

"Yes, ma'am. They brought him over here thinking there wouldn't be as much press and all that. So far, they're right," Jace says.

"I didn't . . ." I lean against the counter. I stayed up all night making brisket for a man who . . . I can't . . . I need to focus on the food. There's no time for that.

"Didn't you wonder what that apple was for?" Jace asks, pointing at the apples I've set out on the counter. I was going to choose the best one.

"No," I say, breathless.

"It was his signature. He left an apple at every crime scene. That's how he got the name," Jace says.

"I didn't know that," I say. So is this now a crime scene? I grow illogically scared. Is this guy planning something? No, Queenie. This is about some sick fuck getting one last hurrah before he dies. That's all. I'll give him his apple. It'll be his last.

"Well, I'll go get the Dent boys for you," Jace says. He leaves. Now I'm alone in the kitchen, in the same building as that monster. With what he did. And now I have to . . . it's fine. I can make barbecue in my sleep. I've already done most of the work anyway. Harlan, Cody, and I will just focus on the guards' supper. We'll cook for us. The kitchen door clicks and Jace walks back through with the Dent boys. Jace takes up his place in his chair and flips open his paper. The Dent boys walk over to me.

"Jace told me," I say, motioning at the reading guard.

"I can't believe it," Harlan says, just shaking his head.

"I remember when they finally caught him, you remember? I mean, everyone was on the lookout for him. Women wouldn't go anywhere alone, everyone was locking their windows at night, I mean—" Cody is getting himself worked up. And he's IN prison.

"The good part is, I did most of this last night. I smoked the brisket, the sausage, and the ribs already. The barbecue sauce is made. So we'll make the potato salad and the fried pies, but I think the key is to focus on cooking for us and the guards' supper," I say, scanning my to-do list. The Dent boys nod in agreement.

"That doesn't seem like a lot at all," Harlan says, disappointed.

"It's not, but it'll keep us busy," I say.

"Yes, Chef," Harlan and Cody say.

"Okay, so, Cody, why don't you get started on those cherries over there for the fried pies," I say. He nods and obliges. I continue, "And, Harlan, why don't we get started on this potato salad," I say.

The morning goes by and I am able to focus on the food. I find myself cruising through the preparation, no heart really going into it. Harlan and Cody are slower today, which is good. We're also not as careful. Not as driven. Not as emotional. Everyone's on edge, but no one is somber like they were the last time. We break for lunch, and I decide to eat my turkey sandwich out by where the guards congregate. I don't want to be alone in that kitchen. Not even for an hour. I sit with Big Jim and Little Jim as they talk about football. LaRue gets in on the action, but I can tell he's nervous. This is the highest-profile convict they've ever had. And in a few hours LaRue is going to be buckling down the left arm of one of the most gruesome serial killers in Texas history. This guy has definitely gotten in all our heads.

Jace is slow bringing the Dents back from lunch and we have only two hours before it's time. We do what we can, but cutting the meat and making the fried pies has to happen at the last minute, so we are stalling at this point. We clean up the kitchen as much as possible, which will be nice in terms of getting out of here faster. We even play a quick hand of Go Fish (Cody wins). When the clock ticks down to just an hour until Shawn walks through that door, we spring into action.

Harlan fries up the pies, and I begin on the meat. The sausage is ready to go and the ribs are glistening and perfect. My barbecue sauce is my best-kept secret. It was Momma's and her momma's before her and on and on up the family tree. A good barbecue sauce should be as complex as the bouquet of a fine wine. It should have notes of sweetness, acidity, and a hint of pepperiness. The kitchen door clicks and Shawn walks in.

"How y'all comin'?" he asks, on edge.

"Good," I say, looking up from the brisket.

"Good. I'll be back in twenty minutes," Shawn says with an efficient nod.

Harlan grabs the tray without any fanfare. He sets it down on the counter and puts a plate in the center. I plate the brisket, sausage, and ribs. Cody scoops up a helping of the potato salad while Harlan cuts a white onion and pulls the pickles from the jar. He sets them on the side. Cody pulls a few slices of white bread from the wrapper and tucks them under the plate. Harlan brings the plate of fried cherry pies over and sets two down on a side plate.

"He didn't ask for ice cream?" Jace asks, wandering over as the plate is in its final stages.

"No, sir," I say.

"He probably forgot to ask for it," Jace says.

"His loss," I say, pouring the sweet tea into a large plastic cup. We stand around the tray.

Two minutes.

We just stand there as the brisket steams and the scent of the barbecue wafts over us. Harlan sets a couple of napkins down on the tray, as well. Cody clears his throat.

One minute.

I pick up the tray and turn toward the door. The door clicks over and Shawn walks into the kitchen.

"Take it," I say, holding it out for him. Shawn nods, takes the tray, and as Jace holds the door open for him, leaves with it.

"Now let's get you some supper," I say, setting down two plates for the Dent boys. I serve up some barbecue, some potato salad, and set a fried pie on each. They pour themselves some sweet tea. Jace walks over just as we finish. The Dent boys' two plates sit in front of us on the counter.

I look from Harlan to Cody then to Jace. We all join hands once more.

"Bless this food, Lord. Let it transport and remind us all of better times. Let it cleanse and purify. Let it nourish and warm. In it, let us find peace. In Jesus' name, amen," I say.

"Amen," the men say.

The Dent boys retire to their table and chairs while I ready the guards' supper. I set up the guards' table and clean the rest of the kitchen while I wait for their return. When Shawn returns, we sit down and can't wait to dig in. Brisket is passed, smoke rings are complimented, and stories are told. Shawn is tense and distant. I chalk it up to the weight of today's events all falling on his (soon to be retiring) shoulders. The guards eat every morsel I've made, but grow tense and edgy as the time nears to do their next job. They don't talk about their charge at all, but from the shared glances, this guy is doing a serious number on them.

They thank me for dinner. And leave. To do their job.

The Dent boys and I quickly clean the kitchen. We want to get out of here as fast as we can tonight. The stench of this man sticks to us all and I can't wait to take a shower and climb into bed . . . with Merry Carole. This guy is freaking me out. The kitchen door clicks and Shawn walks in with the empty tray.

The apple is still there. Uneaten.

Harlan grabs it off the tray and throws it away.

"Cody, why don't you close up that trash bag," Harlan says. Cody pulls the garbage bag out of the can where the apple is. He knots it and stands there.

"I'll take it out back," Jace says, taking the bag from Cody.

None of us mentions the apple again.

Jace takes the Dent boys back to their cells after our good-byes. As Jace is walking out of the kitchen, Warden Dale joins Shawn and me in the kitchen. They exchange a look and Warden Dale passes me a slip of paper. Too bad I'm not a futurist, I'd love to know what all this fuss is about.

Inmate #354-M15:
Chicken fried steak with cream gravy, mashed potatoes,
green beans cooked in bacon fat, one buttermilk biscuit,
and a slice of pecan pie with fresh strawberry ice cream

"Is this some kind of joke?" I ask Warden Dale, the blood rushing from my head.

"No, ma'am," Warden Dale says.

"This is the Number One. My mom's famous meal from her old restaurant back in North Star. It's even written the same, just like on the menu," I say, holding the piece of paper as if it's infected. Warden Dale is quiet. Shawn is watching me. Studying me.

I scan the paper once more.

with fresh strawberry ice cream

My stomach drops as I steady myself on the metal counter. Shawn steps forward. Just in case. Warden Dale holds his ground. The kitchen swirls around me and I can hear my own breathing in my ears.

"This is Yvonne Chapman's order. I'd know it anywhere," I say, my voice desperate and breathless. I hold the paper up and thrust it at Warden Dale. "Why am I holding Yvonne Chapman's order like I'm back working at that damn shack?" My voice gets louder as an explosion inside me ignites everything. All of the delicate rebuilding, all of the intricate emotions I'd started untangling in the past few months go up in flames. Complicated monster or not, this is beyond the pale. My insides will soon turn to embers as I can only continue to stare at the paper.

They wait. As it finally dawns on me.

"No . . . no . . . no way. No fucking way," I say, shoving the piece of paper at Warden Dale.

"Queenie," Warden Dale says.

"You want me to make this meal, my mother's famous meal, for the woman who killed her? You want me to stand in this kitchen while the woman who made my sister and me orphans is just a few feet away from me, just behind that metal door I'm never supposed to go into? What makes you think I wouldn't go over there and do it myself? I mean, if anyone had the fucking right to kill Brandi-Jaques Wake, don't you think it should have been my sister or me? And if we didn't? If we were able to control ourselves, don't you think Yvonne Chapman should have been able to? Was it really that bad? She could have just thrown us out, Warden Dale. Why didn't she just throw us out? She didn't have to kill her!" I scream, slamming the piece of paper down on the metal counter.

"Ms. Wake, you would do well to get in control of your emotions," Warden Dale says. Shawn looks at Warden Dale, his entire body tense.

"You can go to hell. How's that for control?" I say, turning around to pick up my knives. I sling them over my shoulder.

"Ms. Wake, destiny has given you an opportunity here," Warden Dale says.

"Destiny has given me an opportunity? What does that even mean?"

"It means, like so many other victims' families, you can have closure," Warden Dale says.

"Closure is something only people who've never had someone in their family murdered talk about. How is she still even around?" I ask, trying to make sense of something.

"Her case has been in the appeals courts for years, but her time's finally up," Warden Dale says. I would have known this had I not vowed to no longer check that Web site. Is this better? The not knowing?

"Queenie, the meal isn't until the end of next week. You can think about it," Shawn says. My face softens as I listen to Shawn.

I nod and situate my knife case on my shoulder once again. I turn to walk out the back door of the kitchen, leaving the slip of paper on the counter.

"Ms. Wake?" Warden Dale holds up the slip of paper.

"I've been making that meal my entire life, Warden Dale. I'll let you know Monday what I decide," I say and walk through the door without looking back. The door slams behind me. My legs are heavy and I can feel every step I take as I walk to my car. My body doesn't feel connected to my mind, which is somewhere back in that kitchen clutching that slip of paper. I dump my canvas bags and my knives in the hatch and slam it closed. My breathing is slow and I'm pretty sure I'm in some kind of shock at this point. My brain focuses on one thing at a time. Unlock the door. Check. Sit inside the vehicle. Check. I turn the key and the car revs to life. Put the car in reverse. Check. I drive past the guards' tower and see the vigil in front of the prison. A crowd of people holding signs and candles rallies and demands to be seen. I don't look at them as my breathing becomes labored. I get up on the highway and drive in silence all the way to North Star. Through the town square until I'm pulling down Merry Carole's driveway. I walk inside, holding my keys in my hand. My driver's-side door hangs open. I see it from out of the corner of my eye and stumble back over to close it. I walk inside the house again and find Merry Carole and Cal sitting at the dining room table going over his playbook.

"They want me to make Yvonne Chapman's last meal," I say, standing just inside the open doorway.

"Cal, honey, can you excuse us for a second?" Merry Carole asks, closing up his playbook.

"No, Momma," he says.

"What?"

"No." Cal's bravado changes to terror as Merry Carole glares at him.

"Calvin Jaques Wake—"

"Momma, this is my family, too." Cal leans back in his chair and folds his arms. He's staying. Merry Carole looks from him to me. Her fixed stare could cut glass. I walk into the dining room and take a seat. Merry Carole raises her eyebrows.

"Warden Dale came in . . . well, let me back up. Shawn had said that the next two meals I'd be making were going to be more high profile. We were just finishing up today's and Shawn walks in with Warden Dale. He usually just gives me the date and the order at the end of my shift. So I knew something was up. But I just thought it was another high-profile case or something went wrong. He hands me this little slip of paper, and it's the Number One," I say, looking at Merry Carole.

"She ordered the Number One?" Merry Carole asks, bringing her hand up and covering her mouth.

"Can you believe that?"

"How did you know it was Yvonne? I mean, that meal was pretty famous back in its day," Merry Carole says.

"She ordered strawberry ice cream. Fresh strawberry ice cream," I say.

"Dear Lord," Merry Carole says.

"What? Is that bad?" Cal asks.

"Yvonne used to come to the shack all the time and order the Number One. And Momma didn't allow any substitutions. She made it her way, and if you didn't like it she'd run you off. Yvonne would always be going on about how we should have strawberry ice cream. It'd be so much better with strawberry ice cream. She had tons of it in the house when we stayed with her right at the end there."

"And she always said fresh. Fresh strawberry ice cream. Like she knew better. Like she'd tasted the old raggedy kind in the supermarket, but she was so fancy that she liked her strawberry ice cream made fresh," I say. Merry Carole nods in agreement.

"Yvonne thought she was real high class, way better than us Wakes. Of course, the rest of North Star didn't quite agree," Merry Carole says.

"So when Momma took up with Yvonne's husband, well . . . Yvonne lost it," I say in a haze, remembering it all now.

"How do you mean lost it?" Cal asks.

Merry Carole and I don't answer right away. We're off in our own little worlds, staring off into space. Both of us. Cal looks from Merry Carole to me and then back to Merry Carole.

"She took 'em both out," I finally say.

"Both of 'em," Merry Carole repeats.

"Her husband and your momma?" Cal asks. Merry Carole and I just nod.

"And the rest of the town? They couldn't care less. I heard some woman at the store talking about it and she laughed, saying, 'It's not like there was any humans involved,'" Merry Carole says.

"You never told me that," I say.

"Yeah," Merry Carole says, nodding.

"And the thing of it was, if she hadn't shot her husband, too? She would have been out a long time ago," I say.

"Oh absolutely," Merry Carole says.

"How come?" Cal asks.

"Shooting Momma was what any good Texas woman woulda done. They were in his bed; Yvonne was doing the Christian thing by putting us up for a time. She came home early from work and there they were. So she walked into their garage, pulled out the shotgun, loaded the shells, and . . ." I trail off.

"Holy shit," Cal says. Merry Carole doesn't even chastise him for his language.

"So not only was her husband catting around, but he was doing it with Brandi-Jaques Wake. Which—," I say.

"She couldn't allow," Merry Carole says, sipping her tea. Her eyes are distant. Elsewhere.

"Why didn't she just divorce him?" Cal asks.

"Because he'd ruined everything she had worked for and he had to pay," I say.

"But they're dead and now she's the only one paying," Cal says.

"Not true. We're still paying. You're still paying," I say.

"So what are you going to do?" Merry Carole finally asks.

"There's no way I'm making that meal for that woman," I say.

"Why not?" Cal asks.

"It feels like this might bring some weird closure, you know?" Merry Carole says.

"People love throwing that word around," I say.

"Who are you telling? Of course I understand the weight of the decision you have to make. My point is that this—" Merry Carole stops. She gathers her thoughts and continues, "We've let this one event that we had nothing to do with define our lives. Now it feels to me like you came back to North Star for a reason whether you knew that going in or not. This may not be a coincidence at all." Merry Carole leans forward. She reaches across the dining room table and takes my hand in hers. She continues speaking. "I think it's time for both of us—for all of us—to stop paying for something Momma did."

"And how does me making this meal do that?"

"I don't know, but the fact that you don't want to makes me think it's exactly what you have to do," Merry Carole says.

"I'm not even sure that makes sense," I say.

"I think it'd be cathartic. Maybe for all of us," Merry Carole says, clearing the table.

"You don't think this is the least bit twisted?" I ask.

"Oh, it's completely twisted. But it might just be the jolt we need," Merry Carole says.

"How can you be so calm about all this?" I ask.

"Well, first off, I don't have to make the meal, but I think you need to do this more than I need to be mad about Yvonne and what she did and how Momma probably deserved it. I think it's time we put this in the past where it belongs," Merry Carole says.

Later, as Merry Carole bustles around the kitchen and Cal gets ready for bed, tonight's conversation settles around me like dust. I feel inordinately scared. Living in the past has its benefits. Closing the door on this means I have to look to the future.

25

Dairy Queen double-dip swirl cone

As I lie awake the next two nights, I realize I've defined myself by things I can't see and people who aren't around anymore. I've been hunting a ghost for my entire life and so has the pitchfork- and torch-wielding mob of North Star townspeople.

For someone who struggles with faith, I base a lot of my life on things I can't see. All these years looking for the answer and it comes down to the simplest question.

Do I want to go backward or forward?

I believed going on all these adventures meant that I was jumping into my future with everything I had. I left North Star thinking I'd seen the last of the chains and the masks and the pitchfork-wielding mobs. With my two pieces of luggage, I'd brag that I liked to travel light, insinuating that the usual trappings didn't weigh me down. The joke was clearly on me. I hauled the burden of Mom's unceremonious death, my abandonment of Merry Carole and Cal, and my cowardly heart that I never really risked on Everett everywhere I went. It's ironic that after spending my whole life believing in ghosts, I became one.

I didn't live in those cities. I haunted them.

As I sit in church that Sunday, I think about what's real. I look to my left and see Merry Carole, Reed, Cal, and the girls sitting together for the first time. That's real. What's also real is that none of them has urged me to get on my way or leave them be. They've made sure I knew I was family. What's not real are the gossiping ladies and whispering townspeople who snicker behind gloved hands about Reed and Merry Carole: the new, scandalous couple. What's finally sinking in is the knowledge that their opinions are only reflections of themselves and how unhappy they are in their own lives. I should know. I've spent years snarling at people because of how lonely I am. Angry. Sad. Angry is just sad's bodyguard. I gaze up into the high-coffered ceiling and let the sweeping, epic music wash over me. That's real, I think to myself as I relax into the morning.

As we file out of the church, I'm still in a bit of a haze. We all congregate on the edge of the church's front lawn. Reed takes the girls to the table where the punch and cookies are. Rose pointed it out as we walked in. I secretly believe it's why she comes to church. Cal followed them over, but soon got sidetracked by members of the Stallion Batallion wanting to know if he's ready for the big opening game coming up. I saw Everett inside, but haven't yet spotted him out here.

"It's almost Monday," Merry Carole says.

"Yes, Monday customarily follows Sunday."

"Queen Elizabeth, don't be flip."

"I still don't know, but I'm taking it seriously," I say.

"That's it, Momma. Enough," Whitney yells from the other

side of the churchyard. The entire lawn of people screeches to a halt. Merry Carole and I look around and see Cal standing right in the thick of it. Next to West.

Oh shit.

Merry Carole and I immediately hightail it over to where Cal is standing.

"Whitney Shelby Ackerman, this is not the time or the place." Whitney's mother, Cheryl, is all tasteful, matching separates, helmet hair straight from the salon.

"Sweet pea, I know you—" Whitney's daddy, DeWitt Ackerman, always did coddle that girl.

"Momma, my name is Whitney McKay. I'm a McKay. And so is he," Whitney says, reaching up to West's shoulder and pulling him close.

"This needs to stop right here and now, young lady. I am not too old to put you over my knee," Cheryl Ackerman says in a low growl. You could hear a pin drop in this churchyard.

Whitney turns West around and faces him, her hands still on his shoulders. She looks up at him, squinting in the sun, as her chin quivers from tears that are now pooling in her eyes. West shifts and shoots a quick glance at Cal. Cal steps in close. Merry Carole is ready to pounce at a moment's notice.

"Sweetie, I'm so sorry. To be doing this here. Like this. But mommas fight for their kids, and I'm so sorry it's taken me this long to stand up for you. Baby, I—"

"I know," West says, his low voice cutting through the thick humidity like a bell.

"You what now?" Whitney asks, stumbling over her words.

"I know. We've known for a while," West says, looking over at Cal again. Cal steps even closer. Merry Carole inches forward.

"Yes, ma'am," Cal says, now shoulder to shoulder with West.

Seeing them both there. Together. Whitney finally looks at them. Really taking them in. And she just loses it. She claps her hand over her mouth and begins to sob. Wes steps up and takes her in his arms.

"I've never . . . I couldn't bring myself to really look at him," Whitney says, referring to Cal.

"Why didn't you say nothing?" Wes asks the boys.

"It just . . . it seemed really important to you that we didn't know. So we kept it to ourselves," West says, looking from Wes to Cal.

"For how long?" Whitney moans.

"Maybe four years," West says, looking at Cal for confirmation.

"Junior high school, so three years," Cal corrects.

"Three years?" Whitney sobs.

"How'd y'all find out?" Wes asks.

"All you have to do is look at us," West says, voicing what is plainly obvious to everyone.

"We had this long bus ride once, for that all-star Pee Wee League in Dallas?" Cal says. Wes nods. Cal continues. "We sat next to each other and started talking. By the time we got to Dallas, we'd figured it out." Merry Carole pulls a hankie from her purse and swipes at her eyes, cleaning up the now trailing mascara.

"A bus ride," DeWitt says.

"I didn't mind it. I loved living with—" West stops. Not knowing what to call the people he took as his parents for most of his life. He continues, "My grandparents." Cheryl and DeWitt crumple into each other as West's voice cracks. He continues, "I don't ever want y'all to think I thought I was missing out." A single tear makes its way down his face and he angrily swipes it away.

"Come on over here now, son," DeWitt says, pulling West into him and Cheryl.

The entire churchyard is sobbing. Not a dry eye anywhere.

The minister is watching the entire scene from the steps of the church and he's wiping away tears like everyone else. The entire town knew. West and Cal knew. What the hell are we all so afraid of?

West breaks from Cheryl and DeWitt and stands in front of Wes and Whitney. Their two littler kids are holding on to Whitney and Wes, unsure of what's happening, but definitely a bit scared. West looks at the two little kids and then up at Whitney.

"I want you to come home, baby," Whitney says, finally looking up into her son's eyes. Cheryl and DeWitt look on with approval. Pride.

"I'd like that," West says, his chin quivering just like Whitney's. There's an awkward pause as the entire churchyard waits. Please hug him. Please hug him. But it's not Whitney who pulls West in—it's Wes. And he's lost it. He engulfs West in arms as big as tree branches and is telling him how proud he is of him. As the McKays hug and cry, Cal stands by; Merry Carole has finally inched all the way up to be by his side.

Cal takes Merry Carole's hand and whispers so only we can hear, "Thank you for standing up for me. I know it wasn't easy." Merry Carole sniffles and is doing her best to keep it together. She nods as the tears stream down her face, mascara trailing behind them.

"You're my boy," Merry Carole finally ekes out, pulling Cal close.

My cell phone buzzes in my purse. I pull it out and don't recognize the number. It buzzes again. I excuse myself and walk farther down the sidewalk, away from the church.

"Hello?" I ask.

"Queen Elizabeth Wake?"

"It's just Queenie. This is she."

"Oh right. That's much better. Queenie, this is Neal Howard. You e-mailed us a résumé a while back—" Neal is flipping through papers. The churchgoers gather around the McKays/Ackermans and offer their congratulations. Everyone knew. The talk quickly turns to football and all is back to normal after just a few minutes. Fifteen years boiled down to five minutes in a churchyard. Whitney has yet to let go of West's hand. West hasn't moved, but is still leaning toward Cal. I love that through all of this, they had each other. That they'll always have each other.

As I walk a bit farther out of the bustling churchyard, I let my eyes rest on Merry Carole and I'm calm. Family. Love. The promise of time together. Neal continues to flip through papers and I wait for him to tell me that he thanks me for my résumé, but— Neal continues, "Aha, there it is. I'm so sorry. I spoke to Brad Carter over at the McCormick and he had some great things to say about you. We'd love it if you would come to Portland and head up the kitchen here at the Raven." The Raven? I sent out so many résumés, it's hard to remember. I finally land on the little neighborhood grill in Portland. Family owned, really cute place.

"I applied for the sous-chef position, is that—"

"The reason I'm late getting back to you is because we've been restructuring a bit here, which you know is fancy speak for letting our executive chef go. That's where you come in," Neal says.

"As the executive chef?"

"We thought the broad spectrum of your experience made you the clear choice for us." I'm stunned. I continue to walk out of the churchyard.

"This is really an honor and I'm very flattered; is there any way that I can think about your offer and get back to you?"

"Oh sure. Sure. I understand that it's a lot. I have your e-mail. I'll send you the details: pay—the chef's residence is on the same plot of land—hours, and vacation days."

"That sounds perfect," I say.

"Queenie, I'll need to hear back from you by the end of next week, you understand."

"Sure, and once again thank you so much for thinking of me." Neal and I sign off and I look up to find myself just outside the church cemetery. The bustling churchyard is alive with good news and I freeze.

The broken-down picket fence that corrals North Star's departed is covered in vines and overgrown underbrush. I creak open the gate, wiping the dust and dirt from the wood onto my Sunday best. I tuck my cell phone into my pocket and pick my way through the ancient headstones and makeshift crosses, names of cowboys branded onto them as if they were cattle. I swallow hard as the emotion burns in my throat. I chalk the sensation up to what happened with the McKays. Chalk it up to a lot of things.

What am I doing here? Is it curiosity? Not enough melodrama for one day? Do I think after all I've gone through in the last few weeks I'll have a different response to this cemetery than the one I had all those years ago? Is this a test? Some kind of ritual I can put myself through to prove that I'm over her? Is this about Yvonne Chapman and her fresh strawberry ice cream? Black holes and dusty plots of land. Flaming red hair and cruel blue eyes. The first of many tears slides down my cheek.

The humidity settles around me as I make my way to where I know Mom is buried. The grass itches and tickles my legs, the dampness of the air and the earth gather inside my sandals as I walk around the graves and headstones like a cat burglar trying to avoid the laser beams in an upscale museum.

Brandi-Jaques Wake
1963–1998
The Number One

She was only thirty-five? I remember her as being so much older. She was barely older than I am now. Within a matter of seconds, I'm losing control and unable to stop my own bawling. How did I get here? My sobs are coming from a place so deep it terrifies me. The only word that comes to me is why. Why? Why me? Why you? Why did it have to end that way? Why weren't you the mother I wanted you to be? Why didn't you love me? Why wasn't I enough?

"Queenie, sweetheart?" Merry Carole comes up behind me.

"I'm fine," I howl. I'm wailing like a lunatic at our mother's grave.

"Oh sweetie," Merry Carole says, pulling me in close. Rose water and Aqua Net. Home. Love.

"Why didn't she love us?" I ask, my face buried in the crook of Merry Carole's neck.

"I don't know, my love. I don't know," Merry Carole says.

"Aren't parents supposed to love their kids?" I ask.

"Apparently not," Merry Carole says. We break apart from each other and she wipes my tears away, smoothing my bangs down. Cal passes me a handkerchief. I thank him and I'm momentarily embarrassed that he's here to see my full-blown breakdown.

"Aren't you supposed to tell me that people love in different ways and—"

"I don't want to lie to you, sweetness and light," Merry Carole says, her chin up in pure defiance.

"Not even in my weakened state?"

"Especially not in your weakened state," Merry Carole says with a smile.

"I think I'm going to go see the little plot of land," I say, blowing my nose.

"Honey, you don't have to," Merry Carole soothes.

"No, why not make today a hat trick?" I say.

"Do you even know what a hat trick is?" Cal asks.

"Three of something?"

"Yeah, but it's usually three good things; I'm not so sure—"

"No, this is good. These are good," I say. I must look like a wreck. Cal just keeps quiet and takes my word for it.

"Will you tell Reed, Cal, and the girls I'll see them at supper later?"

"Sure."

"You can say something, you know." I motion to Mom's grave.

"I've made my peace," Merry Carole says, entirely calm.

"Am I going to get there?" I ask, envying her cool demeanor.

"Today was a start," Merry Carole says as we walk out of that tiny cemetery and leave Mom behind us. Hopefully for good this time.

"Okay . . . well, I'll be home in a bit."

I walk away from the church and stop at the DQ for a double-dip swirl. I take the side streets, licking my ice-cream cone and observing life in North Star. I feel cleansed. Baptized, almost. I finish my cone just as I make the final turn down the tree-lined street to where the shack used to be.

In the light of day I can see that it's all but gone now. The Hall of Fame, just next door, is closed. It *is* Sunday after all. I walk through the dirt toward what's left of the shack. My sandals are already wrecked, what's a bit more? The rotted-out shack is now just fallen planks of wood that once were walls. They lean haphazardly against the concrete wall at the back of the property line. I shift and move the planks around trying to unearth something that I don't even know I'm looking for. And yet I find it. That old plank Mom nailed to the front of this shithole is just as rotted as the rest of them. WAKE. Four letters. No punctuation. I brush off some of the muck, but think better of it as splinters and spiders threaten to attack at any moment. The branded name is blackened and deep into the wood. Scarred.

"Now I'm just being melodramatic," I say to myself, trying to look around the little piece of land with fresh eyes, just as Merry Carole told me to.

I feel nothing. No swell of emotion like I felt back in the cemetery. I look out to the street in front of the shack, getting reacquainted with the view I stared at day in and day out as a kid while I worked behind that take-out window. And that's when the emotion chokes me. When I think about that kid. The kid who waited and tried to be enough for a selfish, feckless parent. I'd watch down that street for Mom. I remember trying to look busy and proficient as she walked up only to have her shove me aside and tell me I was doing it wrong. I search my memory bank hoping to find some tender nugget of a memory of her and can't find a one.

I've heard people talk about loving their kids or friends or parents, but not liking them. As if love is this inalienable right that trumps a person's bad behavior and neglect. Our society needs parents to love their kids. We joke about how hard parenting is, but there's an understanding that parents would do anything for their kids. It's heresy to suggest anything different. As I stare out at that street, that unchanged street, I realize that I've been wrong this entire time. Just like the movies I'd studied about the Small-town Girl in the Big City, I'd fallen for the mythology of the incompetent parent who makes good in the end. As I stand in the ruins of what Mom once built, I know I won't find some secret letter where she finally proclaims her undying love for Merry Carole and me. I've tried to fit my mother into society's idea of what a parent should be. And within those parameters, I'm cast as the monster. I'm the unlovable child.

What happens if I switch the paradigm?

What happens if I finally see my mother for who she was? A woman so incapable of love that her entire life was about what she wanted, how she'd been wronged, and how the world owed her. Merry Carole and I were just two rusty nails her dress got snagged on as she searched for her real life. This isn't some big philosophical discussion about parents and children at all. It's about one woman. One inexcusable woman who saw people as stepping-stones. Including her own kids. As the ideas run through my head, the leaves rustling in the tiniest of breezes, I feel a coldness run through me.

A woman whose life was only about what she wanted, how she was wronged, and how the world owed her.

The words bump and ping around in my head. How did I not see that these patterns repeat themselves? I'm sure Mom felt the same about her mother. I remember hearing terrible stories about the woman whose recipes I now make by heart.

So here I am. Staring down the same street I did when I was a kid. Who am I waiting for now? Who am I trying to look busy for? Who do I think is going to shove me aside and tell me I'm doing it wrong? I turn the rotted piece of wood over and over in my hand as I replay Merry Carole's simple answer of "apparently not." The quiet settles around me once again.

I choose to go forward.

I throw the rotted piece of wood back in the pile with the rest of the planks and walk down the street, back home to Merry Carole's. I'll call Warden Dale first thing tomorrow morning.

I will make Yvonne Chapman's last meal.

I walk down the manicured path to Merry Carole's house. She and Cal are standing in the kitchen. I walk in and they immediately stop talking.

"What's going on?" I ask, my announcement taking a backseat.

"I was on the computer and your e-mail was open; I didn't know it was yours. I heard a ping and I thought it was mine, you know?" Cal says, looking from me to Merry Carole.

"An e-mail came for you," Merry Carole says, holding out a sheet of paper. I walk over to the kitchen and take the sheet of paper from Merry Carole. It's from Neal Howard at the Raven. He's confirming our conversation about the executive chef position and following up with some details.

"Merry Carole, I—"

"You had no intention of staying," she says.

"No, I mean . . . yes," I say, stuttering and stumbling over my words.

"I actually thought you were . . . no, never mind. You just do what you want," Merry Carole says, opening up the refrigerator. She slams the door immediately. "You told me you were going to at least stay for the wedding."

"Let me explain," I say.

"Are you taking it?" Merry Carole asks.

"I don't know . . . I don't—"

"It says they want you to start next week. So you're also going to miss Cal's opening game," Merry Carole says, steadying herself on the breakfast bar. Cal just looks . . . crushed. Merry Carole walks through the kitchen toward the front door, sweeping past me in a rage. "Cal, why don't we go on over to Reed's for supper." Cal nods and walks out of the kitchen and right past me. He can't even look at me. Merry Carole wraps her arm around the boy, and they walk out of the house, slamming the door behind them.

What have I done?

26

Leftover fried cherry pie and not enough coffee in the world

I wake up early the next morning. Cal's bumping around the house before his morning run. I flip my sheets off and walk out into the rest of the house just as the front door slams.

"Come on," I say to a darkened house. I grab Cal's sweatshirt by the door and run out of the house in bare feet and my pajamas pulling the sweatshirt on over my head. Cal's still stretching just in front of the salon as I come barreling toward him.

"Where are you going?" I ask.

"On my run," he says, bending over for another stretch.

"I know yesterday was weird, but I swear—"

"This whole thing goes away when you tell me and Momma that you're not taking that job. You get that, right?" Cal asks.

"Yeah."

"So . . ."

"You know how when I first got here you asked me why anyone would want to leave New York City and come back to North Star?"

"Yeah."

"And that all you can think about right now is going to UT and getting out of North Star?"

"Yeah."

"But do you know that in-between place? Where you're excited to go to UT, but kinda scared to leave home?"

"Yeah," Cal says, not able to look at me.

"That's where I am right now. I'm in that in-between place. I don't quite know where I want to be," I say.

"Momma wants you to stay here," Cal says, finally taking out his earbuds.

"I know," I say.

"Are you wearing my sweatshirt?" Cal asks, tilting his head as it dawns on him.

"Yeah . . . sorry," I say.

"All right then. I'm going to go ahead and run. I'm not trying to leave without you, but West is waiting."

"No, that's all right. You go on ahead, but I'm back on tomorrow. Say hi to West for me," I say. Cal beams. We're both thinking it. Say hi to your brother for me.

"Yeah, all right," he says, putting his earbuds back in and running out through the center of town. I watch him trot away through the early morning haze. I walk down the driveway and back into the house.

"What are you doing?" Merry Carole asks, standing in the kitchen.

"I was just talking to Cal," I say.

"What were you saying to him?"

"I was just trying to explain to him where I'm at."

"You are so full of shit."

"What?"

"He wants you to stay. I want you to stay. You don't get to ex-plain away why you're leaving again and feel good because you made it sound poetic," Merry Carole says, switching on the coffee-maker.

"I get to figure this out. You don't get to bully me into doing what you want me to do," I say, walking toward her.

"Bully you?!"

"Yes!"

"Oh, that's just fine. That's just fine. We're some stopover every ten years while you get your life together, and if I ask you to actu-ally think about being a part of this family, I'm a bully."

"You're not a stopover," I say.

Merry Carole dismisses me out of hand with flicked fingers and a sniff. She can barely look at me.

I continue, "You want me to pick up right where Momma left off? Is that it? I open up that shack and spend day in and day out making the Number One for the drunks in that bar, all the while being Everett's mistress? You get your life and I get hers? That's your plan?" I walk into the kitchen and face her.

"Of course not."

"Then tell me what my life looks like if I stay. Because from where I'm sitting, I don't see a future except maybe being merci-fully put down by Everett's future wife when she finds us in bed together and then I get a gravestone with my most famous recipe on it. Not that I was a mother, or that I'll be missed. No. Our mother's legacy is a well-made chicken fried steak," I say.

"Queenie, I—"

"I don't know my place here. You say I can have that land, but what am I supposed to do with it? I want to drink the coffee in front of me, Merry Carole. I want to chug it down and luxuriate in it, I swear to God. And I love being here with you and Cal more than anything in the world, but . . . I can't stomach being the spinster aunt who pops up in the background of all of your family photos." Tears stream down my cheeks.

"Come here," Merry Carole says, pulling me in for a hug. I shudder as she holds me tight.

"I become her if I leave and I become her if I stay," I say, sobbing into the crook of her neck.

"All right now . . . all right now . . . shhhhh." Merry Carole holds me tight, rocking us back and forth as she soothes me. I sob and wail as the epiphanies and realizations squirm and infest my entire body once again. I don't know where I belong. I never have. I've been a stray dog trying to find someone to take me in for as long as I can remember. I was thankful just to find a quiet corner I could call my own where the most I could ask for, as far as comfort went, was a warm bed. Acceptance and being enough is my holy grail. So my life became about begging for scraps at the back door.

"I'm so sorry," I say as we finally break apart.

"Don't be," Merry Carole says, swiping my bangs out of my eyes. She kisses me on my forehead, lingering there. I close my eyes as she smooths my hair. She nods; her brow is furrowed, her lips are pursed.

"I decided to make Yvonne Chapman's meal," I say.

"Good. *Good,*" Merry Carole says, her eyes darting around the kitchen as we finally collect ourselves.

"I'm thinking that decision probably has to do with this whole crying-marathon thing," I say.

"I expect that's that closure thing people like talking about."

"We don't have to decide everything right now," I say.

"It's that uncertainty part that I don't like. I like my one hundred percent odds, you know," she says, kissing me on the cheek. She turns around and pulls two coffee mugs from the cabinet. She pours coffee into each and passes me one.

"So we just go forward," I say, trying out my theory. I inhale the luscious coffee smell.

"Right."

"We stop living in the past, just like you said," I say.

"No, I gave you that advice. Remember? I like giving people advice and not taking it myself," she says, finally allowing a laugh.

"Why don't I help out in the salon today?" I say. Merry Carole nods with a cautious smile.

Cal bursts through the front door, pulling his earbuds out as he looks at us standing in the kitchen.

"Are you guys fighting?" Cal asks.

"No, sweetie. We're done fighting," Merry Carole says, smoothing her hand over my arm as she starts making breakfast.

"You need any help?" I ask.

"No, sweetie. Thank you, though," she says.

"So we're not mad anymore? Is Aunt Queenie staying?" Cal asks, walking into the kitchen.

"We don't know yet, honey," Merry Carole says, looking from me to Cal.

"Oh, okay then," Cal says, clearly disappointed. He sits down at the table with me, not meeting my gaze.

"We don't have to decide everything right now," I say. Merry Carole just shakes her head.

I fill my coffee mug once more and grab a fried pie from a Tupperware container in the fridge and meet Merry Carole in the salon later that morning. Cal went off to practice with as many questions as he'd had the day before. I called Warden Dale once the house was empty and agreed to cook for Yvonne Chapman. I also told him that her meal would be my last. I have to go forward and not back. Working at Shine Prison has changed me. I was forced to face some hidden truth that I was in no rush to uncover in each of these meals. With Yvonne's meal I'll exhume the last of the secrets. The experiment is over. It's time for me to leave Shine Prison.

The next step is not as clear. After looking over the Raven offer, it sounds like just what I was looking for. They have a clear (bordering on fussy) vision for their menu, as they should have, but not in all the ways I'd like. They skew toward a more organic fresh fare, which I'm a fan of, but they also pride themselves on offering a healthier alternative to today's comfort food. This is the part I could do without. I can see the clientele now, asking to substitute for the dairy and take off the bread and does this come without the meat and on and on. I'm afraid it wouldn't take long before I was throttling some hipster in a knit cap with a lactose sensitivity problem.

As I said, this is exactly what I *was* looking for. Before. Before the little experiment. As I walk up to the salon, I let that idea bounce around in my head. What am I looking for now?

27

Inmate #354-M15:
Chicken fried steak with cream gravy, mashed potatoes,
green beans cooked in bacon fat, one buttermilk biscuit,
and a slice of pecan pie with fresh strawberry ice cream

I pull Mom's skillet from my canvas bag as the lights flicker on in the Death House kitchen. It's Friday morning. I didn't need any test batches or research for this meal. And yet preparing to come in here today took everything I had. I had nightmares all week of squeaky shoes and muddy cemeteries punctuated by shotgun fire. I finally crawled into bed last night with Merry Carole sometime around three AM. She said she was waiting for me. My morning run with Cal and West felt good, and as I reached the ridge of that mountain I was thankful I saw Everett and Arrow ambling into the horizon. I stopped and chatted, but found myself unable to speak freely. I want to tell him everything and I just don't know how. Instead, I talked about what happened at the churchyard with Whitney and the boys. He said he was sorry for missing that. He hasn't been at church lately. He didn't say why. In the end, I used the boys as an excuse to get out of there. In truth, I felt way too exposed. And once again, I was waiting for him to step in and save me from myself.

The kitchen door clicks and Jace walks in.

"It looks like you're lying in wait," Jace says, motioning to the skillet in my hand.

"Oh yeah," I say, trying to loosen up. Jace walks over to me and just stands there.

"So you're leaving today and Shawn is leaving today. Was it something I said?" Jace's stumbling attempt at a joke is endearing.

"Of course not," I say, smiling.

"Well, if I don't get the chance to say it later, it's been a pleasure," Jace says, extending his hand to me. I set the skillet down on the counter and take his hand, mine quickly enveloped in his.

"I appreciate that. And thank you for being in here with me. It made all the difference," I say, motioning to his chair by the door. I've left something for him. He looks over there and does an immediate double take. He walks over to his chair and looks at the basket I left him, then to me. "Open it!" I say. He obliges. The smell hits him first. An entire batch of churros, a thermos of Mexican hot chocolate, and a pint container of cajeta. And it's all his. He arranges the items back in the basket just as they were and just as meticulously closes the basket back up. He walks back over and hesitates, but then comes in for a hug. His holster and gun bump my hip as he pulls me in close, thanking me for being so thoughtful. He breaks away awkwardly and says he'll fetch the Dent boys for me. He takes his basket with him when he leaves.

I set out ingredients and begin to sketch the day ahead. I imagine Yvonne sitting in that little cell with the chaplain talking about mortality, regrets, and God's mercy. The other night I had the strangest feeling that she'd find out it was me. Somehow there'd be this moment where I'd be unmasked. But maybe that was just an-other one of my nightmares. The kitchen door clicks and Jace walks in with the Dent boys. I smile and know I'm going to miss them. But that thought actually begins to shift and morph into the germ of an idea.

"You're leaving?" Cody asks, walking over to me.

"Yes," I say.

"It's been our pleasure," Harlan says, extending his hand to me. I take it and we shake hands. His hands are calloused and rough, but his handshake is firm and confident. I extend my hand to Cody and he takes it. He won't look at me as we shake hands. I tilt my head down and make eye contact with him and he finally smiles.

"Warden Dale says the Dent boys are going to be in charge of last meals until they get out. He said he was a futurist, I don't know. Something about the future. I can't remember," Jace says from his chair by the door.

"Oh yeah?" I ask.

"Yes, ma'am," Harlan says.

"Y'all will do great," I say.

"Yes, Chef," they say.

"Well, why don't we get started," I say. I made the decision not to tell anyone here about my relationship with Yvonne. I don't need a bunch of hangdog expressions as I work through my last day. I imagine the guards are already on edge simply because Yvonne is a woman. This will be a first for Shine. I lay out the schedule and guide Cody through the mashed potatoes and green beans. I put Harlan on the cream gravy while I start in on the fresh strawberry ice cream and pecan pie. The Dent boys leave for lunch, but I don't stop to eat. I can't. I move around the kitchen, cleaning and busying myself for as long as I can. I know she's just outside these walls. As the day moves on, I'm getting more and more antsy. But I don't dare leave. The pecan pie is in the oven and the ice cream is chilling in the freezer. As the walls settle in around me, I finally sit.

I let my eyes follow the clean silvery lines of the kitchen all the way around the room. I feel the tears begin to fall down my cheeks, tickling their way along the side of my nose. I taste their saltiness on my lips as I swipe at them with my sleeve. I think about that job in Portland. I realize it's not what I want anymore. I'm not the same chef I was just a few months ago. Hell, I'm not even the same person I was a few months ago. I've cried more in the last few days than I ever did in the ten years I was running.

I don't want to work in *a* kitchen, I want to work in *my* kitchen.

I want chairs that don't match and a porch with a swing. I want mason jars filled with wildflowers in the center of rustic wooden tables. I want flickering candles and a fire in a fireplace. I want mismatched dishes and old-timey silver. I want people to be able to smell what's cooking a mile away so that even though they don't know the address, they'll still find us. I want a honky-tonk band and couples dancing under colorful lanterns.

I want a place that feels like home. A place where I belong.

I stare at Momma's skillet, on the stovetop waiting for me to fry up those chicken fried steaks. She may not have loved me. She may not have even liked me. But goddamn if that woman didn't teach me how to cook. I pull my cell phone out of my pocket and dial Neal Howard over at the Raven.

"This is Neal," he answers.

"Mr. Howard, this is Queenie Wake," I say, my voice too loud for this quiet kitchen.

"Oh yes. Hi, Queenie," he says.

"Thank you so much for your offer, Mr. Howard, but I'm going to have to turn you down."

"I'm sorry to hear that."

"Yes, sir. Once again, thank you so much for thinking of m—"

"May I ask why?"

"I've decided to open up my own place here in North Star," I say. There it is. Out loud.

"Well, that's as good a reason as any, I suppose. We're sorry to have lost you, but the best of luck to you," Neal says.

"Thank you," I say. We say our farewells, and I beep my cell phone off and take a deep breath. I tuck my cell phone back in my pocket. I stand up and start milling around in the kitchen. Silence. Everything is in its place. Nothing needs my attention for at least . . . fifteen minutes.

I look at the door to the kitchen. And before I think better of it, I feel the cold metal of the handle under my fingertips and I'm walking out into the main area of the Death House.

"You all right, Chef?" Jace asks, standing up by his desk, his bagged lunch sitting in front of him. Roast beef on white. Mayo. Chips and a soda wrapped in tinfoil. His wife's doing. I smile at him and continue walking forward. He just watches me. Shawn finishes the phone call he was on, hangs up the phone, and approaches me like a wild animal.

"Queenie," Shawn says. A warning.

"Shawn," I say, scanning the room. I don't know what I'm looking for. I don't know why I left the kitchen.

Of course, those are lies. I know exactly why I'm out here and I know exactly what I'm looking for. Shawn sees me find it. A bank of closed-circuit televisions on the far wall by that fateful metal door that I'm never supposed to enter. Black-and-white television monitors. All showing a different angle of the Death Row cell. I walk toward it.

"Queenie, I need you to think about this," Shawn says, following me. The rest of the guards are watching me, but don't move. Shawn is handling it; they're confident of this.

"I just need to see her," I say, still not looking at him.

"Queenie," Shawn says, putting himself between me and the closed-circuit televisions. I stop. I look up at him, finally making eye contact. So soft. So concerned.

"Please?" I ask. Desperate.

Shawn is still. Watching me. I can see him run through a few scenarios in his head, his eyes scanning the outer area and falling on each of the guards. He brings his hands up to rest on his holster; the leather creaks under his strength. Shawn moves his body ever so slightly. Enough to let me pass. A small nod and he follows me over to the grainy, black-and-white TVs.

My eyes shift and flick from one TV to the next. Long, empty hallways. A shot of the empty gurney and the cold, sterile execution chamber. I turn away from that screen as quickly as I can. My eyes finally settle on the cell itself and the two people just inside. I step forward. I lean in, my face now inches from the grainy moving images.

Yvonne Chapman. In all white. Spindly thin as she always was. Her hair is gray now and up in a tight bun on the top of her head. My breathing quickens as my mouth falls open. Her face is wan and those once bright brown eyes are now hollowed out and . . . sad.

"Queenie?" Shawn asks, his voice soft.

"Can we . . . can we hear what they're saying?" I ask, my voice breathy and not of this world. Shawn waits a beat. Weighing his options. This is the last day at the prison for both of us. He turns the volume up just so we can barely make out what they're saying.

"—the past." The chaplain finishes a sentence. He's an older gentleman I've seen only once before. Somber and devout, his mission weighs him down. He leans over and speaks soft and close with Yvonne.

"I just can't," Yvonne says, her voice shaky and frantic.

"This is about relieving yourself of all that weighs on you. Making peace before you go home." Shawn takes my hand, and I squeeze it back. We both step closer.

"How do I make peace? How do I stand in front of my maker after what I done?"

"We are all God's children, Yvonne."

"Not all of us, Chaplain."

"Yes. All of us."

"Even those of us who turned some of God's children into orphans?" My fingers jerk around Shawn's hand, and I can hear myself gasp. I freeze.

"Yvonne, you've confessed your sins. You've done your time."

"And those kids? What about them? You know, Brandi-Jaques and that bastard husband of mine may have deserved what I done. Both of them. Birds of a feather, those two. Didn't care nothing for nobody." Yvonne's voice cracks and chokes. The chaplain passes her a tissue. She continues, "But those girls? What did they deserve?"

"Yvonne, please—"

"I've started a million letters, but how do you say sorry for taking someone's momma? Even if that momma is BJ Wake," Yvonne says, her voice sliding over Momma's name like it's poisonous.

"Do you want to try to write another letter? We can do that right now. Make amends? Ask for forgiveness?"

"Chaplain, no one's going to forgive me."

I look from that grainy screen right up into Shawn's eyes. He just nods. He pulls out his key card, and I watch on the grainy black-and-white screen as Shawn walks down that long hallway and gets the chaplain's attention; then I see them both walk back down the hallway. The metal door I'm never supposed to enter opens up and there are Shawn and the chaplain.

"Chaplain Boothe, this is Queenie Wake," Shawn says.

"Wake," the chaplain says, extending his hand to me. He hesitates as we shake.

"I'm BJ Wake's daughter. One of them."

"I'm not understanding. Why isn't Ms. Wake with the other execution witnesses, Mr. Richter?" the chaplain asks, his voice calm and official.

"Queenie is the chef here in the Death House. She's making Yvonne Chapman's last meal," Shawn says.

"Oh. *Oh my.*" The chaplain situates and re-situates the cuffs on his starched white shirt.

"I'd like to talk to her," I say.

"Ms. Wake, I—"

"She's asking for forgiveness, and I can give it to her. You want her to make peace? I can give that to her. Don't you want that for her?" I ask, my voice edgy and out of control. The other guards are now watching us. None of them moves.

"Ms. Wake, these are someone's last hours here on earth that you're tampering with. I am unsure you grasp the enormity of what you're suggesting," the chaplain says.

I am quiet. My eyes shift back over to the TVs, and I watch as Yvonne lets her head fall into her hands. She's got just under six hours left on this earth. I look back at the chaplain. My breathing is now calm. My shoulders low.

"Please," I say.

The chaplain looks from me to Shawn. Shawn gives the chaplain a nod. And with that the chaplain looks back at me and speaks.

"Follow me, Ms. Wake," the chaplain says, turning and facing that metal door. Shawn puts his key card in and the door clicks open.

Squeaky shoes. The clock moves forward and the click echoes around the long hallway. My breathing is shallow, and I'm beginning to panic. I can see the side of the cell, the stripes of the bars playing tricks on my eyes. I snap my eyes away from the bars, down the long hallway, and they fall on the execution room at the end of the hall. My mouth is dry as I steady myself, planting my feet one after the other.

The chaplain and Shawn stop in front of the cell and both look to me. Shawn opens up the cell and holds the door for me. I breathe in. Deep.

I walk the few steps, past the chaplain and Shawn, and turn to face the inside of Yvonne's cell. She is sitting on the cot just past the door with her head in her hands. At the sound of my shoes squeaking against the sterile white floor, she looks up and it's as if she's seen a ghost. She stands. Then sits back down. Steadies herself. And stands again. She doesn't take her eyes off me. She opens her mouth to speak, but nothing comes out. Tears stream down her face as she searches for something to say.

"How . . . how are you here?" she finally says, her voice a terrified shake of a whisper.

"I'm the chef here. I make the last meals. Your last meal," I say, stepping forward. My voice steadies as I focus on Yvonne.

"The Number One," Yvonne says.

"With fresh strawberry ice cream," I say.

"I always liked fresh strawberry ice cream," Yvonne says, her hand at her chest. She attempts a small smile.

"I know," I say.

"Queenie, I——," Yvonne starts, but crumples to the cot below her as she is unable to finish her sentence. I step forward and kneel in front of her. I wait for her to look up at me. When she does, I can see the tears pooling in her eyes. She continues, "You look like her, you know? Your face—there's something about it. Not the eyes, though, you don't have her eyes." Yvonne brings her hand up and for a small second touches the side of my face with her fingers. A smile. From somewhere deep. "You're okay. Look at you. You're okay." Another smile. A laugh. A relieved laugh and another smile as she pulls me in for a hug. She just keeps saying, "You're okay," over and over again. I wrap my arms around her thin frame and just breathe her in.

"Ms. Wake?" the chaplain says from just behind me, still in the doorway of the cell. Yvonne finally lets me go. Her face is softer. I look at her. It's the oddest realization, especially given where we are. Yvonne's face looks peaceful. She takes a deep breath and gives me one last smile as I creak into a standing position. One last look. Our eyes locked on each other's as Shawn instructs me to follow him back down the hallway.

Peace. She just wanted to know I was okay.

I follow Shawn back down the hallway and hear the cell door close behind me. I don't look back. The metal door opens and closes behind us.

"You okay?" Shawn asks, just outside.

"I'm okay," I say, and the tears explode out of my throat and the crumbling sobs shock even me. Shawn pulls me close, and I'm immediately enveloped. I don't notice the other guards. I'm sure they're observing all of this. I just sob. And repeat over and over. You're okay. You're okay.

I'm okay.

"Chef?" Jace reappears with the Dent boys.

"Yes. *Yes,*" I say, disentangling myself from Shawn and trying to collect myself. Shawn gives me a look. I nod. I'm okay. He gives me

a quick nod of acknowledgment back and then never mentions
again what just happened.

"You ready for us?" Jace asks, gesturing toward the kitchen.

"Yes, sir," I say. I breathe. Deep. Down. The exhalation soars
out of me as I enter the kitchen with Jace and the Dent boys.

I'm okay.

They don't ask me about what happened earlier and I don't tell
them. Maybe one day I will. But not today. We move and thread
through the kitchen like clockwork. The meal begins to take shape.
With each ingredient I lighten. With each ingredient I leave it behind. With each ingredient I take a step toward my future.

With just under an hour I begin the biscuits, cutting round after round. Harlan scoops up the cut biscuits and places them on a
cookie sheet as Cody focuses on the green bean dish. As the biscuits
go in the oven, the kitchen door clicks and Shawn walks in.

"You ready?" Shawn asks.

"Yes, sir," I say.

"I'll be back in twenty minutes," Shawn says. He walks out of
the kitchen, and as the door slams behind him, I turn to the skillet.
It's time for the chicken fried steak.

I begin to fry the chicken fried steak in the lard. After a few minutes, I see Harlan take the tray from the shelf and place it on the
counter. My breathing quickens and I find myself craning my neck
to get a look. The chicken fried steak crackles away in the skillet, but
I can't take my eyes off the tray. I wrench my eyes away and focus
back on the steak. I remember Yvonne's face and calm down.

Five minutes.

I pull the chicken fried steaks from the lard one by one and
place them on the awaiting plate. Cody covers them each with a
paper towel. The grease shines through.

Four minutes.

"Cody, why don't you get the mashed potatoes and the cream gravy. Harlan, could you scoop up some of those green beans," I say, opening up the freezer and pulling out the fresh strawberry ice cream. The canister feels cold against my hands. I blink and refocus. A smile. Her favorite.

Three minutes.

Harlan brings the pecan pie over. I slice the pie and place it on a smaller plate. I scoop the fresh strawberry ice cream out into a bowl and place it on the other side of the tray. I pour a glass of sweet tea for her. She didn't formally request it, but that's what she always used to have a pitcher of in the fridge.

Two minutes.

Harlan brings over the still steaming biscuits while Cody readies the honey butter. Jace sets his newspaper down and walks over. I choose the best chicken fried steak and place it on the plate, finishing the meal.

My last last meal.

We stand around the tray. Just staring at it. Forever in awe. The chicken fried steak will be just as she remembered it. The biscuits will flake just like they used to. The pecan pie will be sweet and will take her back to those times she sat at the tables just outside the shack on a summer's day. And for once, she'll have fresh strawberry ice cream to go with it.

We take one another's hands.

"Bless this food, Lord. Let it transport and remind us all of better times. Let it cleanse and purify. Let it nourish and warm. In it, let us find peace. In Jesus' name, amen," I say. Tears stream down my face as my eyes flutter open.

"Amen," the men say.

The key card clicks and Shawn walks through the kitchen.

"Queenie, it's time."

28

Kettle corn and a Coke

I don't eat with the guards or sit in my car after the meal is done. I clean the kitchen, say my good-byes, and flick off those kitchen lights one last time. I have to get out of here. When Shawn brought the tray back in, he couldn't look at me. I knew something was wrong.

"She said thank you," he said, looking down at the ground.

"What?"

"She said it was exactly like she remembered," he said, his entire body deflated. Shawn set the tray down on the counter and when he finally looked at me, all I saw was pain. His face was tense, the tears mutinously welling up. I just shook my head, unable to say anything. So we just stood there and let ourselves cry. Again.

I speed down the highway, my window wide open. I think about fresh strawberry ice cream and saying thank you. I think about closure and moving on. I think about peace and being okay. I think about complicated monsters and cruel blue eyes—that I didn't inherit. I think about Arabella's ultimatum and a marriage I knew was a sham. I drive through the center of town and continue on toward Everett's. Past the houses and up into the hills. Past the Paragon Ranch gate until I find the dirt road once again. I pull down the long dusty road and my headlights illuminate Everett's home. I turn off my headlights and am stepping out of my car as the door opens and he steps out onto the porch.

"I read in the papers about Yvonne Chapman," he says as I climb the steps of his porch. His white T-shirt and jeans are casual. The glasses and bare feet are downright intimate.

"You know, she ordered the Number One."

"What do you mean, she ordered the Number One? Like the one your mom used to make?" Everett ushers me inside his house as Arrow does his gruff barking routine only to grow weary and plop down on his plaid dog bed.

"Yeah. For her last meal," I say.

"Oh my God," he says.

"I talked to her."

"What?"

"Yeah."

"What did she say?"

"She just wanted to know that I was okay," I say.

He steps forward and speaks. "Queenie, honey, you've been thr—" I stop him. I reach up and I just kiss him. With everything I've got. He wraps his arm around my waist and pulls me into him. I break from him and try to let it all in. I survived the war, but now it's time to take off my armor and set it proudly in its place of honor. It's time for me to choose someone to be in my world without any battlements at all.

"I love you. You've undone me in every way. I don't care how we're together just as long as I don't have to spend another day apart from you. I just don't work without you," I say.

"Does this mean you're staying?"

"Yes."

"For good this time?"

"Yes."

Everett's eyes are fixed on mine. He brings both of his hands to either side of my face. I lean into his touch and close my eyes. He leans down and kisses me. He pulls back only enough to whisper in my ear, his lips centimeters from my skin.

"I'm yours. I've always been yours."

Everett takes me in his arms and I feel it all. The scope and breadth of a love I'm finally allowing to expand to its full size after being kept in a box for far too long.

After however many minutes (hours?), I finally tear myself away from Everett. Merry Carole is going to be waiting up for me for sure, and we have much to discuss.

"So I'll see you at the game?" Everett asks, standing on the porch as I walk to my car.

"Absolutely. And about all the family stuff with your paren—"

Everett cuts me off. "We'll figure it out. We'll make it work." I nod. We'll figure it out. We'll make it work. This time? I actually believe him.

Lighter, I walk down the path to Merry Carole's. Unencumbered. Free. How is that possible? I open the door and walk through the darkened house. I turn on my light and pull my little notebook out of my luggage. I sit down right there on the floor and begin writing. The well-used recipes, the process . . . I clip the pen into the spiral of the notebook and tuck the notebook back into my luggage. I put on my pajamas and turn off the light in my room. I feel my way down the hallway and creak open the door to Merry Carole's room.

"You still up?" I ask.

"Come on, then," Merry Carole says, flipping her blankets back. I tiptoe over to the bed and climb inside. I just sit there.

"I talked to her."

"You what?" Merry Carole sits straight up in bed and looks down at me.

"I talked to her."

"And what did she have to say for herself?" Merry Carole's voice is anxious and terrified.

"She just wanted to know we were okay."

"That's it?"

"That's it. I thought it was going to be this whole conversation about forgiveness and Momma, but she was just . . . she was just worried about us."

"Well, damn," Merry Carole says, leaning over and pulling a tissue from her bedside table. "Damn," she says again, sniffling into the tissue once more. I slide under the covers as Merry Carole lies down. I nuzzle into the pillow, and Merry Carole and I face each other in the darkness of her bedroom. Rose water. I breathe it in.

"She said thank you," I whisper.

"She what?"

"She told Shawn the dish was exactly how she remembered it."

"Oh my God."

"I know."

"How do you feel about it?"

"It's not like—I mean, we've been walking around with this for years. It felt shitty for years, but making this meal did something. Talking to her did something. I can't believe y'all were right, but you were. It's like I've stopped spinning, if that makes any sense," I say.

"No, it does."

We are quiet.

"So were you going to call that guy from Portland tomorrow then?"

"I don't know if I'll have time. I've got to get my Stallion Batallion cheers and big foam finger ready."

"The game is after—" Merry Carole sits up in bed and throws her arms around me. She scrunches back under the covers squealing with delight. She pulls the blankets up over her shoulders and smooths my bangs out of my face. "I'm so glad. I can't wait to tell Cal."

"Me, too."

"Night, Queenie."

"Night night, Merry Carole," I say, snuggling up to her.

"If you don't hurry up, I swear I'm going to leave without you, Queen Elizabeth," Merry Carole says, appearing in my doorway in one of Cal's jerseys, black pencil pants, and a pair of black peep-toe heels. Her blond hair is the closest to Jesus I think I've ever seen it and her makeup is "camera ready" as she likes to say. Rose and Amelia crowd around her as she makes a face at them regarding my unhurried pace. The girls giggle as they shift their Stallion Batallion gear around. Rose and Amelia are wearing the matching gold sundresses Merry Carole bought for them. Merry Carole has done their hair up in pigtails, accentuated with black and gold ribbons that trail down their backs. Merry Carole has a giant gold foam finger tucked under her arm, a pair of pom-poms in one hand, and four gold-and-black seat cushions in the other. Each of the girls has her own set of pom-poms, which they can't help but shake throughout our little sisterly chat.

It's game day.

"I'm ready, I'm ready," I say, sliding into my pair of Converse All Stars. I spin around and let Merry Carole approve my outfit. Jeans and a genuine Cal Wake jersey. WAKE #5. She nods her approval.

"Yes, it's beautiful. Now let's go!" Merry Carole says, rolling her eyes at the little girls like I'm crazy. The girls titter and shake their pom-poms.

It's finally cooling off a bit, so our walk to the high school's football field is turning into a pleasant one. I hold Amelia's hand as Merry Carole holds Rose's. With Reed coaching, it's up to Merry Carole to take care of the girls. She couldn't be more excited. We fall in line with the rest of the town as we queue for the stadium. Merry Carole searches the crowd.

"Dee said she was going to meet us," Merry Carole says.

"I'm sure she'll find us," I say, holding tight to Amelia as the crowd ebbs and flows. Merry Carole picks up Rose as we make our way to the entrance. We're early enough that we get great seats right in front, on the fifty-yard line. Merry Carole settles the little girls on their cushions. I scan the crowd. Whitney and Wes sit just a few bleachers over with their two little ones. We share a narrow-eyed acknowledgment of one another. As the bleachers fill, Dee and Shawn find us. They are both wearing Cal's jersey. They sit their boys down next to Amelia and Rose and settle in themselves. Fawn and Pete weave through the crowd and squeeze in next to Merry Carole. They're also wearing Cal's jersey. Six Wake jerseys all in a row. We are eleven in total. From the back it must look like quite the Wake army.

Shawn and Pete go on a food run and come back with kettle

corn and Cokes for everyone. Shawn looks like a great weight has been lifted off his shoulders. Dee tells me he couldn't be happier with the sheriff's.

I see the Coburn clan gathering on the side of the field for their turn at the coin toss. Even though Reed asked Everett to do it, he'll probably have the entire dynasty come up.

The marching band plays as the crowd gets ready. I'm sandwiched in between Amelia and Dee as we wait for the game to start. The cheerleaders line up on the side of the field, carrying the painted banner that's for the Stallion Batallion to burst through. I take a deep breath and close my eyes, allowing myself this moment. I am surrounded by family. I deposited my savings in the local credit union and managed to secure a small business loan. I have meetings with a few contractors starting next week. I've turned that spiral notebook I hid in my luggage into a journal, a sketchbook, and a menu planner all in one. I've sent two letters to Shine Prison addressed to Cody and Harlan Dent, letting them know that when they get out, they have a job waiting for them in North Star. I even sent a thank-you card to that jerk Brad Carter at the McCormick.

I'm okay.

The cheerleaders run onto the field, pulling the painted banner across the walkway. I sit up straight and crane my neck to see if the team is gathering behind the banner yet. I can see Everett taking his place on the field, flanked by his family. He's talking to Gray about something, resting a hand on his shoulder. Gray bows his head just enough so he can hear Everett over the marching band and growing crowd noise. Everett re-situates his cowboy hat as he leans in to speak to Florrie. He picks up one of her little girls who absently plays with the buttons on his shirt. I notice the kids, and even the grandkids, for that matter, don't really interact with Felix and Arabella. All that childlike joy and exuberance is probably bad for his heart. Or so Arabella would have us believe.

The team gathers behind the Stallion banner and the crowd goes wild. The marching band launches into the school song. We all stand, hooting and hollering. Amelia and Rose stand up on the bleachers shaking their pom-poms and wooohooooing with all their might. The buzz of the team gets louder and louder and louder, sounding like they're going to be blasted on the field from a cannon. The first player tears through the banner and the crowd goes wild. Several confetti explosions burst into the sky and, as the rest of the team runs through the now shredded banner, confetti falls all around them.

And there's Cal. Merry Carole beams. Cal's got his head down and looks rather serious for a boy running through gold-and-black confetti.

"He looks nervous," Dee whispers, leaning over so Merry Carole won't hear.

"I know," I say, watching as he makes a beeline for the sideline. Reed and his coaching staff, all wearing matching black polo shirts with rearing stallion insignia, trot out last. With his baseball cap pulled low, Reed doesn't look into the stands, either. He focuses on the sidelines.

"Isn't that Wes's old jersey?" I ask, pointing at West. Merry Carole tears her gaze away from Cal and Reed and scans the rest of the team for West. She finds him just as he's turning around. MCKAY. In big bold letters. Merry Carole just smiles.

"That's amazing," she says and swoons. We look over to Whitney and Wes and they're also wearing a couple of Wes's old jerseys. As are DeWitt and Cheryl—happily now playing the role of grandparents. I point this out to Dee and Fawn, who launch into a symphony of awwwwws.

The opposing team bursts out onto the field and settles into their sidelines. The referees come to the center of the field, calling the captains of each team as well as the coaches to join them. One of the team parents presents the head referee with a microphone and there is much thumping and feedback as they figure out exactly how this newfangled apparatus works. The referee finally tugs the microphone away and thump, thump, thumps it to make sure it's on.

"WELCOME, oh wow, that sure is loud. Ladies and gentlemen, welcome to a new season of football!"

The crowd applauds. The referee thumps and thuds the microphone as he asks Reed a question. Reed nods and motions to Everett on the sidelines.

"At this time, Coach Blanchard of the North Star Stallions would like to make an announcement." The referee passes the microphone to a very irked-looking Reed. Reed takes it.

"Thanks for coming out, y'all. It looks like the whole town showed up. It's a tradition here in North Star to choose someone from our community to do the opening-game coin toss. This year the North Star Stallions have asked Everett Coburn to do us the honor." More applause as Everett runs out onto the field. He keeps his head down and his cowboy hat low. Fawn, Dee, and Merry Carole all look over at me. Pointedly. I immediately blush, but despite their smug sideways glances, trying to embarrass me, I finally feel free to stare unabashedly at Everett. My man. Reed passes him the microphone and the crowd settles into a momentary silence.

"Thank you, Coach Blanchard, for recognizing Paragon Ranch. We are truly proud to call ourselves members of the Stallion Batallion," Everett says to more applause. Everett continues, "I'd like to bring out the entire Coburn family to help with tonight's coin toss, if you don't mind?" The entire Coburn clan trots onto the field, gathering around Everett. I know I should probably look at this family with disdain. I know Merry Carole, Fawn, and Dee are doing just that right about now. But I can't. I can't take my eyes off of Everett. He turns around and looks at his family as they wait expectantly behind him. He turns back around and looks out into the crowd. He continues, "You know . . . we're actually missing one person. I'm going to ask that person to join me down here on the field. It's the woman I love, and as most of you already know, have loved my entire life."

All eyes shoot to me.

Dee shoves me into a standing position. I look at Merry Carole, who's sitting there with her hand clapped over her mouth. I smile at her and look back down on the field. Cal has taken his helmet off and is looking from Everett to me. I just stand there.

"Queenie Wake, come make an honest man out of me," Everett says, staring right at me.

And before I can think, I thread my way through the various feet and knees of the packed bleachers, the muffled sound pounding in my ears. I hop down the stairs and run across the field looking at no one but Everett. He hands the microphone to Reed and steps forward. I leap into his arms and he catches me. I knew he would.

This is you. This is now.

Damn straight it is.

Acknowledgments

I think as I get older I begin to ask questions about what it's all about, why we are here, and what it is I'm searching for. And then Neil deGrasse Tyson goes and says it way better than I could ever imagine: "We are all connected to each other biologically, to the earth chemically, and to the rest of the universe atomically. That's kinda cool! That makes me smile and I actually feel quite large at the end of that."

This life is about connectivity. People. Love.

Period.

I am thankful—like a quivering mound of flesh when I think of them thankful—for my family. Mom, Don, Alex, Joe, Zoë, and Bonnie. And Poet, of course.

Thanks to everyone at Fletcher and Company.

Appreciation to the team at HarperCollins: Carrie Feron, Tessa Woodward, Lauren Cook, Jean Marie Kelly, Mary Sasso, Seale Ballenger, and on and on.

Thankful praise for Kerri and her adorable fam, Marilyn, Christine, Paige, Henry and Norm, Kim and the Crazies, Kim and Mark, David and Kathie, Nicole and Bekka, Dave and Jen, Mark and Sara, Alyssa, Michelle, Kurt, Matthew, Milly, Mia and Nikki, Scott, Larry and Ricca, Sharon, Jane, Juanita, Donna, Glo, Kit and Margaret, Lynn and Rich.

Thank you to Randy Barbour for helping me not embarrass myself when it comes to all things Texas. Thanks to Nina and Matt for showing me around Austin. Thanks to the Katy House in Smithville, Texas, for putting me up while I soaked in their beautiful city.

Thank you to my readers. You make me teary just thinking about how great you are.

And thank you to Mariage Frères tea, the open road, and great music.

P.S.

Insights,
Interviews
& More . . .

About the author

About the book

Read on

Meet Liza Palmer

LIZA PALMER is the author of *Conversations with the Fat Girl*, which became an international bestseller during its first week of publication and hit number one on the Fiction Heatseekers List in the UK the week before its debut. *Conversations with the Fat Girl* has been optioned for a TV series by HBO.

Palmer's second novel is *Seeing Me Naked*, about which *Publishers Weekly* says, "Consider it haute chick lit; Palmer's prose is sharp, her characters are solid and her narrative is laced with moments of graceful sentiment."

Entertainment Weekly calls her third book, *A Field Guide to Burying Your Parents*, a "splendid novel" and *Real Simple* says it "has heart and humor."

More Like Her is Palmer's fourth

Edwin Santiago

novel. The book received a starred review from *Library Journal* in which they said, "The blend of humor and sadness is realistic and gripping, and watching Frannie figure out who she is and what matters is gratifying."

After earning two Emmy nominations for writing during the first season of VH1's *Pop Up Video*, Palmer now knows far too much about Fergie.

Nowhere but Home is her fifth novel.

One Last Meal

by Liza Palmer

WHEN I FIRST started writing *Nowhere but Home*, I had no idea what my last meal would be. Do you know yours? It's a weird thought, right?

One last meal.

It took writing this book for me to understand what it is we're trying to capture—much like lightning in a bottle. We're trying to re-create a moment, a perfect moment when, as Frank Ocean so beautifully put it, "time would glide."

For me it comes down to three foods. Three foods that transport me, calm me, and surround me with love. These three foods are what I would want in my last moments, not because they're the best things I ever tasted but because in eating them I am loved once more.

Poppa Don's Gnocchi

For Christmas dinner every year my amazing stepdad makes his homemade gnocchi and a beautiful filet. My mom puts out the good china, and we gather around the table in the sparkly light of the season. We talk and laugh. My parents' ridiculous French bulldogs snuffle under the table for scraps. We are tired from Christmas morning, and yet we are all showered and most likely wearing something we were gifted that very morning.

Not only is Poppa Don's cheesy, ▶

About the book

3

One Last Meal *(continued)*

mouth-watering gnocchi at the center of the Christmas table, it's at the center of the entire season.

Sitting around that Christmas table, we are a family.

Alex's Chocolate Chip Cookies

She's one of those bakers who says, "It's easy. It's just the recipe off the back of the chocolate chip bag!" Yet I try to make the same cookies, and they come out sad, flat, and tasteless. (I still eat them of course! I'm not an animal.)

My sister's chocolate chip cookies are the stuff of legend. My family sends urgent texts—ALEX IS MAKING HER CHOCOLATE CHIP COOKIES—and we all drop everything and beeline for her house where we are met with that smelllll, oh the smelllll. Is there anything better than the smell of chocolate chip cookies in the oven?

During a crisis, Alex will bake. She will put the chocolate chip cookies in little baggies and present them to you when you're sad, hurting, sick, or just having a bad day.

They are love embodied.

Mom's Bean and Cheese Burritos

This is probably the food that defines me. It's my all-time favorite food in the world and only my mom *really* knows how to make it.

The pinto beans simmering in the pot, the white cheese (or "Monterey Jack" as some people call it), the flour tortillas my mom would flip on the burner with her deft hands.

This dish is home. Love. The feeling of being safe and sound.

Well, this dish is my mom. ∾

Have You Read?
More from Liza Palmer

FOR MORE BOOKS by Liza Palmer
check out

MORE LIKE HER

What really goes on behind those
perfect white picket fences?

In Frances's mind, beautiful,
successful, ecstatically married
Emma Dunham is the height of
female perfection. Frances, recently
dumped with spectacular drama by
her boyfriend, aspires to be just like
Emma. So do her close friends and
fellow teachers, Lisa and Jill. But Lisa's
too career-focused to find time for a
family. And Jill's recent unexpected
pregnancy could have devastating
consequences for her less-than-perfect
marriage.

Yet sometimes the golden dream
you fervently wish for turns out to be
not at all what it seems—like Emma's
enviable suburban postcard life, which
is about to be brutally cut short by a
perfect husband turned killer. And in
the shocking aftermath, three devastated
friends are going to have to come to
terms with their own secrets . . . and
somehow learn to move forward after
their dream is exposed as a lie. ⌒

An Excerpt from
More Like Her

Prologue

Operator #237: Nine-one-one, what is your emergency?

Caller: I'm a teacher at the Markham School, there's a man here with a gun. He—[shots fired in the background]

Operator #237: Ma'am? Ma'am?!

Caller: [unintelligible screaming] Oh my god. Oh my god . . . Is she dead? Oh my god . . . [unintelligible]

Operator #237: Ma'am, please—

Caller: You need to hurry . . . please. Please, god. Hurry! [unintelligible] Noooooo!!!! So much blood . . . there's so much blood!

Operator #237: Ma'am, I've sent them—the police. Now—tell me where you are in the school.

Caller: [unintelligible] The teachers' lounge. Upstairs. We're on the balc—*Just stay down! Stay down!*

Operator #237: Ma'am, please, I need you to calm down. Is the shooter still in the teachers' lounge with you?

Caller: *Calm down?* He's . . . oh my god [unintelligible] Is he dead, too?

Operator #237: Ma'am, I just want you to stay on the line with me until help gets there. How many people are in danger?

Caller: What? All of us! All of us are in danger! He's got a gun?! What do you think? *Stay down!* Oh my god! No!

Operator #237: Ma'am, is there any way you can block the door? ▶

7

Caller: The doors are glass, there's no
point. *No! Stay down! Frannie!?*
No . . . oh my god. Oh my god . . .
Did he get her? Did he get her, too?
[unintelligible sobbing]
Operator #237: Ma'am, please. Please.
Stay with me. Please. Ma'am?!—
Dial tone—
Total time of call: 1:23:08

Chapter 1

Lipstick and Palpable Fear

I'M NOT THE GIRL MEN CHOOSE. I'm
the girl who's charming and funny and
then drives home alone wondering what
she did wrong. I'm the girl who meets
someone halfway decent and then fills
in the gaps in his character with my own
imagination, only to be shocked when
he's not the man I thought he was.

I'm the girl who hides who she really
is for fear I'll fall short.

SO, WHEN EMMA DUNHAM introduces
herself to me as the new head of school,
I automatically transform into the
version of me who doesn't make people
uncomfortable with her "intensity," who
doesn't need any new friends and who
loves being newly single and carefree. In
short, the version of me that's as far away
from the genuine article as is humanly
possible.

"Headmistress Dunham," she says,
extending her hand. To my horror,
Emma Dunham is cool, like take-me-

back-to-the-fringes-of-my-seventh-grade-cafeteria cool.

"Frances Reid," I say, extending my hand to hers. I won't slip and introduce myself as Frances *Peed*, the moniker given to me as I lurked on the fringes of my seventh-grade cafeteria.

"You're the speech therapist," Emma says, her smile easy.

"Yes," I say, allowing a small smile.

"It's a pleasure to finally meet you," Emma says. I let the silence extend past what is socially acceptable. I take a sip of coffee from my mug—now stained with pink lipstick and palpable fear.

"You two have met, I see?" Jill asks. Her face has *that look*, the one that threatens to reveal all my closely held secrets. All it takes is a simple well-placed smirk from a close friend who knows exactly what you're feeling and thinks it hilarious when your carefully constructed disguise is threatened. I won't look at her.

"Jill Fleming, this is Emma Dunham. Jill is the other speech therapist here at Markham. Emma's the new head of school," I say, averting my eyes from Jill's omniscient gaze.

"Sure. Jill and I met earlier. We're all certainly going to miss Mrs. Kim," Emma says, her white teeth momentarily blinding me.

"Kali is doing just fine, I'm sure. She finally got her dream job at Choate," I say, rebelling slightly by not formalizing an old friend's name.

"Of course with Mrs. Kim gone ▶

there will be an opening as the head of the speech therapy department," Emma says with a smile.

"Will there?" Jill asks transparently.

Headmistress Dunham merely sniffs and tightens her mouth into a prim line.

Jill continues. "Any thoughts you'd like to share with Ms. Reid and I on your hiring process for that position would certainly be welcomed."

"In time, Mrs. Fleming. In time," Emma says. I look past Emma's alabaster skin and beautifully tailored suit as teachers and administrators of Pasadena, California's Markham School for the Criminally Wealthy stream into the library for this year's back-to-school orientation.

"Lovely meeting you, Headmistress," I say, excusing myself from Emma Dunham and her lipstick that never smudges. She gives me what can only be described as a royal nod and quickly falls in with a pack of eager upper school faculty.

"I'm not looking at you or speaking to you for the next ten minutes," I say to Jill as we find a seat in the back of the library. I straighten up and tell myself that my enviable posture is on par with any of Emma's myriad accomplishments.

"Why are you sitting like that? What's wrong with you? Do you have to fart?" Jill asks, her voice dipping with the word *fart*.

I immediately slouch, plummeting back to reality. Even my mimicked perfection looks like I have gas.

"No . . . no, I don't have to fart," I say, clearing my throat.

Jill continues without missing a beat. "She's thirty-four. Originally from Michigan, moved to San Francisco in college. Married to Jamie Dunham— she took his last name. He's a professor at UCLA. I'm humiliated I don't have a picture of him. A wedding picture would have been nice, but there just wasn't any time . . ." Jill shakes her head in frustration. "No kids. This is her first time as headmistress." I "ignore" Jill—meaning I inventory every piece of information relayed to me yet act like I couldn't be bothered.

"Why does it not shock me that you're far more concerned about Emma's marital status than the head of department opening?" I ask.

"It really shouldn't," Jill says, taking a bite of her bagel.

"Is this seat taken?" Debbie asks, motioning to the empty seat just next to mine. Debbie Manners: school librarian and self-proclaimed welcome wagon.

"Yeah, sorry," I say, forcing myself to look apologetic. Debbie walks away in search of another empty seat, preferably next to some unsuspecting fool to whom she'll propose an innocent back-rub. A seemingly chaste request that'll ensure you never let her sit next to you again.

"What are you going to do when the orientation starts and that seat remains empty?" Jill asks. Debbie sits down next to the new lacrosse coach. He instinctively leans away from her ▶

as she whispers in his ear that he looks tense.

"Be relieved," I say.

"I want to thank you all for being here this morning. On time and ready to work, just the kind of orientation I can get used to," Emma Dunham says. Her delivery is relaxed and sincere. I adjust my sweater for the umpteenth time. I can't get comfortable.

Emma continues. "I am Headmistress Dunham and am your new head of school. I am originally from Michigan and no, I'm not as young as you think I am." The crowd laughs and nudges each other. She's funny! She's beautiful! She's humble! She makes me feel like shit about myself! Where's the razor and warm bath?!

"Jeremy couldn't stop talking about you," Jill whispers.

I sigh. Jeremy Hannon. Another setup. Just what every Labor Day barbecue needs: a forced blind date over corn on the cob and onion dip.

Jill continues. "He kept mentioning that mix you made. Said he wanted a copy."

"That was a classic rock CD I got at the grocery store for three ninety-nine."

Jill lets out a dramatic, weary sigh.

I'm letting this golden opportunity slip through my ringless fingers! She's powerless in the face of my indifference! Her unborn godchildren are trapped in limbo and I won't burn a simple mix!

Several people give us looks of deep

concern. We are not respecting the new head of school.

"I guess his cousin is also really into music. He says you remind him of her." Jill's face is alight with excitement.

"I remind him of his cousin?"

"Yeah, isn't that great?"

"No, *Flowers in the Attic*. It is not."

"That's a brother and a sister, and besides—"

"Shh!" It's Debbie Manners. The librarian. How predictable.

Jill continues. "You never know how something is going to start between two people." I shake her off, reminding her that we're in the middle of orientation. I don't want to hear about some guy's halfhearted feelings for me. Halfhearted feelings that depend on a mix of overplayed rock tunes of the 1970s. Not quite the modern-day *Romeo and Juliet* I imagined my love life would be.

Jill persists. "I made sure Martin knew that I wasn't like other girls he was dating. He had to work." I can't listen to Jill's "I made him work" story again. I focus back on Emma just as she smiles, a perfect dimple punctuating her delight. I tried to have a dimple once. It consisted of me sitting on the couch with my finger in my cheek whenever I watched television as a kid. No dimple, just an Everest-size zit where my finger had been.

Jill continues. "He tried to call on a Friday for a date th—"

"I know, but you said that you were reading a book and couldn't go," I say, ▶

interrupting. "I know. Except that you met up with him later at a bar, so . . ." My voice is getting louder.

"Shh!" Debbie again. This time I feel like I should thank her. I look away from Jill and try to focus back on Emma and her ongoing speech about expectations and proper behavior.

"I may have met up with him later, but . . . you know, I told him no first," Jill says, almost to herself.

The truth is, I haven't been seriously interested in any of the legion of men Jill's tried to set me up with since Ryan dumped me. Of course, this doesn't explain why I have entranced none of them. It's much easier to rebuff willing gentlemen callers than to proclaim, "*I didn't like you anyway!*" after they say you remind them of their cousin. Although rejecting Jeremy had less to do with that than it did with his proclivity for saying *exspecially*.

I'm sure my behavior will have dire consequences. Flash forward: I'm living in some seaside cottage in my old age—possibly made entirely out of seashells. I'm clad in a faded housedress, large sunhat and Wellingtons. I make a meager living selling my seashell sculptures at the local farmer's market for tuppence a bag. The locals make up stories about me: I'm a witch, I'm crazy or talk to myself because I'm lonely or I murdered my lover when I was younger. Okay, fine. I made up that last one.

As Emma Dunham speaks, I scan the

library hoping Jill will get the hint that our little conversation is over. I think she's moved on. Apparently someone's put on weight over the summer. I smile at a few familiar faces. Some stare a little too long. A knowing smile here. A rolled eye there. A nervously abbreviated glance from me to . . . *Ryan*. In the front of the library. His leg loosely crossed over his knee. Those white and red vintage Nike Dunks twitch as he struggles to focus. The worn zip-up hoodie and corduroy pants that are a bit too loose for the school's liking yet tolerated (for now) due to an impressive educational résumé that reads like a who's who of top American institutions. The early morning tangle of black hair and the coffee mug he bought in Dublin when we were there last year for his summer internship at Trinity College. I look away. Clear my throat. Sip my coffee. Try to regain my composure.

"You okay?" Jill asks, her voice soft. All evidence of the pep talk slash Spanish Inquisition is gone.

"Yeah. *Yeah*," I say.

"He's been looking at you, too."

"I have no response to that."

"Maybe things are rocky with Jessica."

"Things are never rocky with girls like Jessica."

"Frannie—"

"Don't. Just don't."

Jill is quiet.

I continue. "Exspecially since it won't do either of us any good."

"God, that was driving me crazy. ▶

An Excerpt from *More Like Her* (continued)

I kept trying to say it correctly and he just never picked up on it."

"Of-*ten*-times."

"It's like nails on a chalkboard."

"Shhh!" Debbie again.

Jill and I smile our apologies. Emma is still talking. I focus in just as I see Ryan glance back at us. I act like I don't notice. He swipes his bangs out of his eyes.

Going to be a great year. ❧

Don't miss the next book by your favorite author. Sign up now for AuthorTracker by visiting www.AuthorTracker.com.